W9-BMC-032

ALSO BY TARA ISABELLA BURTON

The World Cannot Give

Social Creature

Strange Rites: New Religions for a Godless World

Self-Made: Creating Our Identities from Da Vinci to the Kardashians

HERE IN AVALON

TARA
ISABELLA
BURTON

SIMON & SCHUSTER

New York   London   Toronto   Sydney   New Delhi

100 YEARS
SIMON &
SCHUSTER

1230 Avenue of the Americas
New York, NY 10020

This book is a work of fiction. Any references to historical events, real people, or real places are used fictitiously. Other names, characters, places, and events are products of the author's imagination, and any resemblance to actual events or places or persons, living or dead, is entirely coincidental.

Copyright © 2024 by Tara Isabella Burton

All rights reserved, including the right to reproduce this book or portions thereof in any form whatsoever. For information, address Simon & Schuster Subsidiary Rights Department, 1230 Avenue of the Americas, New York, NY 10020.

First Simon & Schuster hardcover edition January 2024

SIMON & SCHUSTER and colophon are registered trademarks of Simon & Schuster, Inc.

Simon & Schuster: Celebrating 100 Years of Publishing in 2024

For information about special discounts for bulk purchases, please contact Simon & Schuster Special Sales at 1-866-506-1949 or business@simonandschuster.com.

The Simon & Schuster Speakers Bureau can bring authors to your live event. For more information or to book an event, contact the Simon & Schuster Speakers Bureau at 1-866-248-3049 or visit our website at www.simonspeakers.com.

Interior design by Wendy Blum

Manufactured in the United States of America

10   9   8   7   6   5   4   3   2   1

Library of Congress Cataloging-in-Publication Data has been applied for.

ISBN 978-1-9821-7009-7
ISBN 978-1-9821-7011-0 (ebook)

To the Family
(all of them)

PART ONE

CECILIA GOES TO THE AVALON

CHAPTER ONE

Once there were two sisters.

Cecilia was the elder, though you wouldn't think it to look at her. She rarely washed her face; she never brushed her hair, which had once been pink, and which had once been orange, and which was now a brittle shade of blond. Her tights were usually ripped; her shirts smelled like sweat and cigarettes. She wore heels, invariably, even though she couldn't walk in them, which meant that when Cecilia showed up anywhere, an hour late or else without notice altogether, you'd hear her tramping down the street before you saw her. Cecilia always sounded—Rose said—like a revolution.

God knows, if you met Cecilia, you wouldn't think her an adult at all.

If you met Cecilia—at a bleary Berlin bar, say, or an astral projection workshop or a silent retreat run by nuns or any of the other places Cecilia was usually to be found—you would probably think she was sixteen or seventeen, an underdeveloped twenty at most. It wasn't just her face, either. It was that angelic and infuriating way she had of looking up at you, with blue unblinking eyes, like you somehow had the answers to all the questions she had not yet figured out nobody in their right mind could answer: questions like *what does living a good life look like*, or *why do we always want the wrong things*, or *how do we even know what we want in the first place*. Cecilia was always asking people questions they didn't know the answer to. If you got flustered she'd get confused. If you got annoyed—and of course you'd get annoyed, if a stranger tried to mine your life story for the secret to what to do with theirs—she'd give you this wide-eyed, wounded look, like she was a dog you'd struck. It might even make you feel sorry for her. Then you'd remember that Cecilia was thirty years old, and if you're supposed to learn anything by thirty it's that some questions aren't worth asking.

It wasn't that Cecilia didn't mean well. Even on her bitterest days Rose had to admit Cecilia meant well. It was just that Cecilia was so extravagantly, so idiotically openhearted that you couldn't leave her alone for a minute or two without her plunging them both into some charitable disaster. Tell Cecilia a story about the woman who had broken your heart, and she'd take the sapphire ring she'd inherited from their grandmother off her finger, clasp it into your palm, and beg you to take the next flight to Albuquerque to propose. Tell Cecilia about the seven-part epic poem you were composing, a poem that was going to revolutionize the modern world, but which not a single human being other than you had ever understood or even enjoyed, and Cecilia would open up her wallet and give you every bill she had, and insist that you use the money to get a hotel room quiet enough to grant you necessary repose, without even reading a line. Stand outside the Metropolitan Opera House, looking both bedraggled and receptive to the transcendent power of music, holding one of those signs saying *seeking spare tickets*, and Cecilia would give you the pair she had in her purse. Even if it was Rose's sixteenth birthday. Even if Rose and Cecilia had saved up for them for three months.

"He needed it more than we did," said Cecilia, when Rose protested. "He was in spiritual agony. I could just *tell.*

"Besides," she'd added, with intoxicating certainty. "We'll have an even more enchanted night tonight, because of our sacrifice. The city"—she drew in breath—"will provide."

It did. That was the most infuriating part. New York had always been kind to them; at least, it had always been kind to Cecilia, and it tolerated Rose.

Still, when people asked Rose what it was like, having had her kind of childhood, she found it easiest to say that the city had been their real mother. It was like those myths about the founders of Rome, abandoned brothers who had in their infancy been suckled by wolves. It was a convenient way to explain it without inviting pity. Rose hated pity.

Not that their childhood was a bad one. Their mother had been what people called *an eccentric* when they knew the girls were listening, and what they called *a grifter* when they thought they weren't. To herself she was a *professional muse*.

She knew everybody, and was known by everybody; she'd been something of a model and something of an actress and something of an artist, and she'd been a regular at all those haunts of the seventies and eighties that *New York* magazine regularly lamented were always closing down and being replaced by banks and pharmacy chains, without ever being among the boldface names eulogized. Rose doubted she'd ever paid her own tab. She believed—sometimes Rose thought it was her only conviction—that childhood was an oppressive illusion thrust upon young people by the repressive *bourgeoisie*, and encouraged both sisters to grow out of it as quickly as possible.

What this meant in practice was that the girls fended for themselves, when it came to meals more elaborate than soup cans or cereal; that Rose was allowed to paint murals on the bedroom wall, and Cecilia was allowed to carve her initials into the old tuneless wall piano in the living room; that they spent a lot of time amusing themselves in cocktail party corners; and that they rarely if ever attended school more than a few weeks in row.

The identity of the girls' father (*fathers*, Rose always assumed) was a pleasant mystery: like the existence of God. Their mother always said Cecilia and Rose had been born through parthenogenesis. They never challenged her. There was a parade of stepfathers—some feckless, some avuncular—from whom Cecilia and Rose gleaned odd bits of trivia, occasional periods of discipline, and a taste for Armagnac. *It wasn't*—Rose told a college roommate once—*traumatic or anything.* Only one of the stepfathers had ever been handsy; *and even that*, she'd say, *was innocent, more or less.* After all, he was Italian.

But New York had raised them. Whenever their mother was out or asleep or abroad, Cecilia would march Rose out into the city, convinced that among its munificent strangers the girls would find whatever it was they needed. And whether because Cecilia was charming, or because Cecilia was beautiful, or because the world really was as abundant and glorious a place as Cecilia believed it was, they usually did.

They had protectors in every neighborhood. In Alphabet City they befriended a jazz guitarist with three fingers on his left hand who told them he'd cut off the last two himself in imitation of Django Reinhardt and who let Cecilia practice sonatas on his piano in preparation for her Juilliard audition, which Cecilia aced as splendidly and as effortlessly as everything else she'd ever done. In Bay Ridge they came to know an artist who specialized in self-portraits of himself as various animals—cats, mostly, but also zebras and stags—and who kept his refrigerator stocked with fresh produce and cured meats and hunks of creamy cheese, and who taught Rose how to scramble eggs and also how to shade the contours of a human face.

In their own neighborhood of Tudor City, a little neo-Gothic cul-de-sac between the United Nations and the Upper East Side, they spent evenings at the home of a meticulously dressed old woman from the Balkans they always called the Countess. She lived in the penthouse apartment, at the top of this fantastic faux-medieval tower the girls had spent hours trying to spy on with binoculars, until she had at last called down to the doorman and instructed him to let them in. They never did work out whether she was wildly wealthy or whether she—like their mother—had lucked her way into a rent-regulated apartment; they decided, largely on the basis of her furs, that she must be some kind of European aristocrat in romantic exile. Their grasp of world history—as of most school subjects—was at this point still tenuous, but when Cecilia asked her if she had personally fled the fall of the Ottoman Empire, the Countess took it upon herself to correct the gaps in their education. She checked their homework, lectured them over schnapps and Ferrero Rocher chocolates, let Rose copy sketches out of her coffee-table books from various museums, and once lent the girls a copy of the collected poetry of T. S. Eliot, informing them that they would know they had left childhood behind only when they found themselves preferring "The Waste Land" to "The Love Song of J. Alfred Prufrock."

Rose never ended up making sense of either poem. In any case, she never needed to. As far as Rose was concerned her childhood ended six months later, on the morning of Cecilia's eighteenth birthday, which was the day that Cecilia left for school, without a word to anybody, and then did not return for three years.

Cecilia tried to explain it, later on. There had been this poet—*well*, she faltered, *he thought of himself as a poet.* They'd met on a LiveJournal forum for people who wished they lived in a different century from the one in which they'd been born. He'd written her love letters. (*Well, emails, but—*) He lived out in Montana, working part-time at a rehabilitation center for injured falcons. He'd promised her open sky and the ability to find the beauty in the dirt under her fingernails. His grandfather was going to teach her to play old folk songs on the fiddle. They were going to sit nightly by the fire, and Cecilia was going to learn to recognize every constellation there was, which Cecilia thought was a more robust way of learning about the hidden connection between all things than spending three years at Juilliard. He was thirty-nine.

Cecilia was there five months before she found out about his ex-wife, who was a horse trainer in Missoula, and the two children they shared; she'd thought about returning then, or at the very least writing something longer than a postcard, only by then there was this Austrian concert pianist named Berghardt she'd been emailing after watching his videos, and he lived in this little seaside Slovenian village, and his villa had a piano in it, and it wasn't about true love, exactly, and it wasn't about music, either, and it wasn't about the light of the moon on the Adriatic, either, but it was a little bit about all of those things, and also about something else, something wondrous and indescribable, like the pot of gold at the end of the rainbow or the Holy Grail in the King Arthur stories, and *oh, Rosie?* Cecilia threw up her hands—*I'm no good at putting things into words*—and Rose didn't have the heart to tell her that the first thing you learn when you grow up is that the Holy Grail doesn't exist.

But that was the thing about Cecilia. She never had grown up. She barreled from lover to lover, from continent to continent, from ashram to monastery, in search of the invisible and unnameable thing she could not and would not understand. She was perpetually broke—what little money she earned from odd music gigs she inevitably gave away to causes or communes. She was often sick—once, when she was twenty-six, she got scurvy, which Rose didn't even know was something you could even still get. Whenever Cecilia came home—when she ran out of money; when a lover hit her or left her; when the political activist she'd met on a Transcaucasian railway snuck out of a Yerevan train station with the entire contents of Cecilia's suitcase—she'd show up, white-faced and hollow-checked, on the doorstep of the apartment in Tudor City, with a backpack of filthy clothes and Falstaff, her one-eyed stuffed rabbit, and throw herself once more into Rose's arms. She'd stay for a week or for a month or for three, leaving muddy scuffs on Rose's carpet and festering dishes in Rose's sink; she'd keep Rose up until three in the morning, working out chords on their mother's tuneless piano; then one day Cecilia would vanish like the first breeze of spring, and Rose's life would go on as it had before.

Not that Rose's life wasn't a good one. It was—you couldn't deny this—a success. Rose was proud of it. She had built it up for herself. It was the sort of life a person could point to as evidence of great personal discipline, of self-control, of *seriousness*. Being serious, Rose felt, meant you were the kind of person who chose clear and attainable goals for yourself and worked steadily and methodically toward them until you had accomplished exactly what you set out to do, without being waylaid by self-indulgent narratives about quests or grails or true love. It meant that you made the kind of promises a person could be reasonably expected to keep and that you kept them. It meant being the kind of person other people could rely on. You could always rely on Rose.

Their mother had gotten sick two years after Cecilia's first disappearance, which was the summer after Rose had graduated high school. Cecilia had not been called. Even if Rose had known where she was, she knew better than to ask. Cecilia would have been useless with a bedpan, an IV drip, hospital gowns. She would have spilled pill bottles, confused doctors' addresses, wept at inopportune times. She would have asked her mother, point-blank, whether it was frightening, knowing you were going to die, and whether you believed more or less in life after death, at the razor's edge, and what it felt like to know how your story ended.

Besides, their mother wouldn't have wanted her there. Once, she'd wanted a beautiful life for herself; dying, she wanted it for Cecilia. Cecilia was her favorite. Their mother had taken pleasure in the fact that Cecilia—easily the more beautiful sister—resembled her; *better*, their mother once said, *that she remember me as I was.*

So it was. Rose read Cecilia's postcards out loud. She invented happy outcomes for every love affair. She postponed the start of college in California first one year, then two, and then at last reapplied to college in New York, where she could at least study while living at home.

Rose made up ferociously for lost time.

She double majored in math and computer science; graduated close to the top of her class. She mastered several programming languages. She took a job at a start-up called OptiMyze that helped people make better life choices by encouraging them to input their chosen values into an app and then producing gamified road maps for how to live them out, and then at another start-up called MBody that tracked your health data and told you whenever something about your heart rate or step count or weight gain was sufficiently out of the ordinary that you might want to see a doctor. Now she worked at My.th, which produced a bespoke series of meditation and mindfulness audio tracks to help you focus on the different areas of your life that needed specialized attention, and which customized the specifics of what you heard based on changes in your heart rate.

Rose liked the work. At least, she liked the feeling of being good at her work, and the more general sense that her work was useful, at least to the kind of people who cared about being useful in the first place. Rose always liked to be good at things. She liked when people noticed.

Rose liked, too, the settled calm that came over her when she produced a particularly efficient piece of code; she liked sitting straight-backed at a desk with her earphones in thinking of nothing but what was right in front of her. She liked biking to her office in DUMBO, liked eating salads for lunch, liked dropping by kickboxing on her way home. She liked making money; more, she liked saving it, portioning percentages for retirement and percentages toward an eventual down payment on an apartment and percentages for charitable giving and percentages for scented candles, or else the occasional vacation abroad. A college boyfriend had once told her, not entirely unkindly, that she reacted to spreadsheets the way ordinary girls reacted to sex.

Rose didn't know if this was true. All she knew was that the feeling of serenity that came over her, when she looked at her well-ordered desk, or a well-crafted line of code, was part of the feeling of building a life: something clean and complete and self-contained. It was, Rose felt, what serious people did, people who knew enough to know that out of every ten-thousand-odd girls like her who had dreamed of painting for a living, only one is ever talented enough to make it work.

Besides, Rose reminded herself, on the rare occasions her conviction wavered, it was self-indulgent to live your life for beauty. It was barely better than being one of those people (their final stepfather had been one) who lived only for good food or fine wine. Beauty was just something—like cognac, like heartbreak—a person consumed.

—

Rose was twenty-eight the year Cecilia found the Avalon and vanished for the final time.

That year, Rose was still living in their mother's Tudor City apartment. She didn't particularly like it—it was dated and cramped; the bathtub grout was even more prone to mold than it had been when she and Cecilia were children, and there was always a draft coming from the fireplace— but she knew you didn't give up a rent-stabilized two-bedroom in the middle of Manhattan, no matter how often the boiler gave out. Besides, Cecilia needed a place to come home to, on the rarer and rarer occasions she came home.

In any case, Rose spent most nights at Caleb's.

Caleb was thirty-four. He and Rose had been together for five years. He was the smartest person Rose had ever known. They had met working at OptiMyze, which Caleb had founded, because Caleb was one of those people who dedicates his life to things that matter, and what mattered most to Caleb was helping people make better choices. *People aren't rational*, Caleb always said. *Give them a set of options, and they'll inevitably pick the worst one.* Like how the same people who were afraid of flying regularly underestimated their risk of dying in a car crash. Caleb lived in an expansive one-bedroom apartment on the Lower East Side, with floor-to-ceiling windows and clean marble countertops and blank walls. Caleb liked open spaces. He hated waste. He'd converted one of his bedroom walls into a whiteboard, so that he could write out his to-do list before bed—work tasks, but also exercise, and time carved out for activities, and also the values he most wanted to focus on in the day ahead—so that it would be the first thing he saw waking up in the morning. Rose found this endearing.

Rose and Caleb were happy. They shared the same values, like honesty and frank conversation and solving conflicts by counting silently to fifteen before speaking. They cared about the same things. They were both runners. They both wanted two children. Caleb wanted to one day move somewhere warmer—San Diego, say, or Austin, where a lot of people were working remotely these days—because God knows you couldn't raise one child in this city, let alone two. Rose reminded herself that she liked the Pacific.

They bickered about this, sometimes, because whenever Caleb brought up moving, Rose would bring up the Tudor City apartment, for which she alone was on the lease, and for which she alone paid rent. She wanted to keep the apartment for Cecilia's sake. Caleb would remind her that Cecilia was thirty years old by now, and if fewer people enabled people like Cecilia, there would be fewer people like Cecilia in the world, and then Rose would argue that there was nobody quite like Cecilia in the world. Although Caleb was right about most things and most people and was almost certainly right about Cecilia, Cecilia was still Rose's sister, and there were just some things you didn't do, in this life, and giving up the only apartment your sister could ever afford to live in was one. Caleb said this was deontology, which as far as he was concerned was just a high-level version of operating on emotional impulse. Caleb was probably right about this, too. (Most of what Rose knew about philosophy she'd learned from the Countess, who didn't believe in anything that happened after the Enlightenment.)

Plus, Caleb insisted, it's not like Cecilia would be coming home any-time soon, anyhow. Cecilia had gotten married.

Rose had gotten the letter around Easter. Cecilia's handwriting was so disastrous Rose had to read it three times over to be sure she understood.

His name was Paul Byrd. He was half-English—he'd grown up, Cecilia spent four or five lines explaining, in the same Yorkshire town where the Brontë sisters had once lived. He was an English teacher at a boarding school in coastal Maine. Cecilia had gotten a part-time job teaching piano and violin at their music center, which was well-regarded. They'd met in town, at a bookstore called the Manifest. Right away they knew it was the kind of love people write eight-part poems about. They'd gotten engaged the night they met. Three weeks later the school chaplain married them on the quadrangle, under a trellis of cherry blossoms, because the chapel had burned down three years prior.

Finally, Cecilia wrote, *I've found my grail.*

She apologized for not inviting Rose. They hadn't invited anyone. They'd been too in love to wait.

Rose folded the letter, neatly, in two. Then she crumpled it up and threw it in the trash.

"I don't see why you're so upset," Caleb said. "I mean, it's a good thing for her, right? I mean, she *is* thirty."

Rose didn't know why she was so upset, either. It's not like she and Cecilia spoke often—they hadn't seen each other since six months before the pandemic, when Cecilia was living with a once-well-regarded female artist two decades her senior on a Thames houseboat-slash–art gallery that smelled like a sewer and later sank. Rose had been in London for a conference on technology and society. Cecilia had served her weak tea with curdled milk, and asked her whether she'd made it to the Victoria and Albert Museum, or the Soane's house to see the Hogarths, and Rose had to explain the way you would to a toddler that no, of course she hadn't, because the conference went through dinner, nightly, and then after dinner you still had to linger in the bar to talk to your colleagues, and no, a person couldn't just duck out during a *lunch break*, just to see an old painting, and besides, it wasn't like Rose thought that much about painting these days anyway, but the injured look on Cecilia's face when Rose said this made Rose feel like quitting painting had been some kind of betrayal, instead of just something that happens to everyone who grows up.

"It's just the principle," Rose said to Caleb. "You invite your sister to your wedding. It's just what you *do*." She knew this was probably deontology, too, but she was too annoyed to care.

"On the bright side," Caleb said, and kissed Rose on the forehead. "She's somebody else's problem, now."

—

Cecilia came home on the first cold day of September.

Summer had lingered late that year. The garden boxes that lined the streets of the Upper East Side were still overgrown with daffodils; the trees in Central Park remained defiantly green. The air was still sticky. Rose and Caleb and Grant and Lydia still spent Saturday afternoons in the Rockaways, drinking weak margaritas—except for Caleb, who almost never drank. But there was an amber chill in the air, on the morning that Cecilia came home, and a few russet leaves blew past Rose's face as she made her way to Tudor City.

Rose had not been home in five days. She'd lingered at Caleb's for more nights than usual; she had grown comfortable there, curled up against his shoulder underneath his weighted blanket, on his butter-white sofa, listening to podcasts on surround sound. But Rose had run out of clean clothes, and was also expecting this cashmere sweater she'd impulsively ordered from The RealReal, and so she'd put in her earphones and jogged all the way uptown along the East River.

As soon as Rose opened the door, she knew Cecilia had come home.

It was the smell that did it.

It was the fermentation of dirty laundry, of cigarette smoke, of moth-balls and vintage silk and five different kinds of perfume. Rose had been to the Vatican once, on vacation with Caleb, on the hottest day of August, choking on ecclesiastical incense and other people's sweat. It smelled, Rose told Caleb, *just like Cecilia's room.*

Rose pushed the door open.

Cecilia's suitcase was lying in the middle of the room, underneath a mountain of clothing. The belt of a paisley dressing gown snaked from where it had gotten caught in the suitcase zipper. A trail of dirty under-pants led toward the smaller of the apartment's two bedrooms.

Rose's heart sank.

"Cecilia?" she called.

There was no answer.

Rose took a few steps toward the bedroom door.

"Cecilia—is that you?"

She swung the door open.

Cecilia was sitting at the head of the bed. Her knees were pulled up to her chin. Falstaff was nestled against her chest.

Rose had never seen Cecilia look worse.

She was gaunt. Her skin was yellow, except for a few scabrous patches that might have been acne and might have been eczema. Flakes of dandruff dotted her scalp. She had cut off all her hair—so unevenly that Rose wondered if she'd even used a mirror. Mascara smeared halfway down her nose.

"Rosie?" Cecilia's voice was hoarse. Her eyes were wide and childlike. "What happened to you?"

"What do you mean—*what happened to me*? What happened to *you*?"

Cecilia didn't say anything.

"When did you get here?"

Cecilia didn't meet her gaze.

"Thursday."

"You didn't call me." It was Saturday afternoon.

"My phone was out of credit." Cecilia kept her eyes on the foot of the bed. "And I figured you'd be home soon. So I figured I'd wait." She swallowed. "Where were you, anyway?"

"Nowhere." Rose reminded herself she had no reason to be defensive. "With Caleb."

"Who?"

"My— Jesus, Cecilia, you know Caleb."

Cecilia wrinkled her nose.

"The one with the whiteboard above his bed?"

"It's not ab—" Rose relented. "Yes," she said. "That's him."

Cecilia considered.

"Huh," she said. She pulled her knees in tighter to her chest.

"What are you doing here, Cecilia?"

At first Rose thought Cecilia hadn't heard her. She remained silent, staring straight ahead, chewing on her lower lip. Then at last she looked up. Her eyes were bloodshot.

"I've come," Cecilia said, "to stay."

"Sorry?"

"Here, I mean." Cecilia said, a little louder. "I've come to stay *here*."

"Where's Paul?"

Cecilia's expression didn't change.

"Maine," she said.

"What happened?"

"I don't want to talk about it."

"You broke up?"

"I *said*"—Cecilia's voice tightened—"I don't want to talk about it!"

Rose sank down onto the foot of the bed.

"I'm sorry," she said mechanically.

"Thank you," Cecilia said. She squeezed Falstaff tighter. She took a deep breath. "I can't do this anymore, Rosie."

"Do what?"

"*This.*" Cecilia motioned at the laundry piled on the bedroom chair. "All of this. The coming. The going. The mess. The jet lag. The fuckups. Every new and shiny and exciting thing that turns out to be . . ." Her laugh was dark. "Christ, no different from everything else."

"I'm sorry," Rose faltered, "I don't under—"

"God, Rosie, don't you get it? I'm so goddamned sick of myself!"

Rose fell silent.

Rose had seen Cecilia suffer in so many ways over the past twenty-eight years. She'd seen Cecilia rage and weep and throw things; she'd seen Cecilia pull the blankets over her head and scream into pillows; she'd seen Cecilia insist, feverishly, that there *must have been some misunderstanding*, that the military historian who'd ghosted her at the Prague airport must have just gotten her flight number wrong. Rose had never seen Cecilia despair. She did not recognize the still and steely creature who sat before her, hugging her knees so tightly her wrists left chalky indentations on her skin.

"I want," Cecilia went on, in that same stony voice, "things to be different. I want to *be* different. I want a real life . . ." She wiped her face with the back of her hand. "Rosie?"

"What?"

"Can I stay here?"

"It's your place, too," Rose began carefully. "Of course you can stay."

Cecilia shook her head. "No—I mean—do you *want* me to stay?"

Rose didn't mean to hesitate. But Cecilia's face had already fallen.

"It's fine," Cecilia said. "I'm sorry; I'm sorry; that was stupid of me; I shouldn't have—"

"Of course I want you to stay." Rose was too quick. "Really."

Cecilia didn't say anything for a long time. She fondled Falstaff's ear. She put it, absent-mindedly, between her lips.

"You shouldn't," Cecilia murmured. "God knows I wouldn't blame you if you didn't."

"Cecilia—"

"Come on, Rosie." Cecilia attempted a smile. "All I ever do is mess things up. You know that. Don't you?"

Rose didn't say anything.

Rose hated liars, especially kind ones: there was something cowardly, condescending, even, about telling people only the version of reality they could stand. Caleb had a saying—*everybody endures the truth*, which meant whatever you believed or didn't, you lived in the real world, all the same, and had probably gotten used to it by now. But Rose couldn't help feeling that *everybody*, in this case, didn't quite apply to Cecilia.

"I think," Rose said at last, "you can do anything you set your mind to." This was the most tactful version of the truth Rose could manage. But if there was an evasion, Cecilia didn't hear it. She flung her arms around Rose's neck.

"Oh, *Rosie*," she breathed. "Thank you!"

She drew back. Her whole face flushed. For a moment she was the old Cecilia again.

"I'm not going to let you down," she said. She seized Rose's hand. "I swear, Rosie. You're not going to recognize me. God, you'll be so *proud.*

I'm going to get a job—they're looking for a weeknight pianist over at Mimi's; I already checked; it's tacky but it's *something*, and I could fix up the piano in the living room; it sounds like a sick goose now, but we could fix it up, and I was thinking we could reopen the fireplace, maybe, in time for Christmas, and we could—" She stopped short. She turned Rose's hand in hers.

"Rosie?"

She was staring at Rose's engagement ring.

—

It had happened a month ago. They'd been sitting side by side on Caleb's sofa, listening to this podcast about the top five most common cognitive biases and what you could do about them. Caleb had been nervous. Rose had never seen him nervous, so when he'd started talking about *the shape of the rest of our lives* and *reinforcing our mutual goals* she'd assumed that he was about to break up with her. Only then he'd squeezed himself into the crevice between the coffee table and the sofa, took the ring out from his pocket, and said *will we make each other better, all the rest of our days?*

Even as he was sliding the ring onto her finger, Rose didn't fully believe it. Marriage was something other people did, functional people, people who had grown up with curfews and fully stocked pantries, and fathers. Marriage was for people who were sure of how to live.

Rose had never been more grateful for Caleb.

Caleb would be sure, Rose told herself, for both of them.

—

It's not like Rose planned to keep it from Cecilia. She'd just been waiting for the right time. Besides, it wasn't like Cecilia had contacted her, either.

But now Cecilia was holding Rose's hand in hers, and turning the considerable diamond up to the light, with a look of astonishment on her face.

It has never occurred to her, Rose thought, with such sudden ferocity that she was ashamed of herself, *that something interesting might have happened to me.*

"Caleb?"

"Of course Caleb!"

"How long?"

"Only a couple weeks. I was going to call you; I just—"

"You don't have to explain," Cecilia said. She kept her eyes on the ring. "Do you love him?"

"Of course I love him."

"I mean"—Cecilia tried again—"is he your *soul mate*?"

"What's that supposed to mean?"

"I don't know. Never mind."

"Fine," Rose said. "Sure. He's my *soul mate*. My *one true love*. My *knight in shining armor*. Whatever you want to call it. I love him and I'm happy."

Cecilia only hesitated a moment.

"Good," she said. "Good. I'm happy for you."

Cecilia was a terrible liar. Still, Rose appreciated the effort.

"But you're keeping the apartment?"

"I—" Rose faltered. "We're not thinking about anything like that—until after the wedding."

"And after?"

"I mean," Rose tried. "Caleb's place is nicer." She decided against mentioning Austin or San Diego.

"When's the wedding?"

"Summer," Rose said. "Probably. We haven't set a date or anything." They'd already started touring venues.

Cecilia nodded.

"Well," she said. "That's good." She sat straight up. "I mean—the timing." She cleared her throat. "You could even call it fate. Right?"

Rose looked up at her in confusion.

"What?"

"I mean—that I'm here. Now. Just right when you'll need someone to help you."

"*Help* me?"

"You know. With organizing. And things. Picking napkins. Going to tastings. The bachelorette party." Cecilia was determined to smile.

Rose wasn't sure Cecilia had ever been to a bachelorette party. She doubted Cecilia had ever been to a real wedding.

"I—I could even play something for you," Cecilia went on. "If you wanted me to. I've played church organs before."

"We haven't started thinking about the music," Rose said.

"You'll be a beautiful bride," Cecilia said, patting the blanket for emphasis. "A *princess*."

"I don't really want to be a prin—"

"Fine, a *queen,* then!"

"Thank you." This took effort.

"God knows," Cecilia said. "One of us has to do this marriage thing right."

—

"Be serious," Caleb said, when Rose told him, curled up beside him on his sofa. "She's not going to stay for the wedding."

"She might," Rose said. "She seemed *different*—this time."

"Different how?"

"I mean—people *do* grow up, don't they? Eventually?"

"Come on," Caleb said. "She bailed on her own mother's funeral."

"That was a passport issue!"

"It's always a *something* issue."

Caleb wasn't wrong. Rose couldn't remember the last time Caleb had been wrong.

"I think she really wants to change her life," Rose tried, with a little less conviction than before.

"Everybody always wants to change their life." Caleb shrugged. "Almost nobody ever does."

Rose relented.

"Still," she said. "We should make an effort. While she's here."

Caleb grimaced.

"We'll make an effort," he said. "We can invite her to your birthday? If she's still around by then."

Rose's birthday was three weeks away.

"She's not so bad, you know," Rose said.

"I know, I know," Caleb said. "Your sister's a lot of *fun*." He lanced the word.

"It's not just that," Rose said. "I mean—she *is* fun, but . . ." She tried to work out what she meant. Sometimes, with Caleb, Rose had trouble finding words for the things she meant. She'd somehow find the flaws in her own reasoning before she could manage to open her mouth. "The world's . . . *different*, somehow, when she's around."

"Different how?"

Rose thought of the Countess, the three-fingered musician, the man who painted cats. She tried again. "She makes you feel like you're living inside a story. Somehow," she added, more apologetically than she'd meant to.

Caleb looked at her blankly. "And that's a good thing?"

"Isn't it?"

"I don't know," Caleb said. "It probably depends on what story you're in. I don't think self-narrativizing is particularly healthy. You can convince yourself of a lot of stupid things, if you start thinking of yourself as some sort of hero."

"I don't think Cecilia thinks of herself as a hero."

"A victim, then."

Rose relented. "All I meant was that it's kind of exciting, sometimes, when she's around."

"*Fun*," Caleb said. That settled it.

CHAPTER TWO

Two weeks passed. Cecilia kept her promise.

She unpacked. She hand-washed every article of clothing she owned in the bathroom sink and then hung them from the shower rod in one meticulous row. She scrubbed the dishes after using them, and only rarely did Rose have to sneak them from the drying rack and scour them a second time. She got a part-time job playing at Mimi's, a late-night Italian restaurant-slash-piano bar near Beekman Place, coming home at two or three in the morning with a fistful of cash tips and boxfuls of leftover garlic bread. Sometimes Rose would wait up for her, the nights she still spent in Tudor City, and then the two of them would sit together on the ratty jacquard chaise the handsy Italian had shipped all the way from Venice, and Cecilia would regale Rose with stories of the divorced Slovene diplomat who slipped her a twenty every time she played "Take Me Home, Country Roads" but sang "West Capodistria" instead of "West Virginia," and of the retired literary agent who came in every night and annoyed everybody by asking for Sondheim.

Cecilia didn't mention Paul again. Had it not been for the pale border at the sunburned base of her ring finger you might think she'd never been married at all. Rose tried once or twice to broach the topic sideways—asking about the weather in Maine, say, or bringing up Caleb's friend the divorce lawyer. Cecilia saw through it all.

"I told you, Rosie," Cecilia said, for the fifth time. "I won't discuss it. Don't try to change my mind."

—

Fifteen days after Cecilia's return, she announced that she had made an appointment to take Rose wedding dress shopping. She'd booked them into an exquisitely tiny French shop on Lexington and Sixty-Third called La Belle Dame Sans Souci, which Rose had read about in a *Misandry!* listicle.

The appointment was for ten. When Rose arrived at 9:55, Cecilia was already there with two coffees. Rose had never seen her tidier. She had brushed and slicked back her hair, which a professional had now made even. Her face was clean of makeup. Her tights had no holes.

"Admit it." Cecilia was smiling. "You didn't think I'd show up on time." She handed Rose one of the coffees.

"I mean," Rose began, and then stopped.

"I told you," Cecilia chirped, "I'm a different person now. Besides, a maid of honor has to be organized. It's in the job description."

—

Rose tried on five dresses. She hated them all. The strapless one with the A-line skirt looked self-aggrandizing, like she was pretending to be one half of a royal wedding. A more modest sheath came off apologetic, like Rose was embarrassed to be getting married at all. The one the proprietress called cottagecore (she pronounced it "cot-*age*") was worse still: swaddling Rose in so much fabric she looked like the infant Jesus in a Christmas crèche.

"Don't be stupid," Cecilia said, unzipping Rose from one with tulle frills. "You look beautiful. Besides, it's supposed to be a whole ordeal, finding the right one. I watched a reality show last night where this woman tried on a *thousand* dresses before finding the one she liked."

"You watched *Say Yes to the Dress?*"

"Research," Cecilia said. "Did you know that sixty percent of American couples who got married last year met online?"

Rose did, in fact, know this.

"Still," Rose said, "I don't want to try on a thousand dresses."

"You're the *bride*." Cecilia took a swallow of champagne. "It's your day. You could try on *ten thousand*, and I'd zip you in and out of every single one." She idly fingered the tag on one with a mermaid tail. "How about this one? Christ almighty!" She caught sight of the price. She blanched, then turned the tag over. "Well," she said gamely. "It *does* have a lot of sequins." She shook herself. "Come on. Let's try another."

"I think I'm tired."

"Rosie—come *on*! The next one will be perfect; I can just feel it; I have a *sense* . . ."

"Cecilia—"

"You're going to look like the bride in a fairy tale!" Cecilia thrust a fistful of chiffon into Rose's face. "Caleb is going to take one look at you and faint. Trust me!"

Rose didn't know why she was so annoyed. Maybe it was the heat, or the constricting way the tulle had dug into the flesh of Rose's breasts; maybe it was the limp way her straight, brown hair hung down like a dead branch from her scalp, or the insistent way Cecilia was trying to pretend she knew what would and wouldn't make Caleb faint, like she knew anything about Caleb in the first place, like Cecilia wasn't secretly judging Rose for even considering a dress this ostentatiously *basic*, like Cecilia didn't secretly think that everything Rose had ever done was a betrayal of the person she thought Rose ought to have been.

"For God's sake, Cecilia," Rose snapped, before she could stop herself. "You don't have to pretend to care about the dress."

"I *do* care about the dress!"

"Just because you didn't get to have one—"

Rose saw Cecilia's face and knew she'd gone too far.

"I'm sorry," she said. "I'm sorry; I shouldn't have . . ."

"It's fine." Cecilia kept her eyes on the floor. "You're right. I shouldn't have pushed. I'm sorry."

"I could try this one?" Rose held up a hideous one, studded with Swarovski crystals, in the hopes it would make Cecilia laugh. "You think this one would make Caleb faint?"

A slow smile spread across Cecilia's lips.

"If it didn't blind him first."

—

"As it happens," Cecilia said suddenly, an hour later. "I *did* have a wedding dress."

They were sitting at Bemelmans Bar, at the Carlyle hotel. It was the first time they had ever been there as adults. They had gone there as teenagers, because Rose liked to sketch from the corner booth, and because one of the older bartenders was willing to mix them up soda and bitters at no charge and shoo away the men who sidled up to offer them something stronger.

"It was a nightgown," Cecilia went on. "Technically. I was going to wear this pink silk dress I had, to go with the cherry blossoms; only the night before the wedding I suddenly got this feeling that I absolutely *had* to wear white, that it wouldn't be a real wedding otherwise. Like, I don't know, God wouldn't count it in his ledger unless I had the veil and the white dress and the something borrowed and the something blue; God knows I wasn't doing anything *else* right, but, somehow, it was the most important thing in the world . . ." She snorted. "Of course, the only white thing I owned was this old nightgown I'd found in a thrift shop in Boston and it was covered in coffee stains. And you know what Paul did?"

It was the first time Cecilia had mentioned Paul since the night of her return. Rose tried not to sound too eager.

"What?"

"He stayed up all night, with a bucket of bleach, scrubbing every last stain out of that dress. It was still wet the next morning when I put it on. Paul had to chase me around the apartment with a hair dryer."

Her smile faded.

"No wonder it didn't work out," she said. "You see, he saw me in the dress before the ceremony."

Rose saw her chance.

"What *did* happen, Cecilia?"

But Cecilia was already staring into her Manhattan.

"It doesn't matter," Cecilia said. She took a long gulp. She winced. "Besides, it's *your* day now. I don't want to spoil it. I promise you, it's not a very interesting story."

"You don't have to—"

Cecilia arched an eyebrow. "Rosie, *please*," she said.

Rose knew better than to try a second time.

They drank in silence. They ordered a second round, and then a third. Rose's head was swimming. She could not remember the last time she'd been this drunk; the sensation was pleasant. The rabbits and giraffes and elephants on the mural on the wall were coming in and out of focus. The pianist was playing "New York, New York."

"You know," Cecilia said. "I never get tired of this song. I don't care if it *is* a cliché." She took a sip of her cocktail. "You wouldn't believe the places they play it, either. Tbilisi. Ljubljana. Oxford. Every single piano bar in the whole damn world, they play it." She leaned back in the booth. "Made me homesick, sometimes."

"I didn't think you were ever homesick."

Cecilia's chin jerked up.

"I was always homesick," she said. "Every day."

"Why didn't you come home, then?"

It was easier to ask this when you were three drinks in.

Cecilia shrugged.

"Stubbornness, maybe. I don't know. Maybe I didn't want to come home empty-handed."

"Empty-handed?"

Cecilia arched an eyebrow. "No grail." She blew out her lips. "Not even so much as a shot glass." She gulped another mouthful of Manhattan. "God," she said. "It would be so much easier, if I knew what I was even looking for." Another sip. "You know, Rosie? I've decided something."

"What?"

"Life is probably a tragedy." A dark smile flickered across Cecilia's face. "True love is an illusion. Nobody ever finds what they're looking for. And everybody dies, in the end."

Rose couldn't tell if Cecilia was joking.

"Don't say that."

"Why not? It's true, isn't it?" Cecilia hiccupped. "Besides, tragedies are the interesting ones. I mean, the ones that are true. Think of the opera, Rosie. Nobody goes to the opera to see a comedy, do they? Except *The Marriage of Figaro*, maybe, and that one's sad if you think about it too hard."

"I guess not," Rose said. Rose hadn't been to the opera since Cecilia's first disappearance.

"Now, *that's* a cliché." Cecilia had started, just slightly, to slur. "The lovers reunite. The misunderstandings all nicely cleared up. The spell of the enchanter broken. The Duke or the Prince or whoever comes out from hiding to say some pretty words about how everybody's sins are forgiven, off scot-free and all us fools can just carry on and live *happily ever after*. God, what a crock."

Rose didn't say anything. She had never liked it when Cecilia talked like this. It made Cecilia feel alien to her, like she belonged to a country Rose was not allowed to enter.

"But what am I saying?" Cecilia forced herself to laugh. "*Your* story's going to end in a wedding, Rosie. And I couldn't be happier for you." She squeezed Rose's hand. "It's different for you, you see," she said. "You deserve it."

—

The bill came. It was almost two hundred dollars. Cecilia flinched when she saw it.

"It's on me," Rose cut in.

"Don't be stupid." Cecilia laid out twelve twenties into the folder. "Tips were good this week. And besides—" She swallowed. "I want to do *something* for you, Rosie. Please."

Rose let her.

—

"Something's different this time," Rose said that night, stumbling past Caleb into bed. "*She's* different."

Caleb caught her hand and kissed it. "You know what the definition of *insanity* is, right?"

"Trusting my sister?"

"Doing the same thing over and over," Caleb said, "and expecting different results."

—

Another week passed. Still Cecilia stayed. She took on another two shifts at Mimi's, and a weekly organist gig at an Anglo-Catholic church off Park Avenue. She kept the kitchen sink clean.

—

Then at last it was Rose's twenty-ninth birthday. She and Caleb had made reservations weeks ago at this Korean-Georgian fusion place in Alphabet City called Jjigae Gogo, along with Lydia and Grant, who were the closest thing they had to *couple-friends*. Lydia was a social media strategist.

She worked with Rose at My.th. Grant was a lawyer and knew Caleb from Stanford. Rose and Caleb had introduced them six months after they themselves had started dating. They were not yet engaged. Only Lydia minded.

—

Rose didn't know why she was so nervous about inviting Cecilia. It wasn't that she didn't want Cecilia there. It was just that Cecilia had one of those faces where you could always tell exactly what she was thinking. It meant you couldn't invite Cecilia somewhere without seeing that somewhere, at least a little bit, through her eyes. Rose didn't know if she wanted to see Caleb and Grant and Lydia through Cecilia's eyes.

"Obviously you'll *love* them," she told Cecilia on the phone. "They're great people. I mean—Grant's a little bit . . . he's got a bit of an asshole schtick going on, but it's only because he doesn't believe anything is, like, too sacred. He's not, you know, *sanctimonious*. He and Caleb balance each other out, I guess, in a way. And Lydia—I mean, she's a *lot*—she's very, like, *manicured*, but she's *loyal*, you know, like a terrier, or—"

"If you love them," Cecilia said magnanimously, "then I'll love them."

—

Friday night came. They all met up for a cocktail before dinner at a new and well-regarded martini bar called Swallow's Nest on Avenue B. Lydia had chosen the venue, because Lydia knew everywhere well-regarded and new.

"Christ almighty," Lydia screamed, when Rose and Caleb entered. "It's so goddamn unfair I want to die." She left lipstick marks on both of Rose's cheeks. "How do you look so good?" Her laugh always sounded a little bit hysterical. She seized Rose's hand. "Let me see it again. I swear to God,

Rose, sometimes I feel like one of those piranhas, you know? Like I could bite your finger clean off."

"You think she's kidding," said Grant. "But she's not. She's like one of those snakes that can unhinge her own jaw."

Rose pretended not to hear this.

"Happy birthday, kid." Grant clapped Rose on the shoulder. "How does it feel to be pushing thirty?"

Lydia thrust an envelope into Rose's hands.

"It's a gift certificate for Botox," said Grant.

"Grant!"

"Sorry. I don't know what it is. I just paid for it."

"It's a *spa day*," Lydia trilled. "There's a new place on Governors Island. Apparently they have pools where you can listen to Vivaldi underwater. Not that you need a spa day. God, I hate you!" She pinched Rose's cheeks.

Grant looked up. "Where's the famous sister?"

"She's on her way."

"What's the over/under on her making the reservation?"

"*Grant*," Lydia said again, in the exact same tone. She turned to Rose. "Well, *I'm* looking forward to meeting her."

Cecilia arrived ten minutes later, out of breath.

"Oh my *God*," Lydia shrieked when she arrived. "I can't believe we're finally meeting you!" She flung her arms around Cecilia's shoulders. "Oh my God, it's uncanny; you're like *twins*." Rose and Cecilia looked nothing alike. "I've heard all about you. Like, literally *everything*. Your whole life."

Cecilia's lips jerked into a smile.

"I'm sorry," she said. "I'm afraid I don't know very much about you."

Lydia laughed helplessly.

"You're, like, a singer, right?"

"A musician," Cecilia said, and then flushed. "I mean—not a real musician. I do church services and weddings and things."

"Children's birthday parties." Grant smirked.

Cecilia smiled at him in confusion.

"She's very talented," Rose said with a firmness she couldn't understand. "She plays everything—piano, violin, fiddle."

"That's basically just violin," Cecilia whispered.

"She's a composer, too," Rose said, a little louder, as if Cecilia were a shy child who just needed nudging.

"I'm not a composer."

"She was working on this *wonderful* opera," Rose said. "Weren't you, Cecilia? About the knights of King Arthur?"

Grant cocked his head. "Wasn't that Wagner?"

"I didn't finish it." Cecilia shifted her weight from one foot to the other. "And it wasn't very good." She kept her eyes on Grant's. "Hence the children's birthday parties."

"That's the best part of one's thirties," Grant said lightly. "Isn't it? The reassuring realization that nothing you do, or ever have done or ever will do, is likely to be very good. Unless you're Caleb, of course." He clapped Caleb on the shoulder. "Caleb's going to turn us all into machines, aren't you, Caleb? And all before he's forty."

Caleb winced.

"That's not—*technically*—what we do," he said. But his ears were pink, which was how Rose could tell that he was pleased.

They finished their first round of drinks and were halfway through another when Caleb checked his watch and noticed that they were ten minutes late for their dinner reservation. They spilled out onto Avenue B. Lydia took Cecilia by the arm.

"I want to know *everything* about you," she said as they crossed into Tompkins Square Park. "Your hopes, your fears, your neuroses, your skin care routine, *everything*."

It was already dark. The park was full, the way it always was on a Friday night. An old man was busking with a set of Chinese bamboo pipes; a group of NYU students sat huddled in their sweatshirts on a nearby bench, recording him with their phones. A lesbian couple with matching lace-up boots was making out against a tree. Farther along the path, a skinny Goth girl with purple hair and a cardboard poster was shouting into a bright blue megaphone.

"Christ," Grant murmured. "Not her again."

"*PEOPLE ARE DISAPPEARING EVERY DAY*," the girl shouted. Her voice was raspy and hoarse. "*AND THE POLICE ARE DOING NOTHING.*"

They quickened their pace.

"*THEY'RE TAKING PEOPLE ALL OVER THIS CITY*," the girl went on, without stopping for breath. She tapped her cardboard sign, on which she had scrawled a stick-figure drawing of a canal barge. Underneath, she had written *HAVE YOU SEEN THIS BOAT*, only she'd run out of space halfway through, and instead written what looked like *HAVE YOU SEENTHISBOAT.*

"And they say New York is dead," Grant said as they passed her.

Cecilia looked up at him. "What does she want?"

"Don't worry about it," Lydia said. "It's probably a viral marketing gimmick. We used to do them all the time when I was at Yance and Co. Once, we were doing this launch for this Diable perfume, and we hired this guy to pretend to be a street preacher and stand outside the velvet ropes telling people they were going to hell if they went—"

But Cecilia was no longer listening.

She had gone right up to the girl.

"Hey," she said with a small smile. "You okay?"

"Well," Grant snorted under his breath. "This is going to be interesting."

The girl started in surprise when Cecilia approached. Evidently Cecilia was the only person who had stopped for her that day.

"Nobody believes me," the girl said. "But you have to understand— they're still out there."

Cecilia's smile was kind. "Who's out there?"

"The fairies. They—" She caught her breath. "They—"

"Jesus Christ." Caleb rolled his eyes. He looked from Cecilia to Rose and back again. "We're going to miss our reservation."

Rose didn't hesitate.

"Cecilia!" She yanked her by the elbow so harshly Cecilia yelped. "Let's *go.*"

"Sorry," Rose said to the girl, and felt ridiculous.

As if, Rose thought bitterly, she were the wrong one. As if it were the normal or the right thing for a person to do: going up to strangers in this city and trying to comfort them, no matter how crazy they seemed or how late you were for your dinner reservation; as if there were something cruel or selfish or painfully unsanctified about trying to make it to your own birthday dinner on time.

Somehow, Cecilia always managed to make Rose feel like she was the one in the wrong.

Rose knew she didn't mean to. That only made it worse.

"I just wanted to make sure she was okay," Cecilia murmured as they crossed back out of the park. "That's all."

"She's a nutjob who lives in Tompkins Square Park shouting about fairies," Rose snapped. "Of course she's not okay!"

"Don't worry," said Lydia, patting Cecilia's shoulder. "I'm *positive* it was viral marketing."

They made it to Jjigae Gogo just in time. It didn't start out a disaster. Lydia told Cecilia all about the work she'd done at Yance and Company, and before that at VETD, which was a dating app whose selling point was that you authorized three friends or family members to swipe and message for you, instead of doing it yourself, because (Lydia explained) most people were terrible judges of what they actually wanted, romantically speaking, and maybe overall.

"You should try it," Grant said. Lydia kicked him under the table. Cecilia smiled gamely and said "maybe" without taking noticeable offense, and then Rose felt guiltier than ever about snapping at Cecilia in the park, because God knows Cecilia was making an effort, and Grant didn't exactly make things easy, and of course you couldn't explain to a person like Cecilia that the key to understanding Grant was that you had to not take him seriously. Cecilia took everything seriously.

The appetizers came: a blend of banchan and pkhali. Cecilia asked Grant what he meant about Caleb turning people into machines.

"We don't have to talk about work," Rose tried, but it was too late. Caleb's face had already lit up.

He explained to Cecilia about OptiMyze and how it had developed in the years since Rose had worked there. Originally, he said, it was just a motivational platform: you put down the habits you wanted to form—lowering your screen time, say, or working out every day—and the app sent you reminders at intervals scientifically proven to be effective. Only by now they had five million users, and their mission was expanding. OptiMyze 2.0, he explained, speaking more and more quickly—Caleb always spoke too quickly when he got excited—would let you put down something called a meta-goal: the kind of person you wanted to be, or the kind of life you wanted to have.

"You don't have to have, like, a mission statement or anything," Caleb said. "Bullet points are fine. Or just words that are meaningful to you."

"A mood board," Lydia stage-whispered, loudly, into Cecilia's ear.

"Then what?"

"Exactly!" Caleb slammed the table. He barreled onward. The app would use machine learning to figure out what you actually wanted, or at least, what you *most* wanted, based on sixty or so unique desire profiles, based in turn on Jungian archetypes. Some people, for example, wanted to be Healers; other wanted to be Leaders.

Cecilia blinked. "So it's like a fancy personality quiz?"

"I mean." Caleb coughed. "That's just the beginning. Establishing the meta-goal. Then the app tells you how to get it. We break it down, you know, into measurable steps. You want to buy a house, here's much you need to save each day. You want to run a marathon, here's the best training regimen, customized for your exact body type." They'd already secured a partnership with one of the fitness tracker brands; they were in talks about getting access to various banking apps, so that OptiMyze could see how much money you were spending and whether it was going toward your meta-goal or one of your minor goals, which might or might not be part of your meta-goal. The moral stuff was harder to quantify, of course, but they were putting together a spiritual advisory board. "Rabbis, priests, witches," Caleb said. They were waiting on a couple of Buddhist monks.

Cecilia kept her hands folded in her lap like a schoolgirl. At last she looked up.

"But—how do you know what to put down for the first thing?"

Caleb wrinkled his nose.

"What first thing?"

"The main goal—the . . . meta-goal?"

"Oh." Caleb looked relieved. "That's easy. You get to pick."

"But I could put down anything, right? Like—I could put down that I wanted to be a serial killer, and it would tell me how to do that?"

Caleb winced. "I mean," he said. "Obviously we'll have safeguards."

"Okay," Cecilia said. "Maybe not a serial killer. Maybe something else—something legal. Let's say I want to be—I don't know—a trophy wife. The app will help me do that, too?"

"Worse things," Grant muttered under his breath, "have happened to better people."

"I mean," Caleb said. "It's designed to help you identify your goals and help you achieve them. It's not, like, *magic*." He sighed. "Look—we've got it in beta right now." He took his phone from his pocket. "I'll show you." He fiddled with the screen. He stared her down. "What do you want—more than anything in the world—right now?"

"Come on, babe!" Rose tried to keep her voice light. "Don't put her on the spot."

"No," Caleb went on, even more decisively. "I'm serious." He snorted. "We're in our thirties, for God's sake. We're supposed to know what we want by now." He cleared his throat. "So, what's your meta-goal, Cecilia?"

Cecilia's smile was frozen on her face. She kept her gaze on Rose, in frozen animal terror, as if expecting Rose to rescue her.

"You can just put down adjectives." Lydia nodded. "Like, *vibes.*"

Cecilia did not speak. She now kept her eyes fixed on her silverware.

"Come on," Rose tried one more time. "Let's talk about something cheerful. Grant, why don't you tell us about the messiest divorce case you've had this year?" She rubbed the back of Caleb's shoulder to settle him.

Caleb hadn't meant to hurt Cecilia, Rose thought. Caleb never meant to hurt anybody. It was just that Caleb was so sure of himself, in the way people who were brilliant were always justifiably sure of themselves; you couldn't make him understand that there were kind, well-meaning, thoughtful people in this world who were still mysteries to themselves, any more than he could understand that there were intelligent people who still believed in God. And you had to admit that Cecilia, at thirty, should probably know what she wanted.

Cecilia lifted her chin. A strange, stubborn smile flickered over her lips. For a horrible moment Rose thought she was about to say *the holy grail*, without irony, like that was a thing you could say to strangers at a dinner party. Like that was a thing you could say to Caleb.

"You go first, Rosie," she said. "What's *your* meta-goal?"

"That's easy," Caleb said. "Ro's already filled it out; it's—"

"I want *her* to tell me."

Rose bristled.

"Caleb's right," she said. "It *is* easy."

Cecilia leaned back in her chair. She crossed her arms. "What is it, then, Rosie?" Her eyes flashed. Then, with a hint of acid: "What did you tell him you wanted?"

Rose's cheeks burned. *Even now*, she thought, *she knows how to get under my skin*. She felt as false and as foolish as she'd felt in one of the wedding dresses at La Belle Dame Sans Souci.

"I want a nice birthday dinner," Rose said, more hotly than she meant to, "sitting around the table with people I care about. That's it. That's my meta-goal."

"*A condition of complete simplicity,*" Grant muttered under his breath. "*Costing not less than everything.*"

Cecilia didn't say anything. She twisted her fingers in her lap so violently that thin streaks of red had started to appear on her knuckles.

"And what does your app say," Cecilia said to Caleb, in that same infuriatingly innocent tone, "about how to do that?"

Caleb opened his mouth.

Then Cecilia's phone rang.

Everybody laughed, a little, with relief.

"Thank God," Grant said, clapping. "Unless OptiMyze can tell us what to order for dessert?"

The ringing kept going.

Rose leaned across the table. "Who is it?"

"Unknown number," Cecilia said. "It might be a work thing. I should—"

Grant leaned back in his chair. "Crisis at little Sansa's bat mitzvah?"

Cecilia clambered to her feet. She nearly knocked the chair over behind her.

"I'm sorry," she said. "I have to take this."

She fled into the bathroom hallway.

"Honestly," Grant said once she'd gone, "I'm having a *great* time."

Cecilia came back to the table three minutes later.

Her face was white. Her eyes were red. Her lips were swollen where she had bitten them.

Lydia craned her neck. "You okay, honey?"

"I'm fine," Cecilia said. Her smile was stiff. "Thank you."

Rose looked up at her. "Who was it?"

"Nobody," Cecilia said.

"Work?"

"It doesn't matter," Cecilia said. "We'll talk about it later." She looked up. She smiled. She raised her prosecco.

"Happy birthday, Rosie," she said. "And here's to many more." Her eyes were glassy with tears.

Cecilia did not speak for the rest of the meal. She remained, straight-backed, twisting her napkin into increasingly tortured shapes, forcing un-convincing smiles.

It was only once Grant and Lydia had gotten a car back to Williams-burg that Cecilia at last looked up.

"Will you stay with me tonight, Rosie?" she asked, in a small voice. "Please?"

Caleb and Rose exchanged glances.

"I mean," Caleb said, "it's up to you."

Rose shot him an apologetic look. Cecilia hailed a cab.

Cecilia did not speak the whole way home. She pressed her face against the windowpane as the cab made its way up the FDR Drive. She gazed out onto the East River. The water was black and shot through with moon-light, giving it an obsidian glare. She huddled into herself. Rose knew better than to press her. It was only when the two of them had crossed the threshold of the Tudor City apartment, and Rose had latched the door behind them, that Cecilia sank at last into one of the Italian's tufted arm-chairs.

She hugged a throw pillow to her chest.

"Paul's here," she said at last.

"*What?*"

"My husband," Cecilia said.

"I *know* who Paul is, Cecilia; I—"

"He wants to see me." Tears snaked down her cheeks. "Tomorrow."

Rose sat down in the other armchair. "I mean—is that good?"

"*Good?*" Cecilia rounded on her. "What do you mean, *is that good*?"

"I mean," Rose tried, as delicately as she could manage, "is it some-thing you could work out, maybe, the two of you?"

Cecilia croaked out a laugh.

"God no," she said. "Not a chance in hell."

"Then—I mean—can't you just tell him that?"

"God, Rosie, you don't get it!" Cecilia threw her head against the back of the chair.

"I mean, I get it, it'll be awkward, but . . ."

"No, Rosie, it's not that. It's not that at all!"

"What is it, then?"

Cecilia wiped a palmful of mascara from her eyes.

"I'm afraid of him," she said simply.

"*Afraid* of him?" Rose's chest constricted. "Jesus, Cecilia; you should have t—" She stopped herself. "Grant's a lawyer," she began again. "We can get you a restraining order, whatever you need. We can call the police—make a report—we . . ."

"The *police*? Why would we call the police?" Cecilia looked at her, uncomprehending. Then she burst into hysterical laughter. "God," she said. *"God!"*

"I don't—"

"*Paul*, violent?" Her voice notched higher. "No, Rosie, you don't understand; Paul's a saint. He's a real, bona fide, modern-day saint—it's horrible; God, it's the worst thing in the world; it's *hell*, Rosie!"

"You don't have to see him," Rose tried, more confused than ever, "if you don't want to."

"No." Cecilia shook her head. "I have to see him. I *owe it to him*, to see him."

"Why?"

"I have to explain."

"Explain what?"

"Why I left."

"I don't understand. You guys must have talked about it, right? You must have . . ."

Rose saw Cecilia's face.

Rose understood.

"You just left."

Cecilia's expression tightened.

"Yes," she said softly. "I just left. Without a word."

"Why?"

"It doesn't matter," Cecilia said. "I don't want to talk about it. The point is—I left him without a word. In the middle of the afternoon. Halfway through the third week of classes. He was on campus, teaching a senior seminar on the Nature and Purpose of Love." She grimaced. "I just took my backpack and Falstaff and walked to the bus station and blocked him on everything I owned. I don't know how he got my new number." Her shoulders slumped. "It doesn't matter. It was going to happen, sooner or later."

Rose looked at Cecilia in astonishment.

She was so used, by now, to Cecilia's comings and goings; to Cecilia's rages and her furious heartbreaks and her wordless departures on the winter wind. It had never occurred to her, before now, that Cecilia might have left someone else in the same way.

"Go ahead," Cecilia said in a small voice. "Judge me."

"I'm not judging you."

"You *are*."

"Fine," Rose said. "Maybe I am. It's only—"

"It's a horrible thing to do to someone," Cecilia said. "I know. I *know*. It's one of the worst things I've ever done. Maybe *the* worst thing. But I didn't have any other choice."

"What does that mean?"

"You wouldn't understand."

"Try!"

Cecilia took a deep breath.

"If I'd stayed," she said, "I'd have jumped off the Falmouth cliffs within six months."

"*Why?*"

"I can't tell you." Cecilia's voice was hollow. "Maybe I don't even know myself. I was like an animal chewing off its own leg." She brought her knees to her chin.

"Rosie?"

"What?"

"If I go see him tomorrow, will you stay over and wait up for me?"

"Why?"

"If I knew you were waiting for me," Cecilia said, "if I knew you were here, holding me responsible, God, *judging me* a little, even, I could go through with it, I think. I could look him in the eye; I could explain; without, I don't know, bolting or doing anything stupid."

"You don't—" Rose began.

"I need you, Rosie!"

Rose told herself that this was the exact thing she had promised herself to stop doing. Then she saw Cecilia's face.

"I'll be here," she said.

—

Rose explained the whole thing to Caleb, the next morning, as diplomatically as she could.

"It's just one more night," she said. "And she *is* my sister."

"Seems like a mess to me," Caleb said. He pushed the button on the juicer. "But it's your call."

"I'll be back by Sunday brunch."

"If you ask me," Caleb said, "they deserve each other."

"I'm sorry?"

"Come on," Caleb said. "Anyone willing to put a ring on your sister after, what, a month probably has a couple screws loose."

"Maybe he's a romantic," Rose said. Caleb snorted.

"Please," he said. "There's nothing romantic about running after someone who's made it clear they don't want you."

Rose put her arms around him. She kissed the back of his ear.

"And if I ran away?" she murmured. "Wouldn't you go to the ends of the earth, chasing me?"

"Don't be ridiculous," Caleb said with a faint smile.

He caught her around the waist. He kissed her.

"And besides," he added, "you wouldn't run."

———

Rose spent Saturday night at Tudor City. Cecilia didn't come home.

Rose busied herself being useful. She washed the dishes, which for the first time since Cecilia's return had been left piled in the sink; she aired out Cecilia's room. She threw out the expired milk solidifying in the fridge. She scrolled *Misandry!* articles on her phone, which she rarely let herself do in Caleb's presence: this one personal essay by a woman who realized she was bisexual when she developed an erotic fixation with her ex-boyfriend's yoga instructor, and another one about whether it was emotional coercion to double text. She listened to an improving podcast about evolutionary psychology and physical touch. She streamed a Pilates class on her phone.

At dawn Cecilia finally came through the door.

Her lips were cracked. Her hair was matted. Glitter cascaded from her collarbone to her ear. On the upper part of her cheek, just below the bone, someone had left the ruby traces of a kiss.

"What the hell happened to you?"

Cecilia staggered forward.

"God knows," she said. She couldn't walk in a straight line.

She let her purse fall beside her.

"Did you see Paul?"

"Yes." Cecilia slumped off her coat. "I saw Paul."

"And?"

"God, Paul," Cecilia murmured. "*Poor* Paul."

She pulled herself a few inches forward.

"What happened?"

"I don't want to talk about it."

"*Cecilia!*"

Cecilia took a long, deep breath.

"He wants me back," she said. *"Goddamn him!"*

"What did you say?"

"What do you think I said? I told him he could go to hell!" Cecilia wiped her mouth with the back of her hand. "But he's stubborn, our Paul. God, he's stubborn. He won't sign a single legal document—that's what he told me. He told me I could do *what I liked,*" she did a burlesque of a British accent, "and that the judge could do *what he liked*, but that he had *no interest* in signing divorce papers—*simply couldn't possibly*, you see." She croaked out a laugh. *"Goddamn him!"* she cried again. "God, I'm going to be sick."

She staggered to the bathroom. She vomited with the door open. She gargled mouthwash. She staggered to the sofa.

"Poor Paul," she murmured again. "Poor, saintly, sickening Paul."

"You two didn't—"

"Didn't what?"

"Cecilia, it's five o'clock in the morning."

Cecilia blinked.

"No, Rose," she said, with slurring certainty. "I did not *fuck* Paul Byrd tonight."

"Then where were you?"

Cecilia reached into her pocket.

"Getting this," she said. She pulled out a small, carefully calligraphed card.

She slammed it down onto the coffee table.

Another life, it read, *is possible.*

Beneath it, in larger letters:

THE AVALON CABARET

Rose turned it over.

On the back, it read:

for further particulars:
please send details of your situation.

Beneath was the address of a PO Box in Brooklyn.

Discretion is paramount.

"I don't understand," Rose said. "What is this?"

"How should I know?"

"Where did you get it?"

Cecilia's laugh was hollow. "In a bar," she said. "I just—I couldn't come home, Rosie. I'd left Paul, and I just kept thinking about you waiting for me, and what you'd say, and what *he'd* said, and, oh, Rosie, all I could think about was that I just needed—just a few minutes, you know, an hour, maybe, where I didn't have to be myself any longer. I just wanted to get drunk. That's all. Just to get out of myself. You must know what that's like."

Rose didn't, but she nodded anyway.

"Anyway, Paul's house-sitting for an old college friend all the way out in fucking Red Hook, in the middle of nowhere—it's not even on the *subway*—and there was this old longshoreman's bar, out there, by the water, with Christmas lights up in the middle of October, and I sat at the bar and I had one drink, just to feel better, and then another, and then before I knew it, I was so drunk I couldn't stop crying, and the bartender was looking at me with this awful pitying look, like *just another drunk mess, having a bad night*, and then suddenly I felt this hand on my shoulder and it was . . . her."

"Who?"

"I didn't get her name. Only—Rosie—I thought I was dreaming. She was the most beautiful woman I'd ever seen. She looked like one of those stars, you know, in Old Hollywood movies, Ava Gardner or Rita Hayworth or—I don't know. She had this long black hair, and she was wearing this long red dress, with black feather trim, ostrich, maybe. And she was wearing diamonds."

"*Diamonds?*"

"Well, they looked like diamonds," Cecilia murmured. "I don't know. And, Rosie, the way she *looked* at me."

"Cecilia—you didn't . . ." Rose wasn't ready for another of Cecilia's affairs.

"No!" Cecilia shook her head too violently. "No, it wasn't like that at all. I mean, it *was*. But that wasn't all it was. That wasn't the point of it. She was looking at me like, like she already knew everything, all about me, better than I knew it myself. And she took my hand. And she said *darling, darling, what's wrong?* And—have you ever read the Bible, Rosie?"

"*What?*"

"I mean, I haven't," Cecilia said. "Or only parts, anyway. But there's this bit in Isaiah, when God touches Isaiah's mouth with coal, and then suddenly he has the power of prophecy; suddenly he can *speak*. When she touched me, it was like that. Like I could tell her everything—about me and Paul, about *you*, about you and me."

Rose prickled. "What did you say?"

"She didn't judge me, either," Cecilia went on, as if she hadn't heard her. "She didn't tell me I was a fuckup or a mess or a bad person. Oh, Rosie, she *understood*. I don't know how long we spent there, talking; only at some point the bar closed, and then she took me to the water, and then we kept on talking. And that's when she gave me the card. She told me to write, if I ever needed her."

Rose looked at the card again.

"*The Avalon Cabaret*," she said. "What is it—some kind of theater thing?"

"It's not," Cecilia said. "At least I don't think so. I googled them in the car home. There's no sign of them. All you get when you google *avalon nyc* is the Roxy Music album and some luxury developer in Midtown."

Rose thought of Lydia. "Viral marketing?"

Cecilia shook her head. "No," she said. "No. This woman, she was *real*. She cried—when I told her things—real tears."

"Maybe it's a cult," Rose said with a smile. She and Caleb had recently watched a documentary about a group of heiresses that got involved in what turned out to be a BDSM cult.

Cecilia let herself smile.

"Maybe," she said. "Probably. Maybe she wants me for a human sacrifice." She wiped the last of her makeup from her face. "I'm not pure enough for a human sacrifice."

"Just don't give them all your money," Rose said.

"That's easy," Cecilia said. "I haven't got any."

She picked up the card again.

"*Another life*," she murmured, "*is possible.* Sounds nice, doesn't it?" She shrugged. "Maybe it's viral marketing, after all. God knows, it'd work on me."

She rose.

"We should go to sleep, Rosie," she said. "Everything's always better in the morning."

"It is morning."

Cecilia looked up in surprise. Clear light was streaming through the windows.

"Afternoon, then. Everything's always better in the afternoon."

"I can't," Rose said. "I'm sorry. I'm meeting Caleb for brunch."

Cecilia's lips twitched.

"Of course," she said. "I'm sorry. I've kept you long enough. It was—it was nice of you to wait up for me."

"Don't mention it," Rose said. "I was happy to."

"It's the last time," Cecilia said. "I mean it. I promise."

She took a deep breath.

"I told you, Rosie," she said. "When this is all over. This mess with the papers. I'm going to be so different. You won't even *recognize* me."

She turned and went into the bedroom. She closed the door.

Rose remained a moment, as if waiting for something she could not quite remember, and then turned and walked out into the corridor, then into the elevator, and then, at last, into the day.

CHAPTER THREE

Two more weeks went by. Cecilia did not bring up the Avalon again. She did not mention Paul. Five nights a week she played at Mimi's; Sundays were for the Church of the Resurrection. She played bat mitzvahs three Saturdays in a row, and if, sometimes, Cecilia left a stray mug of milk to curdle or let bluish mold skein the top of a jar of arrabbiata sauce, Rose wasn't there to see it. Cecilia had made it clear that she didn't need Rose to stay over quite so often.

"It wouldn't be fair to Caleb," she said brightly. "You've got your own life to lead. And a wedding to prepare for."

They'd set the date for the end of June.

"It's a good sign," Rose told Caleb. "She's getting more independent. And it will be easier, of course, once they start signing separation papers. Grant says Paul can only hold up the process so long."

"What a waste." Caleb grimaced. "It's not like he's going to *get* anything out of it."

Rose had told Caleb almost everything about Cecilia's night with Paul. She left out only the Avalon.

It wasn't an intentional omission. Rose had almost forgotten about it herself. When it came to mind at odd intervals—when she spotted a woman in red at the unmarked cocktail bar Caleb liked on East

Sixth Street, say, or when she passed the development Avalon Realty was building on a vacant lot on Avenue B—she spent a minute or two meditating on how strange a place New York was, or at least could be, if you were the kind of person who stayed out at longshoreman bars until four in the morning, and then let it pass out of her mind. It had been a long time since Rose had stayed out until four in the morning. She liked it that way. She always felt a little sorry for the people who hit thirty-five or forty or sixty and still hadn't worked out what they wanted to be when they grew up; the kind of people who wandered from bar to bar and party to party, telling frenetic stories that were supposed to be funny, and always needed you to cover their tab, thinking the point of their life was six months in front of them instead of twenty years behind. There were always one or two at Lydia's parties. *Entertainment*, Lydia called them. Rose could not stand the thought of Cecilia becoming one of them.

———

"She's just jealous," Lydia said a few days later, from the next desk over. "That's what I think."

"Cecilia's not jealous of me." If anything, Rose thought, Cecilia felt sorry for her, which was worse.

"Please," Lydia sniffed. "You don't think it's a coincidence—this whole *man drama*—just happening to start up on your birthday?"

"It wasn't on purpose," Rose said. "Believe me."

"I don't believe that," Lydia said. "People always do things on purpose. She wanted the attention. That's what everybody wants. And if they say anything different they're full of shit."

"I don't want attention," Rose said.

"Then you're full of shit," said Lydia. "It's the goddamn human condition, Rose. Like, come on. Caleb wants people to pay attention to *him*—that's why he's so desperate to make his big choose-your-own-adventure machine. I want Grant to pay attention to me—that's why I haven't eaten a carb in six months. Grant wants his parents to pay attention to him— why do you think he's such an asshole all the time?"

"You think Cecilia wants my attention?"

"Your sister," Lydia announced, "wants everybody's attention. She wants to be, like, the main character of Life."

"Cecilia doesn't want to be the main character," Rose said. "She just— wants her life to be a good story, that's all."

"Same difference," Lydia sniffed. She grabbed Rose's hand. She let her fingertips rest on Rose's ring.

"Besides, if anyone's the main character right now," she said, holding it up to the light, "it's you. You're the one who gets the happy ending."

—

The next week was a good one. There were no disasters. Rose and Caleb paid the deposit on a wedding venue: a restaurant Lydia had recommended in Greenpoint, where the inside was full of old books and the backyard was full of fairy lights. Cecilia announced that she wanted to host Thanksgiving.

"We'll host it here at Tudor City," Cecilia insisted over the phone. "I mean, *I'll* host it. You won't have to do a thing. Just bring wine. I'm going to mull some cider, and I'll *cook*. Oh—we'll have a real fire in the fireplace!"

"Are you sure?"

Cecilia had already ruined two of Rose's frying pans.

"I looked up a turkey recipe on YouTube," Cecilia said. "It's foolproof." She cleared her throat. "You should bring your friends, too."

"Are you *sure*?"

"Lydia was . . . friendly," Cecilia said, with effort. "And her boyfriend was—" She tried harder. "Well, he can laugh at himself, at any rate. And besides, if I'm going to be your maid of honor, it's probably a good idea to get to know your friends. And I'll make a better impression this time." She laughed a little. "I can't have them *all* thinking I'm just a fuckup."

"You're not a—" Rose began, but it was too late.

Cecilia had already hung up the phone.

—

"Well," Caleb sighed. "If you're sure."

Rose had gotten so used to that sigh.

"It's Thanksgiving," she said. "It's a family holiday. And—besides—we might not have that apartment for much longer."

"At least book a restaurant," Caleb said. "As a backup. We liked Orsay, didn't we?"

"She insists on cooking. She wants to make s'mores in the fireplace."

Now Caleb raised an eyebrow.

"You know what's so great about marriage, Ro?" Caleb stretched out along the sofa.

"What?"

He kissed her forehead.

"It's family you can choose."

—

Lydia was firmer.

"She'll fuck it up." She swiveled around in her chair. "It's the death drive."

"She won't fuck it up." Rose wasn't sure she believed this.

"Get a caterer," Lydia said. "You won't regret it. There's a guy Grant and I used during the pandemic—he's big on Instagram. He does pre-boxed Thanksgiving meals with, like, individual quails. I want him to do my wedding."

She spun 180 degrees.

"He has an eighteen-month wedding waitlist," Lydia said. "Grant had better fucking propose by Christmas."

—

October blew out. November was balmy. Rose almost started to relax. She and Caleb went upstate for the weekend. They had sex by the fire in their hotel room, and went antiquing, and even Rose had to admit that one of the benefits of moving to a place like Austin or San Diego was that you could get a house big enough for a midcentury credenza or an eight-seat dining table.

Also, Rose started on a new project at work.

She'd been the one to come up with the idea. It was a customized meditation audio track, designed to be listened to by two people at the same time. Officially it was supposed to *bolster intimacy*, since Legal warned them that calling it a sex aid would get them banned from the app stores. In practice you were supposed to use it while fucking. The idea was that it would track your heart rate and your partner's and try to get the two of you to synchronize, to help both of you come at the same time. These two internet-famous podcasters were doing the voices. Rose had been made project lead for the first time.

"It's a really rewarding part of the job," Rose insisted to Cecilia, over the phone. "Using real-world data to help people, you know, get closer to each other."

"I'm happy for you," Cecilia said. Cecilia was a terrible liar.

Still, Cecilia's disapproval bothered Rose less than it usually did. Partly this was because Rose was seeing less of Cecilia. She spent fewer and fewer days at Tudor City. She told herself this was normal, even healthy. Cecilia had a life of her own.

Sure, there were the odd erratic signs. Cecilia had gotten slower responding to Rose's texts; sometimes two or three days would go by before Cecilia answered them. The Tudor City apartment, on the rare occasions

Rose slept over, grew steadily messier. Once or twice, when Rose stopped by, Cecilia wasn't there at all.

The next evening Rose went to Tudor City to pick up her RealReal packages. On a whim she decided to stop by Mimi's, just to say hello. The bar was just a ten-minute walk away. And, she reminded herself, it had been a long time since she'd heard Cecilia play.

Cecilia was playing "I Got You, Babe," singing both parts, when Rose arrived.

She looked up when Rose entered. A nervous, animal expression crossed her face and then passed. She looked back down to her music.

Rose took a seat at the bar. She ordered an acid glass of wine. Cecilia turned to "Sweet Home Alabama." The man on Rose's right told her that he lived an hour away on Long Island. *I'm not ready*, he said, *to face my kids tonight*. He clinked her glass and spilled his. At the next booth there was a Russian woman in a black fur coat on a date with what looked like a rabbi. Rose watched Cecilia play, with the kind of exquisite precision you could hear even when someone was playing "Sweet Home Alabama." She listened to Cecilia sing. Cecilia's voice had always been raspy, even masculine, with the kind of smoky cigarette tinge Rose always associated with old women who sang about ex-lovers. It was not a beautiful voice; nevertheless, people leaned in to listen.

At ten, two men in camel coats came in. They were young, boys, really, twenty-five or twenty-six. Their suits were tailored. They were probably bankers. Their hair was slicked back and parted on complementary sides. They took a table next to Cecilia. They spent ten minutes loudly deciding on the wine. They spilled garlic bread. Cecilia seemed to take no notice of them.

At ten thirty, one of them approached Cecilia's piano. She was halfway through "We Didn't Start the Fire." She didn't look up.

"You got a Venmo?"

Cecilia shook her head. She kept on singing about Joe McCarthy, Richard Nixon, Marilyn Monroe.

One of the boys signaled to the other, who brought him a hundred-dollar bill. He waved it in Cecilia's face.

"You know 'Gold Digger'?"

Cecilia furrowed her brow.

"You know, Ye?"

Her playing remained unchanged.

"That's cool," he said. "We can look it up for you." His friend grabbed the iPad from Cecilia's music stand. Cecilia kept playing by ear: *it was always burning, since the world's been turning.*

Across the bar, Rose's chest tightened. She realized, a moment later, what they were doing.

"Only condition—" the boy went on, replacing it. "You gotta sing *all* the words." His friend snickered.

At last Cecilia understood.

She went red first, and then pale; she looked up at Rose, across the bar, in confusion or else appeal, like Rose had the power to explain why two rich jerks might think it was funny to get a pretty girl to sing offensive lyrics at a bar, or else to get her flustered when she refused. You couldn't explain to Cecilia that sometimes people were just assholes for no reason, because nothing would break Cecilia's heart like the notion that there was no reason for anything at all. Rose shot Cecilia a look of pallid sympathy.

Cecilia took a deep breath.

She picked up the iPad. She slammed it facedown. She sat up straighter. She began to play.

Three notes began it, mournful and low. Rose recognized it at once. Cecilia used to keep her awake playing it on the piano at home. It was a song of Liszt's, one of his *Liebesträume*: those lingering, melancholy songs about love and death and dreams that Cecilia once used to swoon over.

The boys exchanged confused glances. The other patrons started to stare. One by one they fell silent.

Cecilia kept on playing—delicately, defiantly, from memory—her fingers white and long against the keys. Her eyes flashed; her whole face tensed, as if every muscle in her body were taut with concentration.

Rose had almost forgotten how good a pianist Cecilia was. She could make you forget, playing, that a song was just a fortuitous collection of notes; she could make you forget that love and death and dreams were just words you could vaguely gesture at and link, without saying anything real or predictive or actionable about the world.

Rose watched the others, watching Cecilia. She watched the wonder in their faces. For a moment she envied it. She wondered what it felt like, to be watched like that.

Cecilia finished playing. The man from Long Island burst into applause; the others followed him; even the taller of the two boys threw up his hands, in what he doubtless thought was good-natured surrender, and dropped the bill into her tip jar. Cecilia did not acknowledge them. She rose. She inclined her head slightly, as if taking a bow. She marched out into the night. She left the money on the piano.

"You shouldn't have come," Cecilia said, when Rose caught up with her on the corner. "You shouldn't have had to see that."

"They were assholes," Rose tried.

"There are *always* assholes," Cecilia said. "I can handle them."

"You *did* handle them. God, Cecilia, you were wonderful; you—"

"It was a gimmick," Cecilia spat. "That's all." There were tears in her eyes. "It's no different than playing 'Piano Man.' I could have played half as well, and it would still have impressed them! And Liszt is schlock anyhow. Everybody knows that! And if they could only see that there are things in this world—"

Cecilia caught her breath.

"I'm sorry," she said. Her voice was calmer now. "I'm being stupid. It's a job—isn't it? It's good money. It's not supposed to be a vocation, right?"

"You sounded great," Rose tried, again, but Cecilia didn't seem to hear her.

"God, sometimes I can't stand this place!"

She took a cigarette out of her purse. It was the first one Rose had seen her smoke since her return.

"And to think—I might have gone to Juilliard." Her smile was arch. "I'd have probably fucked that up, too. I'd have slept with a professor or something." She puffed her cigarette into oblivion. She ground it underneath her heel.

"Come on," she said. "Let's go back inside. Before I get fired from this one, too."

Cecilia played for two more hours. Rose walked her home. She said goodbye to her, under the awning, and made it three blocks before she realized she'd left one of her RealReal sweaters on the living room chaise and turned back.

Rose could hear the music echoing all the way from the elevator.

She stopped short.

Even at a distance, even on their mother's out-of-tune piano, it was one of the most beautiful pieces Rose had ever heard. She did not recognize it. It was not Liszt or Chopin or Bach or any of the sonatas Cecilia had so dutifully practiced in her audition days. It was more modern—no, it was older, or maybe just stranger, with uncanny intervals, and key changes that did not make sense. It made Rose's spine shiver in a way she didn't understand.

She heard Cecilia fumble with the keys; she heard Cecilia curse; Cecilia started the line over.

The wind blows out of the gates of the day, Cecilia was singing, underneath her breath.

Rose drew closer. She cracked the door open, so quietly that Cecilia did not look up.

Cecilia was leaning over the piano. There was no music on the stand. She tried one version of the line, and then another:

The wind blows out of the gates of the day
The wind blows over the lonely of heart
And the lonely of heart is withered away

"Cecilia?"

Cecilia scrambled to her feet.

"Rosie!"

Her face was white.

"What are you doing here?"

"Nothing," Rose said. "I just left a package. That's all."

"Oh." Cecilia didn't look at her. "Right. Yeah. It's in the kitchen."

"What was that?"

Cecilia looked at her shoes.

"What was what?"

"The song you were playing. Just now."

"I don't know," Cecilia said, too quickly. "I mean—I don't know what it's called."

"Did you write it?"

"Me?" Cecilia laughed. "I couldn't write a song like that in a million years." Her eyes darted back to the piano.

"What is it, then?"

"Just something I heard somewhere," Cecilia said. "That's all."

"Where?"

"I don't remember. At Resurrection, maybe?"

"It doesn't sound like a hymn."

"Rosie!" Cecilia was shrill. "I told you—I don't remember where I heard it, okay?" She slammed down the piano cover. The *CF* she had carved into it as a child glinted under the halogen light. "Anyway," she said, in a strangely vacant voice, "I'm tired. I should get some sleep."

"Okay," Rose said. She hesitated. "Do you want me to stay over?"

"No!"

Cecilia eked out a smile.

"Caleb's probably missing you already," she said.

It was probably nothing, Rose thought, on her way home. Probably Cecilia had written the song herself, and then been too embarrassed to admit it.

Only the song stuck with her, all night, and into the morning. It wormed into her waking. She hummed it, brushing her teeth. She thought she heard a bar or two of it echoing at breakfast, only then Caleb started the juicer and drowned out the sound, and Rose forgot all about it.

—

Thanksgiving grew closer. Cecilia sent Rose the recipes she planned to make, instructed Rose on complementary wine, asked for Grant's and Lydia's email addresses. Rose started to think it might actually happen. She let herself relax. She let herself picture the five of them, around their dinner table with the uneven legs, drinking and eating and talking the way she'd always imagined real families drinking and eating and talking. She let herself picture Cecilia and Caleb, finally getting along.

I'm looking forward to tomorrow, Rose texted Cecilia on Wednesday night.

She read it. She didn't answer.

Rose and Caleb arrived at the Tudor City apartment at twelve thirty with wine.

Cecilia wasn't there.

Laundry latticed the floor. Dishes festered in the sink. A soggy loaf of bread sprouted fungus on the kitchen counter. A pyramid of unopened cans—pumpkin, cranberries, corn—covered the dining table.

"Christ," said Caleb. "What's it like when she's *not* expecting company?"

"She's probably just doing some last-minute shopping," Rose said. She did not recognize her own voice. "I'll just call her." The call went straight to voicemail.

"Grant and Lydia are supposed to be here in half an hour," Caleb said, picking up a can of pumpkin puree. "You think she's going to whip up a whole Thanksgiving out of *this* in half an hour?"

"Maybe she got overwhelmed," Rose said. "She might have gone to Agata's or somewhere to get something premade." This she could picture.

This she could even smile at. Cecilia, in desperation, going from Upper East Side market to Upper East Side market in search of mashed sweet potatoes or the last unreserved turkey; Cecilia, tottering under the weight of a catering tray.

The doorbell rang. Rose's heart leaped. The door flung open.

"We brought gin!"

Lydia barreled in with a bottle in each hand.

"I hope you have mixers."

Grant followed behind, holding her purse.

"Where's your sister?"

"Running late," Rose said quickly. Caleb shot her a look.

"Tell me," Grant said, eyeing the kitchen, "there's *something* in the oven."

"Who needs food?" Lydia set down the gin. "Just tell me where the glasses live."

"Top left," said Rose.

"Jesus." Lydia twirled into the kitchen. "A fireplace! Does it work?"

"When there's no wind."

"And this is *stabilized*? God, you cunt. How much do you pay?"

"The hot water comes and goes."

"For a stabilized apartment," Lydia said, "I'd stop showering altogether." She held Grant's gaze, then burst into laughter. "God knows," she said, with a hysterical hiccup, "I wouldn't need *him*."

"Personally," Grant muttered, "I can't wait to be obsolete."

Caleb made a show of checking his watch.

"She *is* coming," Rose said. "I just talked to her last night."

"Kids these days," said Grant. "No manners. No morals."

Lydia came back from the kitchen with ice cubes.

They drank both bottles of Rose's wine, and started on Lydia's gin, before Rose accepted that Cecilia wasn't coming.

"I'm sorry," Rose said. "I don't know what happened."

"Fuck it," said Caleb, pulling out his phone. "I'm ordering Chinese."

The food arrived. It was overcooked. They ate it anyway. Rose lost track of how many times she refilled her glass of gin. They made desperate conversation. Caleb told everybody about this academic paper he'd read about sports science that suggested you could burn more calories lying in bed and squeezing your muscles like you were constipated than you could by doing ordinary high-intensity interval training, which Grant took as an opportunity to make a dirty joke, and which Lydia said sounded too good to be true.

"It's, like, a law of the cosmos or something," Lydia said. "You have to pay the price for the things you want. Otherwise they're not really worth anything." She wrinkled her nose. "Sometimes I hope Ozempic gives me cancer."

She laughed. Nobody else did. Caleb poured everybody but himself another drink.

They traded stories about other fuckups they had known, which Rose guessed was an attempt to make her feel better. Caleb complained about his first-year roommate at Stanford, an engineering major who tried to make bouillabaisse in a rice cooker. Grant talked about his stepmother. Lydia told an overly detailed story about this witchy-Gothy influencer named Lucinda she'd vaguely known in New Orleans who just two years ago had vanished for three weeks and then turned up drowned in the bayou with three bottles' worth of Xanax in her stomach.

"I remember that one." Grant refilled their glasses. "Her roommate was the one that killed her, right? Posted on her account for like a year?" He poured out a fourth glass, for Caleb, and made a point of setting it down in front of him. "Just in case." Caleb didn't take it.

"Different influencer. This one was suicide."

"It just goes to show," Grant said. "Original fucking sin. Maybe it's the only part of the whole game that's true."

Rose didn't laugh.

Lydia patted Rose's hand.

"If it makes you feel any better," she said in a softer tone, "I hate my sister, too."

Rose drank. She was surprised—it was always a surprise—how good it felt to be drunk. Drunk, nothing existed but what was right in front of you; drunk, there was only Grant and Lydia and Caleb, reading their fortune cookies out loud—Lydia's predicted she'd be married by 2024, but she tore it up and put the pieces in her mouth before anyone else could see it—drunk, Rose could stop thinking about all the places Cecilia could be. Cecilia, passed out in an alley; Cecilia, asleep in a stranger's bed; Cecilia, floating at the bottom of the East River; Cecilia, ten thousand miles away.

"Careful," said Caleb, with his hand on the blade of her shoulder. "You might want to slow down a little." Rose recoiled.

"I'm fine," Rose said. "Really, I'm fine!"

She had a sudden, perverse urge to prove him wrong.

How dare he, she thought, *always be right about everything.*

She took another drink.

The next thing Rose remembered was washing her face in the bathroom while Lydia peed.

"I told you," Lydia said, from the toilet. "Jealousy. That's all it is. You have everything she wants."

And Rose tried to explain, no, it wasn't that at all, because Rose had nothing Cecilia wanted in the first place, and if you didn't understand that, you didn't understand Cecilia, but maybe nobody understood Cecilia, least of all Rose, but she was too drunk to say anything but *no, no*, and then vomit up a stomachful of fried rice while Lydia held back her hair.

When she was done, Lydia handed her an Altoid. She took a baby wipe from her purse and washed Rose's face. She handed her a tube of lipstick.

"There," she said. "Before Caleb smells you."

Rose took it.

"Thank you."

"Men," said Lydia, with a shrug. "They never get it, do they?"

—

It was dark by the time Caleb took Rose home. Rose had lost all sense of time. She leaned on Caleb's shoulder. She clung to his chest.

He led her into the bedroom. He lay her down on the bed, like she was a child.

"I'm sorry," he said. "I don't enjoy being right, you know."

He arranged the weighted blanket over her.

"You know," he said, stroking her hair, "you could reframe this. As a reminder to be proud of yourself."

"Proud?" Rose coughed weakly. Her mouth still tasted like bile.

"You two had the same fucked-up upbringing," he said. "At least some of the same probably-a-little-bit-fucked-up genes. And—despite all that—you manage to turn out like, well, like you."

Rose nodded miserably.

"*I'm* proud of you," Caleb said. He leaned down. He kissed her, on the side of her head. She was suddenly wildly grateful for him.

If only, she thought, as sleep washed over her, *I could always see the world the way he does.*

She curled up next to him. She brought her knees underneath her chin. She let exhaustion take her.

It was only in the last moment of consciousness that Rose heard it: somewhere between a memory and a dream.

The wind blows out of the gates of the day
The wind blows over the lonely of heart
And the lonely of heart is withered away

CHAPTER FOUR

Rose woke up first. She lay there a moment, in Caleb's arms, watching the light beat through the blinds. Then she remembered.

Rose grabbed her phone.

Cecilia had not written. She hadn't even read Rose's texts.

Rose swung out of bed. She threw herself into the shower. Caleb was still snoring when she got out.

Fifteen minutes later, Rose was on the M15 to Tudor City. By nine thirty, she was in the apartment. Cecilia hadn't come home.

The apartment was a disaster. There were Styrofoam take-out containers piled on the dining table; the sink clattered with empty bottles. The bathroom was rancid.

Rose got to work.

She broke down the containers. She tied up the trash bags. She rinsed the last of the wine from the bottles and used hot water to remove the labels, and then threw them, one by one, into the recycling. She put Cecilia's cans into the pantry cabinet. She scrubbed the toilet bowl and the bathroom floor until the whole apartment stank of bleach and lemon verbena. She opened all the windows. She lit a fire in the fireplace.

—

Cecilia came home at eleven thirty.

She looked like she had not slept.

Her hair was damp and matted in clumps. Her eyes were bloodshot. Her lipstick was smeared. Glitter pooled in her collarbones. She'd torn the lining of her coat, somehow, and so a tongue of pink satin lolled from the hem.

"Where were you?"

Cecilia froze.

She dropped her purse.

"Rosie," she said. "Hi."

"We waited for you, you know." Rose did not move from the sofa. "Ninety minutes, we waited, before we gave up and ordered Seamless."

Cecilia looked around in confusion.

"Thanksgiving," she breathed.

"Yes, Thanksgiving," Rose said. "The Thanksgiving you were so, *so* desperate to host."

"Rosie, I—"

"I called you, you know. Four or five times. And I texted. Christ, Cecilia, you could have *said* something; you could have *texted*; anything . . ."

"I lost my phone," Cecilia said. Her voice was hollow.

"Where were you?"

Cecilia staggered forward.

"I asked you a question."

Cecilia looked down.

"I can't tell you," she said. "I'm sorry."

"You *can't tell me*? Jesus Christ, Cecilia—you ghost on Thanksgiving and you *can't tell me*?"

"Rosie, please—" Cecilia sank into one of the armchairs. She put her face in her hands. "It's complicated, okay?"

"How complicated could it be? You just—*bailed*."

Cecilia opened her mouth, closed it, and then opened it again. She sighed. "It wasn't like that, Rosie. I promise. I swear to you, you don't know how excited I was, for Thanksgiving, how badly I wanted—"

"Not badly enough to show up!"

"Rosie, please!"

At last Cecilia looked up. Her face was streaked with tears. She was shaking. There were bruises on all her fingers. Her lips were swollen, as if someone had bitten them. She smelled overpoweringly of ambergris: of cologne, maybe, or perfume.

"You were *with* someone, last night, weren't you?"

"Rosie!"

"Who was it?"

"Please—"

"Don't fuck with me, Cecilia; I can smell you from here." A thought came to her. "Was it Paul?"

"Paul?"

Rose gathered steam. Cecilia had been doing so well, she thought with new clarity, until Paul's return—it was Paul's return, wasn't it, when Cecilia had started acting strangely, when she'd stopped answering her texts, when she'd left dishes piling once again in the kitchen sink. It was a relief to have an answer.

"It is Paul—isn't it?"

"Rosie, please; listen to me. I can't . . ."

"Come on. I'm not stupid! One minute he comes to town; the next you're being sketchy: you don't answer your phone; you just fucking *vanish*, with no warning."

Cecilia closed her eyes. She exhaled: a long, exhausted sigh. At last she nodded.

"Fine," she said. "Fine. You win."

"So you *were* with Paul last night?"

Cecilia hesitated only a moment.

"Yes," she said at last. "I was with Paul last night."

"Since when?"

"I don't know. A few weeks, maybe."

"You're back together!?"

"No—Rosie—"

"I thought you hated him. I thought you said there wasn't a chance in hell."

"Rosie, please!" It was a scream.

"What happened?"

"I—I don't know." Cecilia sounded like she was in a dream. "I went over there, to try to get him to sign the papers; only he said—he said he wouldn't; and, the way he looked at me, God, it was awful, the way he looked at me, and . . ." She swallowed. "Here we are."

Rose relented.

"I'm sorry," she said. "I just, I just don't get it."

Cecilia stared straight ahead.

"I don't get it, either," she said.

"Do you *want* him?"

"No. No!"

"Then what?"

Cecilia curled into herself on the armchair. She wrapped her arms around her legs. She put her chin between her knees. It made her look like a penitent child.

"I told you," she murmured. "I'm afraid of him. I can't be around him. I—"

"Jesus Christ, Cecilia!"

Cecilia began to cry.

It was a hideous, guttural sound, like the keening of a sick animal. It racked her shoulders; her rib cage shook. Rose's anger vanished. You couldn't be angry with someone as pathetic as Cecilia. It was like being angry at a toddler for spilling juice on your carpet. Cecilia, Rose reminded herself, was functionally a child. Of course there were men—there were always men—who used that to their advantage.

Rose stood. Suddenly everything was clear. Rose knew exactly what to do.

"I'll be back," Rose said. "We're going to fix this."

"Rosie, no!"

Rose was already out the door.

—

It was easy to find Paul Byrd's phone number. There was only one Paul Byrd on Google; a cursory search led you to his faculty page on the St. Dunstan's website (*on leave, 2022–2023 Academic Year*), which listed both an office number and a cell phone.

Rose called it.

The first two rings went unanswered. At the third Rose felt a pang of fear, or maybe doubt; she pushed it down. It wouldn't be the first time, she thought, that she'd had to warn off one of Cecilia's men; four years ago, she'd had to call the police on a Colorado bassist who had come to Tudor City in the middle of the night and threatened to break down the doors to get to Cecilia, who was in Paris at the time.

"Hello?"

It was a tight, brusque voice.

"Is this Paul Byrd?"

"Speaking." He still bore the traces of a British accent.

"This is Rose Foster. I'm Cecilia's—"

"I know who you are."

"Can we talk?" Rose cleared her throat. "I mean—I need to talk to you. Today. It's urgent."

He was silent.

"What's this regarding, please?"

"Excuse me?"

"I asked you"—his voice grew brusquer—"what this is regarding."

"Look, are you free or not?"

"Is she all right?"

"I can be there in an hour," Rose said. "I'll come to you."

For a moment he didn't say anything. Then she heard him relent.

"I'll text you the address," he said.

He hung up the phone.

—

Rose spent the whole trip to Red Hook rehearsing what, exactly, she was going to say to Paul. She made some bullet points on her Notes app. She would focus on the legal issue first—the signing of the separation papers (she would drop the name of Grant's firm as soon as she tactfully could). She'd make it clear that if he wanted money—so many of Cecilia's men wanted money—he'd come to the wrong place; nevertheless, she'd be happy to buy him a ticket back to Maine, or England, or the Bahamas, or wherever the hell it was he wanted to go. If he persisted she'd focus on the moral side: Cecilia, she'd explain, *is vulnerable*, the way small animals are vulnerable. She'd name-drop Caleb, if she had to. People had heard of Caleb. At least, the people Rose knew.

Red Hook was one of those industrial and inconvenient parts of New York that nobody ever went to without a reason. Rose had bought a potted plant at the IKEA there once. It had taken her ninety minutes to get home.

The light was white and crisp when Rose stepped off the ferry. The air smelled acrid and brackish: a mix of salt and sea and the fermenting woody smell of the warehouse distilleries on Conover. Rose could hear seagulls.

It was like, she thought, you weren't even in New York at all.

Paul's apartment was in a tenement on Dikeman Street, almost as far down as you could go before hitting the Erie Basin. The building lay between a Pentecostal church and an empty construction lot, in front of which lay an abandoned miniature tractor on which somebody had spray-painted googly eyes and smiling lips. Rats darted underneath the wheels.

Rose steeled herself. She pressed the buzzer. She waited.

A few minutes later, the front door swung open.

"Sorry," Paul said. "Buzzer's out."

He looked nothing like Rose had imagined.

For starters, he wasn't handsome. He was gaunt; spectral, even, with hunched shoulders and a receding hairline. His glasses sat askew on his nose, as if at some point he'd tried to repair them with duct tape. There were moth holes in his sweater. His trousers were too short. He shuffled from foot to foot, as though he could not stand still. Rose couldn't imagine anyone—even Cecilia—being afraid of him.

"You can come upstairs," Paul said. "If you'd like. I'm afraid it's a bit of a state, though." He cleared his throat. "I wasn't expecting visitors. I don't have coffee or tea or anything."

"I don't mind," Rose said. "I won't be staying long."

"Very good," he said.

Paul was almost as messy as Cecilia. There were papers everywhere: on the desk doubling as a dining table; on the piles of books he used as end tables. His suitcase, only half unpacked, jutted out from underneath the futon.

"I did warn you," Paul said, before Rose could say anything.

He cleared a space for her on the futon. He perched himself on a folding chair opposite.

"Please," he said at last. "Is—is she all right?"

It was the *please* that did it. It was an awkward, appealing *please*, completely devoid of power or pretense. Devoid, Rose decided, of self-respect.

"I mean," Rose snapped, "she's not dead or hurt or anything. If that's what you're asking."

Paul's whole body slackened.

"Good," he said. "That's good."

If Rose had been less angry, his relief might have moved her. But she'd spent forty minutes on the subway, and another twenty on the ferry, and seasickness had reactivated her hangover, and all Rose could focus on was the fact that this, *this* gangly matchstick of a man was the reason Cecilia had skipped Thanksgiving.

"But no," Rose went on. "She's not *all right*."

He looked up at her. "What's wrong?"

She rounded on him in astonishment. "Are you kidding me?" she said. "What do you mean—*what's wrong*? You—you're what's wrong!"

"I'm sorry?"

"You—Jesus—you *follow* her here; you demand to see her; you refuse to sign the papers . . ."

"Oh yes," Paul said. "That."

A small, infuriating smile crossed his lips.

"So you admit it!"

"That I won't sign the papers?" He straightened his shoulders for the first time. "Yes. You're quite right. I won't sign them."

"Why?"

"That's really none of your business," he said lightly.

"She's my sister," said Rose. "Of course it's my business!"

He peered at her from behind his glasses. His lips twitched.

"If you must know," he said. "I don't believe in divorce."

"Are you Catholic or something?"

Paul snorted.

"No," he said. "I'm not Catholic."

Rose tried and failed to remember what other religions didn't believe in divorce.

"What are you, then?"

"Nothing," Paul went on, pleasantly, almost as if he was enjoying this. "But that's irrelevant."

"*Irrelevant?*"

"I mean," Paul said, "it's not a God thing."

"Is it a money thing, then? Because—I promise you—Cecilia doesn't have any."

"Of course it's not a money thing!" The jaundiced skin of his nose had turned pink.

"Then what?"

"It's a matter," Paul said, "of principle."

Rose was silent.

"I made a promise," he said. "To your sister. *For richer, for poorer, in sickness, in health, till death us do part.* And—inconvenient though it might be for her—I intend to keep it."

"You're not serious!" Whatever lingering sympathy Rose might have had for him evaporated. Paul was, she decided, a self-righteous prig; probably a little bit insane. No wonder Cecilia had run away without a word.

"I'm perfectly serious." Paul leaned back in his chair.

"You know it's not the Victorian era, right? You can't just, like, *stop a divorce.*"

"I'm aware."

"Sooner or later a judge will just do it for you!"

"I'm *aware,*" Paul said, more firmly this time. "But that doesn't mean I have to sign on the dotted line just to make your sister feel better about herself."

"So you want to punish her, is that it?"

Paul stiffened in his chair.

"No," he said softly. "I don't want to punish her. She's free to do what she likes. I don't intend to get in the way of that. But I'm afraid—as far as I'm concerned—I consider myself a married man."

Then Rose noticed the narrow bronze band on his left-hand finger. She could not stop herself from laughing.

"Are you kidding me? You were together for, what, four months?"

"Five."

"And *how long* had you known each other—when you got married?"

Paul's nostrils flared. "Three weeks."

"Three weeks. And you thought it was a good idea to—"

"I didn't say," Paul went on slowly, "that it was a good idea."

"Jesus, Paul, that's a *fling.* It's not a real marriage!"

He stiffened. "I don't see why not. We said the words, didn't we?"

"A lot of people *say the words.*"

"And when *you* say the words"—his gaze fell on Rose's ring—"I suppose they won't mean anything to you, either."

"That's different!"

"Why? Because you could put an eye out with that thing?"

"I mean—" Rose spluttered. "We *know* each other; we've been together for years; we *talk* about things." Rose didn't know how she'd ended up defending herself.

"And you think I didn't know your sister? That we didn't *talk* about things?"

"After three weeks? I'd be surprised if you knew her favorite color!"

"I knew—I *know*," Paul said, "that your sister was one of the most openhearted, kindest, most *dedicated* people I'd ever met. And that I wanted to spend my life with her."

"Dedicated?" Rose's laugh strangled in her throat. "Please. If you think my sister's a *dedicated* person, then you don't know her at all."

"I disagree."

He said it so calmly.

She rounded on him.

"Look," she said at last. "My sister may be a lot of things—a lot of good things, even—but if there's one thing she's not, it's *dedicated*. Cecilia's an irresponsible, emotionally incontinent *mess* who can't commit to anything for more than three weeks at a time, and maybe if you'd bothered to get to know her for more than a couple of days, you'd have figured that one out!"

Paul's eyes fixed on a warp in the floorboards.

"If there's anyone, *anyone* in this world you shouldn't hold to a lifelong promise, it's Cecilia."

"I'm less interested than you are," his voice was lacerating, "in protecting your sister from the consequences of her own actions."

Rose had never disliked anyone as much as she disliked Paul.

"Do you know what I think?"

"What?"

"I think that's just a fancy way of saying you want to punish her." Rose gathered steam. "You want to make her suffer."

"I don't want her to suffer."

"Please. You want to make her feel so guilty about leaving you that she comes crawling back—that she stays with you out of *pity* or *obligation*. Like she's doing right now."

"Excuse me?"

"Whatever's going on between you—your *friends with benefits* thing or breakup sex or makeup sex, or whatever it is." Rose grew triumphant. "Don't think for a second it's because she wants you back. I know her. If she *is* still seeing you, if she's still *fucking* you, it's only because you've convinced her she owes you, that—"

"Rose—"

"She told me herself—just a couple hours ago." Rose knew she was being cruel now; she couldn't stop herself. "She's afraid of you. That's why she's still seeing you; that's why she was with you last night; because she's *afraid*—"

"Rose!" Paul said, more firmly. "I haven't seen your sister in over a month."

All Rose's breath left her body.

"What?"

"She came here. October. I'd asked her to. I felt I deserved an explanation. And—yes—if you must know, I *did* ask her to come back to me then. Not because she *owed* me, or because I wanted her *pity*, but because I loved her, and for all my sins I stupidly believed she still loved me. She looked me in the eye and told me exactly what you told me: that our marriage had been a disastrous mistake, that the best thing I could do for the both of us would be to forget it had ever happened, *wipe the slate clean*, she said. I said a few choice words I regret and she walked right out that door and, I'm sorry to disappoint you, we've had no contact since."

The worst part was: he was telling the truth.

Even Rose couldn't doubt it. Smug and self-righteous though Paul certainly was, she could tell he wasn't lying. Nobody could fake that look of fury on his face.

"I'm—I'm sorry." She faltered. "I was—" She searched for an ameliorating word. "Misinformed."

"Misinformed." Paul's laugh was horrible. "Very good."

Paul rose. He went to the desk. He rummaged its contents, letting stamps and erasers and stray pencils clatter staccato to the floor. At last he found the papers he was looking for. He took a pen from his blazer breast pocket. He scrawled a few furious lines on the pages.

"There," he said. His face was white. "Give this to your sister."

"What is it?"

"What she wants," Paul said. "Tell her whatever she wants to hear. Tell her she's free, as far as I'm concerned; that she can wipe me clean off her slate, if that's what will make her happy! God knows I don't want her pity. Tell her—" He stopped himself. "Tell her I'm sorry it's taken me so long."

He shoved a folder into Rose's arms.

"Now if you'll excuse me," he said. "I have about twenty-five college admissions essays to edit by Monday morning."

He opened the front door. Rose walked through it without a word. He slammed it shut before Rose could think of a reply.

—

Rose spent the whole cab ride back to Manhattan reeling.

Twenty-eight years Rose had known Cecilia, had protected Cecilia, had put up with Cecilia. She'd put up with Cecilia's messes and Cecilia's heartbreaks and Cecilia's disappearances; she'd put up with Cecilia skipping their mother's funeral, for God's sake. She'd made so many excuses for her. *Cecilia's fragile*, she'd said to Caleb, so many times; *Cecilia's vulnerable*—hadn't she said that to Paul?—*Cecilia isn't like other people*. Whatever else you could accuse Cecilia of, you could never doubt Cecilia's innocence. It was the one quality that made you forgive her everything else—the fact that Cecilia felt so strongly, that she meant so well, that she could never even countenance deceit.

Only: Cecilia had lied.

She'd let Rose make a fool of herself, in front of that infuriating little man.

And he'd had the nerve to mock her ring.

It was late afternoon by the time Rose's cab dropped her off in Tudor City; the sky was violet. The moon, just visible, was dove gray. Cecilia was sitting, motionless, on the living room floor.

She had not changed. She did not look like she'd showered. She was staring into the fireplace, where flames still crackled from the last of the wood.

"Rosie," she murmured, without looking up. "You're back."

"I'm back."

Rose took a seat on the sofa. She put Paul's folder on the cushion beside her.

Cecilia turned around.

"What's that?"

"Divorce papers," Rose said. "Signed."

Cecilia looked up at her in confusion. Then she understood.

"You saw Paul." Her voice was small.

"I saw Paul."

"H-how . . ." Cecilia took a deep breath. "How is he?"

"Well," Rose said, in the nastiest voice she could muster. "A little *con-fused*, you know, that you said you'd been with him last night, when he hasn't seen you in a month."

"Rosie . . ."

"But, you know, *other than that*." She slapped the papers down on the coffee table.

"He signed?" Cecilia said, like it had only just sunk in.

"He told me to tell you he's sorry it took him so long."

Cecilia blinked. Her eyes were unfocused.

"You shouldn't have gone," she murmured.

"You could at least say *thank you*." There was no stopping Rose now. "Do you *know* how much Grant charges?"

Cecilia took the papers. She stared at them, for a moment, uncomprehending.

Then she threw them in the fireplace.

"God*damn* him!" she said, as their edges crackled. Tears streaked once more down her face. "How dare he? How *dare* he!"

"Cecilia!"

"He doesn't mean it, you know! Not really. Oh, he'll *sign*; it won't change *anything*, for him; he'll just go on suffering—the goddamn *martyr*!"

"Cecilia!"

At last Cecilia fell silent.

"Do you want to tell me what's really going on?"

"I don't know what you mean," Cecilia said.

"Don't fuck with me, Cecilia! Where were you, last night?"

Cecilia crumpled.

"I told you," she murmured. "I told you to stop asking."

"Cecilia—"

"I can't talk about it, okay?"

"You can't talk about anything, Cecilia! You can't talk about Paul; you can't talk about where you were last night; Jesus, Cecilia, what *can* you talk about?"

"I mean," Cecilia tried again. "I'm not allowed to talk about it."

For the first time, Rose grew worried. Maybe, she thought, she'd been too quick to judge; maybe Cecilia had gotten herself involved with drugs or sex work or the mob; maybe she'd borrowed money from someone you weren't supposed to borrow money from.

Rose made her voice gentler.

"Are you in trouble, Cecilia?"

Cecilia shook her head.

"No," she said. "No. They're *good*; I know they are . . ."

"*Who's* good?"

"I can't tell you."

"Cecilia—for the love of—" Rose stammered on, stupidly. "You need to tell me *right now* where you were last night, or I swear, I'll—" Rose cast about wildly for a consequence. "Or I'm kicking you out."

"Rosie—please!"

"For God's sake." Rose had never before let herself say this, "I'm the one who pays the rent!"

Cecilia looked, for a moment, like Rose had struck her. Then she took a deep breath. She put her face between her knees. She remained there, huddled into herself, for a moment. Then she looked up.

"If I tell you," she said slowly, "you have to promise me something. You'll believe me—no matter how crazy it sounds. And you have to promise you won't tell Caleb."

"Caleb and I don't have secrets from each other," Rose said. She knew how smug this sounded. She didn't care.

"Promise me, Rosie!"

Rose relented.

"Fine," she said. "I promise."

Cecilia turned back toward the flames. The last of the papers were disintegrating into ash.

"Do you remember the woman in the bar I told you about? With the cabaret? *Another life is possible*?"

"The sex cult lady?"

"Don't call her that!" Cecilia drew in breath. "I mean, she's not. It wasn't . . ." She shook her head. "I wrote them, Rosie. I don't know why I did it. I couldn't sleep, and I was lonely, and I was thinking about Paul, and—well—about everything, and I wrote them and I told them my story and I thought, well, whatever it is, it's another life, right?" Her smile was weak. "Anyway, I put the letter in the mail, and I didn't think much of it. Only—they wrote me back."

"When?"

"A few weeks ago. It was just—a clue, at first. A clue for the location and date, and a time."

"What do you mean, a *clue*?"

"I couldn't work it out; it baffled me for ages; it was these dots, you see, and at first I thought I was meant to connect them; only then I realized it was, it was *music*, and then—"

"Just get to the point, okay?"

"I waited for them," Cecilia said. "At the time and the place they wanted. In Greenpoint, in the middle of the night, right by the Pulaski Bridge. I still thought maybe it was a scam—like, to mug me or something, although I thought it'd be lot of trouble to go to, just to mug someone. And I was waiting, under the full moon, and the water was so black you'd think it went on forever, and just when I started to think, *this is crazy, Cecilia, you've fallen for a scam*, that's when I saw it. Them."

"Who's *them*?"

"Coming toward me," Cecilia went on, as if she hadn't heard her, "on this little red boat—like the one you picture Cleopatra on, you know: *the barge she sat in / like a burnished throne . . .*"

"Cecilia!"

"Sorry. I just don't know how else to describe it. It was—God, it was the most wonderful thing I'd ever seen. *They* were wonderful. There was a boy, all in white, like a harlequin, with a flute, and he was playing the most beautiful song I'd ever heard; and a boatman in seersucker; and they were all like kings and queens, the way they were dressed, I mean, and the way they carried themselves; and—I thought I was dreaming at first, only then the boat came closer, and the boy in white stretched out his hand to me . . ."

"So you got on some stranger's boat?"

"They weren't strangers!" Cecilia's eyes were gleaming. "They were waiting for me. They knew me—all about me—what I'd told them in the letter, but not *just* that; it was like they knew everything about me, all about the holy grail, and about—*why* I do the things I do, when I don't even know myself, and, oh, Rosie, they were so kind to me, and they gave me chocolates, and champagne, and the *music*, Rosie! I've never in my life heard music like that. If I spent my whole life trying to write, I could never, ever write music like that. And *she* was there, the woman from the bar, in the red dress—she was like their leader."

"So, what, it was just a bunch of people having a party on a boat?"

"You don't understand, Rosie! They weren't *people*." Cecilia stopped herself. "I mean, they weren't *ordinary* people."

"Obviously they weren't *normal* people."

"No, I mean, they didn't seem *human*. There were—things they did; the way the light moved, and the shadows, the way things changed color . . ." Cecilia's smile was feverish. "Oh, Rosie, haven't you ever wondered if—you know—it might all be real?"

"What might be real?"

"Magic?"

Rose's stomach plummeted. "Cecilia, please . . ."

"I thought I'd dreamed it, I really did. That nothing like that could possibly have happened to me. Only then they wrote me again, with another date, and another time, and another clue—and then another; and every time, Rosie, it was like the first time, only better, *deeper*, somehow."

"That's where you were on Thanksgiving? Skipping out on us to—what—go frolic with a bunch of people pretending to be fairies?"

"They weren't pr—"

Rose had had enough.

She had bailed Cecilia out: the time Cecilia got really into astral projection; the time Cecilia converted to Catholicism. She'd spent the morning bailing Cecilia out of her own marriage. And still Cecilia was sitting at her feet, babbling about the next great, mad, nonsensical thing, the wondrous key that was at last going to unlock whatever was wrong or sad or broken in Cecilia's fathomless heart, because Cecilia still at thirty hadn't figured out what Rose had learned at sixteen, which is that there are no pots of gold at the end of the rainbow and that the only questions you can get answers to are the ones you're willing to think through yourself.

Caleb was right, Rose thought. People had to want to change. And Cecilia never would.

"You know what your problem is, Cecilia?" Rose's voice was high and cold. "You need to fucking *grow up*."

"That's not—"

"I'm sorry—I really am—that a bunch of drugged-out nutjobs are more, I don't know, exciting or interesting or *fun* for you than your own goddamn family . . ."

"Rosie!"

Rose couldn't stop herself. "Than your own *husband*."

Cecilia went pale.

"Don't you *dare*," she said. "Don't you *dare* talk to me about Paul!"

"You don't think it's a little fucked-up?" Rose knew by now that she was being spiteful; being spiteful felt like relief. "You have to get your kid sister to get your own divorce papers—which you *clearly* don't want, by the way"—Rose motioned toward the last-fending embers—"because *God* forbid, Cecilia, you do anything—even your own fucking *divorce*—you can't undo a second later!"

Cecilia froze.

For a moment Rose regretted what she'd said. For a moment Rose saw the old Cecilia: fawnlike and fragile, the kind of person you couldn't say a harsh word to without them cracking in on themselves.

But then Cecilia looked up at her, with an expression Rose didn't recognize.

"At least," Cecilia said, in an unnervingly calm voice, "I've actually *tried* to do something with my life. At least I'm *looking* for something—something real; not some *meta-quest* Caleb's app can spit out for you." She'd struck bone; worse, she knew it; worse, she seemed to enjoy it. "At least—when I got married, it was because I loved Paul—I mean, *really, truly, deeply* loved him. And even if it *was* wrong, and even if I fucked it all up, at least it was because I loved him, and not because I was bored or lonely or because I needed someone to tell me what to do with the rest of my life!"

For a moment neither of them spoke.

Cecilia broke first.

"I'm sorry," Cecilia began. "God, Rosie, I'm sorry, I didn't mean—"

But it was too late. Whatever regrets Rose had evaporated.

"Of course you didn't mean it. You never *mean* anything. Things just *happen* to you, right? Somehow everything always just *happens*, out of your control . . . ?"

"I just want you to be happy!"

"You can stay here through the end of the year," Rose said. She barely recognized her own voice. "Then I want you gone."

"What?"

"We're moving to Austin," Rose said, with new confidence. "Me and Caleb. After the wedding. We're going to sell his place. We're going to give up *this* shithole." Once she said it she was sure.

Cecilia was trembling.

"But it's our *home*," she said, with infuriating incomprehension.

"Maybe it's your home," Rose said. "It's not mine."

"Where am I supposed to go?"

"That's not my problem," Rose said. "Go back to your husband. Go back to London. Go back to your fairies, for all I care! Unless you get bored of *them*, too."

When Cecilia spoke, at last, her voice was calm.

"I'll leave the keys with the doorman," she said.

She rose. She opened the door. For the second time that day, Rose watched someone slam the door in her face. She heard Cecilia's footsteps fading away.

—

"Jesus," Caleb said, when Rose at last barreled through the door. "What happened to you?"

She had never been more relieved to see him.

"I'm fine," Rose said. "God, I'm more than fine; I'm *great*: I—" She laughed without meaning to. "I'm *fantastic*."

Caleb took a seat at the kitchen island.

"Ro?"

She stood before him. She marveled at him. She marveled at this whole apartment, glorious and gloriously clean, with wide window-panes and white marble gleaming, freshly scrubbed; she marveled at its emptiness.

"I've decided," she said, "to give up Tudor City."

He looked at her in surprise.

"Are you sure?"

"It's a waste of money," she said. "Especially if we're planning to move."

He registered this. He smiled. "And . . ." Caleb grimaced. "Cecilia?"

"Cecilia will do . . . whatever Cecilia does."

"Dare I ask?"

"Don't bother," Rose said. "It's nothing you haven't heard before."

She kissed him on the cheek.

It astonished her how easy it was. She wondered if this was what it felt like, to be a healthy and well-adjusted person. She wondered if this was what it felt like to be Caleb.

"You can say 'I told you so,'" she said. "If you want."

He grinned.

"Just this once," he said. *"I told you so."*

He kissed her on the lips.

"*I told you so*," he said again. He kissed her a second time, more deeply. "*I told you so. I told you so. I told you so.*"

Rose let him take her hand. She let him lead her to the bedroom. She let him kiss her, in all those gentle and familiar ways that meant that this, *this*, was Rose's home now; *home* was Caleb's chest and the sunshine dappled on Caleb's floor and the whiteboard with its clearly delineated goals. Wasn't this what Caleb had always said—that marriage was the family that you chose for yourself?

Rose let Caleb unbutton her shirt, nuzzle her collarbone, kiss her breasts.

I am home, she told herself. She focused on the thought. She meditated on it, the way they were always telling you to do at My.th, picturing it as a wave: letting it fill all the jagged places in her heart; letting it wash away the gnawing centipedes of guilt, the cobweb of regrets. She repeated it, over and over, as Caleb moved inside her, until he had extinguished Cecilia's voice and Cecilia's descending footsteps and the half-remembered echoes of Cecilia's discordant song.

CHAPTER FIVE

December came.

Rose didn't call Cecilia. Cecilia didn't call her. The leaves withered, and the air grew slicing, and every bar on the Lower East Side had either a hot toddy or a mulled wine on their specials menu, and it was like Cecilia had never come home at all.

Rose didn't mind. At least, she told herself she didn't mind. After all, she and Caleb had done holidays together for five years. They had their own routines. They visited his parents in Santa Monica for a long weekend. They went to this German bar in Murray Hill famous for its Christmas lights. They went skating at the ice rink at Rockefeller Center, even though Caleb hated Fifth Avenue this time of year, because it was noisy and full of tourists and you couldn't walk more than a block without having to stop for someone taking a photograph. They went to the Holiday Market at Union Square and bought gingerbread. They watched *White Christmas*. They spent Christmas Day with Grant and Lydia at this new Szechuan tapas place Lydia knew in Williamsburg, because she thought it would be funny and kind of ironic to have Chinese food on Christmas Day, even though none of them was Jewish. Lydia made a few tipsy comments about how New Year's Eve was an auspicious time for a person to propose, and then Grant made a few even tipsier comments about how

Christmas Day was better, for the bride at least, because if you proposed on Christmas the ring was legally considered a Christmas gift, and not a conditional one, which meant that if you broke up before the wedding you wouldn't have to give it back, and then Lydia spent the rest of the meal looking hangdog and hopeful and picking at her uneaten rice until Grant kissed the back of her neck and whispered something into her ear.

This, Rose decided, was what the holidays were supposed to feel like. You were with the people you chose. You didn't waste time missing people who had only ever disappointed you. Or else, if you missed them, you missed them the way you missed believing in Santa Claus on Christmas morning: with a healthily distant sense that what you actually missed was being young enough to believe in the impossible.

"There's some emotions that we're not, like, *evolved* to feel after thirty," Lydia said, when she and Rose discussed it. It was New Year's Eve, and Grant had invited twenty-five people over to his apartment ("I hate that he still calls it *his* apartment," Lydia muttered into Rose's ear), which had a balcony and a guest bathroom and a view of the East River. Lydia had hired the caterer who did the Thanksgivings quails. Grant still hadn't proposed. "Like, personally, I don't really experience *joy*. But honestly I don't think anybody does." She considered. "Maybe during sex. Or if you're on shrooms or something. I don't think it's anything to get, like, worked up about." She popped an edible into her mouth. "Honestly, I'd settle for contentment. Or, like, *peace.*"

She leaned over the balcony railing.

"Like—I want to not give a shit about anything that scares me, ever again."

She laughed, a little too loudly.

"When I get that fucking ring," she said, "I'm going to sleep for a week."

—

Rose went back to work. They had a launch date for the intimacy meditation, which was called *Aphrodite* and was going to come out on Valentine's

Day. Lydia was planning the launch party, which was going to be a big, elaborate Valentine's Day cocktail thing at an immersive theater space in Chelsea.

"Don't worry," Lydia said. "It'll be over by eight."

She wiggled her fingers.

"It had *better* be over by eight. Grant got us reservations at One if by Land, and you know what *that* means."

One of the podcasters had dropped out because she'd converted to Catholicism, and now refused to be associated with anything pagan ("She just wants more money," Lydia sniffed), but Lydia's photographer ex-boyfriend knew the girl who did the TikTok videos of herself reading *The Decline of the West* out loud in her underwear.

"If that doesn't work out," Lydia said, "we've got someone from *The Great British Bake Off.*"

Work came to Rose as a relief. It always did. She could put in her headphones, solve problems like bullet points, and give herself over to the comforting lightness of knowing exactly what she was supposed to do next.

—

The first few days of January passed. Rose did not return to Tudor City.

She told Caleb she was too busy, which was true. The *Aphrodite* launch was taking up most of her time, and her boss was interested in having her take the lead on a second project they were brainstorming called *Persephone*, which was supposed to unlock all your personal traumas from the underworld, and which made Rose feel like maybe she was doing some good in the world.

"Plus, Cecilia's probably left the place a war zone," Rose said. "I don't want to deal with it right now."

"If she *has* left." Caleb wrinkled his nose. "This city makes it a nightmare, evicting someone."

"Believe me," Rose said. "She's probably halfway to Timbuktu right now."

—

Rose and Caleb spent the second Monday of January curled up on the sofa, listening to a podcast about how you could apply kabbalistic techniques in the workplace. Rose's phone rang.

"Jesus," Caleb said. "Who *calls* a person anymore?" He grimaced. "It's not your sister, is it?"

It was Paul's number.

Rose declined the call.

"Spam," Rose said.

She set the phone to silent.

By the time they finished the podcast, Paul had called Rose five times.

Rose told herself it wasn't her problem. Whatever was going on with Paul and Cecilia, it had nothing to do with her. Probably it had something to do with the divorce papers Cecilia had burned. Only, then Paul called a sixth time.

Caleb stretched contently along the sofa. "Do you wanna play *Breath of the Wild*?"

Rose shook her head.

"I think I'm going to run to Whole Foods," she said. "We need milk."

Rose went to Whole Foods. She bought milk, even though there was half a carton in the fridge, so that she would not have technically lied. She called Paul back from Houston Street.

"Thank God," he said. "I was starting to worry you'd blocked my number."

"Just tell me," she began. "Is everything okay?"

"I, I don't know," he said. He was out of breath. "I'm sorry—I didn't know who else to call."

"What's going on?"

"Look, I'm sorry; maybe it's nothing; it's—" He swallowed. "Could I come and see you? Anywhere—anywhere you want."

"Paul—"

"*Please*," he said. He said it as simply, as unselfconsciously, as he had the first time Rose had called him. As if he were not afraid of sounding like a fool.

God, Rose prayed. *Let this be the last time I ever have to do this.*

"Can you come to Veselka? Do you know where that is?"

"I can look it up."

"I can be there in ten minutes."

He hesitated only a moment.

"Thank you," he said at last.

———

Paul arrived at Veselka a few minutes after Rose did. He looked even more haggard than the last time she'd seen him. His stubble was gray. He was drinking a mug of tea.

"I'm sorry," he said as he sat. "I didn't want to worry you. I *don't* want to worry you. And maybe—it's nothing."

"What is it?"

Paul took a deep breath.

"Have you spoken to your sister recently?"

Rose bristled.

"No," she said. "Why?"

"She called me," he said. "On New Year's Eve."

"Okay."

"She sounded—*off*, maybe, or out of it, or—"

"Drunk." It wasn't a question.

"No," Paul said firmly. "Not drunk. She was very clear. Like she'd planned out what she was going to say beforehand. She—told me she wanted to say goodbye."

"I don't see how that's any of my . . ."

"She told me," he went on, more loudly, "that I would never see her again. That I was *free of her*—her words, Rose, not mine. That I was free of any promise I'd ever made to her. *Think of me*, she said, *as dead.*"

Rose's stomach knotted.

"Dead?"

"I thought—I don't want to tell you what I thought."

"I know what you thought."

Rose had thought it, so many times before. She had woken up in the middle of the night, thinking it. She had thought about it so often she had grown numb.

"Don't worry," Rose said, "Cecilia would never kill herself. She'd never do anything she couldn't undo." She saw his face. "Don't look so shocked," she said. "If you'd known Cecilia as long as I have, you'd find that comforting."

"She sounded serious."

"Cecilia always *sounds* serious."

"She said she was going away. Somewhere she couldn't do any more damage any longer."

As if, Rose reminded herself, more forcefully, *Cecilia hasn't said so many things like that before.*

"She said to give you a message."

"Me?"

"She said—I don't know if this means something to you—that she was going *away with the fairies.*"

Rose stared at him for a moment, dumbstruck.

Then she started laughing.

"What? What is it?"

"Is *that* all?"

"I don't see what's so funny."

"Oh, *Paul,*" Rose said, between wheezes. "Poor, poor Paul."

"*What?*"

"She's *fine.* She's totally fine. She's just—you know—gone and done what she always does."

"Who are the fairies?"

"Just some weird friends of hers who live on this houseboat," Rose said.

"That's all. They have some sort of theater performance or something. She's probably crashing with one of them."

Paul had turned red.

"She seemed to think," he said, "that she wasn't coming back."

"That's Cecilia for you," Rose said. "It's always *always* with her. *Always* or *never*. And it never really is."

"You're not even *concerned*?"

The look on his face infuriated her. As if she were somehow the one in the wrong.

"Jesus Christ, Paul! Go *home* already! Go back to New England. Get your divorce. Get—I don't know—a decent therapist. You're not a knight in shining armor, Paul. You're just a sad, sorry man who doesn't know when to let go."

Paul looked down at the table.

"I just want," he said softly, "to make sure she's all right."

"She's as all right," Rose said, "as she's ever going to be." She checked her phone. "I should get back. Caleb's waiting for me."

He stiffened. "I'm sorry to have troubled you," he said.

Rose almost felt sorry for him.

"Just take care of yourself, okay?"

Rose threw down a twenty on the table. She left him sitting there alone.

It was raining as Rose made her way down Second Avenue. The streets were overflowing. There were crowds outside the izakaya place and outside the mezcal bar—couples on dates nuzzling under space heaters and drunk NYU students stumbling against each other's shoulders—and all of a sudden Rose felt horribly lonely and horribly old.

Rose didn't even know why she was crying.

Cecilia wasn't her problem any longer, she thought, and God knows Paul certainly wasn't her problem, and it wasn't her fault that Paul hadn't learned that the more you try to hold a person like Cecilia, the farther they fly; and it wasn't her fault that Cecilia had vanished, the way Cecilia was always going to vanish. The only thing Rose had done wrong was believe her when she said she'd stay.

But there were tears running down Rose's face, and blotches burning into Rose's cheeks, and Rose wasn't ready to come home to Caleb and explain that she'd been stupid enough to worry, even for a second, about Cecilia, after she'd announced with such certainty that she was never going to worry about Cecilia again, because *the definition of* insanity, she reminded herself, as she turned east onto Sixth Street, *is doing the same thing, over and over, and expecting a different result.*

Rose decided to take a walk. Just a quick one, she thought, around Tompkins Square Park, just long enough to listen to one of the My.th mini-meditations she'd worked on last year, just long enough to calm down. There was one she'd always liked, the *Hera*, the first one she'd ever done, which was all about being a kind of queen and ruling your own interior landscape like it was your personal kingdom. They'd gotten this British character actress from *Downton Abbey* to do the voice.

"*There is a castle,*" the voice began, "*inside your mind.*"

It was midnight. The park was still full. The man with the Chinese pipes was there, as usual, competing this time with a young blond doing Dylan on an acoustic guitar. On the path there were discarded needles, piles of rotting leaves, and a slippery mirror or two of ice. A group of Goths were leaning on each other's shoulders next to the Temperance Fountain, smoking weed.

"*From this castle,*" the voice went on, "*let yourself survey the whole landscape of your soul. What does it look like? Where are the mountains? Where are the valleys? Where are the rushing rivers and the mighty forests?*"

Rose kept walking. She had not been in the park since the night of her disastrous birthday, when Caleb had annoyed her by asking Cecilia about her *meta-goal*, as if Caleb hadn't been right, this whole time, about Cecilia, who couldn't even cross this very park without stopping to—

Rose stopped short. The voice continued.

"*Do you see beyond them, the dragonlands, those areas you do not yet dare to go? Those are the parts of your kingdom that are in danger. They are the ones you must prepare yourself to conquer."*

It was a coincidence. It had to be a coincidence, or else Rose was misremembering or else Rose had invented the image altogether, out of a panic or a dream.

Rose jerked the buds out of her ears.

She turned back along the path. She walked to where, three months ago, a girl with purple hair had shouted into a megaphone.

The patch of grass was empty. But the sign was still there: swinging from the branch of a maple tree. Rain had sodden it and corroded its edges.

Rose could still make out the words.

HAVE YOU SEEN THIS BOAT?

The girl had drawn it in a childlike hand: a small canal barge sketched in red crayon.

Underneath were pasted two grainy photographs, seemingly taken from newspapers. A teenage boy, no more than eighteen. A beautiful, middle-aged woman with melancholy eyes.

THEY ARE KIDNAPPING PEOPLE ALL OVER AMERICA
THE POLICE WILL NOT HELP

Rose looked closer at the drawing. The pounding in her chest echoed in her ears.

On the boat's prow, the girl had sketched a name.

THE AVALON.

PART TWO

ROSE GOES TO THE AVALON

CHAPTER SIX

B y morning Rose had convinced herself it was nothing. *Avalon* was a common enough name, she reminded herself, for a boat or for anything else, and even if the boat in the girl's drawing was the same boat that belonged to Cecilia's friends, that didn't mean much. You couldn't put stock in the fantasies of someone shouting into a megaphone in Tompkins Square Park. Probably, Rose told herself, for the fifth time, she was paranoid, or on drugs. Probably Cecilia had gotten bored of them by now.

Rose went into the office. She put in her headphones. She focused on writing the code for *Persephone.* The idea was that the app would know when your heart rate increased, which was supposed to help you figure out when you got close to a thought or memory that really scared you. She made three mistakes in two minutes.

"You look like shit," Lydia said at lunch. "Did you and Caleb have a fight or something?"

"I'm just tired," Rose said. "That's all."

Rose had said nothing to Caleb. She told herself it was because there was nothing to say.

But as dusk came, and the sky paled into periwinkle, Rose's fears closed in.

It is probably nothing, she told herself. She was acting like Cecilia; making molehills into myths, deciding that every other person in the subway was a saint or a prophet or a prince in disguise.

Still, she'd been meaning to go to Tudor City anyway.

—

The apartment was spotless.

Cecilia had washed the dishes. Cecilia had scrubbed the floors. Cecilia had folded the towels into thirds, the way Rose liked them, and scoured the last of the mold from the bathtub grout. Cecilia had taken out the trash.

You might think Cecilia had never been there at all, were it not for Cecilia's suitcase, still under the bed. Were it not for Falstaff, nestled in the pillows. Were it not for Cecilia's passport, on the bedside table, along with her wallet, her ID, her phone.

Rose grabbed it. It was unlocked—Cecilia never bothered to lock her devices—nursing its last percentages of battery. She had seven missed calls, from New Year's Eve onward. All of them were from Paul.

She checked the outgoing calls.

One, to Paul, at 2:36 in the morning of January 1.

None since.

It doesn't mean anything, Rose told herself, more insistently this time. Cecilia was always losing her devices or throwing them away. There had been that three-month period, shortly after Cecilia's conversion to Catholicism, when Cecilia had gone to live with some nuns on a silent retreat and would communicate only by letters, sealed with wax.

But a sick, strange feeling had coiled itself at the pit of Rose's stomach. It tightened around Rose's chest.

She scoured Cecilia's nightstand, her wastepaper basket, under her bed, looking for evidence—any evidence—of the Avalon Cabaret. None came.

You're going to feel so stupid, Rose told herself, *when this is over.*

Rose took a cab to Tompkins Square Park.

The sign was still there, swinging in the winter breeze. There was no evidence of the girl. A young man with a tiny mustache and a typewriter was sitting on a nearby patch of grass at a folding table with a sign saying *POEMS $5.50 $6.25.*

"Excuse me?" Rose already felt ridiculous. "I was wondering—"

"Theme?"

"I—what?"

"Love? Loss?" He tapped his typewriter. "Lust?"

"No—I'm sorry. I'm actually looking for someone."

He scowled.

"Purple hair? Megaphone?" Rose tried an apologetic smile.

The poet gave her a look. "*You're* looking for Franny?"

"I think so. The one who made the sign?"

He raised an eyebrow. "O-kay," he said. He turned back to the typewriter.

"Do you know where she is?"

He shrugged.

"She's here most nights," he said. "Doing her . . . you know . . . *thing.*" He grimaced. "When it's cold she sleeps at a squat nearby. Or so I hear," he added quickly.

"Do you know where?"

He shot her an even more lacerating look.

The night was, Rose thought hopefully, relatively warm.

"I'll—I'll wait."

"You do you," he said. He turned back to his typewriter.

Rose sat on a bench. She waited. She texted Caleb that she would be home late. **Dealing w/ Cecilia apt stuff**, she said, which she figured was technically true. She repeated to herself the words of the *Hera* meditation, in an attempt to still her heartbeat. It didn't work.

At nine the girl appeared. She was older than Rose had realized—thirty, maybe older still, though it was impossible to tell under the flaking layer of makeup. She had tamed her hair into pigtails.

"Francesca," the poet said, without looking up from his typewriter. "You've got company."

"Very funny, Tony," the girl said. Her voice was hoarse. "Go fuck yourself."

"I'm serious," he said. He shrugged in Rose's direction. "Maybe you finally converted someone."

The girl rounded on her.

"What do you want?"

Her eyes were kohl-rimmed and bloodshot.

"I—I'm here about your sign."

The girl eyed her warily. "Yeah?"

Rose steeled herself. "I think I'm looking for them, too."

At once the girl's whole expression changed. Her eyes widened; her shoulders softened; her lips—which had been narrow as arrow slits—began trembling.

"Thank God," she breathed. "Thank God." Her gaze darted from tree to tree, as if she were determining whether they were being watched.

"Look," Rose said, "is there somewhere we can go and talk?"

The girl nodded.

"There's a place on Ninth Street," she said. "It's quiet, in the back."

Rose followed Francesca wordlessly to the café. They sat.

"Get whatever you want," Rose said when the waitress arrived, and then immediately grew worried she sounded condescending. "I mean—it's on me."

Francesca's lips twitched.

"Then I'll have," she said, enunciating every syllable, "the *avocado toast.*" She raised her eyes to Rose's. Rose couldn't tell whether Francesca was making fun of her. Already she was beginning to regret coming. *This is,* she thought, *the kind of insane thing only Cecilia would do.*

"Look," Rose said, once the waitress had gone. "This—this sounds crazy . . ." (*As if,* Rose reminded herself, *anything sounds crazy to a girl who lives in Tompkins Square Park.*) "But I'm looking for someone. Someone who I think got on this—this boat, the *Avalon*. And, well, I need to know how to find them."

Francesca looked up at her. A strange smile spread across her face.

"You don't," she said. "They find you."

"You know them?"

Francesca's expression wavered only slightly.

"I know *of* them," she said stiffly.

"I'm sorry," Rose said. "I don't—"

The last of Francesca's smile died.

"They took my friend."

"*Took . . . ?*"

"Took. *Lured.* Whatever you want to call it. What matters is: he's gone."

Rose's stomach plummeted.

"When?"

"Six months ago."

Francesca rocked back and forth on her elbows.

"His name was Robin," she said. "The sweetest kid you'd ever met. One of those people, you know, no matter what life did to him; and believe me, life did a lot—he never lost his innocence. People used to call him my puppy. *Hey, Franny, watch out for the puppy; don't forget to bring home extras for the puppy.*"

"How did you know him?"

"He was always around." Francesca searched Rose's face for recognition. "He used to come into this gay bar I worked at, cruising for middle-aged daddies to take him home. Not that it went well for him. Kid was so nervous he could barely put in a drink order without stammering. Barely eighteen, with the shoddiest fake ID I'd ever seen. I told him I wasn't going to let him do that shit—not in my bar. That's when he told me he didn't have anywhere else to go. It was one thing when *my* folks kicked me out, you know," she said. "But that was the nineties, right? You'd think things had changed."

"His parents kicked him out?"

"I wish"—color rose to Francesca's cheeks—"they'd *only* kicked him out. The things they did to him—for years—first. God, sometimes I used to think, maybe it'd be worth my whole soul, just to take an ax to their throats." Her eyes blazed; Rose shivered.

"But we took care of each other," Francesca went on, "Robin and me. He used to follow me around. I let him work at my bar. I let him sleep on my sofa. No more hustling—*you fuck someone,* I told him, *it's because you want to fuck them.* Careful with the hard stuff—I'd been up and down that road before, and I knew how it goes. We even had a place together for a while, over in Cypress Hills. We had it all worked out. He was going to get discovered, as a singer—kid had a voice like a goddamn castrato—and I was going to be his manager, and we'd move out to LA and do all that, like, *wellness* shit." She winced at the memory.

"What happened?"

Francesca closed her eyes. She exhaled: one long, exhausted breath.

"It was spring," she said. "We were rich—I mean, we *felt* rich. Tips had been good, and we'd been putting out some videos, you know, of Robin singing, and they were getting traction or whatever. And we decided to go blow it all and have a night out on the town. Pretend we were rich NYU students living on Daddy's dime. We got all dolled up and went to this, like, kitschy 1920s night they do above the KGB Bar over on Fourth Street, with music and burlesque and shit. And the pianist is playing ragtime, or whatever you call it, and Robin, he asks if he can sing; and he sings—you know 'Paper Moon'?"

Rose shook her head.

"Say it's only a paper moon / Sailing over a cardboard sea." Francesca's voice was raspy and off-key; a couple at the next table turned toward them in irritation. *"But it wouldn't be make believe / If you believed in me.* God, that was his favorite. He broke your heart, with that one. He broke his own heart. Every time he sang that, he'd start to choke up a little. I used to always have to redo his makeup afterward. Maybe that's why they picked him, I don't know." She swallowed. "I was chatting up some girl at the bar.

Usually I kept an eye on him, you know, but it was late, and I was drunk, and he was talking real intently to this girl. I remember—because she didn't look like the rest of them. Everyone else, you know, we were wearing, like, shitty boas and drugstore rhinestones, only she looked like she'd walked straight out of the 1920s. Tiny thing, barely looked older than twenty, with this little bleach-blond bob down to here." She indicated her cheekbones. "After, he told me the girl had given him something."

Rose's heart sank.

"A card?"

Francesca nodded.

"We figured it was just, like, some self-promotion shit. Robin told me he threw it out. I'd forgotten all about it. Only then he started acting weird."

"Weird?"

"Disappearing. Staying out all night. Missing shifts at work. Refusing to say where he'd been. He'd get distracted—like, one minute we'd be in the middle of a conversation, and then the next he'd be staring off into space, like I wasn't even there. At first I thought—*don't ride his ass,* you know, *he's probably got a real boyfriend, it's about time.* But—I got this feeling, you know? Like, *psychic,* right?" She tapped her temple. "Something wasn't right. He started talking about how he hated this city and everyone in it, how they were all liars and cheats. How he hated the music we were making—how it didn't sound like it was *supposed* to sound. How it didn't live up to the music in his head.

"One night I woke up, two, three in the morning, to the sound of him tiptoeing out of the apartment. Only he hadn't taken anything with him. No keys, no phone, nothing. So I followed him. I trailed him through the Brooklyn Navy Yard like I was in a goddamn film noir. I followed him, all the way to the end of the pier. That's when I saw them."

An uncanny gleam had come into Francesca's eyes.

"I thought I was dreaming," she said. "This red boat, floating toward us, with *THE AVALON* right there in black letters, and all around it these flames that were, like, floating in midair, like magic. And all over, flowers that changed color. And the *music . . .*" Her voice trailed off. "For the rest of my life," Francesca said, "I'll remember that music."

Rose remembered the discordant song echoing from Cecilia's piano. Nausea crashed over her.

"I watched him get on." Francesca's voice grew unsteady. "I watched them vanish, into the mist." She swallowed. "And that was the last time I ever saw him."

"Did you go to the police?"

"*The police?*" Francesca scoffed. "Yeah, sure, I went to the police." She snorted. "Some junkie punk walks in, says her friend disappeared on a mysterious magic boat—sure, they sent the goddamn coast guard after him."

"You're right," Rose faltered. "I'm sorry."

"I waited, you know. For weeks, I waited. I couldn't afford the place on my own, only I couldn't leave, because I thought he'd come back. *Any day now*, I thought. I had an old girlfriend in Philadelphia; she tried to get me to crash out there for a while. Only, I kept thinking, *what if he needs me; what if he comes back and finds me gone.* He didn't even have his phone!" She emitted a keening, animal sound: something between a laugh and a shriek. "Of course. I couldn't work; I couldn't think. That I'd made it up. Sometimes I thought I'd even made *him* up—that I'd lost my mind altogether. I thought maybe I'd started using, and blocked out the memory or something. Then I *started* using, again, because it was the next best thing, you know, to that music. You can only imagine how my landlord took that one." She scoffed. "I threw every grenade you can throw into your own life, trying to find them again.

"Only—"

"Only?"

The whole room was swimming.

"He wasn't the only one." Francesca fixed her gaze on Rose's face. "I started digging. Every day I'd go to the library; I'd look up newspapers, articles, anything I could find. And then I found her. Constance Nelson. Google her."

The name sounded vaguely familiar. Rose half remembered scrolling the *New York Times*, sometime in the pandemic: a few days' worth of articles, about a hunt for a woman who'd gone missing one night off the Coney Island Boardwalk, then silence.

"They never found her, either," Francesca said. "They thought the husband did it—apparently he had a history—but he had an alibi." She gnawed at her lower lip. "Motel. Other woman."

"I don't understand."

"He told the police she'd been vanishing for weeks. Same story. Strange hours, refusing to say where she'd been. Finally the police figured she'd run away with someone. They closed the case."

"Maybe—" Rose tried. "Maybe she *did* run away with someone."

Francesca shook her head. "The *Fiddler.* January 10, 2021. *An eyewitness reported seeing the missing woman boarding a red boat.*" She grimaced. "Of course, nobody trusts the *Fiddler.* And the eyewitness was just some drunk who lived on the boardwalk. And there's no such thing as boats that spirit people away." She seized hold of Rose's hand. Her nails pressed into Rose's fingers. A harsh laugh rattled her throat. "But I know what happened. They have her. And they have Robin. And they have your friend, too. And they won't let any of them go!"

Rose could not speak. Her heart was in her throat. *None of this*, she thought, *is real*; it was all viral marketing, or one of those TikTok stunts where somebody is secretly recording your reaction.

"But you—" Francesca went on without stopping for breath. "You get it—you believe me; we could help each other. We can keep watch—I've made a list of all the piers in . . ."

But Rose was no longer listening. The table, the plates, the brick of the wall were all doubling and redoubling before her like the fragments of a kaleidoscope; the patterns on the ceiling were all mingling together. Rose was spinning—no, the whole room was spinning; she was suddenly hot, so hot she could not breathe, and all Rose could think was that if she did not get out of the café that very minute the earth would split beneath her and swallow her whole.

Rose threw down all the cash in her purse.

"I'm—I'm sorry." She could barely get the words out. "I have to go."

———

Rose spent the night googling Constance Nelson.

Francesca had told the truth. Constance Nelson had—her husband said—behaved erratically for weeks; *not*, he said, *that she wasn't always a bit erratic to begin with*. She'd been secretive: going for walks at all hours, leaving her wallet and phone and keys behind. She'd grown so obsessed with the arrival of the mail that he started wondering if she was dealing drugs. Security cameras had last caught her at three in the morning, on the Coney Island Boardwalk, heading toward the water. A homeless woman told the NYPD she'd seen a woman getting on a boat, but then again, so many crazies come out of the woodwork every time a beautiful woman disappears. They'd waited for a body to wash up on the shore. None came.

A coincidence, Rose told herself. *Cecilia is probably halfway back to London by now.*

She no longer believed it.

———

"You okay?" Caleb said, over breakfast the next morning, as Rose tapped her fingers frantically on the kitchen island.

He took a fistful of carrots from the crisper. He took down creatine powder from the cabinet. He began to scoop it into the blender.

"I'm fine," said Rose. "Just tired. Only—"

"What is it?" He looked up at her.

Last night, she'd said nothing to Caleb, who was thankfully too busy emailing potential OptiMyze funders to notice. She had justified it to herself on the grounds that she was tired, probably hysterical; she hadn't been thinking clearly, and in any case, how could you explain to a person like Caleb that you'd picked up a stranger in Tompkins Square Park and asked her to tell you about the fairies?

Still, they had never lied to each other.

"Cecilia," Rose began.

"Jesus—Ro."

Rose tried harder. "Paul got in touch. He said she's gone."

"Of course she's gone! Isn't that what you wanted?"

"It's just—" Rose tried to put it into words that made sense. "These people she's been seeing lately; I don't like the sound of them."

"What else is new?"

He put his hand against her cheek.

"I thought we were aligned on this, Ro," he said.

He said it so gently. If she'd known him less well, she might even have missed the disappointment in his voice.

"I know." Rose tried one final time. "I'm sorry. I—"

There was nothing worse, Rose thought, than disappointing Caleb. Disappointing Caleb was what the old Rose would have done: the foolish, heedless Rose who dragged Caleb down into dramas any well-adjusted person knew enough to avoid. Like Rose's birthday. Like Thanksgiving.

He had forgiven her so much already.

"Never mind," Rose said. "You're right. I'm overthinking it."

He kissed her cheek.

"Good girl," he said.

—

Rose went to work. She put her earbuds in. The last of the *Hera* meditation echoed into silence. The numbers and letters on her screen scrambled together. She suddenly felt savagely lonely. It was as if Rose had gotten lost on her way home from work and wandered into another world where she was the only human left alive.

She tried to concentrate. She gave up. She took out her phone.

She called Paul.

———

By noon Rose was back at the front door of Paul's apartment. She'd told Lydia it was stomach flu.

"I'm sorry—it's still a bit of a state," Paul said, opening the door. "I've been packing." His suitcase lay on the futon.

"Where are you going?"

Paul shrugged. "Back to Maine, probably," he said. "Or to England, for a while. Wait out my academic leave in peace." He looked up at her. "What is it? Have you heard from her?"

Rose shook her head.

"Look," she said. "You're probably going to think I'm crazy. You can tell me—if I'm crazy. I just needed to tell *someone*."

"What?"

"Please know, I don't do, I don't know, *woo* shit. I don't believe in ghosts or witches or *energy* or anything. I don't even believe in astrology!"

"Rose." His voice was firm. "What in God's name are you talking about?"

Rose told him everything. She was detailed; she was methodical; she left nothing out, from the typewriter poet to Constance Nelson's husband's alibi to the haunting song Cecilia had played that night after Mimi's.

Paul listened without a word.

When she finished, he took a long, deep breath. He sat for a moment, on the futon's edge, closing his eyes. A strange, wry smile began to form at the edges of his lips, and then vanished as quickly as it had come.

"What is it?"

"Nothing." Paul shook his head. "Nothing." He put his face in his hands.

"You think I'm crazy, don't you?"

At last he looked up at her.

"No," he said softly. "I don't."

"Come on, you—"

"Did you ever read *The Lion, the Witch and the Wardrobe*," he said suddenly, "when you were a child?"

"I'm sorry, *what?*"

"The ending. When the children are telling the old Professor about the land of Narnia. Implausible, of course. The other grown-ups think it's all bollocks. Only the Professor says—there are just three options. They're mad. They're lying. Or they're telling the truth." He nodded, as much to himself as to her. "I don't think you're crazy. And I don't think you're lying, either."

"And the girl? Francesca?"

"She might be crazy," Paul said. "She might be lying. Or she might have seen something—*something*—she doesn't altogether understand."

"She said her friend's been gone for six months! And this other woman—Constance—it's been two years! No word. No contact. Her cards, her accounts, untouched; no clue whether she's alive or dead, whether *any* of them . . ."

Paul blanched.

"She's not dead," he said flatly.

"How do you know?"

"She just isn't," he said. "That's all."

"Because—what—you'd just *know?*"

Paul didn't say anything, and Rose felt a fresh wave of irritation.

As if, she thought, *it were true that people just know, when someone they love is dead.*

As if, she let herself grow bitter, *he would be the one to feel it first.*

"Right." Paul banished the thought. "So what do we do?"

"*We?*"

"Obviously we can't go to the police—no doubt they'll tell us a somewhat politer version of *fuck off.*"

Rose opened her mouth to protest. She closed it again.

"Do you have the card they gave your sister?"

Rose shook her head.

"I checked Cecilia's room," she said. "There was nothing."

"Anyway," Paul sped on, before Rose could say anything more. "The girl said they found the boy at a bar."

"KGB," Rose said. "In the East Village."

"And your sister, too?"

"A longshoreman's bar? Near here? With music, maybe?"

Paul looked amused.

"Sunny's," he said. "Not much of a longshoreman's bar these days. But your sister enjoys poetic license." Rose registered the present tense. It made her feel better. "We'll start there. It's the most recent place they've been spotted, so it's the most likely."

"*Start* there?"

"Well," Paul went on, "if they are looking—*hunting*—for people, who-ever and *whatever* they are, it stands to reason that the best way to find them is to turn up where they—well—*hunt.*"

Rose gaped at him in astonishment.

"You're not serious," she said.

"Do you have a better idea?"

Rose sighed. The weight of two sleepless nights pressed in upon her. Her resistance waned.

"Look," she said. "You don't have to do this. I mean, I'm grateful—really, I am. But this isn't your mess to fix."

"I'm sorry?"

"She's not your responsibility."

"Of course she's my responsibility!"

Rose remembered the sermon he'd given her about principle. Once again it vexed her. "What, because she's still *technically* your wife, you mean?"

"I made a promise." Paul's voice was tight. "And I intend to keep it."

"Is that *really* all it is?"

Paul was silent a moment longer.

"No," he said. "That's not all it is."

"Because if you're expecting to ride in on your horse and rescue her, and you think she'll—"

Paul rounded on her. There was a look of quiet fury in his eyes.

"I don't expect your sister to come back to me," he said. "I'm not quite as much an idiot as you think."

"I didn't mean—" Rose began.

"And I *certainly* don't want her back out of some sense of obligation." The look on his face made her ashamed.

"I'm sorry," she said. "I didn't mean to insult you."

"Is it really so very difficult for you," Paul said, acidly, "to imagine loving someone, and wanting nothing in return?"

Rose didn't answer him.

Paul rose. He went to the window. He stood there a moment, looking out toward the harbor.

"We'll go to Sunny's," he said. "Eleven thirty, maybe? When's *the witching hour* supposed to be, anyway?"

Rose felt a sudden shiver down her spine. It was the same uncanny feeling she'd felt in the corridor of Tudor City, listening to Cecilia's song.

"I'll be there," Rose said.

—

Rose took the bus back to work. She tried to concentrate. She texted Caleb and told him—truthfully, *technically*—that she planned to spend the night at Tudor City. **Cecilia**, she said, **has left a mess behind**. He responded with a thumbs-up emoji.

—

At eleven thirty, Rose came to Sunny's. Paul was already there. He was sitting in the middle of the bar's three rooms, in a rickety booth overlooking the garden, where a pockmarked statue of St. Francis of Assisi stood in a corner under a Texas flag. Christmas lights hung from a wooden sign above the bar. In the back a band was playing old American folk music. There was a skinny girl with a fiddle, and for a moment Rose missed Cecilia so much she couldn't breathe.

"I took the liberty—"

Paul motioned at a second whiskey beside his.

"I figured we'd be here awhile. This table has the best view."

Rose sank into the banquette opposite.

"What are we supposed to do now?"

"Watch? Wait?"

"For what? Someone to waltz in in a red ball gown?"

Paul didn't answer.

It wasn't, Rose had to admit, like they had other options.

They watched. They waited. At the next booth a date went badly. At the bar, a girl with a bleach-blond pixie was arguing with an Australian she accused of cutting her in line.

"So," Rose said, after thirty minutes of silence, "you're originally from England?"

He gave her a look.

"Come on," Rose said. "We have two hours until last call. We might as well make conversation."

Paul sighed. "My mother's American," he said. "My father was from Yorkshire. She came to England for a nursing conference and never left."

"How long have you been in the States?"

"Six years."

"All in New England?"

"Three in North Carolina. Two in Maine."

"You've always been a teacher?"

Paul's eyebrow twitched.

"I wanted," he said, "to be an eminent professor. Once. I was going to *revolutionize the study of literature.*"

"What happened?"

"Nothing very interesting." Paul shrugged. "Turns out I didn't have very many new things to say about the study of literature. I got as far as a serviceable draft of my mediocre doctoral dissertation and then threw it in the dustbin."

"Why?"

"*Principle*," Paul said with a smile. Rose couldn't tell if he was making fun of her. But he went on: "I was stubborn. *I* knew I didn't deserve to pass. I couldn't have stood it if anyone else had dared tell me otherwise. It would have felt like cheating." He took a sip of his whiskey. "Besides," Paul said. "I didn't mind teaching high school. Children don't know if you're not original. To them, everything's new." He shrugged. "What do you do, anyway?"

"I code for a wellness app."

"Yoga and things?" Paul looked dubious.

"I mean—it's more scientific than that. We make guided meditations that track your heart rate—you know, fostering mind-body connection?"

"Ah," Paul said.

"We help people get to know themselves better." This didn't land, either. "We've got someone from *The Great British Bake Off* doing the voices," Rose added, in desperation.

"And did you always want to . . . code for a wellness app?"

"I wanted," Rose admitted, "to be an artist."

"What happened?"

She kept her eyes on her drink. "Nothing very interesting. Family stuff."

"Your mother, you mean?"

She looked up at him in surprise.

"Your sister told me."

"It wasn't *just* that," said Rose, more tetchily than she'd intended. "I mean—either way, I'd have grown out of it. I wasn't very good."

He leaned forward on his elbows. "What kind of art did you make?"

"I don't know; it was years ago." Paul's eyes remained on her face. "Drawings, mostly portraits."

"Of who?"

"I don't know. People. Around the city. Strangers." She thought, briefly, of the artist in Bay Ridge, who had taught her about proportion and the proper shape of the skull. "We used to work together, you know. Me and Cecilia. We'd go out to places we thought were bound to have interesting people, and I'd pick out the person I'd draw, then she'd go up and talk to them and distract them from the weird kid sketching them in the corner."

"That," Paul said, with a melancholy smile, "sounds like your sister."

Now it was midnight. The man at the next booth was on his second date of the evening. At the bar a gray-bearded man was showing the bartender a collection of objects he'd found with his metal detector. Rose was grateful for the whiskey. It warmed her nerves. It calmed the churning in her heart. It made her bold.

"Why did you do it, anyway?"

"Do what?"

"I mean—come on—*three weeks?*"

"Ah," Paul said. "That."

"I mean—I get it, with Cecilia. *She* does things like that, always has. But you—"

He pushed back his glasses with a smile. "I don't strike you as the impulsive type?"

"Not really."

"I'm not," Paul said. "At least—I wasn't. No." He considered. "Quite the opposite. I had—well, I had a good little life, I suppose. I liked my job. I liked my students. In another era I might have been one of those *confirmed academic bachelors* everybody always assumes is a closeted homosexual." His eyes danced. "Which, of course, was what my parents assumed of me. Of anyone, really, in the middle of rural Yorkshire, who wore blazers and liked books." He took another sip of whiskey. "They needn't have worried. I tried *that* exactly once, at Oxford, and promptly ruled it out. I was sorry, too. It would have made things easier."

"What do you mean?"

"There would at least have been a *reason*," Paul said. "For whatever was *wrong* with me."

"*Wrong* with you?"

"I wasn't altogether joking," Paul said, "when I told your sister about my *great tragedy*. Call it—coldness or shyness or *avoidant attachment style*; maybe you'll come up with a better word than I ever have. Point is: I preferred books to people, and solitude to company, and imaginary loves to real ones. Don't get me wrong—I dated. I probably frustrated the hell out of many well-meaning women, who figured I just needed to be chased. But . . ." He paused for a moment, as if searching for the right words. "I didn't want to settle for anything less than exactly what I wanted."

"Which was?"

"A love that made the whole world make sense?" Paul shrugged. "I don't just mean passion, or sex. I mean—the kind of love that makes you understand what love is supposed to be *for*, that throws everything else into relief. That makes you understand why—I don't know—why human beings have ten fingers or why birds have beaks or why there are however many stars there are in the heavens. You know," he added archly, "*simple things like that*."

"But that kind of love doesn't exist," Rose said.

"I know that," Paul said. "That didn't stop me from wanting it. It was all-or-nothing with me. If I couldn't have it, I mean, *all of it*, the right way, the real way, then I didn't want it at all. And I was happy enough, you know, in my little monk's cell up in Maine. Only—then I met your sister."

A new gleam came to his eyes.

"Perhaps you're picturing love at first sight," he said. "*I saw her across a crowded bookstore and had to have her.* It wasn't like that. At least, I don't think it was. I found her beautiful, of course, but it's not like I haven't kept my head around beautiful women before. We got talking in the poetry section. I was in her way—or she was in mine. She looked at me, with that gaze of hers—you know the one—and told me, without a trace of irony, mind you, that she couldn't get more than three cantos into Dante's *Inferno* because she couldn't stand to picture all the poor souls in hell. If he really had been to hell and really had seen their suffering, she couldn't understand how he could do something as self-serving as writing a poem about it. *Sometimes I'm afraid*, she told me, *that if God exists, He must be evil. Or else hate us. And I can't see how that doesn't amount to the same thing.* She hadn't even told me her name."

"That," Rose said, "sounds like Cecilia."

It was a relief, somehow, to talk about her. As long as they kept talking about her, she was not missing, but only absent: on a steamship, say, or an ayahuasca retreat. Talking about her, Rose could almost believe that this vanishing was like all the other ones that had happened before.

"We spent all night talking," Paul said. "Went out into the woods with a bottle of cheap wine, and looked out at the water, and watched the sunrise come over us. It was easy to talk to her. She took everything I said seriously. Kindly. She didn't treat me like I—like there was something broken about me, for the way I'd lived my life. She didn't tell me I was a fool or a sullen child or that I put women on a pedestal or any other version of the recriminations I'd heard a hundred times before. She listened, very quietly, and then afterward she said, *I know exactly what you mean.* And then she told me about the grail."

Rose stiffened. *That*, she thought, with sudden possessiveness, *is our word*; it was like the Countess or the three-fingered guitarist or Tudor City. It was for the two of them alone.

"She told me everything about her life," Paul went on. "Her disappointments. Her disasters. You."

"Me?"

But Paul hadn't heard her. "We made quite the pair. Two broken people, too old for our dreams, who had never quite managed to find our way in the world. Me in my cloister. Her—everywhere. At dawn she took me to the music building. She played me a song she said she'd been working on—part of the opera she was writing about the Knights of the Round Table. Guinevere's aria."

Rose looked up in surprise. Cecilia had, she'd been sure, given up on that project years ago.

"She told me it had been years, and she'd never managed to get it right. *I can't keep my head on straight long enough to focus.* She grew quiet, and still; for a moment I thought I'd done something to upset her. Then she looked up at me. And she said, *I think we should just get married.*

"I thought I'd misheard her at first. But she said it again. There wasn't a doubt in my mind she was serious. *It's the only solution,* she said. She had a whole logic worked out. It was going to be our salvation. *If we can just commit to something,* she said. *If we can just decide.* Throw our lives together, in a moment, *do something stupid and brave and glorious,* the way nobody in this day and age, she said, did stupid or glorious or brave things. We needed something to live for—*fine,* she said. *Let's just live for each other.* The whole world would look different, she said, on the other side."

"And this sounded like a good idea, to you?"

Paul kept his eyes on the table.

"It seems ridiculous now, doesn't it? But—blame the moon, blame the wine. Blame her beauty, maybe, after all. It was like . . ." He stopped himself suddenly.

"What?"

"I was going to say *it was like we both were under a spell,*" said Paul.

It was twelve thirty. The booth next to them was empty. The musicians were playing "My Old Kentucky Home." There was no sign of a woman in a red silk dress or a girl with a flapper bob.

"Yes," Paul went on quietly. "I said yes."

"Why?"

"I didn't have anything better to do."

Paul downed the last of his whiskey.

"We weren't total idiots," he said. "At least, we tried not to be. We got the license, that day. We agreed to wait a couple weeks, until Easter—in case one or both of us came to our senses and backed out of this grand, mad experiment. She insisted she wouldn't. *I'm tired of backing out of things*, she said. *You're sensible; you'll change your mind before I do.* Like it was a game of chicken—to see which one of us would see sense. But—you see—I'm a stubborn old fool. And those three weeks—well—" His voice caught in his throat. "They were the happiest three weeks of my life. I like to think they were the happiest of hers."

"And then?"

"I should have known," he said. "Of course, there was a part of me that *knew*, that had always known, that you *can't* just change your life on a dime, just because you've decided to throw in with someone as broken and as lost as you are. But—well, Rose, I did a very stupid thing. I let myself hope. And once you've done that—"

He stretched out along the banquette.

"I'm sorry, Rose," he said. "I've talked your ear off. You probably think I'm off my rocker."

"No," said Rose. "I don't."

Rose didn't know what she thought. She still didn't like Paul, exactly; his sanctimony still infuriated her. And you couldn't feel too sorry for anyone—could you?—who had blown up his whole life based on a bottle of wine and one searching conversation. Probably, she reminded herself, there was nothing special about Paul. He was just one of those insufferable romantics who expect ordinary women to live up to their erotic fantasies, and punish them when they don't.

Still, Rose felt more tender toward him than she'd expected.

Probably, she told herself, it was the whiskey.

Probably it was the fact that he could talk about Cecilia.

"I think," Rose said, "that the two of you deserve each other."

—

Last call came and went. The woman in red did not appear. A drunk girl slumped sobbing over the bar stool. The man with the metal detector was putting his treasures back into his satchel.

"Well," Rose sighed. "That was a bust."

Three whiskeys had made her nauseous.

"We can try again tomorrow," Paul said as they stepped out onto the street. "Or we can go to the other place—the one the girl mentioned. We can split up, maybe—maybe it's better if we go alone; cover more ground."

"Come on, Paul! We don't know who these people are; if they even come back to the same place twice!"

Paul stopped short.

"What else would you have me do, Rose?"

The water was black before them. In the distance they could make out the southern tip of Manhattan, white-lit in mist. The air smelled like brine. The stars were clear. On a night like this, Rose thought, you could almost believe in a little red boat, sailing under changing flames.

Paul held out his hand. It took Rose a moment to realize he intended her to shake it: as if, she thought, they were conspirators.

"We'll talk tomorrow," he said. "Good night, Rose."

—

It was almost three by the time Rose made it back to Tudor City. The whiskey had worn off by now, leaving in its place a mounting feeling of terror. It was like the sky had cracked open; like the ground beneath her feet had turned to water. The world had stopped making sense. And somewhere, on the other side of it, was Cecilia; Cecilia, who had never not believed in all the creeping and uncanny things at the margins of consciousness; Cecilia, who if she were here, who if only she were here, would know exactly how to find them; Cecilia, who summoned down magic everywhere she went.

Rose locked the door behind her. She stumbled onto the sofa. Her whole body was numb.

It was all her fault. Rose could see that so clearly now.

If she hadn't kicked Cecilia out; if she hadn't been so smug, so *vindictive*; God, how easy it would have been to just let Cecilia stay. She could have afforded it; she could have put Cecilia on the lease, or done any other of a hundred reasonable things that did not involve throwing your vulnerable sister out on the street. If she had only listened when Cecilia had told her about the mysterious red boat, about the music, instead of barreling on with a self-righteous sermon about responsibility. As if Rose had been responsible.

All Rose was responsible for was the fact that she might never see Cecilia again.

Then Rose saw it.

Cecilia had made a fire in the fireplace. There were still ashes, not yet disintegrated into dust. Among them were a few scraps of paper, seared at the edges.

Rose looked closer.

She could make out cream card stock, elegantly engraved. Odd letters swam into view, segmented dates:

—*esence is requested*

—*ember*

—*23;*

Rose's heart began to beat faster.

Of course, she thought, with dazed relief, Cecilia would have tried to burn them; of course, it was exactly the kind of stupidly sentimental thing Cecilia would do: Cecilia, for whom everything was a kind of rite; of course, Cecilia would never have managed to do it properly. Rose had never been more grateful for her carelessness.

Rose reached into the fireplace.

She pulled out a little card with singed edges.

On one side: the address of a PO Box.

Rose turned it over with shaking hands.

Another life, it said, *is possible.*

CHAPTER SEVEN

Rose wrote the Avalon the next morning.

She had spent another sleepless night trying to work out what to say. She'd curled up on Cecilia's bed, with Falstaff in the crook of her arm and Cecilia's coverlet up to her chin, reading over and over the few visible words on the charred paper, tracing them with her fingertips.

Rose told herself she had lost her mind. Even if she *did* write them, maybe they would know at once that she was an imposter. Maybe they would tear up her letter. Maybe they would arrange to meet her, somewhere as secluded as the pier where they'd sent Cecilia, and kidnap her or knock her out or worse.

Or maybe it was just viral marketing after all.

At last Rose went to Cecilia's nightstand. She got out a few mismatched sheets of Cecilia's stationery. She sat down at the dining table. She clicked her pen open. She stared, for a while, at the paper.

First she wrestled with the salutation (*how are you supposed to address a bunch of mysterious beings, anyway*), deciding in despair on *To Whom It May Concern:*

She made a few stray marks on the paper.

She tried to remember everything Cecilia and Francesca had said about the Avalon. Both Cecilia and Robin had encountered the woman in bars—late, past midnight. There had been music playing. They had both been emotional—hadn't Francesca said Robin had burst into tears after singing? They'd pretended—surely it was pretending—to offer comfort.

How dare they, Rose raged. Finding lost people—*vulnerable* people—people who were drunk or sad or alone, at places and hours nobody who had a real life ever went; stroking their cheeks; drying their tears. Kidnapping people they thought nobody would miss.

Rose tried to come up with a convincing story: something that would make them think she was a likely candidate for whatever it was they did. They liked music—she'd gleaned that much—but Rose didn't dare risk pretending she knew anything about that. They liked love stories, too, or at least stories of unhappy love: Hadn't they gotten Constance Nelson to run away from her husband?

Thank you so much to the beautiful stranger, Rose began, *who comforted me at the bar the other week.* (That was suitably vague.) *You made me feel* . . . ink blossomed on the page . . . *like I was not alone.*

For the first time, Rose felt lucky to have a forgettable face.

She wove what she hoped was a compelling paragraph. She was an artist—a frustrated one, of course—who had given up on her dreams. She lived with her boyfriend, no (she crossed that out), *husband*, no (she crossed it out again), *boyfriend*, but she wasn't sure about him. She ached for something more, something else, something greater, something she didn't even know how to name. She wanted—she gratefully remembered Paul's phrase—*a love that makes the whole world make sense.* She wanted a feeling that could tear her in two—Rose briefly worried if that was too bathetic, but she figured anyone desperate enough to write the Avalon Cabaret in the first place probably didn't worry about sounding cringe.

I want, she concluded, *another life.*

Rose wondered if Cecilia had written a letter just like this one, at this very dining table, with this same pen. She wondered what Cecilia had told them. She wondered what Cecilia had said about her.

Of course, she couldn't sign her real name.

She thought for a moment. An old memory came to her—a song their mother used to sing about Rose-Red and Lily-White, who went hand in hand into the forest and never returned.

She signed it: *Lily Forrest*

Then there was the question of the return address. She couldn't put down Tudor City—they might recognize it as Cecilia's. Putting down Chrystie Street meant risking Caleb seeing it, and Rose hadn't even started to fathom how she was going to explain any of this to Caleb.

At last she decided:

91 Dikeman Street, #4

Rose dropped the letter in the mailbox on her way to work.

She watched it vanish into the slot. She stood there a moment, trying to calm the beating of her heart. *This is not really happening*, she thought; things like this just didn't happen; the letter would come back "return to sender," or else she would receive no reply at all.

Or else, she thought, *they will summon you.*

She didn't know which outcome unnerved her more.

—

Work was disastrous. Rose made so many mistakes in her lines of code that her boss sent her a message on Slack reminding her to check her work. Rose had never before needed to be reminded.

"Wedding brain already?" Lydia craned her neck to look at Rose's screen. "That was fast."

"I'm just tired," Rose said. "That's all."

"Don't crap out on me," Lydia sniffed. "I'm shitting bricks about Valentine's Day as it is. I don't need to worry about *Aphrodite*, too."

"I'll be fine," Rose said. "I promise. It's just stress."

"Like *you* have anything to be stressed out about," Lydia muttered, as she turned back to her screen.

—

Rose came home. She kissed Caleb and made vague noises about being too tired to cook, offering to Seamless something instead. She said nothing about the past twenty-four hours. She did not know where to begin. Whenever she imagined telling him, she saw his face contort with confusion, then contempt. He would think she'd lost her mind—maybe she had—or that she was on drugs, or that she'd found some new excuse, however outlandish, to let Cecilia keep ruining her life. Maybe he was right. Caleb usually was.

—

Four days passed. Rose heard nothing from the Avalon. She sent Paul so many obsessive texts, *just checking in,* that he called her back in a quiet huff to inform her that he'd barely left the house in five days, so petrified was he of missing the mailman.

"For God's sake, Rose," he said. "You don't think I'm just as frantic to find her as you are?"

Rose stopped sleeping. Rose couldn't eat—she told Caleb it was a new pre-wedding diet. Rose spent her workdays in a haze. Every time she tried to play a test section of *Aphrodite* into her earbuds, she registered instead Cecilia's uncanny melody:

The wind blows out of the gates of the day, the British bake show contestant sang into Rose's ear.

The wind blows over the lonely of heart
And the lonely of heart is withered away

—

"It's my fault," Rose said to Paul. "I screwed up the letter. They probably thought I was an idiot."

They were sitting on a bench overlooking the Brooklyn Bridge. It had by now become a lunch-hour routine. Rose would slip out from work; Paul would bike up from Red Hook; and for twenty or twenty-five minutes they would sit, shoulder to shoulder, and Rose would feel slightly less insane.

At times Rose was almost grateful for him.

"You don't know that. It could be anything."

"We should have done it your way," Rose said. "Staked out Sunny's or the KGB Bar."

"For all we know they've never been back there, either."

Rose looked out over the water.

"Sometimes," she said, "I'm afraid we're never going to find her."

"We'll find her," Paul said.

"How do you know?"

"Because," Paul said, "we have to. That's all."

"It's that simple, is it?"

Paul kept his eyes on the water.

"I won't accept anything less," he said.

———

Rose accidentally skipped two Zoom meetings. Rose picked a fight with Caleb over the dishes. Rose went out running, at dawn, because she could not keep herself still.

———

At last a week after Rose had sent the letter to the Avalon, Paul called her.

"Well," he said. "The good news is there's *something* for you."

"What's the bad news?"

"I can't work out what the hell it means."

—

The first part was straightforward enough. It was on the same meticulously engraved cardstock as Cecilia's invitation had been.

Dear Miss Forrest,

The pleasure of your company is cordially requested at the

AVALON CABARET

Please be ready for us at the pickup point designated on your ticket in the early morning hours of

Saturday, January 14
2:05 a.m. <u>sharp</u>

Please see the attached for the location of your ticket.

Come alone.
Tell no one.

The letter was signed *M.F.*

There was only one problem. The invitation had given no indication of where the pickup point might be.

Rose turned to Paul. "What's *the attached*?"

He handed her a second piece of paper. It was thinner than the first—printed, as if it had been torn from the pages of an old book. It contained a fragment of what appeared to be a poem.

This I would do for you, it read, *knowing the end*
But following always your voices
Piercing sweet above the woodwinds
Compare me with the cautious man-love
That will be yours.
Remember me as you lie in your

Monotonous beds.
Remember the forest and the spears
Upon my white and shining chest.

"Tell me," Paul said, "you have some idea of what that means."

"Aren't you the professor?"

Paul's nostrils flared slightly.

"When the fairies send along a quotation from *Middlemarch*," he said stiffly, "I'll be sure to let you know."

"I'm sorry." Rose sank down onto Paul's futon. "It just—doesn't make any sense." Half a memory came to her. "Cecilia—she said something about *clues.*"

Paul looked up.

"What did she say?"

"I don't remember."

"What do you mean, you don't remember?"

Paul shot her one of his more insufferable looks. By now Rose recognized it. It was a look of injured confusion, like he couldn't possibly understand why a person might behave anything less than perfectly.

"I wasn't really listening," Rose admitted, defeated. "I cut her off. I thought—" Even without looking at him, she could feel his gaze burning through her. "Come on, Paul, she said a lot of crazy things, okay?"

"Okay," Paul said.

"Go ahead. Judge me."

"I'm not judging you," Paul said. "You're right—you couldn't have known."

Somehow Paul's pity was worse than his judgment. "Stabbed by a spear—a white and shining chest. Could that be a soldier, maybe? Or a statue of a soldier?" She thought for a moment. "There's a statue of Joan of Arc on Riverside Drive."

"Burned at the stake," Paul said. "Not stabbed."

"St. Sebastian?"

"Arrows. And that doesn't explain the part about the forest."

"Well, there aren't any forests in New York. Not unless you count the parks."

Rose hoped the Avalon didn't expect her to go trudging through Prospect Park.

"And what's *monotonous beds* supposed to be about, anyway?" Rose remembered what she'd told the Avalon about her unhappy relationship. She remembered the joke she'd made to Cecilia about the BDSM cult. She remembered the kiss on Cecilia's cheek. "God—if this is a sex thing . . ."

"A sex thing?"

Paul looked flummoxed.

"I mean," Rose said, "if that's how they get people. If they seduce them—or . . ."

Paul cleared his throat and looked down. Rose regretted having said anything.

"Well," he said. "We're looking for a soldier having exciting sex in the middle of the woods. How difficult could that be?" His voice was like acid. "After all, we've got three days."

———

Rose spent the next two days working out the clue. Google was no help—there was no trace of the poem anywhere online. There were statues of soldiers, to be sure—Rose even stopped by the one of General Sherman at the bottom of Central Park—but none of them had white chests or spears, and certainly none of them had anything to do with sex.

Rose tried every brainstorming technique she'd ever learned. She went for a run with the *Athena* meditation playing in her ears. She made a word association list on her phone, looking up the thesaurus matches for every single term in the poem. She made a mind palace. She even wrote the poem out by hand on Caleb's whiteboard while he was at the gym.

"*Monotonous beds*?" Caleb said, when he came home. "You trying to tell me something?"

"It's for work," Rose said, without thinking. "Mood board stuff for *Persephone.*"

It was the first true lie she'd told him. Everything else had been omission. She told herself it was forgivable. The truth would have made no sense.

He considered the poem. He grimaced.

"What does it mean?"

Rose felt a sudden stir of hope.

"What do *you* think it means?" she asked. "I mean—what does it make you think of?"

Caleb, she thought, was an observant person; he was always picking up on things Rose missed. Maybe he'd see something she couldn't.

Caleb shrugged. "So—this guy," he said. "His girlfriend's left him for someone worse than him. And he's telling her what she's missing out on." He sat down on the edge of the bed. "I don't see what this has to do with, like, repressed trauma or whatever."

"We're still brainstorming," Rose said quickly.

Caleb kept looking at the whiteboard. His face was blank.

"Do you mind?" he said. "It's taking up a lot of room."

———

Another day waned. Rose didn't sleep. She felt more lost than ever.

She tiptoed into the living room. She left Caleb snoring.

She took out the paper with the poem. She looked it over.

Surely, she thought, *there must be something I'm missing.*

She closed her eyes. She tried to let her mind go blank. She repeated the words of the poem over and over to herself under her breath.

This I would do for you, knowing the end

But what was *the end*? Was it death—a spear to the heart? Or was it a breakup, like Caleb had said: someone who knew the person he loved was going to leave him? And who were the *voices*? Was that the woman—his lover—or someone else? Had the woman betrayed him? And—if she *had betrayed him*—was he condemning her to loneliness or to regret or to *cautious man-love*, whatever that was supposed to be? Only—Rose thought—*he says he'd do it all over again.* Knowing the ending. Expecting nothing else. A martyr, Rose thought. Maybe she'd been on the right track with saints.

Rose thought of Paul. She tried to extinguish it. She tried to keep her mind as still and dark and receptive as a cave.

A martyr. A forest. A betrayer—a woman. A white and shining chest.

Then a memory broke open her darkness.

Morning light. Cecilia—fourteen, maybe fifteen; Rose couldn't remember—beside her on a bench, her face turned upward. Rose's pencil tracing the outlines of a tree, a gate, a hunting dog, a flank. Cecilia, overcome, staring up at the tapestry with glassy eyes.

This is why, Cecilia had whispered, *I'm afraid to fall in love.*

This is always how it ends.

—

At three o'clock on Friday morning, Rose called Paul.

He picked up at once.

"I think," Rose said, "I know where to go."

—

Rose told her boss she had a doctor's appointment. She took the subway uptown. She was there by ten.

It had been years since Rose had been to the Cloisters. It had been years since she'd been to any museum at all. She'd blamed work; she'd blamed the city—wasn't that what people were always saying about New York, that it had the best museums and the best theater and the best opera in the world, only anybody who actually lived there was probably too busy to go?

The truth was that Rose couldn't go without Cecilia. Museums were where they had gone those days—so many days—that they'd skipped school; museums were where Rose had perched and sketched and lost herself in worlds she did not have words for. She'd drawn the Singer Sargents at the Met, the Klimts at the Neue Galerie. The tapestries at the Cloisters.

—

Rose followed a school group down the corridor. Their footsteps clattered on the stone. Their teacher was holding forth about the history of the museum, and of the medieval era more broadly, pointing out the stained glass, the courtyard that had once belonged to monks, the wooden altar-carvings, and the suits of armors. Two of the girls were giggling at a naked saint. Rose quickened her pace, accidentally elbowing one of the girls in the ribs. The girl yelped; Rose stammered out an apology; she ran on.

"Rude." Rose could hear the girl's voice echoing off the archways.

Then, at last, Rose was in the room of the tapestries.

There it was, just as Rose remembered it. Seven tapestries, hanging side by side. The unicorn, free in a field. The unicorn, tended to by a maiden, putting his trusting head in her lap. The unicorn, betrayed, assailed on all sides by hunters with swords, with spears, *upon my white and shining chest.* The unicorn that had made Cecilia weep.

Rose raced from one tapestry to the other. She checked the plaques, the spaces below.

There was no sign of a ticket or a card or another clue. There was no sign of anything out of the ordinary.

Maybe, Rose's heart stopped, *I have gotten it wrong.* She sank down onto the bench. By now the school group had made it into the room; now the teacher was droning about medieval allegory and how the unicorn was supposed to be a Christian symbol, and the schoolgirls were crowding so tightly that Rose could not see the tapestry at all.

Rose had been so sure. The spears, the chest, the untrustworthy virgin—it had all *fit.* A wave of rage came over her—*as if*, she thought, *you expected these people to play fair.* For all she knew they had sent her here intentionally, to throw her off the scent; for all she knew they were watching her now, laughing at the stupid tears that came to her eyes.

She put her head between her knees. She took a few breaths.

Then she saw it.

The envelope had been taped to the bottom of the bench.

Rose looked around. The school group was busy gazing up at the final tapestry: the one with the unicorn alive again. The teacher was busy explaining how this was supposed to represent the Resurrection.

Rose grabbed the envelope.

For Lily, it said.

Rose didn't stop to open it. She ran.

—

Rose was halfway into Fort Tryon Park when her hands stopped shaking long enough to open the envelope. She nearly tore it in half.

Inside was a small ticket, on the same elegant cardstock as the invitation. *ADMIT ONE*, it said.

On the reverse someone had written, in pen, finely calligraphed: *40.66662072; -740005374*

Rose googled the coordinates. A corner of industrial wasteland, just off the Gowanus Canal.

Rose began to laugh: wildly, ecstatically. She told herself it was relief. It was only that she was a little closer to finding Cecilia, and if there was a little bit of pride mixed in, or some savage feeling of exhilaration Rose did not recognize, it was only because Rose had spent so many sleepless hours finding the answer. It was the kind of joy, Rose told herself, she got from solving a coding issue at work. It was only that she liked being good at things.

It didn't mean she was enjoying it.

Still, as Rose took out her phone to call Paul, her hands still trembling, the sky seemed brighter. The air seemed somehow crisper, cleaner than before.

"*I did it*," Rose said, as soon as Paul picked up. "I was right—I got it!"

Paul didn't say anything.

"Paul, are you listening? I—"

"Rose." Paul's voice was hollow. "I need to show you something."

—

Her name was Lucinda Luquer.

Paul had emailed Rose the article from the *Fiddler*. He'd heard the story two or three years ago—some of his students had talked about it; he'd forgotten it, until now.

She was from New Orleans. She'd been big on TikTok, a while back. She made videos about magic and witchcraft and voodoo—all filmed against shadowy arcades in the French Quarter. She did tarot readings over DM. She had a brand deal with a votive candle company, and a cameo role in an HBO series about vampires.

She was twenty-seven when she died.

—

They found her in the bayou. They said it was an accident, or else a suicide—equal parts drowning and the drugs in her system that had rendered her unable to swim. The *Fiddler* had published some of the speculation at the time; the comments section did the rest. Her ex-boyfriend told police she'd been acting strangely for months. She'd had fantasies about mysterious otherworldly creatures—*the time travelers*, she'd called them. She'd started vanishing—once every couple weeks at first, and then more often. Then she'd vanished altogether. She'd left behind everything she owned. A month later a tour group found her body.

Her family had deleted her socials, afterward. A few of her videos were still online, grainily rendered on a video-hosting site in Vanuatu.

"*There are things*," she told the camera, "*beyond what the human mind can comprehend.*

"*All over this city,*" she said, "*there are people who have experienced the time travelers. I've already met a few. They told me their stories. And their lives were changed forever.*

"*Now it's my turn.*"

—

"It could be a coincidence," Rose tried, on the phone to Paul. "I mean—it looks like she was into all sorts of crazy stuff." She'd done ayahuasca in Peru once. She'd gone into Yosemite to do shrooms. There was a whole series of videos where she'd tried to summon demons at Marie Laveau's grave. "That doesn't mean it's *them.* Or that they're— you know—magic."

"It doesn't sound *good,* though, does it?"

"We can't panic," Rose said. "Not yet."

"Of course I remember Luci Luquer," said Lydia, at the office later that day. "Everybody in the industry knew her. I even met her, once or twice." Rose had tried so hard to keep her voice casual, to hide her mounting panic. "God, what a mess."

"What happened?"

Lydia looked delighted to be asked.

"Honestly," Lydia said, "it was pretty tragic."

"Drugs, right? It was a drugs thing?" Rose tried not to sound too hopeful.

"Well," Lydia said. "*Mostly.*" She wiggled an eyebrow.

"What do you mean—*mostly?*"

"So, *I* knew her ex-boyfriend," Lydia said. "At Tulane. We even hooked up a few times. He was like the world's only straight photographer. Seriously, his photos were incredible; everyone always looked so *thin*—"

"Lydia!"

"Right." Lydia shook herself. "Luci. She was always into some weird, like, occult shit."

"The time travelers, right?"

"Deep cut!" Lydia looked impressed.

"Who were they?"

"Nobody," Lydia snorted. "She found a couple of people around the city who claimed to have met them. Some, like, speakeasy or secret show or something?"

"A cabaret?"

"It was 2019," Lydia sniffed. "*Everything* was a speakeasy or a secret show."

"On a boat?" Rose's heart began to race.

"How did you know?"

"I must have read it somewhere."

Lydia's brows knitted together.

"The *Fiddler*," she breathed. "Probably. They used to print all that speculative shit—I mean before the lawsuit. Anyway." She grinned. "Luci became *convinced* that this mysterious boat was, like, a portal into the 1920s. She was going to find it, film it, do some big series."

"Did she find it?"

"Of course she didn't find it!" Lydia crowed. "Or, if she did, it was probably just, like, I don't know, some lame Mardi Gras cosplay thing. I mean, she was doing a lot of shrooms at the time, so." She saw Rose's face. "What?"

"Nothing." Rose felt her gorge rise. "Go on."

"Point is," Lydia said, "she was messed up before, and she kept on getting *more* messed up, the more drugs she did, and one day she did one too many drugs and went off into the wilderness or whatever. I mean. Shit happens. TikTok makes people crazy. Or possessed. One of these days—I swear to God—I'm going to get a flip phone."

"Lydia!"

The room had started spinning. Lydia's face swam in and out of focus.

"Jesus, Ro." Lydia cocked her head. "Does Caleb *know* you're into influencer drama?"

Rose didn't answer.

"Thank God," Lydia said. "You have *one* goblin quality." She thwacked Rose on the shoulder. "I was starting to really worry about you."

"Obviously," Paul said, an hour later, "you can't go. It's too dangerous."

Rose had left work early, claiming a headache. She had gone straight to Paul's apartment.

"We're not just going to *not show up!*"

"Of course not!"

"What do you suggest, then?"

He sank down beside her on the futon.

"I'll go."

"You can't be serious!"

"Why not?"

"Well—for one thing, they're expecting *me*."

"It's not a social call, Rose!"

"Look," Rose said. "I'll be fine. I'm sure of it. It's the same story—with all the others. The first disappearances—they're temporary, just a couple of hours . . ."

"Unless they already know you're a fake. And they're waiting for you to go with them somewhere isolated so they can . . ."

"Well, I can't do anything about that now, can I?"

"God!" His voice was rough. "Why the *hell* didn't you let me write them, Rose?"

"What, so *you* can go off and get yourself killed?"

A strange look flickered across Paul's face.

"Better me than you," he said.

"What, because I'm the woman?"

"*Because*," he snapped, "you have an actual *life* to go back to!"

They fell silent.

"I'm sorry," Paul said, after a moment. "That—that was an idiotic thing to say."

"It's fine," Rose said. "You were upset."

"It's just—" Paul sighed. "Sometimes I think back to who I was nine months ago—and I can't even remember what it was like, to be that person."

"You miss it?"

"No," Paul said. "*God*, no." He sighed. "You'll find it hard to believe, Rose. But I *was* happy. Or, at least, I thought I was happy. But going back—to Maine, to St. Dunstan's. Even if we *do* find her. It's unthinkable."

"Why?"

Paul reflected. "It would mean," he said at last, "that none of it mattered."

"You and Cecilia?"

"Me and Cecilia. The Avalon. *You.* All of it. Just imagine—going *back*, after that. Grading papers. Writing college recommendations. Ice cream student socials and strip mall vermouth. Shutting myself up in my cloister again, with the comforting idea that the reason my life looked nothing like I wanted it to is because nobody's life ever does." He grimaced. "Romantic, isn't it, though?"

"What is?"

"Dying a meaningless death trying to save the woman you love?"

"Now *that's* self-indulgent." But Rose said it gently.

They fell again into silence. Paul tapped his foot. He drummed his fingers on the armrest.

"You know," he said. "I can't help feeling like all of this is my fault."

"*Your* fault?"

"I came back, didn't I? You said it yourself. She was happy, until I came back. She was doing well—"

"She's always doing well," Rose said, "until she isn't." She felt a sudden rush of pity for him. "Look, if it's anyone's fault, it's mine."

"Yours?"

"I kicked her out. In December. She tried to tell me about the Avalon, and I wouldn't believe her. I told her I was sick of her bullshit. I told her I wanted her out by New Year's." She steeled herself for his judgment. "It's my fault she's gone, Paul. And it's my job to find her."

Paul's expression was gentler than she'd expected. His eyes—hazel, in dusklight—were kind.

"Just keep your location tracker on," he said.

———

Night drew nearer. They formulated a plan. Rose would go to the location. Paul would wait, hidden, on the opposite bank of the canal—*at least that way*, he'd said, *I can keep an eye on you.*

Rose texted Caleb and told him that she and Lydia were getting cocktails. They'd be out late, she said, and in Greenpoint to boot, so it made more sense for her to spend the night at Tudor City.

He responded with a thumbs-up.

———

At half past one in the morning, Rose and Paul set out for the Gowanus Canal. It was a twenty-minute walk; they took opposite sides of the street, in case—*just in case*—they were being watched. They didn't look at each other.

The streets were empty, at that hour. In the distance Rose could make out the elevated train, black against the sky, like the skeleton of some prehistoric bird.

Rose and Paul parted ways at Hamilton Avenue. Rose watched him turn down Smith Street, fear prickling across her shoulder blades. She huddled against the cold. She walked on.

The pickup point was just south of Nineteenth Street, between a closed Home Depot and a vacant industrial lot, at the very bottom of the canal. The only sign of life was the occasional roaring of a truck going over the expressway. Rose waited. The water was black. The fog was thick. Rose had a sudden, savage urge for a cigarette.

A few minutes later, Paul appeared across the canal. Against the mist he looked more spectral than ever. He stopped short, as if to acknowledge her, and then disappeared behind a parked truck. Rose checked her phone: *2:03.* She clutched her *ADMIT ONE.* She steeled her nerves. She watched the water.

She'd spent the night talking them both down from their fears; now that she was alone, they returned. Maybe, she thought, Paul had been right all along; maybe this was all some ploy to get her somewhere nobody could hear her scream; maybe they would drug and drown her, the way they had drugged and drowned Lucinda Luquer, the way maybe—*please, God, no*—they had drugged and drowned Cecilia.

Then she heard the music.

At first it was faint: a whispering tinkle so soft Rose thought she had imagined it. Then it grew louder. It was a light, haunting sound, reedlike, as if coming from the wind itself.

It was the song Rose had heard Cecilia play.

Then came a voice, out of the darkness.

The wind blows out of the gates of the day. The voice was high and androgynous.

The wind blows over the lonely of heart
And the lonely of heart is withered away

Then Rose saw a red barge, coming through the fog.

It was just as Cecilia had described it. The boat was long and narrow, with an open deck stretching from a wooden cabin at the stern. There were flowers, everywhere, armfuls of them, roses and magnolias and jasmine and hyacinths and lilies, garlanded on the prow and all along the sides. Their petals gleamed in the moonlight and shimmered, and after a reeling moment, watching the dance of shadows, Rose realized that they were changing color. Above the boat four white-hot flames swung back and forth, seeming in midair, casting their light onto the deck, illuminating the figures on board.

The boat drew closer. Rose gasped.

They were the most beautiful beings Rose had ever seen. There were six or seven of them: although so many of their limbs were twined together, dancing or swaying or reclining on red velvet divans that lined every side, that it took Rose a moment to disentangle them. A slender, white-faced man in a top hat and tails was dancing with a skinny, blond girl in a beaded orange dress that swung as she moved her hips. An older woman in a green-sequined gown, her hair piled into a beehive, stood at a microphone. At the piano sat an androgynous figure, laden down with pearls, wearing a red silk dressing gown and a tasseled fez. A boy in a harlequin ruff and diamond hose held a tray of champagne. At the prow stood a man with an exquisitely waxed gray mustache, wearing a boatman's cap, with rope twisted around his hand.

Rose's breath caught in her throat.

None of this, she told herself, *is real.*

She was dreaming, or else it was the cold, or else it was some kind of phantasmagorical hysteria. She searched in vain for Paul, but the fog had grown so thick she could no longer see beyond the *Avalon*'s edge.

The boat drew up to the edge of the water.

Then, all at once, they looked up at her.

"Oh, thank *God*!" cried the blond girl, stretching out her arms. "We were afraid you wouldn't come!"

She scrambled to the gangway.

"Cassidy said you wouldn't come," the girl barreled on, a luminescent grin spreading across her face. "He said it was too bitter a night—that you'd get cold feet! But here you are!"

Rose gaped at her in astonishment. She wasn't sure what, exactly, she had expected. But she certainly hadn't expected this guileless, gleeful girl, who showed no signs whatsoever of wanting to murder her.

"I—"

"Well, come *on*!" The girl stamped her foot. "What are you waiting for? Thomas—get her down here!"

The boatman approached. He bowed to Rose, just slightly, from the shoulders upward. He offered her an arm.

Rose took it. She noted with some relief that his flesh was solid and—despite the weather—warm. He hoisted her onto the side of the boat, nearly catching her heel in the crevice between the boat and the concrete. His eyes flickered over her.

"Really," he said. "You should consider flats."

Rose couldn't speak.

"There's just one *tiny* thing," the boatman went on. "And I am sorry about this . . ."

Rose's mouth went dry. All her fears came flooding through her.

The boatman slipped Rose's purse strap from her shoulders.

He threw the purse into the water. Rose's phone, Rose's keys, Rose's wallet all plummeted to the bottom of the Gowanus Canal. Rose stifled a yelp.

"You can never be too careful," the boatman said.

"It's not that we don't trust you," the girl trilled, slipping her arm into Rose's. "But—you know what people are like." She laughed. "*Other* people, I mean. Out there. Now come have a drink."

The boy in the ruff stepped forward.

"We only have champagne, I'm afraid," the girl went. "Red wine and boats don't really mix." She handed Rose a glass.

Rose hesitated.

"Don't worry, honey," said the figure at the piano, in the kind of Southern drawl Rose had never heard outside a Tennessee Williams play, "it's not poisoned. At least—it's the kind of poison you pick."

Rose looked around, one last helpless time, for Paul. But the mist had shrouded her vision, and the boat was already moving, making its way out toward open water.

"You're Lily. The artist."

Rose nodded mutely.

The girl stuck out a hand. "I'm Jenny. This is Cassidy." The man in the tuxedo had appeared at her side. "And Rebecca and Nini!" She motioned at the two older women. "And that's Ralphie, at the piano. He's *brilliant*—you know he can play Chopin, *backward*?"

Ralphie played a single discordant bar.

"If only," he sighed, throwing up his hands, "I could play him forward."

Rose felt her knees buckle under her.

"Don't worry." Cassidy caught her. "Everybody gets dizzy, their first time."

Jenny nodded intently. "You'll get used to it."

"I—" Rose began, dazed. "Where *am* I?"

"You can't read?" Thomas's mustache twitched.

"I—"

"You're at the Avalon!" Jenny exclaimed.

Ralphie played a flourish.

"*The carnival,*" he began, in a barker's shout, "*of lost souls; the sanctuary of straying spirits; the ship of fools!*"

"Hear hear," Jenny cried. The others applauded.

Rose steadied herself against a divan. She at last let herself look around. The boat was by now out into New York Harbor. All that was visible, through the fog, was the faint pearly gleam of the torch of the Statue of Liberty. There was no sign of Cecilia.

"A toast." Cassidy raised his glass. "To Lily."

They all turned to her, beaming.

"To Lily!"

"I—" At last Rose dared to speak. "I don't understand. Why—what did I do?"

"You *came,*" Jenny said, like it was the most obvious thing in the world. "And, oh, we're so, so happy that you did."

"It means," Cassidy said, "that you're a dreamer."

"A seeker," Ralphie cut in, from the piano.

"It means," said a voice, from the corner, "that you've been looking for us, your whole life."

Rose whirled around in surprise. The others fell silent.

A woman Rose had not noticed before was sitting at the barge's edge.

She was older than Jenny—how old Rose couldn't tell—and tall, with long, black hair that rippled down her back. She was holding a gargantuan peacock fan, so enormous that it seemed to obscure her altogether. She wore long, black gloves and diamonds and a long, red dress. Her eyes were catlike; feline, too, were her movements. Her cheekbones were high and sharp. Her lips were dark. To call her beautiful would be to miss the point. She had the kind of face that drew you, not because you wanted to look at her, or because you liked looking at her, but because you needed, in some animal way, to look.

Even if she had been ugly, Rose thought, Rose would have been unable to look away.

This, she was certain, was their leader.

She fixed her gaze on Rose. She folded her fan. She rose. She came toward her, with the slow and luxuriant gait of someone unaccustomed to rushing. She took Rose in, inch by inch, as if she were committing her to memory.

Once more, Rose grew afraid.

"Haven't you?" the woman murmured. "Been looking for us, your whole life?"

"I—think so?" Rose wondered if there was another right answer. "I mean—yes, I . . ."

The woman put a finger to Rose's lips.

"What you think you're looking for," she said, "and what you *are* looking for, are two very different things."

Rose nodded dumbly.

The best thing, she told herself, as her first sips of champagne took hold, was to play along. There was no chance of searching the boat—it would be obvious; and it was evident that, wherever Cecilia was, she was not on it. Nor, Rose knew, would it be particularly easy to ask questions with any subtlety.

"You've come to us," the woman went on, "because you want to find out the difference."

Rose nodded a second time. She kept her eyes carefully, reverentially, downcast. Beneath her fear she felt the anger crest. As if, she thought, this stranger could have possibly understood what Cecilia wanted.

"My name," the woman said, "is Morgan. And everything you see or hear or *feel* tonight is a gift we have prepared for you." She motioned to the divan. "Sit."

Rose sat.

"Your glass is empty."

"I'm sorry!" Rose said, without thinking.

"Rebecca—" The woman in the emerald sequins looked up. "Why don't you get Lily another glass of champagne."

Rebecca complied with a curtsy.

She refilled Rose's glass. She peered at her. A slight sourness came to her smile.

"*Where* did you say we found you again?"

Rose's heart began to beat a little faster.

"At a bar." She had memorized this part. "Downtown." She cleared her throat. "Manhattan, I mean. A c-couple weeks ago, maybe?"

Rebecca's expression did not change.

"Which bar?"

"There was—" Rose prayed. "Music? Jazz, maybe? I don't remember the name. I was—I was having a bad night; I was upset . . ."

"Mona's!" Jenny clapped her hands. "Oh, I *knew* you were one of mine! I always find the artists."

"Mona's," Rose echoed her. "Right. On Avenue B." The three-fingered guitarist had played there Tuesday nights.

Rebecca's expression remained grim.

Morgan sat down at Rose's side.

"Are you ready," Morgan whispered in Rose's ear, "for the show to begin?"

"Y-yes?"

Morgan smiled. She snapped her fingers. Then all was darkness.

For a moment there was silence. Then from the piano: a lower, more mournful melody. A blue flame sprang up above them.

Rebecca was standing at the microphone. Her eyes were downcast, half-closed. Her sequins shimmered with the firelight.

She looked up at Rose. The acidity had vanished from her face, leaving only a transfixed look of joy.

She leaned into the microphone. She took a single deep breath, as if inhaling the music.

Then she began to sing.

—

Years later, when Rose tries—as she so often will—to tell the story of the Avalon, she will be able to describe so much. She will be able to describe the beading on Jenny's orange dress, and the way the changing colors of the flame make Rebecca look as if she were made of glass. She will be able to describe, as accurately as she can remember, the layout of the boat—though the size will always vary in her telling—where the pillows lay on the divan and where stood the little wooden tables, carved into the shapes of elephants and giraffes. But she will never be able to explain, not to her satisfaction, what it was about that song that turned her inside out. She will be able to tell you that the song was a kind of ballad, low and slow, and maybe if you had to describe the music with any human genre, you might say it sounded like blues, but of course that is not exactly right, either. She will be able to tell you that the song was a story. She will even be able to recall its outlines: *once there was a traveler, who spent his whole life on a long journey, to a sea he has only ever heard in other people's songs.* He climbs mountains; he scours valleys. He chases the sunset westward. He goes to the bottom of the world's deepest cave and comes out the other side.

Somewhere along his journey (so Rebecca sings) the traveler grows weary. His face becomes chalk. His flesh cannot carry him. He collapses at the home of a kindly innkeeper, in a small and landlocked village between two unprepossessing hills. The innkeeper's daughter tends to him. He marries her. He stays. They have a child. They are happy.

Still, he dreams. He dreams of water the color of glass. He dreams of the reflected light of the moon.

Sometimes Rose remembers some of the words. She writes them down, when she can, but she knows she has gotten them wrong. The lines do not scan the way she remembers them. She will never recall the melody. She never had Cecilia's ear.

Imagine, she will tell you, when none of her other explanations will do, *that somebody can look into your heart—yours specifically, I mean, and not anybody else's—and turn it into a song, the way enchanters turn metals into gold.*

That, she will say, *is what the song did to me.*

—

But Rose, shivering on the divan, had none of those words. All she knew, watching the tears form like diamonds on Rebecca's cheeks, was that there was a fissure inside her, that the pieces of her soul did not fit together as neatly as once they had. All she knew was that, for a moment, after Rebecca had finished her song, and the flames in the sky had exploded into thousands of tiny silver shimmers, after the others had all applauded and shouted *brava* into the starless air, Rose became a stranger to herself.

Of course, Rose had an explanation for it. She was tired; she was drunk; maybe they had put something else in the champagne. And wouldn't you feel anything, if a group of mysterious dancers in fine dresses came up to you and kissed your cheeks and told you that they had been waiting for you, all this time, because tonight you were the most important person in the world, and what you were looking for was the only thing that mattered? She had spent so many sleepless nights, over the past few days, electric with terror; she had come to the industrial park half-certain someone was going to slit her throat; relief made a person vulnerable, vulnerable to forgetting who you were or why you had come.

Rose pushed down the feeling. Shame came next.

There had been a moment when she'd even forgotten Cecilia.

"You're trembling." Morgan's hand was on her shoulder.

"I'm cold."

Morgan made a gesture. The boy with the tray put a black fur stole around her shoulders.

"Do you know," Morgan said, smiling, "that is the only time, in all of history, that that song has ever been sung. And it is the only time it ever will be."

Rose stared up at her, uncomprehending.

"It is the only copy that exists," Morgan said, "and at dawn, we will burn the music."

Still Rose did not understand.

"You see," Morgan said. "We wrote it for you."

She is lying, Rose thought. *She has to be.* Maybe somewhere, someone could write a song like that, once in their lifetime. But nobody, she thought, could write a song like that for a stranger, and then throw it away.

"It's true," Jenny said, as if she'd heard her. "We throw them into the flames."

Rose saw an opening.

"How often do you do these—cabarets?"

Morgan's eyes glimmered.

"When we find people who need them."

Rose knew the discussion had been closed.

"And now," Morgan went on, "Act Two."

—

The cabaret continued. Rose's head was spinning. The boy refilled her glass. Jenny did a high-wire act, on what would have been a tightrope, only there was no tightrope, just Jenny, cartwheeling in midair. The woman called Nini sang another song, this one about the peregrinations of a swallow, which would have wrenched Rose almost as violently, had she not now been on guard against it. Ralphie played a ragtime, and then something slower, sultrier, which caused a stout man in a three-piece suit to wheel Jenny onto the dance floor. Rebecca and Nini were locked together, swaying. Morgan watched them from her perch. She was smiling. It was a gentler smile than the terrifying look she'd given Rose the moment they met. It was almost maternal.

—

Cassidy came toward Rose. He held out his hand.

"Shall we?"

"I don't know how to dance."

"That doesn't matter," Cassidy said.

It didn't. He was an expert lead. He put his hand on Rose's waist, and another to steer her shoulders, and then it did not matter that the boat was swaying slightly on the water, because wherever Cassidy's feet went Rose's followed.

Cassidy leaned in.

"So." His lips curled into a smile. "What do you think of our cabaret?"

"It's—" Rose wasn't sure what she thought about anything. "It's wonderful." She saw they were out of earshot of the others. "How do I come back?"

"Steady on," Cassidy said, with a wink. "Aren't *we* presuming?"

"I'm sorry." Rose knew she'd gone too far. "I didn't mean . . ."

"It's not up to me, darlin'," Cassidy murmured. "If it were, I'd be dancing with you every night this week."

She was suddenly conscious of his hand on the small of her back.

"Who is it up to, then?"

"Our Lady."

"Morgan?"

His nod was almost imperceptible.

"She separates the wheat"—he pronounced it *hwheat*—"from the chaff."

Rose wondered what that meant. She thought of Lucinda, floating facedown in the Louisiana bayou. She thought—with renewed panic—of Cecilia. She cast about for the right question.

"And—" Rose kept her voice as light as she could manage. "What happens to the wheat?"

Cassidy spun her around. "Pretty girls shouldn't worry so much."

Clearly, Rose thought, Cassidy was no likelier to give her a straight answer than Morgan. She was beginning to grow frustrated with herself. She had been at the Avalon for hours—she could not tell how long, but the fog had cleared, and the sky was growing more pallid by the minute—and she was still no closer to any sign of Cecilia.

Rose tried another tactic. "I bet you say that to every girl who comes here."

"It's our whole philosophy," Cassidy said lightly. "Beauty should be protected from pain."

"You want to *protect* people?"

He drew back. A shadow of confusion crossed his face. His eyes, kohl-rimmed, grew wide.

"Of course," he said. "What else?"

He is lying, Rose thought, as the music slowed, as he drew her close enough to smell the ambergris at his neck. *All of them are lying.* Of course nobody had been waiting to welcome her, like an absent friend; of course they hadn't written songs for her, and only her; of course—she knew this—there had to be a trick, hidden like a spring in a machine. They'd taken Cecilia; they'd taken Luci and Constance and Robin and God knows how many others; *and here you are, dancing with them, like an idiot.*

He wheeled her toward the piano.

Then Rose saw the *CF*. It was small and messy and uneven, carved on the wood of the piano, just above the music stand. The same spot where Cecilia had carved it, once, on the piano at Tudor City, because of course Cecilia believed that you could play a piano properly only once you'd left your mark on it, maybe even a bit of yourself.

Rose acted quickly.

"Is that you?" Rose smiled up at him. She nodded at the mark. "Cassidy . . . what?"

She saw him register it. He blanched only slightly.

"No," he said. "I don't play piano."

Rose took a chance. "Who is it, then? Someone here?"

"This boat," Cassidy said, too quickly, "is full of all sorts of mysteries, my darling."

She had, at least, unnerved him.

He spun her back to the center. The music came to a halt.

"I hope," he said, "you'll come to know more, one day soon." He leaned over her hand. He kissed it.

—

Dawn came at last. The sky splintered pink. The boat came once more toward the city. The sky was clear. Jenny was yawning. Rebecca and Nini had taken off their shoes and were huddled in conversation on one of the divans. The boy in the ruff was sleeping in Morgan's lap.

The boat came to a stop at the very edge of Coney Island. The Ferris wheel was rosy in the morning light.

Thomas extended his arm once again. Rose stumbled as she took it. His body did not feel real to her. Nothing in the whole world felt real.

"You see," he said lightly, "why we recommend flats." His mustache seemed to curl even more than it had before. "Sorry again about the purse."

Then Rose felt sand underneath her feet.

"Wait!" She turned back. Everything she should have said, every clever question she ought to have asked, every piece of evidence she had failed to attain, came flooding over her.

But the *Avalon* was already halfway out to the horizon, then farther still, until it vanished into the dawn as if it had never existed at all.

CHAPTER EIGHT

It took Rose two hours to get back to Tudor City. She'd staggered from the water's edge, making her way, her feet blistering, to the subway. She hadn't hopped a turnstile in a decade. She watched the sky split orange from the elevated train. Its rumbling made her stomach turn. Still, nothing seemed real.

There were so many people in the train car: two Russian women, with their hair in kerchiefs; delivery cyclists with e-bikes; a Chinese family; a young couple with their heads leaning together; a group of Hasidim. People commuting to work; people on their phones; people staring blankly at the same sunrise Rose saw, as if the world were the same world that it had been last night, as if this were not a world where sometimes a boat came bobbing to your feet, and strangers stretched out their arms, and you danced until dawn under flames that changed color. Rose wanted to scream.

Rose made her excuses to the doorman. *I must have left them at the office*, she said, as he retrieved the spare keys. She made it as far as the armchair before her legs gave out.

She sat, for a while, staring at the empty fireplace, trying to make sense of what she had seen. *Of course*, daylight told her, *they can't have been*— there was no such thing as—fairies or sirens or time travelers. She'd taken Thomas's arm; she had heard Cassidy's heartbeat, when he'd pulled her in for a dance (*oh God, that dance!*). But then again—the way the flowers had seemed to blossom and wither and then blossom again. Then again— the flames, and Jenny cartwheeling in midair (*you could do it with wires, couldn't you?*). Then again, the music.

It was the music that vexed Rose most. The way it had snaked down her throat and coiled itself around her heart; that was something, she thought, nobody could fake.

Rose tried to call the song to mind. In daylight, she was sure, it would move her less.

Only: Rose could not remember it.

She racked her brain; a fragmented line came to her; she could not work out how it sounded.

And not just that. Already her memories were less solid than they had been; already Rose was forgetting whether Jenny's acrobatic act had come before or after Nini's song about the bird; she was forgetting Cassidy's face and the color of Rebecca's eyes; in a moment, Rose thought, with new panic, maybe she would forget even the *CF* on the piano.

She ran to her nightstand. She grabbed a pen, some paper.

She began to draw.

By the time Rose was aware of what she was doing, her pen had already sliced the outline of the prow; it had caught the face of the silent, wide-eyed boy with the harlequin ruff. She drew everything she could remember: the roses and the bowl of chocolates, Jenny's button shoes, Morgan's eyes. She drew furiously, fervently, without thought.

When she had finished, she stared at what she had done.

Morgan stared back her.

—

"Thank God," Paul said, when Rose opened the door an hour later. "I've been trying you all morning." Rose had never been more relieved to have kept her landline. "I was ready to call the police!"

He embraced her. It was an awkward hug—at once too timorous, too forceful; nevertheless, Rose let him.

He took off his coat. He looked around, taking the place in.

"So, this is Tudor City."

"This is Tudor City."

He sat. His cheeks were hollow, and there were bags under his eyes.

"Tell me everything," he said.

Rose did. She told him as much as she could remember—more fragmented, now, than it had been even an hour ago. She showed him the drawings. She told him about the *CF*, which matched the same carving on the piano here.

"Of course, we don't know if it means anything," she said, fingering the initials. "She could have put it there when she was—you know—*visiting*." The word sounded ridiculous, but Rose didn't have a better one.

"Still," Paul said. "It *is* something. I presume it wasn't something she was in a habit of doing with random pianos?"

Rose shook her head. "It was sentimental," Rose said. "She always said she wanted to store a part of her soul in every instrument that meant something to her."

"Then she's alive," Paul said firmly. "Or—was. If they let her play—" He grimaced. "Or *made* her play." He considered. "Did they give you *any* indication—anything at all—of what they wanted?"

"One of them said something about beauty. Protecting beauty." She tried to remember the wording, but this, too, was vague. "They seemed to think that they were helping people. I guess?"

"And you believed them?"

"I—" Rose faltered. "No, no, of course not. Only—"

"Only."

"They weren't like I expected."

"What does that mean?"

"They seemed—I don't know. Innocent." She thought of Jenny. "Childlike." She shook away the thought. "No, no, I'm being stupid." She

149

was being, she thought, like Cecilia, trusting instinctively anyone who looked at her with kindness. "Obviously they're dangerous—we *know* they're dangerous. That poor girl—Luci."

Rose picked up the drawing. She tried to imagine Lucinda Luquer among these sylphlike figures. She tried to picture them holding her head underwater. For a moment Lucinda's face became Cecilia's.

"God," Rose said. "It's like I'm losing my mind—like they put me . . ."

"What?"

Rose could not bring herself to say it out loud.

Paul took the drawing from her. He stared at it for a while. An inscrutable expression came over his face: a look, Rose thought, like longing. Then he shook it away.

"Right." Paul looked up. "What do we do now?"

"They said they'd be in touch."

"That's *it*?"

"They'll write another letter, probably, if they decide—if Morgan decides—"

"*Who?*"

"Their boss, or their *queen*, or whoever." This, too, sounded ridiculous.

Paul made a sound between a laugh and a scoff.

"What?"

"They're certainly committed to the bit," he said. "I'll give them that."

"What are you talking about?"

Paul reached into the breast pocket of his blazer. He unfolded Rose's invitation.

"Signed *M.F.*"

"Okay?"

"*M.F.* Morgan. The *Avalon*?"

Rose had a vague stirring of memory. A childhood story came back to her, mingled with the few completed fragments of Cecilia's abandoned opera. King Arthur and his valiant knights. The grail. The witch queen.

"Morgan le Fay?" Rose's voice was dull. "No, Paul, come on, that's—"

Paul didn't answer. He went to Cecilia's piano. He fingered the keys, the cover, the *CF.*

"The isle," he murmured, "of apple trees. That's what *Avalon* means, you know." A laugh caught in his throat. "What a joke. What an enormous cosmic joke." He hit the keys. The piano groaned. Paul sighed.

"You know," he said. "It's so strange to be here."

"Here?"

He nodded.

"She told me everything about this place." He rose. "This piano. This fireplace." He went to the bedroom threshold. "This."

There, in the doorframe, was a series of height markers: red for Cecilia, blue for Rose. The dates had been penciled in.

"Are your murals still on the walls?"

"No," Rose said. "I painted over them years ago."

"Pity." Paul kept his eyes on the doorframe. "You know, she really loved this place."

"Did she?" Rose couldn't conceal the doubt in her voice.

"Oh yes. She told me all about it. Your midnight walks. Your misadventures. Your—was it a princess, next door?"

"The Countess." It had been years since Rose had thought about her. "She's probably dead by now."

"You're lucky," he said. "To have grown up knowing people like that."

"Really? Most people feel sorry for us."

Paul shook his head. "Where I grew up," he said, "you couldn't see another human being for miles. Let alone a countess." He turned back at her. "You can tell I'm an only child."

He entered the bedroom.

"Falstaff," he said with a smile. "It's been a minute." He looked back—almost nervously—at Rose. "May I?"

"Go ahead."

He picked up the rabbit. He pressed it to his cheek. For a disconcerting moment Rose thought he was about to cry. But he replaced it, carefully, on the pillow.

"Sometimes," he said, "I think it's why she married me."

"For *Falstaff*?"

"For a home."

—

Rose told Caleb that her purse had been stolen at a nightclub.

"It was my fault," she said. "I was drunk. I wasn't paying attention."

"*Ro.*" She bore Caleb's grimace.

"It's fine," Rose said. "Lydia got me a car home."

"*Lydia.*" Another smirk. "You're lucky she didn't send you to Hoboken by mistake."

"Actually," Rose said. "We had a pretty good time."

Caleb looked dubious.

"Just be careful," he said. "I don't even want to think about what she'll do at your bachelorette."

—

Rose got through the weekend. Rose went back to work. She tried to concentrate on her screen.

Her fingers flew under her. Drawing garlands, drawing tendrils of flowers with no name.

"I have a bone to pick with you," said Lydia, on Monday afternoon.

Rose's head jerked up. She'd been trying to re-create the layout of the boat. She could no longer remember what the cabin door looked like.

"What is it?"

"Who is he?"

"*What?*"

"Friday night. You told Caleb we were at Le Bain."

Rose froze.

"Don't worry. I covered for you. You're lucky I was at Night Spin. And that Grant thinks people still go to Le Bain."

"Lydia—" Rose began. "It's not, I mean, it's not what you're thinking."

"It's okay," said Lydia brightly. "Baby, I don't judge; you know that."

"I wouldn't!"

Lydia gave her a look.

"Don't worry," she said, in a burlesque of conspiracy. "I *get it.* Relationships take work. And sometimes you need something that's just, like, *yours*, you know? Just for *you*." She shrugged.

"I'm not having an affair, Lydia."

"What is it, then?" Her eyes widened. "You're not doing, like, *drug* drugs, are you? Because I knew this girl . . ."

"It's not drugs."

"Then *what*?"

"I don't want to talk about it."

"I thought so." Lydia looked triumphant. "Just *tell* me next time, okay?" She patted Rose's hand. "Life's hard enough, lady. You've got to take that happiness anywhere you can." She stopped short. Her gaze fell on Rose's drawings. "Christ," she said. "You're good." She made a face. "Sometimes I *really* hate you."

—

Rose came home. Rose cooked dinner. Rose kept calm, with more difficulty than before. Caleb didn't notice. He was, as he always was, genially distracted; OptiMyze was gearing up for another funding round. He kissed Rose on the side of her head when he finished dinner, and then put his headphones in and sprawled out along the sofa, his laptop on his chest.

It astonished her how easy it was to lie to him.

—

The second letter from the Avalon came on a Tuesday afternoon. Paul brought it to their bench in DUMBO.

"On the bright side," Paul said dryly, "at least this one has pictures."

Rose's second cabaret was scheduled for Thursday night.

The clue was even more perplexing than the first.

It was a series of cards—a little larger than playing cards—with images drawn in, so dark and delicately rendered that they looked as though they'd been assembled from stained glass.

The first was a shipwreck. In the background, the ship's mast reared up as the stern began to shatter into a whirlpool. In the foreground, a desperate sailor—submerged from the shoulders down—clutched at the air.

The second was a beautiful woman, in queenly raiment, sitting on a seaside promontory at the onset of a storm. Her hair was dark, her expression severe.

The third was a middle-aged man with a mustache, grimacing under the weight of three beams of wood.

The fourth was the prow of an old-fashioned ship. There were no figures in this one, but rather a wooden steering wheel.

The fifth was a tall, stout man, richly dressed in a Renaissance doublet and oxblood hose, with an eye patch over his left eye and jewels on his fingers.

The sixth was blank.

Paul looked up at her. "Tarot cards?"

"They're not tarot cards," Rose said. Lydia had read her fortune enough times for her to know that. "At least, I don't think they are. For starters, tarot doesn't have blank cards."

Rose turned the cards over. They had identical backing: calligraphed gold, in a paisley pattern, surrounding a single apple tree.

"Great. Helpful," she sighed. "How are we supposed to figure this one out, in two days?" She looked at the cards again. "Maybe it's them somehow?" The woman on the rocks looked a little like Morgan; she could see Thomas in the man with the mustache. "Or we're meant to find what the blank card is supposed to be? Maybe that's the answer? Like—if there's a pattern."

Paul didn't say anything. He took the cards. He held them to the waning light.

"God," he said. "A man feels useless sometimes."

—

Rose took the cards back to Caleb's apartment. She arranged them on the kitchen counter. She shone her phone flashlight on the blank one. She tried to remember everything she knew about invisible ink. She spent twenty minutes fishing Caleb's UV flashlight out of the bottom of his closet but this, too, yielded nothing.

Maybe, she thought, it was a narrative—you were supposed to use the cards to tell a story, although Rose couldn't see how the cards fit together, how this was supposed to lead you to a location.

Rose picked up the card with the drowned sailor.

His face was cherubic. His eyes were blue.

He looked—Rose pushed down the thought—so much like Cecilia.

—

"Don't tell me," Caleb said, when he got home, "that Lydia's got you into witch stuff now."

"Of course not!" Rose said, shuffling them away. "I just think they're pretty, that's all. I don't, like, believe in them or anything," she added.

"Of course not," Caleb said. "They're archetypes." He leaned over her shoulder. He seized them before she could stop him. He rifled through them. "Which one are you?"

Rose was flustered. "I—I'm not sure."

"Well," Caleb said, grinning. "There's only one woman, so . . ." He held it up next to her. "No, I don't see it. She's too old."

"That's not how it works!"

She had not meant to snap at him. But Caleb drew back, stung. Rose opened her mouth to apologize. But Caleb had already started shuffling the cards.

"You're the blank," Caleb said, at last, with a conciliatory smile. "The wild card. You can be anyone."

He nodded, satisfied, and handed the cards back to her.

—

At two thirty in the morning, Rose's phone rang.

It was Paul.

"Jesus," Caleb moaned, from the other side of the bed. "Who is it?"

"Wrong number," Rose whispered. "Go back to sleep."

She waited until Caleb's breath slowed. Then she tiptoed into the living room.

"Paul?"

"Are you at home?" His voice was rough.

"No," Rose whispered. "I mean—I'm at Caleb's. Why?"

"Be downstairs in twenty minutes," Paul said. "And bring the cards."

—

Rose met Paul at the corner of Chrystie and Houston. It was an insalubrious hour to be out on a Wednesday morning. A girl in black leather minishorts was puking into a trash can.

"Let me see them," Paul said. "God—what a fool I was—I should have taken a picture."

"You found something?"

"Maybe."

Rose handed him the pack of cards. Paul rifled through them twice. Then he broke into a laugh.

"*What?*"

Paul reached into his bag. He took out a slim hardback book. He handed it to Rose.

"Here," he said. "I thought so. Page thirty-three."

It was *The Collected Poems of T. S. Eliot.* Rose found the page.

"I've marked the section," Paul said. "It's from 'The Waste Land.'"

Rose squinted in the darkness.

"*Madame Sosostris, famous clairvoyante—*"

"Skip down a bit. To the part about the cards."

Rose read: "*Here, said she,*

"*is your card, the drowned Phoenician Sailor,*

"*(Those are pearls that were his eyes. Look!)*

"*Here is Belladonna, the Lady of the Rocks,*

"*The lady of situations.*"

"Keep going."

"*Here is the man with three staves, and here the Wheel.*" It was beginning to make sense.

"*And here is the one-eyed merchant, and this card,*

"*Which is blank, is something he carries on his back,*

"*Which I am forbidden to see. I do not find*

"*The Hanged Man.*" She looked up at him. "We're looking for a hanged man?"

"Go on—" Rose had never seen Paul so excited. "Read to the end of the line."

"*Fear death by water?*"

"Right. Right!" Paul's face was shining. "God, they're *clever*, aren't they?"

"Death by water . . ." Rose thought for a moment. "There's a mariner's memorial, isn't there? By Battery Park?"

Paul was already on the curb, hailing a cab.

The second envelope was underneath one of the memorial statues at the very edge of the pier. They'd taped it to the chest of a prostrated sailor.

His bronze arm stretched off the jetty toward his drowning companion, whose body vanished into the water of New York Harbor.

In the envelope was the card of the Hanged Man. The coordinates were on the back.

"But—" Rose asked, when they were back in the taxi. "How did you figure it out?"

"Finally." Paul shrugged. "A use for my degree."

"Let me see the book."

He handed it over. Rose fingered the pages. A disconcerting thought struck her.

"It's funny," she said. "We were just talking about the Countess the other day."

"I don't understand."

"She loved poetry. She used to make us read to her—me and Cecilia. She always said that we'd know we'd grown up when we started preferring 'The Waste Land' to 'Prufrock.'"

She read the lines over.

"It's just funny," Rose said again, without knowing exactly what she meant by it. "Cecilia loved that poem. And she loved that tapestry."

Paul turned to her.

"What are you saying, exactly?"

"I don't know what I'm saying," Rose said. "It's probably a coincidence. It just seems—I don't know—like *everything's* connected. I can't tell what's real and what I want to be real."

The cab came to a stop outside Caleb's building.

"I'll call you as soon as I can," Rose said. "I'll tell you everything."

"It wouldn't do any good, would it? Asking you to be careful?"

"They won't hurt me," Rose said, with more confidence than she felt. "At least—not *yet.*"

Paul took her hand. He held it in his.

"I don't think I could stand," he said, "to lose both of you."

—

The light was on, when Rose at last tiptoed back in. Caleb was sitting up in bed.

"Where were you?"

"Couldn't sleep," Rose said. "I decided to go for a run."

"At two in the morning?"

"Stress," Rose said. "I just can't seem to turn my mind off, that's all." She sat down at the foot of the bed. "It's just—a lot, you know. Wedding stuff . . ." She suddenly ached to tell him the truth. "Family stuff." It was as close as she could get.

"Oh, *Ro*." He cupped her cheek. "Poor Ro."

He took her hand. He nudged her ring from side to side.

"Stuff can only get to you," he said, "if you let it."

—

On Thursday night, Rose set out for the Avalon a second time. She had left her new phone and keys in Tudor City—she'd learned from her mistakes—taking with her only a few cash bills and a MetroCard. She'd dressed warmly, worn flats. She'd enlisted Lydia for an alibi.

"Just be careful," Lydia said, when Rose asked her. "There's a difference between, like, a *frisson*, or whatever, and fucking up your whole life."

This time the pickup was at the southern tip of Roosevelt Island. The night was a clear one. Stars studded the sky. The *Avalon* was right on time.

Rose had thought the sight of it would affect her less, the second time. She'd thought that now that the shock had worn off, and some of the fear, she would be able to tell at once whether or not the flames that danced upon the prow were real or illusion, whether the rings of flowers that hung over the water really changed when you looked at them. But as soon as Rose heard the music, light and lancing on the wind, the old, enthralled exhilaration took hold of her. Her spine shivered. Goose bumps puckered on her skin.

The boat drew nearer.

"Lily!" Jenny jumped up and down. "Oh, Lily, you *made* it!"

Then once more she was among them. Then Ralphie was playing a fanfare, and Cassidy was kissing her on the cheek and lingering there; then Nini and Jenny and the stout man they called Julius were hugging her and telling her how much they'd missed her and how badly they'd been hoping that she would solve the riddle, because *if anyone could*, Nini said, with flashing eyes, *it's you*. The boy in the ruff poured her champagne. Only Rebecca hung back, considering Rose with birdlike detachment.

Ralphie raised his glass first. "To Lily's second time!" Today he was wearing a blond wig, done in marcel waves, and an eyeliner mustache. He wore a different-colored ring on each finger. "May it outstrip the first, as the sun doth the moon!"

"To Lily!" everybody echoed him.

"To Lily"—a softer lilt overtook the rest.

The others all turned at once.

Morgan raised her glass. She was sitting, as last time, on the central divan. Tonight she wore a white fur cape over her oxblood dress, with a matching hat, that gave her the air of some arctic queen. "They say," Morgan began. "I mean, of course, *elsewhere*"—she lanced the word—"that nothing ever quite lives up to one's first time." She fixed her gaze on Rose. "I hope you will not find that true of us, here."

"No," Jenny cut in insistently. "It just keeps getting better and better!"

Morgan motioned for Rose to sit beside her. Rose obeyed. The boy refilled her glass, although Rose could not recall having finished it.

Morgan spread her fur around Rose's shoulders.

"You were," she murmured, "so kind to come."

Rose looked up at her in surprise. God knows, she thought, the Avalon hadn't exactly made it easy for her to get here in the first place.

"What do you mean?"

"You've given us your attention," Morgan said. "A few hours of a finite life. Whatever we give you, here—is simply our attempt to repay your generosity to us."

You could almost believe she meant it.

—

Tonight's song was as haunting as the first.

This time it was Nini who sang it. This one was a love song. It was an old-sounding ballad, something someone might have sung by a fireplace, or in the highlands. It was the story of a prince made entirely of glass.

He fears many things, Nini sang, rats and snakes and thunderstorms, but above all things he fears going out into the world.

Only, there is a nightingale who'd fallen in love with him. She comes each morning to his window; she tries to sing him a song of her love, chirping and beating her wings; every morning, the prince has his faithful valet close the shutters, lest the sound make him shiver, lest the shiver make him break.

But one morning the valet leaves the shutters open. The song doesn't tell us why.

The bird beats her wings. The bird sings her nightingale song.

The prince listens at last.

He takes it all in: the wingbeat and the smell of the spring and the feeling of sun on his iridescent skin. He takes in the song of the nightingale, who has pecked her breast bloody in the wanting of him. He closes his eyes. He shatters into a hundred million pieces.

The valet finds the pieces the next morning. He sweeps them away—with difficulty, for he is hunched and old. He finds the body of the nightingale, huddled on the windowsill. He tells his wife that tonight they dine on fowl.

Rose was the nightingale. She was the prince. She was one hundred million pieces of glass.

Rose tried, once again, to hold on to the melody; it slipped away like sand.

—

"My dear," Morgan said, when it was over. "Those are the wrong kind of tears."

Morgan touched Rose's face with her fingertips. Rose hadn't even realized she was crying. It must have been the champagne, she thought; the exhaustion; the cold.

"Is there a right kind of tears?"

Morgan nodded. "Cry for the prince," she said, "if you will. Cry for the nightingale. Their story deserves our tears. But to cry for yourself . . ." Her eyes searched Rose's face. "That is a waste of hours."

"I'm not crying for myself," Rose said, before she could think better of it.

"You have no lost lover, then."

It was not a question.

"No," Rose said.

"And the one you do have?" She motioned at Rose's ring. "What kind of tears do you cry for him?"

Rose's stomach plummeted. She had gotten so used to wearing it by now that she had forgotten to remove it. She felt suddenly defensive.

"I don't cry any tears for him," she said hotly, before remembering what Lily had said in her letter. "He doesn't make me cry at all!"

Morgan pursed her lips. "More's the pity," she said.

Rose didn't say anything.

Morgan took Rose's hand in hers. She turned it over.

"This man of yours," she said. "Would you peck your own heart of your breast, for him? Would he let you shatter him, like glass?"

Rose stiffened.

So that, she thought, *is what they want.* That was the point of the champagne, the music, the way Cassidy had let his hand linger on the small of her back, the way Morgan was looking at her, right now, unblinking, as if she were the only human being who had ever existed. Hadn't Francesca said that the Avalon seduced people? She reminded herself of her mission. At least an hour had passed since she had come on board; already they had sailed out into the harbor, and she had learned nothing that would help her find Cecilia.

"I don't know," Rose said, with careful neutrality. "I don't know if I want that kind of love."

Morgan's eyes searched Rose's face.

"I think you know more," she said, "than you think you do." She touched the last of Rose's tears.

Rose seethed inwardly. She betrayed nothing.

"It was," she said truthfully, "a beautiful song."

"Beauty," Morgan said, "must always be protected."

She brushed Rose's hair from her face.

"This world has so few safe places," she said. "We can never forget how lucky we are."

The cabaret continued. Rebecca sang a jazz number about a dove who becomes a star. Julius juggled swords. Jenny pulled a squalling rabbit out of a hat. Ralphie played a waltz with no words. The boy refilled Rose's glass so many times she grew dizzy. The dancing began. The city glittered in the distance.

"Well," Cassidy said, as he steered Rose into a spin. "How does your second night at the Avalon compare to the first?"

"Oh." Rose tried to imagine how Cecilia might have sounded on a night like this one. "Oh, it was *wonderful*! I could—I could dance a week, without stopping. Oh, I could simply dance *forever*."

Cassidy leaned in closer.

"Maybe one day," he whispered into Rose's ear, "you will."

A jolt shot through her.

"What do you mean?"

Cassidy drew back. When he spoke again it was with more care.

"Nothing," he said. "Simply that, at the cabaret—from time to time—a dream or two comes true."

"Darlings!" Jenny came up abruptly behind them. She shot Cassidy a smile. "We've got to vary our dance cards—don't you know?"

She led Cassidy away before Rose could stop him. No sooner had she gone than Nini was at Rose's side. Tonight her bright red hair was pinned up, with ringlets around her face; she wore a high-necked purple dress, in the Edwardian style, from which protruded delicate black leather boots.

"Would you like to keep dancing?"

Nini's smile was gentle. There was just a hint of melancholy in her eyes.

"Don't worry," Nini said. "I can lead."

She could. She was short—easily three or four inches shorter than Rose—but certain in her movements, steering Rose in a waltz. She smelled like orange blossoms.

"It's a lot," Nini said in a conspiratorial whisper. "Isn't it?"

Something about her tone struck Rose. It was less theatrical, less polished, somehow less certain, than that of the others. It made Rose bold.

"Sometimes I wonder what I'm doing here at all," she confessed.

"Don't worry," Nini said. "It's ordinary to feel like that—at first." She squeezed Rose's hand. "Like the whole world's a kaleidoscope you've just shaken, and you haven't yet worked out what it looks like on the other side."

Out of the corner of her eye Rose could see Rebecca, perched at Morgan's side, watching them. She did not smile.

Rose waited until Nini had steered her with her back to Rebecca.

"I just—" Rose whispered. "Sometimes I have to pinch myself to believe it's all *real*, you know. That *you're* real." She tried to work out the best way to get Nini talking about the Avalon's other visitors. She could bring up one of Lucinda Luquer's videos—no, too dangerous; better to ask Nini, innocently, if *she* knew the identity of the *CF* on Ralphie's piano, and register her reaction. She pretended to stumble in the direction of the piano.

"I *know*," Nini whispered back. "I feel the same way myself, some-times. The first night I came here . . ."

Rose's breath caught in her throat.

"The first night *you* came here?"

Nini blushed.

"I mean," she said quickly, "the first night *you* came here." She was poised once more. "I saw it on your face. The disbelief. It's—it's such a gift, really. To be able to watch that dawning of realization."

"And you?" Rose pressed harder. "When did *you* first come?"

Nini hesitated.

"I don't like to think," she said, "about that." Her laugh was airy. "Any-way, it was a long, long time ago. Shall we get something else to drink?"

She signaled to the boy, who came with the tray.

"Thank you," she said. The boy bowed his head.

Rose had a flash of instinct.

"I don't think we've properly been introduced," she said. "I'm Lily. What's your name?"

The boy shot her a helpless smile.

"Oh, Robin doesn't talk!" Jenny appeared at Rose's side, cradling the rabbit in her arms. "He says everything he needs to with his eyes."

"Robin." Rose's heart skipped. "It's nice to meet you."

Robin clicked his heels. He looked down at the floor.

"Don't worry," Jenny said, dandling the rabbit's ears. "It isn't you. He's frightened of outsiders." She touched Rose's shoulder. "But you won't be an outsider for long. I hope." She stole a glance at Morgan, who was still watching them from the divan. "Let's have one last dance!"

Rose tried, desperately, to think of how to ask all the questions form-ing at the edge of her consciousness: what Robin was doing there, and whether they were keeping him prisoner, whether Nini, too, had once been a visitor, like her, and what it was that she—they—had become now, and why, oh God, *why*, Cecilia wasn't with them.

But the boat was already pulling once more back into the harbor.

"Oh, *blast*," Jenny murmured. "And we were having so much fun, too." She pressed her lips into the rabbit's fur.

Nini took Rose's hand.

"My dear," she said. "It's been a great delight."

There was something so familiar in her smile.

———

An hour later Rose was on Paul's doorstep.

"Rose?"

Rose had no time for pleasantries. "I need to use your phone."

Paul let her in without a word. He handed his phone over.

Rose typed in the search terms. Her heart was pounding.

"What is it?"

She did not answer him.

"Rose?"

There it was, at last.

A *Fiddler* article from January 2021 about the disappearance of Constance Nelson from the Coney Island Boardwalk. Rose scrolled faster, down to the photograph.

Nini was staring back at her.

CHAPTER NINE

Rose kept going to the Avalon. A third letter arrived, on Monday—that clue was simple enough, a line from *Alice in Wonderland* that led Rose to an envelope hidden under the statue with the toadstools in Central Park.

"I've learned how they think now," Rose told Paul, the morning before her fourth visit. "And I'm getting closer. I'm sure of it."

Only: Rose still wasn't sure what, exactly, she was getting closer to. On her third visit she'd coaxed out of Nini an uncharacteristically brusque admission that yes, once, she'd been a visitor to the Avalon, but nothing more concrete about who, or what, she had become now. Getting Robin alone was a lost cause; no sooner would she make eye contact with him, taking another glass of champagne, than he would jerk his head into a bow and scurry toward Morgan or Rebecca. The others had been even less forthcoming.

"The *past*?" Jenny had trilled, when Rose had ventured to ask whether she, too, had had a life before the Avalon. "God, who wants to talk about *that*?"

"As if"—Cassidy made a face—"any of us had any interest in *elsewhere*."

Rose had tried other tactics. She'd asked Cassidy—so playfully—

whether they all slept on the boat, after the cabarets, or whether they had more comfortable accommodations somewhere else.

"*Here?*" Ralphie had cut in, from the piano. "Please. We only sleep on satin."

"So—you *do* sleep sometimes, then." Rose tried to make it a joke. Maybe even a flirtation.

Cassidy put his hand to Rose's cheek.

"*Where no one gets old and godly and grave,*" he said, "*where nobody gets old and crafty and wise, where nobody gets old and bitter of tongue.*"

He let his eyes meet Rose's.

"You could," he said, "do worse."

Out of the corner of her eye, Rose could see Nini, her head on Rebecca's shoulder. Her smile was tinged—was it the moonlight?—with silver, with sadness, with something like regret.

"I can't get *anything* out of them," Rose admitted to Paul, in one of her more despairing moments. "Everything I ask, they have an answer for. And it's never the one I need."

Every time Rose thought she'd worked out an answer, something else would make her doubt. At times she convinced herself that Nini and Robin were prisoners—that would explain, at the very least, Nini's melancholy, Robin's silence, although it wouldn't explain why Nini was allowed to dance and sing and why Robin stood mutely with the tray. Other times she wondered if all of them had come, the first time, as visitors like her. Only when Cassidy steered her, with his hand on the small of the back, to one of Ralphie's tarantellas, so deftly that Rose never once stumbled or skipped; when Rebecca sang about a brown bear or an old soldier or a world-engulfing flame with that smooth and sultry voice that made Rose's heart stop, just for a moment, Rose could not imagine that these uncanny creatures could ever have been as flustered, as uncertain, as *human* as she was. Nor could she fathom the reverse.

And there was still no sign of Cecilia.

Rose had done her best, of course. She'd asked Jenny, so casually, about other people who had come to the Avalon, in the past, but this, too, yielded little.

"Right now," Jenny said, pressing Rose's hand, "I don't want to pay attention to anyone but you."

By the end of her third visit to the Avalon, Rose was beginning to despair of finding Cecilia altogether. In her worst moments she feared that Cecilia had somehow—like Lucinda Luquer—been tried and found unworthy; that she, too, at this very moment, was floating facedown somewhere in the Erie Basin; that the day would come when she, too, would wash up onshore.

Still, Rose kept going.

"They trust me now," she told Paul. Even Rebecca had stopped peering at her with that wary, hawkish look. "They'll let something slip." After all, she'd insisted, she'd learned a few valuable things already. She'd overheard Jenny and Thomas talking in low voices about plans for their next *raid*, which she'd gathered meant one of the nights that the denizens of the Avalon went out into the city, in search of despairing souls.

Rose told herself that this was the only reason. Why else would someone keep coming back, in the middle of the night, piling lie upon lie, to a place full of strangers who had very probably killed someone—she could not let herself wonder if they had killed Cecilia—and who might kill again? And if, from time to time, the sound of Ralphie's piano or Rebecca's voice made Rose feel like her soul had been dashed against the rocks, if from time to time Rose found herself sitting on Caleb's butter-white sofa, or staring at her My.th deck, humming strands of melodies she yearned for more than she could fathom to recall, then it was only because things affected you—didn't they?—when you were sleepless or stressed, because Cecilia was gone and with her all of Rose's defenses, because Robin kept refilling her champagne between every song.

There was something else, too, that gave Rose hope. The clues—all of them—had been things Rose associated with Cecilia. Hadn't Cecilia once wept in front of the unicorn tapestry; hadn't Cecilia loved "The Waste

Land"; hadn't she and Cecilia once spent a whole night tucked together under the toadstool of the *Alice in Wonderland* statue in Central Park, drinking vodka they'd charmed off the three-fingered guitarist, the night Cecilia had admitted to Rose that she wished she could draw the way Rose could?

It's different with music, Cecilia had said. *With music, you feel it on the inside. But you, Rosie—artists know how to really look at things.*

I can never keep my head on straight, Cecilia had said, *long enough to look at things.*

Only then, Rose would remind herself that a lot of people visited the Cloisters, and that "The Waste Land" was on every single college English syllabus, and that the *Alice in Wonderland* statue was always thronged with tourists taking photographs, and that if all three clues had pointed to things Cecilia had once loved, it was only because Cecilia loved so many things to begin with, and you couldn't just start assuming that everything you loved or remembered was connected, just because, sometimes, now, when Rose was on the subway to work, or hauling groceries home from the Whole Foods on Houston, there were moments when the world seemed to come together in a flash of connection, like a lightning bolt had struck everywhere on earth, all at once.

Rose had heard, once, on this cognitive science podcast, that this was how schizophrenia started. Some wires got crossed in the part of your brain that recognizes patterns, so that you start to think everything relates to everything else. You start seeing connections that don't exist. You start believing fairies are real.

Or maybe, Rose told herself, *you just want to think that Cecilia is alive.*

—

Rose kept drawing. She drew what she could remember, and what she could not remember but whose outlines passed like shadows through her memory. She drew Jenny's midair pirouettes and the blue-gray fox fur

Rebecca always wore. She drew the swords Julius swallowed. Only when she was drawing did Rose's panic temporarily quell, the dread dissipate. It was as if by drawing she could fix them to the page: to stop them from whatever they were doing or—*God, no*—what they had already done.

Rose drew, over and over, Morgan's face. She tried to capture that inscrutable expression, the one she had witnessed every night as Morgan watched the cabaret from the divan. She never could. Either Rose could capture the severity—that discomfiting queenly stare that never failed to make Rose a little bit afraid—or she could capture the joy, which when Rose tried to re-create it made Morgan look too girlish, too vulnerable, too young.

—

The fourth clue came on a Tuesday. It took Rose almost two days to solve it. A series of stray marks on a page turned out to be musical notes, which led her to an opera called *Rusalka*, about the love of a water nymph for a prince—which led Rose in turn to the statue of Dvořák in Stuyvesant Square, where a card awaited her with the coordinates of an Inwood pier. Rose had never seen *Rusalka*. As far as she knew, Cecilia had never even mentioned it.

Still, when Rose dressed at Tudor City on Friday night—this time she'd invented a weekend business trip—she told herself that this, *this* would be the time. She would at last figure out the right question to ask, the right moment to look closely at one of Jenny's magic tricks, that would at last unravel the whole mystery of the Avalon.

If Rose lingered at the mirror, putting on her earrings, applying perfume and darker lipstick, it was only because dressing a little more like them, for her fourth night at the Avalon, would help her to gain their trust. If she let herself hum the fragmented phrase of flute song, it was only because she had gone by now so often that the sound of that high, ungendered voice, coming out of the darkness, had coiled at the edges of her consciousness. If she blushed, a little, when Jenny and Nini and Cassidy and Julius and Ralphie and even Rebecca, by now, flung their arms around her, when Thomas helped her onto the boat, and Ralphie told her that she looked just like Hedy Lamarr and played a few sinuous bars of a shimmy ("you clean up decently, I guess," Thomas muttered), and Jenny whispered in her ear how much she'd missed her, it was only because it is natural to be flustered, when a whole riotous group of beautiful people embrace you, as if they had been waiting for you their whole lives, as though you had ever been the kind of person worth waiting for. Even if you know it is almost certainly a lie.

If Rose felt, when Morgan extended her hand toward the place she had prepared for her, a new kind of reverence, mingled with her fear, it was only because Morgan moved with such luxurious certainty. Robin filled her glass; Rebecca arranged the furs about her shoulders; all she had to do was incline her chin, in a particular direction, and Thomas would at once steer the boat this way or that into the nighttime waters. And yet, when Morgan took Rose's hand and asked her *are you happy here*, or when she turned with Rose toward Rebecca or Nini or Julius at the microphone, listening rapt to one of those songs that even now made Rose's heart unravel, with diamond tears mingling with the glitter on her face, Rose could almost believe that Morgan was as affected by the Avalon as if she had been a visitor, taking everything in for the first time.

"Doesn't she ever perform herself?" Rose asked Cassidy, later that night.

"Morgan?" He gave a little laugh. "Never. She's too busy writing the songs."

"*She* writes the songs?"

"Every last one, darlin'. Music *and* words. Including the incidentals."

"But—*how*?"

Cassidy's eyes danced. "Magic," he said.

That night there was a full moon. They had gone out farther than usual, and the lights of the city seemed smaller and more distant, almost indistinguishable from the stars. Ralphie was playing a slow song.

"Tell me, Lily," Morgan said to Rose, as the first blot of dawn began to spill across the sky. "Your man? How is he?"

"My man?" For a moment Rose had forgotten about Caleb altogether. "I mean—he's fine, I guess. He's—good—erm—thank you?" she added, as an awkward afterthought.

"And your wedding? It is soon, is it?"

"June." Rose was too flustered to lie.

Morgan nodded.

"Tell me," she said. "About the world he is the heart of."

"I'm sorry," Rose said. "I don't understand."

"Every love," Morgan went on, as matter-of-factly as if she'd been talking about the weather, "is the heart of a world. It gives it birth. It gives it seasons. It separates its mountains from its oceans. It gives it spirits, demons, gods. Your man—what is the world like, with him at its core? Are there gods there?"

Rose had no idea what Morgan was talking about. She felt embarrassment, first, as if she'd failed to know something she should, then irritation—as if all this cryptic talk of hearts and spirits and gods wasn't as much a part of the Avalon's trickery as the roses, the flames, the music.

She tried to remember what Lily had written in her letter.

"He's a good man," she said carefully. "I mean, we have a good life. It's a good world." No, that sounded too defensive. "Of course," she hastily added, "it's nothing like—you know—*all this*."

Morgan searched Rose's face. Her fingers were cool against Rose's cheek.

"One day, Lily," she said, "you will have to decide what world is the one you can stand to live in."

———

"As if," Rose raged to Paul in Tudor City on Saturday afternoon, "she even knows me—as if she knows the *first thing*, about me *or* Caleb."

"I don't see," Paul said quietly from the armchair, "that it matters."

"Of course it matters!" Rose rounded on him. "That's what they *do*, you see—they try to convince people not to want what they want. That their lives are empty or boring or magic-less or . . . Don't you get it? That's how they got C—"

"I don't care *how* they got Cecilia!" Paul grew louder. "What I *care* about is finding out where she is, getting her *back*! Which, by the way, you might have bothered to do last night. Or were you too busy getting punch-drunk and dancing the tango, or whatever the hell it is you do out there?"

"That's not fair!" Rose sank into the armchair. "The only way we're going to find out *anything*," she tried, "is if I keep going."

"And you've found out so much so far, have you?"

"She uses that piano!"

"Used."

"What do you suggest, then? I start interrogating them?"

"If you'd just let me come with you—!"

"Two against nine. And—besides—as soon as they saw you they'd just sail away again."

Paul stared, for a while, into the empty fireplace.

"Caleb," he said suddenly.

"Excuse me?"

"That is his name, isn't it?"

"Yes, but—" Rose realized, too late, what he meant.

"If there's three of us." Paul had grown manic. "I mean, next time, you could wait, the two of us could hide; you could give us a signal; we—"

"That's insane," Rose said flatly.

"I don't see why!"

"Because! For starters, we can't just *intimidate* them into telling us where Cecilia is."

"Charming them's working so well."

"We don't know they'd tell us anything useful. And besides—" She stopped herself.

"What?"

Rose didn't say anything.

"Don't tell me he doesn't know?"

"Paul—"

"You haven't told him?"

Rose felt suddenly, childishly sullen.

"It's complicated," she said.

"Where does he think you were last night?"

Rose avoided his gaze.

"Work trip," she said.

Rose did not have to look at Paul to feel his judgment.

"Look," she said. "It's a delicate situation, okay?"

"I don't see how!"

"Caleb's—a very particular kind of person." She knew how cowardly it sounded out loud.

"Meaning?"

"Meaning," she began, "that if I tried to tell him I've been spending my nights on a *magical fairy boat* trying to track down Cecilia, he'd have me in an Uber to the psych ward before I'd finished!"

Paul drew back. He looked at her with bafflement.

"But surely . . ." he began. "He loves you. He trusts you. Surely—"

"Jesus, Paul!"

"I'm sorry," he said. "It's none of my business."

"You're right. It's not."

"I just think it's a pity," Paul said, looking at the floor. "That's all."

"A *pity*?" Rose rounded on him. "Seriously?" As if, she thought, Paul knew the first thing about what normal, adult relationships were like; Paul, who had gotten his idea of love from stories about paladins and princesses; Paul, who was willing to throw his whole life away on somebody,

175

just because he was too stubborn to admit that sometimes adults broke their promises, and it didn't make the universe close in on itself. "As if," she said, out loud, before she could stop herself, "you and Cecilia talked about *anything* real before you got married."

"Rose." His voice was a warning; Rose couldn't bring herself to heed it.

"For Christ's sake, Paul, she couldn't even tell you she was leaving!"

She saw his face.

He looked like she'd slapped him.

Rose knew, at once, that she had gone too far.

"I'm sorry," Rose began. "I'm sorry; I'm tired; I'm stressed; I haven't slept."

Paul inhaled sharply.

"It's fine," he said. "Don't worry about it."

"Paul—"

"In any case," Paul said. "You're entirely right. I'm not in a position"—his voice was bitter—"to lecture anyone about anything."

He rose. He went to the door. He took his coat from the rack.

"I'll call you," he said, with clipped formality, "when we hear from them."

———

Rose went back to Caleb's apartment on Sunday morning. Rose kissed him on the cheek. Rose went to the farmers market. Rose cooked dinner. Rose told herself that it was not really a lie.

Of course, she told herself, *I will tell him, one day*; when Cecilia had been found—she *would* be found—when she at last herself had words for what had happened, those strange green nights where she had danced until dawn. She would have an explanation then, one that Caleb could understand; by then she would understand, too, why it was that when she looked out at the East River now, a wild thrill came over her, and why when she slept she dreamed of music. Rose would understand why, sometimes, when she could not sleep, even when Caleb wrapped his arms so tightly around her, she tiptoed to the kitchen counter and let her pen fly across the pages of her sketchbook, as though of its own volition, as though whatever appeared on the paper, Thomas's cap or Nini's button boots or the way the stars looked when you gazed up at them from the middle of New York Harbor, would be the key that would allow Rose to at last make sense of herself.

She would understand, too, why she had grown so irritable, on the days the Avalon did not write her, or on the days it did not come. She would understand why sometimes when she and Caleb sat on the sofa, listening to a podcast about the evolutionary basis for polyamory, she found her gaze drifting to something beyond the window; why, when they tried together the beta version of *Aphrodite*, when Caleb's heart rate indicated he was pounding toward climax, and the voice of the contestant from *The Great British Bake Off* talked about *the unity we all crave, the moment when two become one*, Rose's own would quicken and then slow in all the wrong places, and the leftist podcaster would start repeating the section about *focusing on your own breath*. She would understand why, when Rose and Caleb and Grant and Lydia all went out together for Lydia's thirtieth birthday, at the beginning of February, to a rooftop bar in Williamsburg with a swimming pool underneath the water tower, and Grant made the same dark joke that Rose had unthinkingly laughed at so many times before, about how believing in marriage was just as preposterous as believing in God—*isn't it lucky*, he said, as Lydia struggled to smile beside him, *that I'm an Episcopalian; all I have to do is show up and mouth the words*—Rose could no longer stand it.

"What are you saying? That you plan to fake your way through marriage, too?"

She felt Caleb's hand on her forearm, tightening.

"I mean," Grant said, "I plan to *show up*. Don't I get points for that?"

Lydia laughed too loudly. "A-plus," she said. "For attendance!" She shifted her tiara.

Valentine's Day was less than two weeks away. Lydia had been getting a manicure every other day in anticipation.

"Don't you ever get tired," Rose snapped, "of shitting on everything everybody cares about, all the time?"

"I'm always tired." Grant shrugged. "It's the condition of man."

"He works too hard," Lydia said, to nobody in particular.

—

"I don't see what you're so worked up about," Caleb said, when they got home. "All he's saying is that marriage is a useful institution."

"A *useful institution*?" Rose kicked off her heels. "Seriously? For what, exactly?"

"It ensures that, well, people like Grant, and people like Lydia, have a framework for how to relate to each other," Caleb said. He began to unbutton his shirt. "Besides, it keeps them safely out of the dating pool." He grinned at her. Rose didn't grin back.

"She loves him." Rose couldn't stop herself. "She loves him—and he treats her *horribly*!"

"Come on, Ro." He set a hand on her shoulders. "She knows what she's getting herself into. They both do."

"Sorry, what does that mean, exactly?"

"It means," Caleb said, "that Lydia wants a big ring, and Grant wants someone who won't ask too many questions, and we should let people make their own choices."

"So, what, we're *post-love* now, is that it?"

Caleb gave her a look. Even now it had the power to make Rose curl in on herself.

"You're starting to sound," he said, "like your sister."

They are getting to you, Rose told herself. That was what they had done to Constance, to Robin, to Cecilia, to God knows who else. They had made her restive; they had made her sloppy. Already they'd made Rose make so many mistakes, in the run-up to the *Aphrodite* launch, that her boss had started to make vague noises about a Performance Improvement Plan—Rose, who had never in her life gotten less than *excellent* on a performance review. It was as if, Rose thought, they wanted to uproot her from everything she had ever cultivated or cared for; all the easier, she thought, for them to spirit her away.

She would not let them.

—

Rose apologized to Caleb the next morning. She blamed wedding stress, the wedding diet.

"I don't know what came over me," she said. "Probably I just need more carbs."

He smiled down at her. He stroked her cheek.

"Dinner's on me," he said. "We're getting pasta."

Caleb took Rose to an Italian restaurant they both liked on Tenth and First called Agli Donfrancesci. It was an unseasonably warm night, for February, and so Caleb had them sit outdoors, in the heated dining shed. Caleb ordered a bottle of Nero d'Avola and two plates of carbonara before Rose had even looked at the menu.

"Believe me," Caleb said. "You need it."

The taller Donfrancesco brother brought out a bread basket. The other opened the wine. Caleb lifted his glass.

"To the institution of marriage," he said with a smile. "There's no institution I'd rather be in."

"To marriage."

They drank in silence.

The brothers brought out the carbonara. Caleb began to tear into his guanciale.

"Thank *God*," a voice echoed from just outside the shed. "I was starting to think maybe I'd made you up."

Rose whirled around.

Francesca was standing before them.

She looked even worse, if possible, than the last time Rose had seen her. Her hair had grown more matted; the purple had washed out.

Caleb stiffened.

"Christ," he muttered. "Not *her* again."

"I've been looking everywhere for you," Francesca went on, with shining eyes. "I even went back to MUD a few times—they said you hadn't been in."

She leaned in toward Rose.

"Did you find them?"

Rose kept her eyes on her plate. She could feel the color burning through her cheeks.

"Do you *know* this person, Ro?" Caleb hissed. Rose didn't move.

"You *did*, didn't you?" Francesca barreled into the shed before the shorter Donfrancesco could stop her. "I can see it on your face. You—you look just the way *he* did, after . . ."

"Excuse me." Caleb cleared his throat. "We're trying to have dinner here."

But Francesca took no notice of him.

"Was *he* there? Did you see him? Is he okay?"

"Ignore her, Rose," Caleb said. "Just ignore her."

"Signorina!" Both brothers were hovering at the shed entrance. *"Gentile Signorina, per favore."*

At last Rose looked up at her. She tried to convey, with her look, something like *please* or *not now* or *just give me a second, to figure out what to do,* but Francesca was beyond noticing. She seized Rose's hands.

"Tell me about the music. I keep hearing it, you know—every night— it's the same dream . . ."

"Ro!"

"I'm sorry," Rose said at last. "You must have me confused with someone else."

"Hey." Caleb held out a crisp dollar bill. His smile was genial. "We don't want any trouble, okay?"

For a moment Francesca stood there, stunned.

Then she pulled their tablecloth clear off the table.

Two plates of carbonara, a bread basket, and a bottle of Nero d'Avola clattered to the floor.

"You *liars*!" Francesca cried. "You're all liars!" A hysterical laugh escaped her lips. "You're all the same—every last one of you!"

"*Signorina!*" Both brothers were at her side.

"I'm going!" She threw up her hands. "I'm going!" She made as if to leave. Then she turned back toward Rose. Her eyes burned.

"You know," she said. "Sometimes I think he's better off, where he is."

Rose kept her gaze on her lap.

"At least he doesn't have to deal with people like you."

Rose and Caleb waited for the brothers to sweep up the broken glass, to replace their meals. Rose smiled gratefully when the waiters brought out apologetic glasses of limoncello, and nodded when Caleb launched into a tirade about how this city had gone to the dogs, ever since the pandemic, and now you couldn't even go out for a nice dinner in your own neighborhood without some crazy junkie ruining your meal.

"Thank God," he said, "we're getting out of this dump."

—

Rose couldn't sleep that night.

How easy it would have been for her, she thought, to say something, to somehow reassure Francesca that Robin was alive, if not exactly *well*, to offer to give him a message. How easy it would have been to look her in the eye, the way Cecilia had once so done, to tell Francesca that she believed her, that she was not mad, that the world was so much stranger and wilder and more wondrous than a person could ever have dreamed of.

Rose felt a sudden yearning to call Paul, to tell him everything. Pride stopped her, or maybe shame.

After all, she knew, Paul would have told Francesca the truth.

———

Rose went to Tompkins Square Park before work.

The sign was gone. The poet with the typewriter was hunched over his desk. He scowled when he saw her.

"I'm—I'm looking for Francesca," Rose said. "Can you tell me where she's gone?"

"Philadelphia," he said. "Cleared out last night, apparently."

Rose's heart sank.

"Did she leave you any contact information?" Rose tried desperately. "A phone number, maybe?"

"You know what?" Tony looked up at last. "She *did* leave a forwarding address."

Rose waited.

"The Ritz-Carlton."

———

Another letter from the Avalon arrived the next morning. Paul came to their usual bench to deliver it. Rose slipped out between meetings.

"You'll find I haven't opened it," he said.

"Thank you," Rose said. She tried to catch his eye, but he avoided her gaze. "Look—about the other day."

"Don't mention it," he said. He was so much colder with her now, with the same brusqueness she had not seen since the first time they'd met.

Rose opened the envelope.

Please join us, it said, *for one final cabaret*
In the evening of February 14, 2023
8:00 p.m.
please note that no return journey will be provided

"*Goddamn* it!"

Of course the Avalon would have chosen Valentine's Day, at an hour so uncharacteristically early that there would be no way to lie to Caleb about where she was going. It was exactly the sort of day you'd chose, Rose thought, if you were trying to ruin somebody's life.

And then there was that *no return journey.*

That part made Rose's spine shiver.

Had Lucinda Luquer, she wondered, gotten a letter like this one? Had Cecilia?

The clue was a drawing, this time, done in pen.

It was of a young, fair woman in a long, medieval-looking kirtle with roses on the bodice, and a crown of roses in her hair. One hand was pressed to her breast. The other was outstretched, before her, only the artist had ceased drawing at the wrist. The woman looked beautiful, and vaguely familiar.

"You've seen her before?"

Rose shook her head. "I don't know," she said. "I think so. But I'm not sure." Every face looked like Cecilia's now.

"No return journey." He turned to her. "Will you go?"

She looked at the invitation.

"What choice do I have?"

Paul sighed.

"We'll think of something," he said.

"And if we don't?" Rose hoped he wouldn't bring up Caleb again.

"For all we know, she could be dead already!"

He said this softly. He kept his eyes on the water.

"She isn't. She can't be."

"Sometimes," Paul said, "a person gets so tired of hoping."

He rose.

"I won't keep you," he said. "Let me know if you need anything."

Rose wanted to call him back; to say something, *anything*, that would make things right between them.

But he was already cycling away.

Rose told herself she would find a way. She'd pretend to come down with a stomach bug at the *Aphrodite* launch; she'd make her excuses to Caleb before the dinner he'd booked uptown; maybe—she told herself she would think about it later.

There was no use worrying about an alibi before she'd figured out the clue. At least they'd given her more time than usual.

Rose spent the afternoon studying the drawing.

She had—she was increasingly certain—seen it before, long enough ago that the memory was hazy. She had a vague sense, looking at the way the roses garlanded the girl's head like a diadem, that it was not the girl's face that was familiar, exactly, but the meticulous curling of the petals, the elaborate lattice at the neckline.

Rose's heartbeat quickened. She slipped into one of the empty conference rooms. Once more she took out her sketchbook. Her pencil. She set out the drawing before her. She began to copy it. She traced the line of the neck, the soft jaw, the narrow lips, the wavy hair that cascaded down on either side of the woman's head, then swooped around to where it had been pinned, in the back. She closed her eyes; she kept her hands tracing the folds of the woman's cloak. She tried to remember where, exactly, her fingers had traced this shape before—a museum, maybe, the Met, or the Cloisters again, or the Neue Galerie, where she and Cecilia used to spend hours splitting a single Viennese coffee, and licking the whipped cream off their spoons, or any one of the places they had gone, when the whole world was before them, and they were the only two people in the world.

A slicing fall night. The smell of fresh earth. Cecilia, breathless, her scarf full of leaves, bursting with a story about how she thought she'd seen a ghost, shimmering in the cypress trees by Leonard Bernstein's grave.

Rose texted Caleb she was going out for cocktails with Lydia. She texted Lydia a plaintive **cover for me?** She took a cab to Green-Wood Cemetery.

The sun was setting by the time Rose arrived. The guard at the entry point warned her they'd be closing before too long. Rose quickened her pace. She passed the grand mausoleums of merchants and industry captains, topped by angels or grotesques, passed the pockmarked markers of the middle class, passed cypresses.

Then at last, it was before her. An enormous vaulted archway, topped with two spirals as delicate as lace. The plinths decorated with grieving angels. The statue of Charlotte Canda, thrown from a horse carriage in 1845, on her way home from her own birthday party. Her head, garlanded with seventeen roses: one for every year of her life. Her delicately patterned neckline: the dress she'd worn that day.

Charlotte had wanted to be an artist, an architect. She'd been working on sketches for her late aunt's monument when she died. They'd used them for her own instead.

Charlotte Canda had designed her own grave.

Rose came closer.

Surely, she thought, this couldn't be a coincidence. This wasn't like the others—the unicorn tapestries, the Eliot, the *Alice in Wonderland*—things anyone in this city, or anyone who loved art or books a little too much, could reasonably know. Charlotte Canda had always been *theirs*, one of the secrets of the city that she and Cecilia had shared like a language. It had been a refuge only they knew.

There, at Charlotte Canda's feet, was an envelope.

Rose picked it up with shaking hands.

Then she heard footsteps behind her.

Rose whirled around. The cemetery was empty. There was nothing but shadows and stone. Probably, Rose thought, it had been a squirrel or a rat, or maybe just the wind.

Then Rose saw her.

A slim figure, all in black, standing behind a pillar of stone.

She had hidden her hair under a hat. Half her face was obscured by a scarf.

Rose would have known her anywhere.

"Cecilia?"

The figure stood still, for a moment, staring back at her.

Then she started to run.

"Cecilia!"

Rose tore after her.

"Cecilia—wait!"

Rose rounded one corner, then another; she followed Cecilia uphill, to where the graves grew smaller and narrower; she sped up, only Cecilia did, too, sprinting faster than Rose had ever seen Cecilia run in her life, until she was only a flash in the distance.

"Cecilia—wait—*please!*"

She came, panting, to a crossroads. She looked around wildly, desperately, for any sign.

Cecilia was gone.

Rose stood there for a moment, dazed, trying to catch her breath.

It had been Cecilia—she was sure of it. Cecilia, alive; Cecilia, *here*, on solid land; Cecilia, not a captive or a prisoner or a strange, silent figure, with nobody here to stop her from throwing herself at last into Rose's arms.

Cecilia, running away, once again.

Then Rose remembered the envelope.

Maybe, she thought. Maybe Cecilia had brought her here, after all, for a reason; maybe Cecilia had left her some note, some sign, some explanation, for what she was doing here, alone in a cemetery at dusk, for what she had been doing the past few weeks.

She opened the envelope. Her fingers, half-frozen, could barely tear at the paper.

Inside was a fragment of paper.

No coordinates. No map. No missive from Cecilia.

Just a single handwritten line.

no earthly path leads to it, and none could tread it.

Rose stared at the paper for a moment. She took in the words.

Then she put her hands against her mouth and screamed.

CHAPTER TEN

An hour later Rose was at Paul's doorstep.

They went to Sunny's. Rose told Paul everything, sitting in the garden next to the statue of St. Francis. Cecilia was not floating facedown in the Gowanus Canal. Cecilia was not imprisoned, in some secret Avalon trapdoor or under some implausible magical spell. Cecilia had brought Rose, for some outlandish reason, to Green-Wood Cemetery, just as— Rose was sure of this now—she had brought Rose to the Cloisters, to the mariner's monument, as part of whatever perverse game she had been playing this whole time. While Rose had been breathless with worry, while Rose had been lying to Caleb and nearly getting fired from My.th and spending increasingly nonsensical midnights trying desperately to work out the mystery of the Avalon, Cecilia had been watching her. Maybe even laughing at her: laughing at poor, hysterical, idiotic Rose, who had once again nearly blown up her whole life for someone who barely cared about her own. Whatever the Avalon was, whatever the hell it was they wanted, from her or from Cecilia or from anyone else, for that matter, whatever had happened to Lucinda Luquer in the New Orleans bayou, Cecilia had stared Rose in the face, and heard her call out to her, and still she had turned on her heel and run away.

Paul listened without a word.

When she had finished, he rose. He went inside. For a moment Rose thought he'd gone altogether.

Then he returned, with an enormous glass of whiskey in each hand.

"Right," he said. "Let's get drunk."

They drank without a word.

"God," Rose said, when she could speak again at last. "Aren't we the two biggest fools in the whole goddamn world?"

Paul took another sip of his drink.

"I mean—my God," Rose went on. "Here we are, working ourselves up into hysterics, convincing ourselves that she's dead or kidnapped, and there she is, just *hanging out*, alone, in a cemetery, you know, *as you do . . .*" She gulped her whiskey down. The burning felt like relief. "We should have known. She *told* us, where she was going; she *told* us, not to follow her; and still we ran around after her, chasing her, hunting down magical clues, like this was, I don't know, Dungeons and Dragons or something, convincing ourselves that this was all *real*."

"But it was real—wasn't it? I mean, you were on the boat. You saw it!"

"I don't know what I saw!" Already Rose's memories were mingling together; already the drink was taking hold; already she was telling herself there must be some explanation for the flames and the flowers, for Jenny's trapeze, for the music that even now echoed in her ears. "Don't you see? It doesn't *matter*. Maybe they *are*—I don't know—fairies or time travelers or whatever. Maybe Morgan is the literal, actual Morgan le Fay. Or maybe they're just a bunch of whack jobs with a boat. God, Paul, I don't *care* anymore! She's alive; she's not obviously injured; she's *clearly* well enough to sprint a fucking seven-minute mile—what more would you have me do?"

He looked at her for a long time.

"Nothing," he said at last.

"Nothing?"

"You're right," he said slowly. "We agreed—didn't we? We were going to find your sister, make sure that she was alive and safe, and then we were going to get on with the rest of our lives." He took another drink. "I believe you accused me, once, of expecting to charge in on my shining steed, and hoping she'd finally swoon into my arms."

"I'm sorry," Rose said quietly, "about that."

"Well, you needn't worry. Our *duty*"—his tone was lacerating—"is discharged."

He raised his glass.

"To freedom, Rose," he said.

"To freedom."

They drained theirs dry.

"I don't know about you," Paul said, "but I'm having another."

Rose and Paul kept drinking. A light snow had started to fall in the garden, but the whiskey warmed them, and in any case Rose was grateful for the fresh air. Inside, the band had started to play a set of Scottish border ballads; the sound threaded in, submerged by voices.

"What will you do now?" Rose asked.

Paul set down his drink.

"Go back to Maine," he said. "Grovel at the feet of administrators, beg them to let me back for Trinity term. Get on the *apps*. Find a nice girl."

"I thought you didn't want to go back?"

Paul shrugged.

"As much as I enjoy cramming the children of Cobble Hill for their SATs," he said, "it's not really a living, is it? And besides"—he looked up at her—"it's ice cream social season."

They drank some more. The night seemed warmer. The statue of St. Francis had two heads.

"Do you want to know," Paul said, on their third double, "something very foolish?"

"Shoot."

"I think a part of me enjoyed it."

"Enjoyed it?"

"Not in the moment, of course. Not—the worry, the fear. But the rest of it. The letters. The clues. The midnights. The sense that there was—

something. It was the first time since your sister left that I knew what I was *doing* with my life. Maybe the first time at all. Selfish—I know. And your sister had the nerve to call me a saint." He set down his glass again. "You know, after all that, I still don't know why she left."

"It's Cecilia." Rose could, once more, be angry with her. "Who knows why she does anything?"

"I can work it out, of course. I'm not a total idiot. What a dull little life for her it must have been, after the thrill wore off. Moldy faculty apartments with intermittent heat. Students knocking at your door at all hours, asking for recommendation letters. Having to drive as far as Howlham for a decent coffee. And—of course—a dull, doddering husband, an old man at thirty-five, who'd used up his lifetime's supply of bravery on a single senseless decision. Not exactly someone you'd want to be saddled with for a lifetime."

"Don't say that!"

"Why not? It's true."

"You're not dull!"

"You're very kind," he said. "I am, however, old."

He lifted his left hand. He slid his wedding ring off his finger. He tossed it down onto the table.

He rose.

"Right. Another?"

Rose lost count four drinks in. The stars were doubling and redoubling; she no longer felt the snow. The band indoors had begun the sentimental melodies: "Danny Boy" and "My Wild Irish Rose." Paul had started, only slightly, to slur his words. Couples had gathered in the garden, swaying side to side.

Then the band struck up a new song. It was one Rose had not heard before, an old border ballad about a girl named Janet who sets out to rescue her lover Tam Lin from the fairy kingdom, how she holds on to him as he transforms beasts and birds into every shape there is.

For a moment Rose felt the old thrill: that shivering sense that behind every moment, in this world, lay some underpinning enchantment. Then she began to laugh: a wild, helpless laugh.

"What?"

"*Imagine*," she gasped, between wheezes, "*imagine* being so goddamn full of yourself, you think that fairies care about the set list at your local bar!"

Paul looked at her, for a moment, in bafflement.

Then he began laughing, too.

"Come on, Fair Rosamund." He reeled to his feet. "Let's show them how it's *really* done."

He pulled her up. He put one hand on the small of her back, the other on her shoulder blade. He steered her into the center of the courtyard. "Do they dance like *this*," he murmured into Rose's ear, "in fairyland?"

They danced.

It was not like the dancing on the *Avalon*. Paul might have been a decent dancer, sober, but drunk he stumbled every other step; Rose's knees buckled under her. Sweat made Paul's shirt cling to his chest, and there was whiskey on Rose's breath, and still, somehow, when he moved she moved with him, and when he pulled her close she felt his heartbeat.

Somewhere across the water, Rose thought, as the band started a slower one about a village lass and her lad, there was a boat, with flames through the mist. Maybe Cecilia was on it; maybe she wasn't; it didn't matter. All that mattered was that Cecilia had left her, once again, the way Cecilia had always left her, and always would; all that mattered was the way her heart collapsed in on itself, the way the ground collapses in an earthquake.

"Cheer up, Rose," Paul murmured into her ear. "We've got the music. We've got the moonlight. We've got plenty of booze. We've got everything *they've* got, haven't we?"

She leaned into him. She let her head rest on his shoulder. She let him pull her in; she rested her fingers on his chest; *tomorrow*, she thought, *everything goes back to normal*; tomorrow she would go early into the office; she would stop lying to Caleb. Tomorrow her life would be free of beings who sang songs that tore your heart out, of people who ran away because real life was too challenging for them, of people strange enough and stubborn enough and wonderful enough to think that just because you'd made a promise, once, you owed it to the world to keep it until the world went up in flames around you; tomorrow or the day after or soon, Paul would go back; everything would go back; only tonight, tonight, Paul and Rose were dancing, and the snow that fell around them seemed to change color in moonlight, and the stars were as lapidary as they had ever been from that midnight boat, and Rose was disintegrating into a hundred million pieces, and Paul understood each one.

Rose kissed him.

It lasted only a moment. Rose was past thinking. All she wanted, in that moment, was to stop time: for the past and the future to quicksand into nothingness, so that nothing existed but Paul's heartbeat, and his sweat, and the stars, and the band still playing Tam Lin.

Paul was the first one to pull away.

"I'm sorry," he began, his face reddening, stammering out some humiliating combination of *I shouldn't have* and *I didn't mean to* and *that is not what I meant at all.*

"No—I'm sorry. I didn't."

"The booze—"

"We're drunk."

"It wasn't—"

"I should go."

Rose couldn't look at him.

"Let me call you a—"

"It's fine. I'll get it myself."

"At least let me—"

"Paul, *don't!*"

She left him standing in the courtyard.

It was the Avalon, Rose told herself in the taxi. It was the drink and the moonlight and the aching bone-loneliness; it was the lack of sleep and the

relief and the anger and the way Cecilia had run. She did not love Paul—
she barely even *liked* Paul—she loved Caleb; *your fiancé, what's wrong with
you*; Caleb, who was good and strong and who loved her for all the right
reasons, the intelligible reasons, and not out of sentimentality or stubbornness or a desire to prove that things could really happen, sometimes,
like they did in stories.

Besides, Rose thought, *Paul still loves her.*

—

The cab arrived back in Tudor City at one in the morning. Rose stumbled
past the doorman. She could barely keep herself upright in the elevator.

The door was unlocked.

For a moment Rose's heart stopped.

Maybe, she thought, *she has come home after all.* Maybe she would cross
the threshold to find Cecilia curled up once more on her bed, with her
knees to her chin and Falstaff in her arms.

She pushed the door open.

"Cecilia—" she began, but the sound caught in her throat.

Caleb was sitting on the sofa. There were dark circles under his eyes.

"Ro," he said. "You're back."

"Caleb," Rose said dully. "Hi."

"Did you know?" His voice was low. "That Grant and Lydia are in
Aspen for the weekend?"

"Caleb—"

"Just tell me, Rose! Is it just a sex thing?"

She stared at him for a moment, flabbergasted.

She sank onto the sofa beside him.

"It's not a sex thing, Caleb."

"Jesus Christ!"

"I mean—it's not *anybody*!"

"Come on, Ro," Caleb said. "You sneak out in the middle of the night;

you lie to me about where you've been; you get fucking *Lydia* to cover for you . . ."

Rose could still feel Paul on her lips.

"I'm not—" she began. "I'm not having an affair, Caleb."

"What, then? Drugs? Because, Jesus, I never thought you were that stupid!"

Rose looked down at her lap. She didn't say anything.

I deserve this, she thought. *I deserve all of this.*

"That junkie the other day. Did you *know* her? Did you *buy* something from her?"

"No!"

"*What*, then?"

Rose took a long, deep breath. She looked up at him. His eyes were wide and almost childlike, now, in astonishment.

"Cecilia," she said.

"Oh, for *fuck's* sake!"

"She was in trouble," Rose went on, in a flat, gray voice. "At least, I thought she was in trouble. She got involved with some—messed-up people. And I needed to find them, to make sure she was okay."

"And?"

"I found her. She's fine. She doesn't need my help. She doesn't need *anything* from me."

It was the truth, after all. She saw it, for the first time, through Caleb's eyes: prosaic and repetitive and dull.

"That's it?"

"That's it."

"It's over?"

"It's over."

Caleb didn't say anything for a moment. Then he made a sound between a scoff and a laugh.

"What?"

"I think I wish," he said, "that it had been an affair."

"Look, Caleb, I'm sorry; I—"

"I just don't *get* it, Rose!" He threw up his hands. "I don't fucking get it."

"Get what?"

"It's like you're always, what, two drinks away from blowing up our whole lives!"

He saw her recoil. He softened.

When he next spoke his voice was smaller, gentler.

"And I *like* our life, Ro," he said. "I really do. It's a *good* life. Isn't it?"

"It is."

"And *we're* good for each other, Ro? Aren't we?"

He reached out for her hand. He held it, there, in the darkness, like he was afraid to let it go.

"Yes," Rose said. "We are."

Caleb pulled her to him. He pressed his face against the palm of her hand. A single, sharp sob escaped his chest.

They did not speak again until morning.

—

Rose did such a good job, forgetting about the Avalon.

She went for a run every morning. She listened to the *Hera* meditation on her commute. When she got to the office she put in her earbuds and scanned her screen without a word. She found every remaining bug in the *Aphrodite* code. She went to kickboxing. She stopped drinking. She and Lydia ate salads for lunch.

"I'm sorry," Lydia said. "I tried. But Grant has a code about this kind of thing! Bros before hos and all that."

"It's not your fault," Rose said. "Anyway, we're working it out."

"Good," Lydia said. "I'm happy for you." She considered. "But if you want my advice, just have a threesome next time." She shrugged. "It makes everything so much simpler."

Rose came straight home after work. She and Caleb curled up together on Caleb's sofa and listened to a ten-episode podcast series about the assassination of JFK.

She reminded herself that she'd been lucky. Since that hideous night in Tudor City, Caleb had not brought up Cecilia again. He was unfailingly kind to her—maybe gentler, even, than he had been before. He brought her green tea in the mornings. He arranged the weighted blanket around her shoulders. He volunteered to set up their wedding website.

It was as if it had never occurred to him, before now, that he could lose her.

The worst of it—Rose told herself—was over. Already, her memories of the Avalon were fading; already, she was humming, less often, bars of half-forgotten music; already she had started to forget the sound of Ralphie's ragtime and Jenny's laughter. She had started to forget Morgan's eyes. Soon, she would forget Paul.

He had texted her the morning after Sunny's: brusque and businesslike. He'd told her he planned to head back to Maine later that week. They were letting him off leave early.

thank you, he said, **for everything**

He didn't mention the kiss. Maybe he didn't even remember it.

Better, Rose thought, *if he doesn't remember it.*

Rose shoved the Avalon's final clue into the back of her underwear drawer. Sometimes she felt it there, mocking her: that *no earthly path leads to it, and none could tread it*, because God forbid the Avalon do anything straightforward, instead of worming into her brains with riddles. Once, she caved and googled it. It was a line from a Wagner opera about—*of course*—the Holy Grail.

Rose tore up the paper and threw the pieces in the trash.

———

Valentine's Day grew closer. Rose did not give in. She and Caleb sent out their wedding invitations. She asked Lydia to plan the bachelorette. She put the finishing touches on *Aphrodite.* She picked out her dress for the Valentine's Day launch: a pink halter minidress she'd found on The Real-Real. She chose matching heels.

Rose passed her performance review. *We're glad to see,* Rose's boss told her, *you've finally got your head back in the game.*

"Honestly," Lydia sniffed, when Rose told her. "Wedding brain should be protected by the ADA."

Rose tried not to think about a little red boat or a journey with no return.

—

Rose and Caleb did a tasting with the quail caterer. Rose chose a wedding dress. Rose thought she saw a man with a gray mustache coming out of a Tribeca Paper Source, and ran halfway down Franklin Street after him before reminding herself that some things were just coincidences, after all.

—

Valentine's Day came at last. Caleb had made dinner reservations at a French restaurant on the Upper West Side that was supposed to be reviving classic *haute cuisine.* Rose and Lydia changed for the launch party in the office bathroom.

"Tonight's the night," Lydia said, putting on her lipstick. "I'm manifesting." She was wearing a white bandage dress that ended, improbably, in a tutu, and a tiara that said *PRINCESS* on it.

—

The *Aphrodite* launch party was at the upstairs bar of an immersive theater space in Chelsea called the MacIntyre Hotel that only pretended to be a hotel. They'd bought out the whole floor. Lydia had hired a bunch of burlesque performers she followed on Instagram: a six-foot-tall woman named Athena Maidenhead who undressed behind a pair of enormous ostrich fans, a fire-eater, and this former data scientist Rose knew who'd worked at OptiMyze who now did burlesque under the name Mobius Strips. The walls were red velvet; so, too, were the floors; there was a band in the corner that did 1920s-style covers of current pop hits. There was a waitress with a hoop skirt made out of champagne flutes. You could almost believe you were at the Avalon. If you were drunk. If you half closed your eyes. If you didn't pay too much attention to the music.

—

"Everybody's here," Lydia trilled into Rose's ear. "Unity is *in*, baby." The actress who did *Hera*, and also the woman who read *Decline of the West* in her underwear. *The Great British Bake Off* had sent its entire season 13 cast. There was a problematic YouTube historian who had been cancelled for having a "The Sun Sets on the British Empire" birthday party. There was a former dominatrix who'd written a business self-help book. The Catholic podcaster was explaining to three girls from VETD that the reason their app was so successful was that human beings weren't wired to be free. There was the son of a once-famous novelist. A woman read tarot cards for guests by the light of a battery-operated candle. Rose's boss was drunkenly telling people that she'd personally disrupted sex.

Lydia had come up with the tagline, which hung from a banner across the center platform:

Be My.th
Be Your Own My.th.

—

Thank God, Rose told herself, *Cecilia isn't here.*

It would be like Rose's birthday all over again. Rose could only imagine

Cecilia, staring up at her boss, at the podcaster, at *Lydia*, with those enormous innocent eyes, asking all the wrong questions, like *do you believe that you can ever love someone so much you'd peck out your own breast for them* or *can two people spend an hour together and decide to be together for the rest of their lives* or *what is it all even for?*

Rose could only imagine Cecilia: judging all this.

"Well," Caleb said, coming up beside her. "You've got to hand it to Lydia—she pulled it off." He kissed Rose on the side of her head. "You feel good?"

"I feel great," Rose said. "Never better."

It was six thirty. The Avalon expected her at eight. Rose didn't care. It was her night, she told herself—*mine, and not Cecilia's*—Caleb had forgiven her; she was surrounded by her closest friends; she had done so well.

Caleb was holding her hand. Grant had his arm slung around Lydia's shoulders. He shot Rose a glare.

"*Gli promessi sposi*," he said in a lacerating tone, "reunited at last."

He grimaced.

"Now," he said, bringing Lydia's fingers to his lips, "to pair the spares."

———

Rose and Caleb left the party at seven thirty. Caleb hailed them a cab to the Upper West Side. There had been an accident, on the highway, and so the car took them up Broadway. Rose was relieved. She didn't think she could stand to look at the water right now.

The night was gray and blustering. Flecks of rain hit the window like spit. They stalled in traffic.

"So this place," Caleb began. "I read about it on the *Fiddler*. Apparently they, like, wear lab coats and do the chemistry stuff table-side."

"It sounds nice," Rose said. "I'm excited."

She tried to ignore the feeling at the pit of her stomach. She tried not to look at the clock on the taxi TV, its numbers shimmering toward eight.

She tried to meditate upon all the good and sure things in her life, the ones she had spent so much time cultivating, the ones she had chosen for herself, that she had won.

Caleb went on, "Grant says the wine list is top-notch."

He patted her knee. His hand lingered there.

He was trying, Rose thought, so hard, to keep things normal. It was the first time in five years she had ever felt sorry for him.

Traffic slowed. The cab stalled outside Lincoln Center.

"God," said Caleb. He threw his head back. The honking of horns was deafening. "Sometimes I really hate this city."

Rose looked out the window. She brushed it clear. She watched the spurting of the fountain, the people in their ball gowns and tuxedos, heading slowly into the Metropolitan Opera House.

Then she saw it.

An enormous poster—larger even than a tapestry—unfurled from the Met's rooftop, hanging halfway down to its doors.

PARSIFAL
Premiering January 2023

The golden, sacred cup, glimmering under the light of the moon.

It was five minutes to eight.

Almost time for the curtain.

"What is it, Ro?"

The driver of the car behind them had given up honking, pressing his horn instead in one unyielding drone.

"Rose?"

Rose watched another group of people vanish inside. The traffic had eased; the car was starting up again.

She told herself she could do this. She could turn back to Caleb with a smile, as though nothing had ever happened, as though the Avalon had never existed. They could go to dinner. They could pretend Cecilia was simply on a hawk rescue in Montana or on a houseboat in London or in a coastal town in Maine. They could go home, sprawl on the sofa, talk about intelligible things, and not talk about the things they did not know how to talk about, and not want the things they did not know how to want. Rose could spend the rest of her life living in this world. She might forget she'd ever known another one.

"Stop the car!"

"Ro?"

"I said—*stop the car*!"

The car braked at the curb.

"What's wrong? What is it?"

Caleb's face was blank, uncomprehending. It was four minutes to eight.

Rose could spend the rest of her life trying to explain, and still she would never be able to explain it in a way Caleb could understand.

"I'm sorry," Rose said. "I have to go."

"Go where?"

"I don't know," Rose said. "I'm sorry. I'm so sorry, Caleb."

Caleb gaped at her.

"You're serious," he said.

She slid the ring off her finger. She held it out to him. She accepted the look she had always known would come.

He took it. "What do you even want?"

"Another life," Rose said. "That's all."

Rose was halfway across Lincoln Center when she realized she'd left her purse, her wallet, in the cab.

The xylophone was already chiming, signaling the impending curtain. The last few audience members filed in. There was nobody left outside but the usual lingerers: the students and late bookers and the same few grifters who always waited outside with their handwritten signs saying *Seeking Spare Tickets*. Rose took her place among them. She felt strangely, exhilaratingly calm. Her feet felt like they were floating.

When Cassidy appeared outside the opera house, in a top hat and tails, Rose wasn't even surprised.

"Madam." He inclined his head to her. He was smiling.

"I hope you don't mind," he said, offering her his arm. "We're going to miss the opera."

—

They sped together through the night. Cassidy led her wordlessly to the Greenway, at the water's edge, then up the path, and then farther still: past the Boat Basin, past Riverside Park, past—even—the George Washington Bridge. They walked, side by side, as if they were two ordinary people, on an ordinary Tuesday night, as if Rose were still the same person she'd once been, as if the world were the same world.

The streets were empty by the time they reached the base of the little red lighthouse. The boat was already docked. Thomas was standing, rope in hand, on the shore.

He took one look at her shoes.

"*Really*," he said. He rolled his eyes. He hoisted her aboard.

—

Rose didn't know how long they spent upon the water. The wind sliced at her cheeks. The spray studded her hair. She was no longer in her body. Maybe she slept. Maybe she dreamed. Maybe she was no longer human at all, but another kind of thing, something for which time did not exist.

Thomas sang as he steered.

The wind blows out of the gates of the day
The wind blows over the lonely of heart
And the lonely of heart is withered away
While the fairies dance in the place apart

—

At dawn the boat came to a stop.

The dock was at the rocky edge of an enormous, overgrown rose garden. At its back border, on three sides, Rose could make out an iron gate,
so trellised with vines that Rose could not see past them. Closer, in the
heart of the garden, was a small, ordinary-looking yellow house, fronted
by an equally ordinary-looking blue veranda.

Thomas hoisted Rose onto the dock. Cassidy remained beside her.

"Are you ready," he said, "to go behind the curtain?"

They drew closer. Now Rose could make out the figures on the veranda, gathered under a heater. Jenny in yellow flannel pajamas under a
peacoat, her hair limp around her face, with a cup of coffee. Rebecca, in
an apron. Ralphie, his face clean of makeup, in a plain black bathrobe.
Morgan, in a red negligee and a dressing gown, with her hair tied up in
a bun. On the table were plates, bread, jam, as if they were just ordinary
people, having an ordinary breakfast.

Morgan looked up when she saw them come. She rose. She extended
her arms.

"Lily," she began with a smile. "Welcome. We're so glad to finally be
able to—"

"Rosie?"

A voice, echoing from the upstairs window. A scamper of descending
feet.

"Rosie?"

Cecilia was standing on the threshold, in a nightgown.

She pulled up her skirt and ran toward her.

PART THREE

ROSE AND CECILIA COME HOME

CHAPTER ELEVEN

Cecilia threw her arms around Rose's neck. Cecilia kissed Rose's cheeks. Cecilia pressed Rose's hands to her lips.

"I knew it," Cecilia kept saying, over and over. "I knew it was you."

Rose just stood there, dazed.

"At first I wasn't sure," Cecilia was saying. "They didn't tell me much— just that it was a girl, an artist, *Lily Forrest*, oh, oh, Rosie, I *hoped*. But I didn't know for certain—not until I saw you."

Rose's mouth was too dry for words.

"But you understand now," Cecilia was saying. "Don't you? You've heard the music—you've felt it—oh, Rosie, you're finally *here*."

She stopped at last for breath. She took Rose's face in her hands. "Let me look at you!"

Rose looked back at her.

Relief flooded through her and anger and exhaustion, all at once.

"Cecilia—" She could form words at last. "What's going on?"

"Please"—Rebecca's voice came from the veranda—"enlighten us."

Rose turned around. For a moment she'd forgotten the others—so ordinary, now, in daylight. They were all staring at her with bafflement.

"You *know* her?"

Rebecca marched closer. Fury blanched her. Thomas trailed after her.

Cecilia hadn't even heard.

"Oh—Rosie—you'll stay, won't you? Tell me you'll stay!"

"Stay?"

Rose's legs were weak under her.

Then Rebecca's hand wrenched Cecilia's shoulder.

"You brought her here?"

Cecilia's eyes were shining. "I didn't! I swear. I wasn't sure myself; not until—"

"She's her sister." The voice came, soft but unmistakable, from the veranda. "Aren't you?"

Morgan was standing on the stairwell. She came toward them. Her gaze was inscrutable.

"Rose," she said. She extended her hand once more.

Rose nodded mutely. She was even more confused than ever. Last night, under the stars, adrenaline coursing through her, the magic of the Avalon had overwhelmed her; there had been moments when Rose had been willing to end up floating facedown in the Erie Basin, so long as it meant knowing what was on the other side. But everything was different by daylight.

"What a nightmare!" Rebecca was raging. "It's a mess—it's like New Orleans all over again!"

Rose stiffened. She became suddenly conscious that they were eight against two, that it would be so easy to hold one of them—both of them—down in the water.

By now the others had appeared in the doorway. They were staring at Rose.

Morgan's face betrayed nothing. She turned to Cecilia.

"You contacted her?"

Cecilia grew pale.

"I didn't," she said. "I didn't even know—not at first. It was only later—that I started to suspect, I swear." Her voice grew agitated. "I didn't know for sure. Not until the other night. When Jenny and I went to the cemetery to leave the envelope, I told her I'd forgotten something; I doubled back . . ."

Jenny, on the veranda, made an injured sound.

"She's telling the truth," Rose cut in quickly. "I came by myself. I found one of your invitations in her fireplace. I found the PO Box."

She could hear Rebecca scoff without looking at her.

Morgan regarded her with new interest.

"You—found us?"

Even in a dressing gown, even without her makeup or her silks or her ostrich feathers, she could still make Rose shiver.

Rose forced herself to be bold.

"Yes."

"Why?"

"I wanted to find Cecilia. To bring her home."

If Morgan looked uneasy, for a moment, the moment passed.

"Are you sure," she said, in the same low, controlled voice Rose had heard so many times at the Avalon, "that *that* is why you came?"

It was easier now, to withstand it—sober, in daylight, next to the little yellow house that looked just like any other wooden colonial house you might find all over the Hudson River Valley, with people who—Rose was certain of it now—were no less human than she was herself.

"Of course I'm sure!" Her fear gave way to anger. "Now—can someone *please* tell me who you are, and what I'm doing here?"

Morgan looked from Rose to Cecilia and back again.

"I think it's time," Morgan said, "that you and I speak in private. Robin!"

He jerked to alertness in the doorway.

"Why don't you bring the two of us some tea?"

Morgan led Rose into the house. She led her through the parlor and the kitchen, to the back stairwell.

Inside, too, the house was ordinary—if slightly bohemian, as if a particularly eccentric artist had boarded it up sometime in the middle of the twentieth century and not returned since. There were silks and furs strewn on the sofa; necklaces and brooches filled the mantelpiece; in the kitchen—*modern appliances*, Rose noted, with dazed surprise—about six or seven mixing bowls crammed the countertops. The windowsills overflowed with herbs. Lace curtains fluttered in the morning breeze.

Rose followed Morgan up the stairs, to the third floor, and into a small room just off the landing, with a narrow green velvet daybed, a mirrored vanity, and a piano. The red walls were barely visible under dozens of gilt-edged drawings. The red silk dress and the ostrich cape shimmered down from a clothes hanger, perched atop a weather-beaten set of gold silk screens.

"I understand," Morgan said, as they sat, "that this must all be very confusing to you."

Rose stifled an astonished laugh.

"In this case," Morgan went on pleasantly, "you've given *us* something of a shock, yourself."

"Where *are* we?"

"The Avalon, of course."

Rose couldn't tell if Morgan was mocking her.

"No—*where* are we? I mean, literally, where."

"An idyllic country estate," Morgan said. "Somewhere in the rough vicinity of New York City." Her smile flickered. "We're not in the habit of giving out our address. Even most of us here don't know it."

"And who is *us?*"

"It's all very simple," Morgan said, pleasantly. "We're . . . an intentional family of like-minded individuals who have chosen to dedicate our lives to the preservation and protection of the lost, the lonely, and the brokenhearted, and who, in the service of that vocation, operate a small traveling cabaret."

She spoke lightly, fluently, as if she had said it many times before.

"And you're not—"

"What?"

It seemed so implausible, out loud.

"Magic," Rose said, feeling foolish.

Morgan's smile narrowed.

"If you're asking," she said, "whether or not we conjure spirits or lift objects with our minds or control the sky or the sea, then I'm afraid I'll have to disappoint you."

"And the others?"

"Visitors like yourself—once upon a time. Who found themselves sympathetic to our aims and desirous of living a life of service."

"A life of service? Are you serious?"

"What else would you have us call it?" Even now, every one of Morgan's gestures was exquisite. "We give up our lives—our ordinary lives—to live extraordinary ones. We comfort the afflicted. We bring beauty to the forlorn. Good, our tea. Thank you, Robin."

He looked younger, in jeans and a T-shirt, without the harlequin makeup, although his eyes still bore that same rabbity expression. Still, he bowed—just as he always had—when he left them.

Morgan poured the tea. She handed Rose a cup.

"So, what—" Rose's head was still spinning. "You're, like, a cult or something?"

Now Morgan smiled.

"I prefer to call us a family."

At last Rose had had enough. All the exhaustion, all the manic strangeness, of the past twelve hours came flooding back to her, along with the overwhelming shame of her own vulnerability.

"I don't care *what* you are!" she cried. "I've come to get Cecilia—and I've come to take her home."

"I'm afraid that won't be possible."

"Why? Because you'll do to us what you did to Lucinda Luquer?"

For the first time, Rose saw surprise in Morgan's eyes, followed by fear. Then Morgan was composed once again.

"What happened to Lucinda Luquer," she said, "was a very great tragedy. It was also an accident. One we don't intend to let happen again. You may find this hard to believe, Rose, but everything we do here, we do from a place of love. Our business is to protect those who cannot protect themselves."

"Then why won't you let Cecilia go?"

"*Let* has nothing to do with it. Cecilia is here because she wishes to be."

Rose's heart sank. She could not deny, by now, that Morgan was telling the truth.

"Nobody is a prisoner here," Morgan went on. "Everybody who is here is here because they have chosen to come. Everybody who stays is here because they choose to stay."

"And if they change their minds?"

"Nobody ever has."

"But *if* they did?"

Morgan sighed.

"Then we would take them on the boat back to the city and wish them well."

"I don't believe you."

"You will," Morgan said. "When we take *you* back, tonight. Assuming, of course, that you wish to leave."

Rose rounded on her.

"*Excuse* me?"

"I don't presume. You might prefer to stay."

If Morgan had told Rose, point-blank, that she was in fact the queen of the fairy realm, and that the tea they were drinking had the power to make Rose eternally young, Rose would have felt less flabbergasted than she did right now. It was one thing, somehow, for Morgan to talk like this, in elegantly anachronistic riddles, on the boat, with the music echoing from the piano and the sound of footsteps. It was another thing entirely to listen to it in this cramped and paint-flaking parlor, with morning light streaming through the walls and feathers shedding from the hanger.

"Stay? Why would I *stay* here?"

"To remain with your sister, perhaps. Or because you think you might find our way of life to your liking."

"Your *way of*—"

"After all"—Morgan took no notice of the interruption—"what do you really have to go back to?"

Her eyes fell on Rose's left hand. They registered the absence of a ring.

Rose remembered.

Last night, she had hardly been aware of what she was doing. She had been manic; she had been mad; she had half convinced herself that she had been under a spell, *as if,* she thought bitterly, *there is such a thing as spells,* that the Avalon had drawn her with such inexorable power that she had not even had a choice.

Now, at last, it hit her.

"You—you *tricked* me . . ." she began. "You . . ."

"We did nothing of the sort," Morgan said. "We sent you an invitation. You chose to come. In fact"—she smirked—"you rather invited yourself."

"I was looking for Cecilia."

"Did she ask you to look for her?"

"No, but . . ."

"Did she tell you to come? Call you on the phone? Send you a letter? Tell you directly she was in danger?"

"No," Rose admitted miserably.

"You came," Morgan said, "because you wanted to come. Because something in our ways, in our music, spoke to you. Because you decided you would rather live in our world than in your own."

Rose didn't say anything. Even now, she thought bitterly, the Avalon had a way of turning all her words back in on themselves.

"Now," Morgan went on. "There are doubtless some among us who think I shouldn't even give you the choice. That I'm making a mistake, even speaking with you here, when you could already be blindfolded on the boat, halfway back to the city. But you solved your clues, just as the

213

others did. You came to the cabarets. You wept at the music. As far as I'm concerned, you earned your right to remain."

Rose gaped at her.

Surely, she thought, Morgan had to be insane. You couldn't live like this, couldn't spend every night on a little red boat, trawling for lost souls; you couldn't expect *other* people to throw away their lives; unless there was something so wrong with you that no human intervention could fix it.

Only, she thought, other people had.

"Take your time," Morgan said. "Think about it. Thomas has already taken the boat out for a grocery run."

"Groceries?" Even now Rose couldn't imagine that boat getting groceries.

"We do need to eat, you know." Morgan finished her tea. "In any case, the boat won't be ready to take you back until nightfall. You can make your decision then."

"And Cecilia?"

"That," Morgan said, "is between you and Cecilia. But I daresay I already know what her answer will be."

She rose. She opened the door.

"Your sister's room is on the second floor," she said. "I'd advise you to get some rest, before you decide anything."

Rose stumbled out into the hallway, still reeling. She needed the banister to steady herself on the way down.

Now, she thought, *I really have lost my mind.*

She had to get out of here. She would convince Cecilia—she would grab her by the shoulders and shake her, if she had to—and get them both on the boat, tonight. She prayed that Morgan was telling the truth about keeping nobody a prisoner. She doubted Morgan had been truthful about Lucinda Luquer.

"I just want to say," a voice said, from the second-floor landing. "It's all right—if it's a bit overwhelming at first."

It was Nini. She was wearing an apricot nightgown. Her hair was in curlers. She was smiling the same gentle, nervous smile that Rose had noticed her second night at the Avalon.

"For the first week," Nini said, coming down the stairs, "I thought—any minute, I'd wake up, and bam, I'd be right back in my old life. I thought it was—well, *too good to be true*, I guess." She put her hand on Rose's shoulder. She didn't notice Rose recoil.

"You don't have to get the hang of it right away," Nini went on. "It was weeks before I was ready to go out on the boat, and even then I just served drinks like Robin. Do *you* sing? Or play an instrument?"

"No."

"That's all right." Nini patted Rose's hand. "You can learn. If you want to. Or you can do something else. I'm sure Morgan has something in mind for you already." She saw Rose's blank expression. "For the cabarets, I mean."

Now Rose could not stop herself from laughing. As if, she thought, these people all seriously expected her to spend the rest of her life doing *cabarets*, performing for strangers like a circus animal.

"Are you kidding? I'm not performing in any of your fucking cabarets!"

Nini's brows knitted with concern.

"My dear . . ."

She reached out to touch Rose's face. This time Rose jerked away.

"Don't touch me!"

"I'm sorry," Nini faltered. "I didn't mean . . ." She drew back. She looked down. "I'm sorry," she said again. She hurried past Rose down the stairs.

"You shouldn't have spoken to her like that."

Cecilia was standing in the corridor. She had changed out of her nightgown and was wearing a ruffled shirt and a pair of black breeches, which together gave her the look of a Shakespearean boy.

"Nini's an innocent," she said. "She's gentle. She's suffered a lot, you know. It's unkind to be so rough with her."

She was quieter than when Rose had seen her earlier, more contained. Rose took her in.

Her hair had grown; the close-cropped pixie she'd worn when she first came home was now a curly cloud about her head. There was color on her cheeks. Her face had lost its anemic look. There were no more bags under her eyes. She looked somehow older.

"I want," Cecilia said, "to explain everything."

Cecilia took Rose into her room. It was small—smaller even than Morgan's—with peeling floral wallpaper and chintz curtains. There were fresh flowers in a little vase under the window. There was a view of the water.

"I didn't want," Cecilia began, "to worry you."

She took a seat on the bed. Rose sank down beside her.

"To tell you the truth, I thought you'd be relieved."

Cecilia's hands were folded in her lap. Her spine was straight.

"It was a mistake," she went. "To call Paul. Of course he'd have worried. I wanted—" She stopped herself. "I don't know what I wanted. To tell him goodbye. To let him go. For him to tell you—" She searched for the right words. "Not to worry. Not to follow me. That you were free, both of you. That you wouldn't have to clean up my messes any longer."

Rose opened her mouth to protest; she closed it again. How many times, she thought, had a part of her been relieved every time Cecilia had gone?

"When your letter came," Cecilia continued, "I wondered. I hoped. An artist—*ambivalently yoked*. And the name. I tried to check the address, the handwriting, but Thomas wouldn't let me see the letter. They're very strict here, about things like that. I told myself I was being silly. *Come on, Cecilia*, I told myself, *how many regretful artists are there in this city?* Only when we were working on the clues, Jenny and Julius and me—I suppose, I got to thinking about the sorts of clues someone like you might be drawn to. The sort of places someone like you might go—that might make you feel . . . the way we try to make people feel."

"Which is what, exactly?"

This Cecilia—soft, certain, self-possessed—was almost a stranger.

"A sense of enchantment," Cecilia said. "A sense that suddenly the whole world's opening up before you. Morgan says it's like—cracking open the top of an egg. Only from the inside."

"Why weren't you on the boat?"

"Morgan didn't want me there. She's careful with newcomers here. She says we need time to adjust. Not to risk missing our old lives too soon. We start on the simpler things first. Working on the clues. Rehearsals. Learning to make the costumes." She laughed a little. "You know I can sew now?"

"But you were at the piano?"

Now Cecilia smiled.

"Yes," she said. "At the piano. She had me do some of the cabarets—giving Ralphie a night off. But only for the one-offs. People we knew probably wouldn't return, or whom we didn't *want* to return, necessarily. People who could go home, having had one wonderful, glorious night—like a dream—and could face the rest of their lives. There's a lot of people like that. More than the other kind. But—your letter. From the beginning they thought you were one of the people who might stay. Morgan told me I wasn't ready for that. But I asked Robin what Lily Forrest looked like. It wasn't much to go on—*brown hair, brown eyes*. But it was something. And I suppose I kept hoping. Kept pushing for clues for *you*. The others listened to me—they don't know the city as well."

A thought occurred to Rose.

"They're from New Orleans?"

"Yes. And California before that. We move around, you know. We have to." She said *we* so instinctively. "Or people get suspicious."

"Like about Lucinda Luquer, you mean?"

Cecilia stiffened. The corners of her lips twitched. "It wasn't their fault. It *was* an accident. But—they had to get out of there, quickly. It would have been awful. Police, detectives—putting their noses into our world, demanding to come on board the boat, dragging us into interrogations, trying to make it out like we were all just crazy. It would have destroyed the magic."

"For God's sake, Cecilia, there *isn't* any magic!"

"Rosie—"

"I mean—it's just tricks, isn't it?"

"It's not just tricks," Cecilia said. "Rosie—it's everything. We're creating a whole *world*. You should see their faces, some of them, when we play."

"You're fooling people. Vulnerable people! Making them think . . . things no sane person could think. Luring them out to this—this—compound . . ."

"They didn't. I chose to come."

"They lied to you!"

"They didn't lie!" Cecilia's voice was firm. "They promised me *another life*. And that's what they gave me."

She saw Rose's face. She softened. "Oh, Rosie," she murmured. "I wish I could make you understand what a good place this is. I know it sounds crazy . . ."

Color rose to Cecilia's cheeks. Still, she continued.

"I'm *doing* something, Rosie. I'm happy here. I'm useful. When I play, at the cabarets, I play for people for whom it *matters*. It's not just a drunk night out for them or a big joke or some chance to get dressed up and take pictures and show off to their friends that they've been somewhere worth going. It changes them. You saw it. You felt it—I know you did. And the others—they're kind; they're *good*; they're my friends; we're like a family . . ."

"A family!" Rose could stand this no longer. "Are you serious? While Paul and I have blown both our lives up, looking for you, you've been hanging around on a compound with a family of—"

Cecilia froze.

"Paul was with you?"

Rose felt suddenly, irrationally defensive. "He was worried," she said. "We both were."

"Where is he?"

Cecilia had gone white.

"Back in Maine. Moving on with his life."

Cecilia hesitated. Then she relaxed.

"Good," she said. "Good. I'm happy for him. He deserves that." Her gaze darted to the window. The morning light was clear on the water. Rose remembered her mission.

"You can't stay here."

Cecilia turned back to Rose. "Why not?"

"Because—" Rose had so many reasons. "Because it's crazy; because it's a *cult*; because people can't live like this."

"*Why* not?"

"Because!" Rose was starting to feel like she was the crazy one. "Because you can't just run away from everyone in your life!"

"But that's the thing, Rosie!" Cecilia took her hand. "I don't have to. Not if you stay."

"I'm not staying!"

"Is it Caleb? Is that it?"

"No, it's not Caleb—"

Rose saw Cecilia catch sight of her left hand. She grabbed it.

"What happened?"

Rose wrenched her hand away. "It doesn't matter."

"I'm—sorry."

"So am I."

They sat like that for a moment, in silence.

"I'm sorry, Rosie," Cecilia said softly. "I really am. I don't want to let you down. I don't want to make you unhappy. But I'm not leaving. I can't. And I don't want to. God, Rosie, my whole life—all I've ever wanted is to know what I'm doing, and why I'm doing it, and to know that it matters. And I've made so many messes; I've made a mess of everything I've ever tried, until now. And finally, finally, I've found something I won't destroy."

Rose knew, then, that Cecilia would not change her mind. Cecilia was staring up at her with a quiet, fervent expression, a look of stubborn, mystic certainty, that reminded Rose of paintings she had seen of Joan of Arc.

It was the same expression Rose had seen, so many times, on Paul.

"So"—there was a lump in her throat—"what happens to us?"

A shadow crossed Cecilia's face.

"You go back," she said. "I stay here."

"And do I ever see you again?"

Cecilia was silent for a long time.

"Maybe." She forced a smile. "Across a crowded bar, at two o'clock in the morning." She shook her head. She looked, once more, at the light streaming in the window. "Can't we just pretend, Rosie? For a little while? We've got a few hours left. Can't we just pretend that you'll stay?"

Rose didn't say anything. She took Cecilia's hand. She took her in her arms.

They lay like that for a while: Rose's arm around Cecilia's shoulder, Rose's heart against Cecilia's back. Rose could have held her there forever. She listened to the tidal variations of Cecilia's breath. She did not know which one of them was leaving the other behind.

—

When Rose woke up the sun was setting. Cecilia was snoring, gently, beside her. Rose could hear birdsong. Through the window Rose could see the boat, bobbing on the water.

Rose tiptoed out of the bed. She placed the coverlet over Cecilia's shoulders.

The house was quiet now. The only sound was the odd footsteps, or the clattering of jewelry, coming from behind the closed doors of the other bedrooms. The parlor and the veranda were empty.

Rose came out into the garden.

Even in the February barrenness, it was beautiful. Pansies and primroses protruded from lattices of vines, their buds dormant. There were the remnants of what must once have been a fountain, topped by a cherub with a sheared nose and broken wing. There was a small gazebo with a swing set, and a few hammocks arranged around a fire pit. There were two apple trees, not yet in bloom, between the house and the iron gates, which were so tall and overgrown that Rose could not even make out where the door was located, or whether there was even a door at all.

Rose looked out over the water. The horizon was pale, so that the yellow-green of land in the distance—seemingly uninhabited—melded into the gray-green of the sky. They could be anywhere, she thought— she had been too overcome, last night, to register the boat's direction. If Thomas brought her home, she knew, there was little chance of her finding the Avalon again.

"*Great God,*" a voice said behind her. *"I'd rather be a pagan, suckled in a creed outworn."*

Rose started. Cassidy was standing beside her. He had already dressed for the evening, in his top hat and tails; nevertheless, his voice was different, rougher. She could make out for the first time traces of a Midwestern accent.

"It's Wordsworth," Cassidy said, with a dark smile. "You get a lot of time to catch up on your reading here. Jenny's making her way through all of Malory, at the moment. And of course it's helpful for the clues."

Rose didn't say anything.

"I hear," Cassidy went on, "you've decided to leave us. Shame."

"Not really."

"I liked our dances. You're not bad, you know. When you relax." He turned out toward the water. "We had a good time."

"Just tell me one thing."

"Shoot."

"How do you do it?"

"Do what?"

"The flowers. The fire. Jenny's tightrope."

"Ah." Cassidy smiled. "That. Good lighting. Hidden motors. Motion sensors. Clever rigging. Julius was an engineer, before he came out with us. And Thomas knows a thing or two about chemicals."

"And the music?"

"What about the music?"

"Is it drugs? Ecstasy or shrooms or something? In the chocolates, maybe, or—"

Cassidy shook his head.

"The music," he said, "is the music."

"But you don't really—"

"I told you the truth," he said. "Morgan writes the songs herself. Always has. New for every cabaret."

"And you really burn them, after?"

"Come out yourself," Cassidy said. "And see."

He put his hands in his pockets. He came closer, to her side. For a moment Rose remembered, flustered, how he had once pressed his fingers into the small of her back. But there was no sign of flirtation in him now.

"I just don't see how you stand it," Rose said. "Knowing it's all a lie."

"Everything's a lie," Cassidy said. "You just have to choose the kind of lie you can live with. Do you know what St. Ignatius of Loyola used to say?"

"What?"

"*Perform the acts of faith,*" he said. "*And the faith will come.* My spiritual director was fond of that one. Then again, he was a Jesuit, so—"

"Your spiritual director?"

His smile glimmered. "I was a priest, once."

"What happened?"

"The faith stopped coming." Cassidy leaned against the trunk of one of the apple trees. "My bishop—he told me not to worry. It was common, he said. *Let it go.* He doubted a third of the priests in the diocese believed in all the things they were supposed to. Episcopalians, right?"

Rose thought briefly of Grant. She still could not bring herself to believe that, less than twenty-four hours ago, the four of them had been laughing at the MacIntyre bar.

"But if there's one thing that links all of us here," Cassidy continued, "it's that we're all pretty rotten at letting things go. *The carnival of tortured souls, darlin'.*" For a moment he was the cabaret's Cassidy once more. "The box of broken toys." He made a contemptuous noise. "We don't do so well with disappointment."

Cassidy sounded almost ordinary now. He almost sounded sane.

"What happened?"

"Funny thing," he said. "You can't really *be* an ex-priest, not in the Episcopal Church. Even the Catholics have a way out. But us? They get you for life. You can quit. You can go back to your ordinary life. But you've still got a little voice, in your disbelieving soul, telling you the God who doesn't exist still has you on the hook. I tried to do what I could, after. I considered grad school. Hospice work—rough gig, for someone who can't believe in life after death. Hell, I even thought about learning to code. But—still that little voice. Telling me I couldn't leave it all behind, the same moment I couldn't stay. I took—as they say—to drink. Started in the shallow pool with drugs. Hurt my share of women. And that's when she found me. Brought me in."

"Morgan?"

He nodded. "She was the one who found me. In an absinthe bar at the French Quarter at dawn. All in red." He affected a voice. "*Gams like gazelles and a stare that could knock you six ways to Sunday.* I think I fell in love with her a little then. We all did." Something melancholy came into his face and then vanished. "God, those first nights. Sometimes I wish I could bottle that feeling, like a brandy, take a hit when I'm feeling low. I hadn't felt that way since seminary. Like the world was shot through with stardust."

"You weren't angry when you found out?"

"Found out what?"

"That they weren't real?"

Cassidy chuckled.

"I knew they weren't *real*," he said. "At least, not *real* how you mean it. I was under no illusions." He smirked. "For one thing, I recognized Jenny. *Geneviève,* as she was."

"You knew her, before?"

"I'd seen her across the room at parties. She was a grad student when I was in seminary. One of those prodigies everybody envies and feels sorry for. Doing physics PhD work by nineteen. Something to do with black holes. She had a breakdown, two years in. Developed a fear of death so bad she couldn't cross the street, in case a car hit her. When she went missing we all figured she'd just burned out, gone somewhere to start over. She wouldn't have been the first."

"You knew—and you kept going?"

Cassidy shrugged.

"I figured," he said, "whatever it was—whoever *they* were, spirits or cultists or just a bunch of whack-job actors with a vision—it was a hell of a lot better than anything else I could do with my life. And she has a gift, you know, Morgan. She can see, within a moment of meeting you, what it is you want, what it is you need, more than anything in the world. Most priests, they don't have the power to do something like that. It's why she can write the songs."

"But they're lies!"

Cassidy raised an eyebrow. "You know what Dostoyevsky said," he said. "*Beauty will save the world.* And he didn't even look like our dear Morgan le Fay." He looked up. "Speaking of . . ."

Morgan had appeared in the doorway.

She had dressed now for the evening. Once more she had put on the red silk dress, the ostrich cape, the earrings that glittered in the moonlight that now settled over them. She looked as regal, as unearthly, as she had the first time Rose had come to the boat.

The others followed behind her. They had all dressed, too, Ralphie with blond finger-waves in his hair and a white mink around his neck; Nini like an eighteenth-century courtesan, with stays and panniers and her hair piled and powdered on her head; Jenny in a velvet doublet and hose, with an Elizabethan ruff around her neck; Julius in a double-breasted suit. Rebecca, gold sequins clinging to her hips, glowered at her. Only Cecilia had remained unchanged: still wearing the simple shirt and breeches from the afternoon.

Morgan approached the dock. Thomas was already there, unrolling the rope. She beckoned Rose over.

"We'll leave," she said, "in fifteen minutes. We can't be late—we have a pickup in Long Island City. A widow. So if you want to say your goodbyes"—she nodded toward Cecilia—"I'll give you a moment."

Thomas helped the others into the boat.

Cecilia came to Rose's side.

"Looks like I have the night off," she said with forced gaiety. "What should I do? Take a hot bath, you think?"

Of course, Rose thought, *Morgan has arranged it this way*—the way Morgan arranged her cabarets—so that she would have to watch Cecilia waiting, alone on the shore, as the boat spirited her homeward.

Rose told herself she would kiss Cecilia goodbye. She would walk down the dock without hesitation. She would let them take her back to her whole life, her good life—at least, what was left of it. By tomorrow she could be walking into the My.th office; maybe Lydia would be there; maybe she could talk to Caleb; maybe she could explain, or try to explain, or at least come up with some story that sounded like an explanation; or else maybe she could go home to Tudor City, sink alone into the bed that had once been Cecilia's, stare alone at the cracks in the ceiling, and try to move on with her life, the way Paul—*oh God, Paul!*—had moved on with his. She would get on the apps. She would go running. She would finish the *Persephone* meditation. It would be so much like it had always been. What was the difference, she thought, between Cecilia in a London houseboat and Cecilia on a Montana hawk rescue and Cecilia in a garden you could not get to unless by boat, that nobody knew how to reach?

"I'll see you." Cecilia tried to smile. "You know. Around."

She stuck out an awkward hand, like she expected Rose to shake it.

"*Goddamn it!*"

"Rosie!"

"Rose?" Morgan was at her side.

"You win, okay? I'll stay. I'll do whatever you want; I'll write your little clues; I'll wear your costumes; I'll be the cocktail waitress at your *fucking* cabaret. Are you happy now?"

Rose was suddenly so tired. She wanted to sink down into the grass, among the primroses, and sleep for a hundred years.

Morgan brushed the hair from Rose's face. She took Rose into her arms.

"There," she murmured. "There. It'll be all right. Everything's all right."

As if Rose were a child, having a tantrum in the middle of the garden. "You'll be all right."

Somehow, Rose let herself believe it.

"You can't be serious!"

Rebecca was making her way down the dock. Her eyes blazed.

"She can't just stay here!" By now she was at Morgan's shoulder. "What's she going to do—hang around, painting her toenails, while the rest of us . . ."

"She'll do the shows," Morgan said. "Like anyone else."

"She'll call the police. First chance she gets. We send her out on a raid . . ."

"She won't call the police," Morgan said, with perfect certainty. "Will you, Rose?"

Rose looked over at Cecilia.

She knew, as well as Morgan did, that Cecilia would never forgive her.

She prayed that they'd been telling the truth about Lucinda Luquer.

"No," Rose said slowly. "I won't. So long as you promise me one thing."

"What?" Morgan looked amused.

"If Cecilia changes her mind—if she decides to go home . . . you won't try to keep her. Either of us. You'll let us both go."

"I'll take you on the boat myself."

"But—" Rebecca tried.

"My decision," Morgan said quietly, "is final.

"Come," Morgan said. She put her hand on the small of Rebecca's back. "We're expected." She turned away. She led Rebecca down the dock, onto the boat, where the others still stood waiting. Thomas blew the horn, once, and then the boat was pulling away, into the gathered darkness.

Rose and Cecilia watched as it sailed out of view, until there was nothing left on the still water but the reflected light of the moon.

CHAPTER TWELVE

On Rose's first full morning at the Avalon, Thomas came to her room with a bag.

"You'll be needing these," he grunted, and threw it down on the bed. It contained a toothbrush, a few haphazardly chosen skin care products, and—mercifully—a set of clean underwear.

He explained the rules.

They usually took the boat out three times a week, usually late enough that the piers would be empty and they would meet few other boats on the way. Cabaret nights were full—there were rehearsals, all day, and then a strictly timed departure; arriving a minute early, Thomas said, or a minute late counted as a promise broken.

Other nights—when they went out to leave clues, say, or when they went out on raids—were more flexible; Rose could do what she liked, then, provided that she didn't leave the grounds of the estate.

That, Thomas said, was the first and most important rule of the Avalon. Nobody entered or left the estate except by water. Even Thomas—who bought groceries, did all the repairs, and picked up the mail from the ever-changing PO Box—never left by land. The gates were always locked. Not even Thomas had the key.

"Why?"

"To preserve the magic."

To preserve the magic, Rose soon learned, was at the heart of every rule at the Avalon. It was why nobody at the Avalon had phones or computers or televisions; it was why nobody was permitted to know where, exactly, the house was located; it was why nobody, once they'd come, was permitted to contact anyone from their old lives; why nobody was ever allowed to have a wallet or a bank account or go out into the city alone. Raids were always done in pairs, in case anyone was tempted to borrow a stranger's phone.

"So if you're thinking about getting in touch with that old fiancé of yours," Thomas said, "don't."

"I'm not," Rose said. She meant it.

"Anyone else we should be worried about?"

Rose thought, briefly, of Paul.

"No," she said.

There were other, more prosaic rules. Chores and cooking were done in a rota—the latter under Rebecca's ministry. Everybody had to contribute to the upkeep of the garden. There was a budget—Thomas declined to elaborate on its source—for costume pieces, books, or varied personal items, for which anyone could make a request, and which Thomas could purchase on his regular trips into the outside world, but Morgan had final discretion.

"And what happens," Rose said, "if somebody breaks the rules?"

"Nobody breaks the rules."

"Never?"

A cloud passed over Thomas's face.

"Almost never."

"What happens then?"

"It doesn't matter," Thomas said. "It won't happen again."

"How do you know?"

Thomas's face softened.

"Because," he said. "We have too much to lose. Now stop asking questions."

—

It was easy to lose track of time at the Avalon. Already Rose had stopped counting the days. She had not yet—on Morgan's instructions—gone out onto the boat; still, she had grown accustomed to the Avalon's rhythms: the way everybody ran from room to room at dusk, in search of Nini's spare rouge or Julius's bowler or Ralphie's pearls; the way everybody staggered home, with feathers falling and smiles on their faces, at dawn; the way they all stood at the fire pit in the garden, with their torn costumes and their makeup smeared and their hair disheveled, consigning that evening's music to the flames.

Even without the cabarets, Rose kept busy. Upon discovering Rose could sew a decent hem, Morgan had sent her to Nini, who received her with no trace of rancor over Rose's outburst on the day of her arrival, and who presented her with a wardrobe full of mismatched chiffons and torn silks that Thomas had picked up at an estate sale the week before. Rose served alongside Cecilia in the kitchen—to Rose's surprise, Cecilia had by now learned to chop a decent onion—and tried to ignore Rebecca's scowl burning into her back. She fed the rabbit, who was called Mab, and who lived in a hutch by the kitchen door. She set up Jenny's tightrope—gossamer-thin but visible, now, by daylight—between two birch trees in the garden. She weeded the primroses. If, from time to time, Rose stopped short, mid-prune, to gaze at the way the afternoon light speckled on the water, or to listen, rapt, to the thrush that nestled in the apple tree, nobody—not even Rebecca—chided her to hurry.

Plus, there were the clues. Every few afternoons, Rose would gather in front of the parlor fireplace with those of the others not rehearsing songs or acrobatic acts—Cassidy, usually, and sometimes Jenny or Julius—and armfuls of reference books from the shelves, and they would go through Thomas's handwritten list of the visitors who'd written in that week. They would debate what kind of clue you wrote for the boy you found sobbing in a West Village piano singalong, who had told Jenny he couldn't understand why everyone there was so happy, as if the whole world weren't going through an apocalypse ("nihilists," Cassidy whispered into Rose's ear, "are the most picky about clichés"); and what kind of clue you wrote for the girl who'd found her boyfriend—she had confessed, sobbing into Nini's chest—in bed with the barista at the coffee shop where the two of them had first met; and what kind you wrote for the old man closing up a dive bar in Ozone Park, whose daughter didn't speak to him with good reason.

The art was delicate. Make the clues too difficult and you risked people not solving them at all—one month they'd let Julius take over the clues, and not a single person had managed to show up. Make it too easy and you risked destroying the thrill.

Rose only watched at first as Jenny and Cassidy debated whether you could reasonably expect a person to figure out that a series of dots referred to the constellations on the ceiling of Grand Central station, or whether it was too obvious to make a line from Dante's *Purgatorio* lead to the statue in Dante Park. There was a part of her that still bristled at the idea of luring someone—as she had been lured—across the city on a whim, as if they were nothing but maneuverable dolls. But Rose had to admit that, when a clue for a lawyer regretting that she'd never had children was supposed to lead to a painting of Demeter and Persephone at the Met, there was something meditative in drawing the soft lines of Persephone's lips, the way her vision lingered, as she turned back toward the underworld, toward something she could not see.

"But you're *marvelous*," Jenny exclaimed, leaning over Rose's shoulder. "Oh, we've been needing another artist—we have all these ideas, you see, for painting different scrims, and Ralphie's always too busy on the piano . . ."

Rose had to admit, too, that Cecilia had been right about the others. They were all—with the exception of Rebecca, who remained icy—extravagantly kind, as delighted to see her, each morning, as they had been when she had first stepped onto the *Avalon*.

"But of course we're overjoyed you're here," said Jenny, linking her arm into Rose's. "Who wouldn't be? To have found someone else, in this big, cold world of ours, who *understands*?" She grinned. "Every new person who comes to be part of this," she said, "is a reminder that we're doing something that can really last."

Even Robin—still silent—approached Rose with a shy smile, once, after rehearsal, with four new-budded apples from the garden, before he hurriedly set them down and fled.

"He *does* talk," Cecilia said. "If you get him alone. He's just nervous around people he doesn't know."

Rose remembered what Francesca had said about Robin's parents.

She knew better than to ask.

—

Rose told herself that she wouldn't be at the Avalon for long. Surely, Cecilia would grow bored any day now; the novelty of cooking and sweeping and weeding would turn to restlessness; any dawn she would come stumbling off the boat after a long cabaret and declare that she was done with the Avalon forever. But Cecilia was always on time, when it was her turn for kitchen rota, always assiduous when weeding the garden, always five minutes early—her costume meticulous—when they all gathered at the dock under the stars.

"It's easier, here, somehow," Cecilia told Rose, as they sat together one afternoon on the bottom of the bunk bed Thomas had contrived for them in Cecilia's room. "I know exactly what's expected of me." She had spent that afternoon practicing a new song, for a failed actress, and there were calluses on her fingers. "And I know what I'm doing it *for*. Besides—whenever I'm tired or nervous or . . ."—she swallowed—"melancholy, then I just think about the others. About what it would mean to break the spell *for them*."

"What do you mean?"

"All it takes," Cecilia said, "is one wrong note on the piano, one mo-ment when I'm not paying attention, one moment where I say the wrong thing and confuse the brokenhearted girl whose boyfriend's left her with the unhappily married housewife—and *poof*!" She snapped her fingers. "It all comes crashing down.

"We owe it to one another," she said, "not to let that happen."

There were moments, listening to Cecilia, or else seeing Cecilia's ex-pression, when she tramped in at dawn with glitter on her face and a rapturous smile on her lips, that Rose felt, once more, a strange tug at her heart: the same pull that had once kept her awake, lying next to Caleb in bed, trying to remember the bars of the Avalon's song. There were mo-ments, when Rose was curled up, by the fireplace, while the others were out on a raid, at last making her way through the whole of "The Waste Land," or else when she was lying in bed and heard Cecilia snoring con-tentedly beneath her, that Rose felt the cessation in her heart of something she had not even known existed, as if she had grown so used to the sound of whirring machinery or rumbling pipes in her apartment walls and now, at last, heard silence for the first time.

—

"That doesn't mean," Rose said to Morgan, for the third time, "I'm stay-ing."

They were sitting once more in Morgan's parlor. Morgan had invited Rose—as she did every week or so—for tea.

"Of course," Morgan said. "That's your prerogative."

"She'll change her mind," Rose said. "Eventually. She always does."

"Maybe," Morgan said. "Perhaps not. Sugar?"

Even after weeks at the Avalon, as the others had become more human to Rose, Morgan still managed to vex her. Rose had gleaned nothing of Morgan's personal life, or even whether *Morgan* was her real name. As far as anyone seemed to be concerned, she hadn't existed at all before the

Avalon. Her accent, her affect, never once altered from the regal role she'd played on board. Even in a bathrobe with her hair twisted into a messy chignon, or eating breakfast at the kitchen table, she still stalked through the world with the same pantherlike placidity: like she was a different kind of being from the rest of them.

"I've decided," Morgan went on, "you're going out on the boat."

"When?"

"Tonight."

Rose rounded on her. *"Tonight?"*

"Robin's ready to start singing," Morgan said. "We need someone to hold the drinks tray."

She searched Rose's face.

"Is that a problem? If you feel unready, of course; if it's too much for you—"

Rose knew what Morgan was doing. It worked anyway.

"I'll do it," she said.

—

That night's cabaret was for a woman named Yvette Thornbill. She was fifty-three years old and believed that her husband no longer loved her. Rebecca had met her last week at the King Cole Bar, at the St. Regis hotel, where she'd attempted to buy Cassidy a drink and burst into tears when he refused. Rebecca had offered her a handkerchief. They'd ended up in the bathroom, with Yvette sobbing into Rebecca's chest that maybe nobody had ever really loved her, and that maybe nobody ever would. They'd sent her a more straightforward clue—"Rebecca's a softie at heart," Cassidy told Rose—a line of Shakespeare that led her to the statue of Romeo and Juliet in Central Park. She was supposed to wait for them in Bay Ridge.

Rose's role was simple. She would be as silent, holding the drinks tray, as Robin once had been; improvising conversation, Cassidy informed her, was a skill that took weeks to master. She would refill glasses. She would offer chocolates. From time to time, when Yvette Thornbill was distracted by the music, she would sneak into the cabin, where a small freezer held a bagful of fresh ice, to replenish the champagne, which turned out to be prosecco ("we *are* on a budget," Thomas muttered). She was not—Rose was relieved to hear—expected to wear a harlequin's ruff or makeup; instead, Nini had found her a simple peach dress, bias cut, from the ever-overflowing wardrobe, and a pair of patent-leather shoes.

Cecilia did Rose's makeup at the small vanity in their bedroom. She'd put Rose's hair in curlers, which she now brushed into waves; she put rouge on Rose's cheeks.

"There," Cecilia said, finishing the outline of Rose's lips. "You look perfect, Rosie." She was wearing a halter-necked midnight-blue gown that gave her the vague air of a pagan priestess. "Oh, Rosie, you look like *yourself*!"

Rose turned to the mirror. She wasn't sure what Cecilia was talking about. She looked, she thought, like a stranger. Her makeup was delicately rendered; her jewelry shone; her hair, brushed out now, held the kind of geometric curls Rose had seen in old silent movies.

She looked exactly, she thought, like them.

—

They gathered on the pier.

"Rosie!" Jenny scampered toward her. "You look like a vision—doesn't she look a vision, Cassidy?"

"*As fine a sight*"—Cassidy used his debonair voice once more—"*as I ever did see.*"

Thomas looked Rose over.

"Hm," he said. "You'll pass."

"You ready"—Ralphie wiggled his eyebrows—"to make some magic?"

Out of the corner of her eye Rose could see Morgan, coming down the dock. On her face was a small but triumphant smile.

They sailed out onto the water. One by one Thomas lit the flames, suspended by wicks, whose thread had been twisted into the vines. He put the lighting gels in place. He checked the motors hidden within the silk-paper flowers, which furled and unfurled with different colors on each side.

The night was balmy and clear. The stars were diamond bright. Waves foamed at the prow. Cecilia was playing a bagatelle on the piano. Jenny was leaning out over the railing, letting the salt spray redden her cheeks. Rebecca was fiddling with Robin's bow tie—he was in a tuxedo, tonight, his hair combed and slicked back, traces of a mustache above his lip.

She brushed the hair from his face. She kissed his cheek.

"There," she murmured. "Now you're perfect."

Thomas handed Rose the tray. He showed her how to best hold it, to resist the rocking of the boat.

"Remember," he said. "Look sharp. And don't say a word."

They passed under an elevated train line, crossing below first one bridge, then another. Then they were in open water. From time to time they passed another boat—the cargo ships, the fishing boats, and the odd private yacht—then they passed onward, and the darkness stretched in all directions. In the starboard distance, Rose could make out Coney Island: the neon of the Wonder Wheel, the parabolic skeleton of the Cyclone, and all the fairground colors phosphorescent against the night. A stray thought—that she ought to have been keeping track of the directions, to work out the location of the house—came to her; it passed.

Thomas checked his watch. "Midnight," he said. "Places."

Jenny pirouetted to the divan. Cassidy leaned against the railing. Cecilia, at the piano, straightened her back.

"Are you ready?" Morgan purred into Rose's ear.

"I think so."

"It's easy," Morgan said. "All you have to do is remember that you're giving someone a very great gift. The greatest."

"Magic?" Rose could not hide her doubt.

Morgan shook her head.

"Attention," she said.

At ten minutes past twelve they came to Bay Ridge.

Yvette Thornbill was standing on the pier.

She was blond and busty, with a face so buttressed by intervention it was impossible to tell her age. She was huddled in an extravagantly dated mink and weighed down by jewels, as if she had dressed for a tryst with a lover. She was looking in the wrong direction.

On the prow, Thomas lifted the flute to his lips.

Nini began to sing:

The wind blows out of the gates of the day
The wind blows out of the lonely of heart
And the lonely of heart is withered away

Rose steadied her grip on the tray.

The boat drew nearer. Yvette Thornbill looked up at them.

Her eyes were full of wonder.

Then everything happened at once. Rebecca was dashing toward Yvette, with her arms outstretched, and her face alive with a tenderness Rose had not seen before. Cecilia was playing a flourish; Jenny was calling for champagne. Rose prayed she would not drop the tray.

Oh, my dear one, Rebecca was saying, *we're so relieved—so relieved— you've come.*

Yvette tottered toward the divan. Nini seized two glasses from Rose's tray and placed one into Yvette's hands; dazed, she accepted it.

"What . . . ," she began. "What—is . . ."

"We're your guardian angels, beautiful!" Ralphie cried.

"We've had our eye on you," Cassidy cut in.

Yvette stared back at them all, in mystified delight.

Then Julius was at the microphone, introducing the *cabaret of lost souls, the speakeasy of broken dreams*, and Yvette was at Morgan's side on the divan.

Then Robin made his way to the microphone.

Cecilia caught Rose's eye. Her face was flushed. Her eyes were shining. On her face was a look of luminescent joy.

She turned back to the piano. She began to play: a sultry, shivering melody, something between a bolero and a chanson.

Robin opened his mouth. He began to sing.

It was the story of a swallow in winter, in search of a home, who traveled from house to house, from barren tree to barren tree, with frozen beak and brittle wing, and who found nothing but naked branch and panes of glass, shut against her.

His voice was high and crystalline. He sang like Rose had once imagined angels sang: like his voice did not belong to a body at all. It caught Rose cold.

She had not expected this. It was one thing, to let music overtake you when you were bewildered, when you were surrounded by strangers and flames whose wicks you could not see. But as Robin's voice grew stronger with every bar, the song slipped between Rose's ribs; it filled, once more, her empty places. For a moment, Rose let herself wonder if there really was magic, after all.

Robin went on:

The swallow kept searching. She grew weak from hunger, half-frozen from wind. Then, at last, when she was almost ready to give up, to let herself sink into the ice-clotted river and drown, it appeared before her: the open window. The warm room. The feast ready. The nest prepared.

When Robin sang, Rose could smell the burning of cedar logs and the new-baked bread. She could feel the fire on her skin and the softness of the blanket, wrapped around her, like the certainty of home.

Robin sang like he could feel it, too.

And never more to roam, he sang. Tears dappled his cheeks.

Rose looked over at Yvette Thornbill.

There were tears on her face, too. But she was smiling.

She kept smiling—through Jenny's aerial act and Julius pulling roses out of her ear, through Rebecca's ballad about the jewels in an old woman's dresser, and the stories they could tell—her hand tight on Morgan's, her chest heaving with gasps of wonder and intermittent sobs. She kept smiling when Rose refilled her glass of champagne, when Ralphie caressed each of her earrings and told her she looked just like Rita Hayworth, when Cecilia started up a tango beat and Robin sailed to Yvette's side.

He bowed, deeply, from the waist. He took her hand. He pressed it to his lips.

"Madam," he said, in a voice so low and deep Rose started when she heard it. "Would you do me the honor of a dance?"

They moved together, across the dance floor, Robin holding Yvette to his chest. His fingers stroked her hair.

Rose watched them. She kept her tray aloft.

She tried to remind herself of everything she knew: that the flowers were motors and paper, and that the flames were suspended, and that they were only actors, with paint on their faces, and that there was no such thing as fairies or as angels, and that all of this was a lie. But as she watched how Cecilia leaned over her keys with such tender precision, how Robin touched so gently the small of Yvette's back, how he looked up at her with such ecstatic reverence, as if she were an unexpected creature and he were the one marveling that she existed at all, Rose believed in it anyway.

—

At dawn they brought Yvette to Sunset Park. Thomas and Rose helped her to land.

She seized Rose's hands and kissed them.

"Thank you," she murmured, between sobs. "Thank you!"

Then they set sail once more.

They waited until the pier was no longer visible. Then, at once, they burst into laughter.

"Oh, Robin!" Jenny flung her arms around him. "You were wonderful! A *sensation*!"

He turned bright pink. He reached out for Morgan's hand.

Thomas turned the boat around. Cassidy began clearing away the champagne coupes.

Cecilia caught Rose's eye. Rose couldn't speak. It didn't matter.

"Oh, Rosie." Cecilia's eyes were dazzling. "Oh, Rosie, I *knew!*"

Then Julius was clapping Cassidy on the shoulder; then Rebecca and Nini were giggling and whispering into each other's ears; then everybody was laughing and crying all at once; then Jenny seized Cassidy's face between her hands and kissed him.

She drew back, hastily, as if surprised at what she had done.

Then she kissed Julius in the same fervid way, then Ralphie, then Nini, then Rose herself.

For years afterward, when Rose tells this part of the story, she will stop short. Her breath will catch in her throat. She will try to hold on to what she remembers. She will try—she will keep trying—to explain.

Sometimes I think, she will say, when she at last finds words, *it was the grail, after all.*

It is not, exactly, what Rose means. But it is as close as she can ever come.

Cecilia leaned her head on Rose's shoulder. She squeezed Rose's hand.

"Come on," she said. "Let's go home."

CHAPTER THIRTEEN

Spring came. Rose stopped counting the weeks. All she knew was that the air was warmer; the breeze was balmy instead of bracing. Buds and then blossoms appeared in the garden: so many roses and daffodils and hyacinths that Rose had to hike up her skirts, every time she came down to the dock, to avoid catching them on thorns. Cecilia's hair had reached her shoulders. Every day was the same. Every day was glorious.

The Avalon had become part of Rose now: the way the smell of Rebecca's fresh bread wafted into her room in the mornings—or rather, the early afternoons that passed for mornings at the Avalon; the way the garden hammock rocked when Rose curled up in it, some evenings, with the copy of *The Brothers Karamazov* Cassidy had picked out for her from the bookshelf in the parlor; the sound of Cecilia rehearsing at the piano, echoing all the way to the veranda. The way the salt wind tasted on Rose's lips, as the boat made its way across the water.

Rose had done so many cabarets by now. For weeks she had remained in silent, spellbound service: pouring drinks for the ballet dancer who couldn't stand the feeling of her own flesh; the novelist convinced his best days were behind him; the young Hasidic husband who lay awake nightly beside his wife and three children, wondering which parts of his life were a lie. She grew more adept at balancing the tray, even on rougher waters, at noticing the exact right moment to refill a visitor's glass, at knowing just a moment before they did when they would in their rapt distraction knock a coupe over or spill champagne on the floor, at cleaning the pieces away before they even noticed what they'd done. Most of the visitors came just once—either Morgan would decide that once was enough, or else they'd fail to solve the clues. A few came two or three times. Nobody was asked to make a journey with no return.

"You have to be careful," Thomas said, one morning, as Rose helped him repaint the side of the boat. "You never know, with new blood. Look at what happened with *you*." She could not tell whether there was a smile behind his mustache. "All it takes is one wrong person . . ."

Time had made Rose bolder. Even now the shadow of Lucinda Luquer still sometimes flitted across her mind.

"Were there other—mistakes, then?"

He turned to her.

"You're asking me about Luci Luquer."

It wasn't a question.

"What happened to her?"

Thomas made a gruff, guttural sound.

"A mistake," he said. "Not one I'm interested in revisiting."

"But—if it was an accident—"

"If you know what's good for you," Thomas said, "you won't bring it up again—and especially not in front of Morgan."

He heaved a long, exhausted sigh.

"It just about broke her heart," Thomas said. "And that woman's heart isn't made for breaking."

Rose did not ask again. In time the question faded entirely. Whatever happened to Lucinda Luquer, she told herself, the Avalon couldn't have been responsible—she couldn't imagine Julius or Jenny or Ralphie intentionally hurting anybody. They were innocents—that was the beauty of them—and Rose no longer doubted, watching Rebecca's face, when a runaway bride stepped onto the *Avalon* for the first time, or Nini's soft, startled smile when a depressive NYU student threw his arms impulsively around her neck, that they believed in protecting those who needed it most.

—

Soon after the tulips bloomed, Morgan summoned Rose once more for tea.

"I've finally decided," she said. "That you're ready."

"To do what?"

Morgan smiled.

"What you've always wanted," she said.

They set an easel up in the corner of the boat. Thomas nailed it to the deck, so that it would not heave with the winds. He brought her pencils, brushes, paint. He brought her a black sequined beret and a long, velvet emerald robe: the sort of thing Rose imagined an eccentric lady artist might have worn in the Jazz Age.

"The trick will be," Thomas said, "to only lie a little. You want them to be pleased when they look at themselves. Not frightened. You think you can manage that?"

"I think so?" Rose said.

She went to the easel. She felt the brush between her fingers. She looked out over the water. She remembered her furious, fervid drawings, back in the city.

"Yes," she said. "I can manage that."

—

Rose drew an aging actress who was afraid of her own daughter. Rose drew a man whose wife had left him while he was on a business trip. Rose drew a writer who compulsively walked so many city streets at night that he'd left blood in his shoes. She watched them watching the stage, with shining faces; she watched them overcome. She captured their fear and their joy; most of all, she captured their wonder. She left out their blemishes: small

243

eyes, a bulbous nose, a jutting chin. She made them beautiful. She loved making them beautiful. When she handed them the sketches, she loved to watch the amazement take shape in their eyes.

By summer Rose had even grown comfortable talking as the others did: crying *darling!*; telling them, in a rapid, anachronistic pattern, that *it's been simply ages since we've had so much fun.* It was easier than she'd expected. By and large the guests were too astonished to ask questions; those they did ask were simple enough to evade, with a laugh and a joke and a call for more champagne.

—

One day, Thomas informed Rose she would be joining them on that night's raid.

"She's decided," he said, handing her a wad of cash and a MetroCard, "that you won't do a runner."

"I won't!"

"I believe you," Thomas said lightly. "Whereas *the proverbial millions . . .*"

He shrugged. He handed Rose her fake ID.

It was only when he'd stalked off to the boat that Rose noticed he'd put her name down as *Lily Forrest.*

"Don't worry," Cassidy said, as they disembarked at Coney Island. "Your first return is always the hardest."

It was the first time Rose had been back in the city since arriving at the Avalon. The pavement beneath her feet felt like it was caving in.

The city was so strange to her now. As she and Cassidy sat side by side on the subway, heading in the direction of a late-night cigar bar Morgan had chosen on the Upper East Side, Rose could hardly believe there had been a time when she had sat, with her laptop in her satchel, among the tourists, the nighttime commuters, the drunk students in their NYU sweatshirts scrolling the *Fiddler* on their phones.

The subway car crossed over the Manhattan Bridge. For a moment the whole city was before her: a fractal of lights, doubling and redoubling against the stars. Rose's breath caught in her throat. For a moment—just a moment—she wondered whether, in one of those lights in the distance, Caleb was sitting, scowling at his whiteboard; whether—somewhere, farther still—Paul—

She stopped herself.

"Remember," Cassidy whispered into her ear, "you're *in* it. But you're not *of* it anymore."

Cassidy was right. It got easier. After Rose's third or fourth raid, at the KGB Bar, at Mona's, she began to find them exhilarating. She began to revel in the way the Avalon slipped through the city; the way strangers sometimes gawked at and sometimes ignored their clothing.

But what Rose loved most was the deciding. The way you could look across a sweltering dive bar or the lounge at an old hotel and find the person whose eyes or whose stance or whose gestures betrayed their suffering: the one person—in the noise and the crowds and the clamor that was so overwhelming to Rose now—you could save.

—

In late summer, Thomas paired Rose on a raid with Rebecca.

"Sorry," Thomas said, seeing both their faces. "Orders."

Rebecca had learned by now to be outwardly cordial, at least at cabarets; in private she still treated Rose as frostily as the day Rose first arrived.

"Right," Rebecca said, as they disembarked just north of the Wards Island Bridge. "We might as well get this over with."

They rode the train from East Harlem in determined silence. Morgan had assigned them to a place none of them had been before: a trendy new rooftop bar on Beekman Place with a moving terrace that was supposed to rotate 360 degrees.

"As if," Rebecca muttered, "we're going to find *anybody* worth bringing in there."

They pretended not to know each other. They sat at opposite ends of the bar, taking turns watching the elevator for newcomers. Rose bristled at Rebecca's eyes upon her, as she ordered a drink, as she made conversation with a promising-seeming aspiring actress next to her at the bar. When Rose got up to use the bathroom, Rebecca scowled and turned her bar stool to face the restroom corridor until Rose returned.

"You know you don't have to do that," Rose said.

Rebecca said nothing.

Rose returned to her seat. She ordered another drink. She scanned the room. Everyone there was in pairs or in larger groups, everyone loud and riotous and jolly with drink. As much as Rose hated to admit it, Rebecca was almost certainly right. They wouldn't find anyone here.

Then Rose heard it.

"You've got to be *shitting* me!"

Rose froze.

"I *knew* it! I fucking *knew it*!"

Rose spun her bar stool around. Lydia was standing before her.

She had dyed her hair a paler shade of blond. She was tanner. There was a diamond ring on her left hand.

"Lydia—" Rose began. Out of the corner of her eye she could see Rebecca glowering at them both.

"Grant was convinced you were in rehab. He thought it was, like, a fentanyl thing. Wanted to put money on it. I knew he was full of shit." Lydia saw Rose's face. "Oh God—I'm an asshole—it was rehab, was it?"

"I—" Rose shot Rebecca a helpless look. "No, it wasn't rehab."

"Good. You're too smart for that shit. I *told* Grant"—her voice reached a glass pitch—"*She's too smart for that*. I told him it was probably burnout. You know, a lot of people are getting that, these days. There was this piece, in the *New Misandrist*, you probably saw it."

Rose had not seen a newspaper in months.

"No," she said mechanically. "Sorry, I didn't."

"What was it, then?" Lydia's smile tightened. "Was it the guy? Grant was telling Caleb . . ." She paused a moment too long. "Oh. Sorry."

Rose couldn't stop herself. "How is he?"

Lydia stood up a little straighter. "He's good. He's in Austin now."

"Good. Good!"

Lydia kept nodding, like a bobble-headed doll. "We text sometimes."

"And you're—" Rose motioned toward Lydia's ring.

"What can I say, right?" Lydia's laugh was dark. "I finally wore him down, right? *Go me!*" She waved her hands, awkwardly, in midair. The ring caught the chandelier light.

Across the bar, Rebecca made a show of clearing her throat.

"Congratulations. I'm happy for you."

"Sure." Lydia wrinkled her nose. "Okay." Then her face softened. "What *happened* to you, Ro? One minute we're, like, living it up in the MacIntyre; the next—"

"It's a long story."

"Really?" Lydia's voice was too bright. "*Is* it? Because, like, I don't have work tomorrow or anything, so, you know, we could get a . . ."

Out of the corner of her eye, Rose could see Rebecca glaring at her.

"I just needed to start over," Rose said, as brusquely as she could. "That's all."

"Oh. Sure." Lydia looked down. "Yeah. Totally. Good for you."

She drained her cocktail in one gulp.

"You know," she said. "I really missed you, Rose." The alcohol made her shudder. "Cringe, right?"

"Lydia, I—"

"I was going to ask you to be my maid of honor." She let loose a laugh like a hiccup. "But, you know. Whatever, right? I'm not, like, mad about it. Life happens. Just—" She exhaled. "Rose?"

Rose spoke as carefully as she could. "What is it?"

"Was it worth it?"

For a moment Rose thought Lydia was being sarcastic. But Lydia barreled on.

"I mean—*really*, Rose. I'm asking. Was it worth it?"

Rose hesitated.

"Yes," she said at last. "It was worth it."

Lydia didn't say anything at first. She looked down. A shadow of something Rose had never seen before flitted across her face.

"It was good talking to you, Rose," Lydia said. She made a vague gesture toward a group of girls on the terrace. "I should—"

"Of course."

Rebecca was at her side. They watched, together, as Lydia vanished into the crowd.

"I'm sorry." Rose turned to Rebecca. "I swear, I didn't know she'd be here."

But Rebecca's lips had curled, for the first time, into something like a smile.

"Come on," she said. "This bar's a wasteland. Let's go have a cigarette."

—

"You know," Rebecca said, as they stood side by side on Beekman Place, staring out at the water, "I thought I saw my kid on a raid once."

"Your *kid*?"

It had not occurred to Rose, before now, that anyone at the Avalon might have children.

"Rick. My oldest."

"How many did . . ." Rose faltered. "Do you have?"

"Two. One of each." Rebecca puffed out a smoke cloud. "He wouldn't be old enough to drink, of course. But he'd be eighteen this year. Old enough to go to college. NYU? Columbia? Old enough to get a fake ID, sneak into a bar on the Lower East Side. He was that kind of kid, too. You know the type. It was me and Jenny, on a raid, and in walks this—this *man*. Same blond hair. Same eyes. Same hulking way of walking."

"How long since—"

"Seven years." Rebecca shook her head. "It wasn't him, of course. Just a cookie-cutter jaw and low lighting. But those were the worst thirty seconds of my life." She took another puff of the cigarette. "Thinking I'd have to explain—"

"Why you left?"

Rebecca nodded. "God knows, I can barely explain it to myself." She leaned out over the railing. She shook out an ember. At their feet, the river was still. "I'm not Nini or Robin. I don't have a tragedy to point to. I was bored, maybe. Selfish? Absolutely. Unhappy?" She shrugged. She kicked out her feet under her. "Unhappier than I wanted to be. And that was enough." Her lips twitched. "I wasn't cut out to be a mother. My husband used to say that he'd married a bachelor who couldn't even boil an egg. It used to be our joke. Until it stopped being funny. Until I went out one night on a bender in the Haight and heard a song I couldn't shake echoing from an alley." Smoke lingered in the air like mist.

"It wasn't like it is now," Rebecca said. "We didn't have Julius, for the illusions. We didn't do clues. We didn't even have the boat. Just Morgan and Thomas and a rickety old piano, and a smoky basement room, and a microphone where they had me sing until morning. But it was enough to cut me loose. Maybe anything would have been enough. Maybe I was as desperate for happiness as a stray dog is for food. I don't know. What matters is: I made my choice." She turned, just slightly, toward Rose. "We all had to. Except you."

Rose felt suddenly ashamed.

"I didn't ask for this," she said.

"Doesn't change anything." Rebecca rubbed the last of her cigarette into the railing. She lit another. "You're lucky. You get it all."

She fell silent. She watched the fishing boats crossing the water.

"You don't understand," she said, after a moment, "the kind of sacrifices we make here. The people we leave behind. The decisions we have to live with." A darkness had come over her face.

"You're talking about Luci."

"Poor kid." Rebecca's voice had grown cigarette hoarse. "That's what

Morgan said. Poor, manic, tweaked-out little kid who just needed some kindness and a place to call home. But Morgan's an innocent."

Rose remembered what Thomas had said about Morgan's heart.

"The rest of us—" Rebecca said. "We may be in exile from the world. But we *have* lived in it. We know exactly what it is we're walking away from. But Morgan?" She shook her head. "Sometimes I think if she ever went out into the real world, she'd shatter like a pane of glass. She'd seen Luci so many times—haunting the bars we haunted. Morgan knew she wanted it. And it's Morgan who makes the rules." She blew a trapezoid of smoke into the air. "So we brought her in. We made her one of us. We gave her a bunk in Jenny's room—oh, it was a glorious house, the one we had. Twice the size of this one. Magnolias everywhere. A porch swing. We'd even started to talk about doing cabarets in the garden—making a whole *fairy ring*, among the jasmine and the honeysuckle. She was a sweet kid—jumpy, maybe, but always, always kind. Morgan loved her. We all loved her." Her voice tightened, for a moment, then she went on: "We knew a little about her past—her videos—but she swore she'd given it all up. She said she wanted to never be looked at, ever again. *I want to be a ghost*, she'd say. Invisible. And for a few weeks, we believed her." She let the cigarette fall from her fingers, as if she'd forgotten she was holding it altogether.

"I don't know if she'd planned it, from the beginning. Or if she got bored of us. Or found the temptation more than she could stand. We were less careful, in those days; we sent people on raids right away; we didn't think . . ." Rebecca shook herself. "Somehow she got herself a phone. A little camera. She started recording—the cabarets, the raids, the burning of the music; everything that was sacred to us, everything we'd given up everything for. I was the one who found it, the one who had to tell Morgan . . ." She regained her composure. "God, the way we looked, through that girl's eyes. Like a bunch of fools. Like a bunch of whack jobs at a Renaissance faire.

"We came up with a plan, me and Thomas. We'd take her out on a raid, somewhere out of the way, declare it a bust. I'd get her drunk, slip some pills into her glass—nothing worse than what she used to take, all the time. Just enough to make it easy to get the phone off her. Then we'd leave her in the bar, and take the boat back alone. We told Morgan. *I trust you,* she said, *to do what's right for the Avalon.*

"And so we brought Luci out. Some sports bar in Chalmette. I put the pills in when she was in the bathroom. Bought her a couple more shots of tequila. Waited for the Xanax to kick in. Got her to hand over her phone.

"She started to cry, of course. Begged me to give her another chance. Told me it was a mistake, a moment of weakness; she hadn't sent them to anyone; she'd changed her mind, thought better of it. She was hardly coherent enough to be convincing to anyone. I left her there, sobbing into her drink." Rebecca's voice had grown cold.

Rose could see it now: that pale, hysterical figure from the video, hunched over a bar banquette.

"Only . . ." Rebecca went on. "She followed me. I don't know how— God knows she could barely stand when I left her. She arrived at the pickup point, just as Thomas was pulling away. She was standing there, on the shore, shouting *please.* Begging us not to leave her behind. Thomas— he almost turned back then, but I told him to keep going. Only then she started to swim . . ."

She kept her eyes fixed on the horizon.

"There were so many things we could have done, of course. We could have gone back, pulled her onto the boat. We could have calmed her down, brought her back to shore, left her there. We should have known she was too drunk, too high, to make it. But all I could think, that moment, watching her paddle through the darkness, is that the dawn was coming, and that someone might hear her crying out, and that she had already made us risk so much. And so Thomas and I kept going until we could no longer hear the sound of her wailing. We'd convinced ourselves she'd given up, turned around, gone back. We didn't tell Morgan, at first. Better not to upset her. Until the next raid. Morgan was the one who saw it. A news channel on a bar television. It was the closest we've ever come to losing everything. Two days later we'd packed up the house, put that boat up for sale. A month later we were here. Starting over."

"I'm sorry," Rose said. And she was; she felt suddenly, wildly sorry for all of them.

"It is what it is," Rebecca said. "I'll answer for it, one day. All of us will. When it finally comes crashing down around us. And it will."

Rose started in surprise. She had always thought everyone expected the Avalon to last forever.

"I have no illusions," Rebecca said. "We're on borrowed time. We were on borrowed time before Lucinda died; we're on borrowed time now. And hell, maybe it won't even be you. Maybe it'll be Cassidy or Julius or sweet little Jenny or someone new, years from now, we haven't met yet. Maybe it'll be me. The spell *will* break, Rose. All I want is to delay that moment, as long as possible."

"And what will you do—when it does?"

Rebecca turned to look at her at last.

"Pay the piper," she said. "As best I can."

———

Rose barely slept that night. She counted the cracks in the ceiling. She listened to Cecilia snoring under her. When she dreamed, Lydia's face became Lucinda Luquer's.

It was, she reminded herself, *an accident.* Rebecca's reasoning had been impeccable; maybe she herself would have made the same decision. In the real world, sometimes, there were difficult decisions, impossible ones, even, and people strong enough to make them. It was just that it had not occurred to her, before, that the Avalon was part of it.

But in the morning the tiger lilies had bloomed, and dawn showers had called forth a rainbow over the water; in the morning the light was clear and the smell of fresh bread, tinged with cinnamon, suffused the whole house, and the enthusiastic patter of Jenny's footsteps on the stairwell was so full of anticipation that by the time Rose came down to breakfast she had managed to push her doubts away. Surely, Rose thought, watching Cassidy sneak one of Jenny's peaches, watching Jenny hit his shoulder in mock indignation, watching Julius showing Cecilia a sketch for a puppeteering act he'd been developing, they could make this last forever.

The days grew sweltering. The cabarets continued. Rose drew portraits of a children's book illustrator who'd grown to hate children, of a gay lawyer who'd fallen for a con artist half his age, of a woman who'd run away with her husband's best friend and found the world she'd thrown her life away for was no different from the one she'd left behind. They were happy—fervently, insistently happy—and if from time to time Cecilia's smile faded, a little, while they were sailing to a pickup or a raid; if, from time to time, Cecilia crept to the downstairs piano and played a few halting bars of an unfamiliar song, Rose thought little of it. Maybe Cecilia had gotten back into composing, the way she herself had gotten back into painting: her watercolors of the garden, which Thomas had framed, now lined the stairwell walls. Cecilia was always a little distracted when composing.

It was only that, one night, when the sisters were dressing together for the cabaret, and Rose was rummaging in the vanity for a pair of Venetian earrings Cecilia had worn the night before, to pair with the Japanese-print gown Nini had made for Rose, when Rose found a small lacquered box at the back of Cecilia's drawer, containing a plain gold band. Cecilia snatched it out of Rose's hands with such violence that three strands of pearls clattered from the vanity to the floor.

"That's not," Cecilia said, too quickly, "for the cabaret."

It took Rose a moment to realize what it was.

"You kept your wedding ring?"

"It was in my coat pocket," Cecilia said. "When I came here. That's all. I'd had it there for a month, telling myself I'd make it to the post office . . ."

She did not meet Rose's gaze.

"You see, Rosie?" She gave a forced laugh. "What a disaster I used to be? You couldn't count on me for *anything*. Not even to put my wedding ring in the mail." She turned toward the window. She looked out on the water. "God," she said. "I hope he's finally happy now."

She put the box back in the drawer. She slammed it shut.

Cecilia didn't mention Paul again. Rose found this a relief. She tried not to think about Paul, either. The few times Rose let herself remember, she reminded herself that whatever had happened between them was best buried. Two lost and lonely people, drunk on disappointment, rarely meant true love.

Rose hoped he was happy, too.

—

Robin's nineteenth birthday came when the days were still long. They had a party for him on the veranda. Rebecca baked a plum cake. Nini made him a flower crown. Ralphie and Rose had worked together on an enormous banner, the size of a scrim, that featured a drawing of Robin in his harlequin's costume, surrounded by smaller, comically caricatured portraits of the others, holding up their glasses in a toast, with conversation bubbles converging in *MANY HAPPY RETURNS*. Thomas presented Robin with a model train set he'd picked up on his latest grocery run. Cecilia played "Happy Birthday" on the piano. Everybody sang. They watched as Robin blew out the candles, his cheeks pink with elation.

They watched, in surprise, as he stood, at the head of the table.

He raised his glass.

"I—I'd like"—his voice grew stronger—"to make a toast."

"Will wonders never cease," murmured Cassidy. Jenny shot him a look.

"To all of you," Robin went on. The depth of his voice still startled Rose every time she heard it. "For making the impossible real. And for saving my life."

"Hear hear!" Cassidy cried. Everybody raised their glasses.

"And—especially—" Robin went on, "to Morgan." She was sitting at the opposite end of the table. There was a softness in her eyes Rose hadn't seen before. "You're the closest thing to a mother I've ever had. Thank you."

He looked down. He sat, abruptly, as if he had surprised himself.

But it was Morgan Rose couldn't look away from.

She was staring back at Robin in stunned wonder. Her eyes were like glass. The coupe of champagne trembled in her hands. She laughed, a strange, uncomfortable laugh, and then looked down, as if she could not stand to see the others watching her.

It was the first time Rose had ever seen Morgan look human.

Then Morgan strode to Robin's side. She took him in her arms. She kissed him once, almost violently, on the side of his head.

"Happy birthday, Robin," she said.

She went into the house without another word.

The others looked at one another for a moment in disbelief. Then Cassidy raised his glass again. "Well, look at you, kid," he said. "You've got the gift of the gab after all. You've even managed to cast a spell on *her*."

Robin made a shy noise of acknowledgment.

"She'll have you writing some of the songs, next. She'll—"

"Steady, Cassidy!"

Thomas had risen to his feet. His voice was so low it was almost a growl.

"Come on, Thomas," Cassidy began. "I was only—"

"I'd advise you," snapped Thomas, "not to talk about that of which you know jack shit."

He followed Morgan into the house.

The party continued. Ralphie took over at the piano in the parlor, still audible outside. Julius lumbered over and asked Cecilia to dance on the makeshift dance floor in the garden. Rebecca and Nini danced together. Jenny dragged Cassidy onto the dance floor as well.

Soon only Robin and Rose were left at the table. They watched the others dance. The moon was full and extravagant: its light overflowed onto their cheeks, their ankles, their shoulders. Jenny had closed her eyes and was leaning her head against Cassidy's chest, her expression rapt. An image of the garden at Sunny's drifted, briefly, into Rose's mind; she pushed it away.

"You know," Robin said suddenly. "We didn't do birthdays, when I was growing up. Jehovah's Witnesses, you know."

It was the longest sentence Robin had said to Rose in months.

"I hope," Rose said, "it was a good one."

He nodded. He kept watching the dancers. "First time I ever had a real birthday," he said, "I was eighteen. It was my first birthday after my—" He stopped himself. "After I left home. My friend Franny decided to go all out. Sparklers. Candles. The works. She made a big sign—not as fancy as that one, obviously—out of an old sheet, and she hung it on the walls of our apartment. We didn't take it down for weeks."

Rose had thought little about Francesca since arriving at the Avalon. She, like Caleb, like Lydia and Grant, like so much of Rose's old life, had dissolved like fragments of a dream. In any case, Rose had thought, nobody at the Avalon wanted to talk about the people they'd left behind.

"That sounds nice," she said.

"She was always doing stuff like that, Franny. She looked out for me. Made sure—made sure the trouble I got into, I could handle." He grimaced. "She did what she could," he said steadily, "with the life we had."

"She sounds—" Rose felt a pang of guilt. "She sounds like a nice person."

She wondered if Francesca had made it safely to Philadelphia. She prayed she had.

"Whatever." Robin shook his head, as if wrenching the thought away. "She turned out the same as the rest of them, in the end."

"What do you mean?"

Robin fiddled with a stray birthday candle.

"She was supposed to come out here," he said. "With me. *Where you go, I go*—that's what we told each other."

Rose started. "She told you she was coming?"

"No. Not exactly. But when I was on the boat. The last time. When Morgan took me—for real. I told her everything. I told her all about Franny, how we'd made a pact, the two of us, to stick together. How I couldn't leave without her. I told her I wanted to come to the Avalon, more than I'd ever wanted anything in the whole world. But I'd promised. And Franny—oh God, she'd have loved it. You see, she was a dreamer, too."

"What did Morgan say?" A sick feeling of dread had taken residency in Rose's stomach.

The light had faded from Robin's eyes.

"She listened. Morgan always listens—you know. She thought about it, for a moment. She asked me about Franny, about our life together, about whether Franny sang or danced or played an instrument, or anything like that. And then—" He swallowed. "She told me she'd make an exception. Just for me. She'd go in person, she said. The very next raid. I told her the bar Franny worked at. She'd talk to her. No letter. No clues. Tell her—tell her I was waiting for her, somewhere more wonderful than she could imagine, more wonderful than anything we'd ever dreamed . . ."

"And?"

"She went. She saw her. She told her everything. Franny didn't believe her, at first, but Morgan gave her a letter from me, to prove it. And Franny agreed. The next night, she'd come wait for the boat in Domino Park. She'd share my room, just like we always had. I'd already started thinking what she could do for the cabarets—she wasn't much of a singer, but . . ." His voice trailed off. "Anyway. It didn't matter. She didn't show. We came, Morgan and me and Thomas, in the boat. We waited twenty minutes. I kept begging them to stay—Franny was always running a little late. But finally Thomas said she must have gotten cold feet—or maybe she'd never planned to come in the first place. And that was that."

Robin finished his champagne. He shot Rose a dark smirk. A wave of nausea washed over her.

"It just goes to show," he said. "You can't depend on anybody out there." He rose.

"Anyway," he said. "It doesn't matter now."

Then he, too, went into the house.

Surely, Rose thought, watching the dancers, *there is some explanation*; maybe Francesca had lied to her, or had been drunk or high and forgotten—it's not, she reminded herself, like Francesca was the most reliable person to begin with. But she knew, already, that this was a delusion.

Surely, she thought, *Morgan has her reasons.*

Rebecca had said it herself, hadn't she? You had to be so careful. The Avalon was in danger of obliteration, at any moment; it was like one of those hothouse flowers you couldn't expose to the light for too long.

Soon Ralphie ceased playing; soon the dancers had filed, pair by pair, into the house, until even Cassidy had turned on his heel and gone upstairs, leaving Jenny to wander alone toward the apple trees in the back of garden, the hem of her dress catching on the vines.

"You didn't feel like dancing?"

Morgan had reappeared in the doorway. She had changed into a red dressing gown with a dragon on the back. She had reapplied her makeup. Whatever composure she'd lost earlier, she'd regained.

"Not tonight," Rose said. "I'm not much of a dancer. Not on land, anyway."

Morgan took a seat beside her.

"It was a good party," she said, as if confirming this to herself. "They were happy."

"It was a very good party."

"Robin liked his cake." A small smile came to Morgan's lips. "Plums are his favorite."

Rose could not quell her fear.

"He told me," she said. "About Francesca."

"Francesca?"

"His friend. The girl."

"Ah yes." Morgan nodded. "Sad story, that." She exhaled. "It's why we have rules here," she said, after a moment. "To protect each other. It was my folly, thinking we could break them."

"She's still looking for him, you know."

Morgan's chin jerked up.

"Excuse me?"

"Francesca. Or was. She had a sign up in Tompkins Square Park. She blew her whole life up, looking for him."

Morgan didn't say anything for a long while.

"Her mind," Morgan said, at last, "was lost already." Her sigh was long and resigned. "I told Robin the truth. I considered her, I really did. The next raid, I went myself—to watch her. I said nothing. I only watched." She turned her gaze back to Rose. "You've met her?"

"Yes."

"Then you know—how she is."

"Yes."

"And could you have pictured her on the boat? At one of the cabarets?" She waited for Rose to answer. Her eyes lingered on Rose's face.

"Well, no," Rose admitted, "not at first, but—"

"He told me she'd done so much for him. But what *had* she done for him? She hadn't protected him from the life he'd led. The life he'd been *made* to lead. She'd given him half a rat-infested apartment and made sure his drugs weren't cut with worse ones."

"That's not fair."

"Isn't it?" A flash of anger crossed Morgan's face. "Or perhaps you think there's something romantic, about certain kinds of degradation? Perhaps that's the view from a luxury condo on the Lower East Side."

"You could have told him the truth."

"You're right," Morgan said. "I could have. And risked him staying, with the guilt gnawing at his heart, until he became as much a liability as she was. Or risked him going back to a life that would have destroyed him in a matter of years." She shook her head. "He needed us, Rose."

"She needed you, too!"

Morgan flinched, just slightly. Rose had at last struck bone.

"Perhaps," she said. "At another time. In another world. We could have done something for her. But—"

"What?"

"Even here, Rose. Even here, there are compromises, to protect the ones we love." She looked up at Rose. "You know that now. Don't you?"

Rose remembered what Rebecca had told her, on Beekman Place.

"I just have one question," Rose said.

"Go on."

"You took me. After Lucinda. You wouldn't take Francesca. But you took me."

"Yes." Morgan poured the rest of the champagne into Rose's glass. "I did."

"Why?"

"Because," Morgan said, "your sister had told me all about you already. You were all she could talk about when she came here, you know. How *thoughtful* you were, she said. How you were the kind of person a person could always rely on. How you understood the quiet, ordinary work that goes into making a life. It was what she admired most about you. *Rosie just gets things done*, she said."

Rose felt a sudden rush of affection for Cecilia, asleep in their bedroom upstairs.

They looked out, together, at the water. Rose could not tell, in the moonlight, where the sky ended and the ocean began.

"This place is full of dreamers," Morgan said. "But it can't *only* be dreamers. And Thomas is getting older . . ." Her voice trailed off. "All of us," she said, "are getting older." She gestured with her glass to where the dancers had been. "They must never be allowed to grow old."

She turned back to Rose. She raised her glass.

"To magic, Rose," she said. Her eyes met Rose's.

Rose hesitated only a moment.

"To magic," Rose said.

CHAPTER FOURTEEN

Still, it was summer. Still, Rose was happy. Still, the garden was in bloom, and Jenny had set up an aerial hoop in the apple trees; still, Ralphie played ragtime at dinner.

Rose had new responsibilities now. She had repainted an entire wall of the living room with murals; there had been talk about setting up a proper stage in the garden, as they'd once hoped to do in New Orleans, so as to make what Ralphie called *a real production* of the arrival of the next new member of the Avalon—whoever that might be. Thomas had started taking her along on grocery runs, or to buy cardstock for the invitations.

It was as if there had never been a time that Rose was not part of the Avalon. As if there had never been a time that Rose had had a life outside of it. And if, from time to time, Rose wondered, looking out at the sun dancing on the ocean, whether Paul was watching it from the Falmouth cliffs, or Lydia, leaning precariously off Grant's balcony, or Francesca, from a squat or a park or a lover's bed, she pushed the thoughts away. The Avalon was her world now. She had come to love it. She had come to love them. Sometimes you had to protect the people you loved.

She said nothing to Robin about Francesca.

Morgan, she concluded, after a single sleepless night, had been right. Robin was better off here. All of them were. Here, Rose thought, there was music that shook your heart to smithereens; here there was dancing that left you breathless; here there were always new flowers in the garden, always new fruit on the trees; here, even errands had their magic: the knowing smile Thomas gave the cashier at Paper Source when she asked if they were planning to throw a big party. Here you knew, every morning, what you were waking up for; here you never wondered whether what you were doing mattered, or whether you loved the wrong person, or whether you loved the right person but in a wrong way, or whether one morning you'd wake up to find the bedroom window open and the person you loved gone.

Cecilia seemed happy, too. The nights she played the cabarets, her face still lit up with exultance; still, she chopped and swept and weeded with the same graceful precision: as if she were a priestess performing a rite. If there were nights, or somnolent afternoons, when Cecilia rose and tiptoed downstairs to play unfamiliar songs on the parlor piano, Rose did not let herself worry too deeply about it. She no longer feared Cecilia would fly away.

—

The air grew cooler. The leaves and the light turned gold. Julius kept tinkering with his marionettes. They kept doing cabarets.

Then, one night, it was cold enough that, for the first time since her arrival, Rose had to put a fur cape over her marigold velvet dress, and Cecilia had to play the piano through fingerless gloves. The pickup that night was in Astoria; the visitor was a man whose wife had left him. Rebecca was doing the first song, which was about a man who traps a selkie and who must return her to the sea. Rose, at her easel, could see her breath crystallize in the air.

Ralphie was on champagne duty. Cecilia was at the piano. Her face was flushed.

"I don't know what's wrong with me tonight," she said to Rose. "I'm a little nervous. I can't feel my fingers."

"It's just the cold," Rose said. Her hands, too, were numb.

"It's not like I haven't done lost love before."

"Oh, lost *love*." Ralphie drew nearer with the tray. "Never gets easier, does it, darling?"

Thomas called places. He lit the flames.

Everybody got into position. Cecilia straightened her spine at the piano. Cassidy took Jenny into his arms just in front of Rose's easel; Julius lowered Rebecca into a dip. Nini reclined next to Morgan on the divan. Thomas took out his flute. He played the first few bars of the melody.

The boat drew nearer.

A single figure was waiting, mist-shrouded, in the distance.

Robin sang out into the night:

The wind blows out of the gates of the day
The wind blows over the lonely of heart
And the lonely of heart is withered away

The boat began to turn starboard.

"It's going to be a good one tonight," Jenny whispered into Cassidy's ear. "He's a real seeker. I can tell. When I met him at Sunny's . . ."

Rose's head jerked up.

"What did you just say?"

"Shhhhh!" Rebecca's finger was on her lips.

The boat was almost at the shore. Rose's cry stopped in her throat.

Paul was standing on the pier before them.

For a moment nobody noticed anything was wrong. Cecilia's eyes were still on her music; she kept on playing; the dancers had already started their circulation of the deck; Nini had already stretched out her arms in expectant welcome.

"Darling," she began. *"We've been waiting so—"*

"Cecilia!"

The music stopped.

Cecilia froze.

All the color had drained from Cecilia's face. Her hands trembled, suspended above the keys. She was staring at Paul, transfixed.

"Cecilia!"

She rose, mechanically, when he called her name.

"Cecilia!" He tore to the water's edge.

The boat was ten feet from shore. Nini looked back at them, in astonished appeal, her hands still outstretched.

Cecilia took a few halting steps forward. Then she looked back, dazed, toward the others, then again toward where Paul stood: his face flushed, and his eyes wild.

"I—" Nini stammered. "I . . ."

"Go," Cecilia whispered. Then, with more strength. "Go!"

For a moment nobody said anything. They stared at one another, at Cecilia, dumbfounded, as the boat bobbed nearer.

Then Rose sparked to action.

"She said *go*!" Rose leaped up from behind her easel. "Go! Go! Get out of here!"

Paul's eyes fell on Rose at last.

"*Rose* . . ." His voice was ragged. "Rose, wait. Please. *Wait*—make them wait!"

But Thomas was already turning, so sharply that Ralphie's tray of champagne coupes went flying to the floor; Jenny and Cassidy lurched across the deck.

Rebecca turned to Rose.

"What the *hell* is going on?"

"Faster!" Now Morgan was on her feet. "Faster—the lights; damn it, turn off the flames!"

Julius dove toward the cabin.

The boat sped faster. Paul was still calling, out into the mist.

"Wait—wait—please!"

"Watch out," Cassidy said from the railing. "I think he's about to swim."

Paul was stripping off his jacket, his shoes. He was still calling Cecilia's name.

Rebecca's face went white.

"No—" she began. "No, he can't."

Rose rushed to the railing. At last she caught Paul's eye.

She shook her head. For a moment they stared at each other—in astonishment, in apology, at last, in understanding. He nodded, almost imperceptibly.

Then everything was darkness. The only light came from the moon.

All Rose could see was a shadow, standing motionless, as the *Avalon* sped away.

"What *was* that?" Nini cried, when they were at last once more on open water. "Who *was* he? Cecilia—who was that?"

But Cecilia said nothing. She was sitting, huddled, on the piano bench, her knees curled up all the way to her chin.

"Cecilia—who *was* he?"

"Leave her alone!" Rose was at Cecilia's side. She put her hands on Cecilia's shoulders. They were shaking. "Let her breathe!" She wrapped her arms around Cecilia's body. "It's okay," she murmured into Cecilia's ear. "It's going to be okay. You're okay." Cecilia shook her head. She said nothing. Tears were running down her cheeks.

Rose sank down beside Cecilia on the piano bench. Shock had made her numb.

Then Cecilia looked up. She turned to Jenny.

"What did he say?"

"What?"

"On the raid. When you met him. What did he say?"

Jenny looked wary.

"What did he *say*, Jenny!"

It was the first time in months Rose had heard Cecilia raise her voice.

"N-nothing . . ." Jenny stammered. "Just that—that his wife had left him, a while ago, and that—that he'd tried to move on."

"What else?" Cecilia's voice was ferocious.

Her gaze darted, apologetically, to Morgan, who had come by now to

265

the other side of the piano. "That he realized he didn't *want* to move on. Th-that, after everything, he still loved her. That loving her had been the best thing he'd ever done." She caught her breath. "That he'd rather be lonely in the world where that mattered than happy in the world where it didn't matter at all. Oh, Cecilia, I'm sorry; I didn't know—I swear—I didn't!"

Cecilia caught her breath. She made a strangled sound, something between a laugh and a sob.

Now Morgan took Cecilia's hands in hers.

"Oh, my darling," she murmured. "It's all right—it's all right. They all love, my darling; they all lose; they all forget; even the ones with the prettiest words; even he will forget, with time . . ."

"No!" Cecilia wrenched away from her. "He won't—you don't understand."

"He *will*," Morgan purred. "He loved a dream. He could only love a dream—how can a dream be expected to love, in return? You have nothing to feel guilty over."

She kissed the tears from Cecilia's cheeks.

But it was too late.

Rose understood.

Cecilia loved him. Of course she still loved him. Rose was astounded she had not realized it before. How many times had Cecilia blanched at the mention of Paul's name? Rose saw it all, now—Cecilia tearing up the longed-for divorce papers and throwing them into the flames; Cecilia slamming the box with her wedding ring back into the dresser. Rose had thought—God, she had been so stupid!—that it had been guilt or anger or whatever strange perversity had always made Cecilia do whatever it was she least wanted to do, at the moment she least wanted to do it. Now it was clear. Cecilia loved Paul—she had always loved Paul—in that desperate, destructive way that only Cecilia could.

Nobody said anything, the rest of the boat ride home.

When they arrived, at last, on the dock, the moon still high and silvery above them, Cecilia went into the house without a word. A few discordant bars echoed from the piano.

"Let her be," Morgan said, when a tearful Jenny tried to follow her. "It will all seem better in the morning." She put her fingers to Jenny's cheek. "I promise."

"Come on, old girl." Cassidy put his hand on Jenny's back. "No harm done. There's only eight million people in this city, after all."

The others filed upstairs. Rose remained in the doorway, watching Cecilia hunched over the piano. She waited a moment on the threshold. She steadied herself. The blow was less immediate now; now Rose could feel, mingled with her pity, a new kind of pain.

She went over to the piano. She kept her voice soft.

"What are you playing?"

Cecilia didn't answer for a moment. Her fingers kept moving under her.

"You know," she said at last. "I played this for Paul, the night we met. In the music building at St. Dunstan's. 'Guinevere's Lament,' I called it."

"From your opera?"

"My opera," Cecilia echoed her. Her voice was hollow. "My great, unfinished opera. My magnum opus." She scoffed. "Just something else I couldn't see through."

"You love him."

It wasn't a question.

Cecilia played a few more bars.

"I really thought," she said. "I thought—if I just *leaped*. If we just leaped, straight onto the other side. If we did something we couldn't undo. I thought the feeling would finally stop, you know? The fever. The black dog. I thought—*if we could only decide that this, this* is the rest of our lives. I was going to read every book in his library. I was going to finish my opera. I was going to be the kind of person who knows how to keep a promise. And he was *good*, Paul. No, not just good. He was wonderful." She hit a false note; she started over. "For the first time I thought, *finally,*

finally, someone as crazy as I am. Someone who wanted the grail as badly as I did."

Rose put a hand on Cecilia's shoulder.

"The problem is," Cecilia went on, "you always *can* undo things. Even if you don't want to. Even if, more than anything in the world, you want not to want to. The moment we got back to the apartment, after the wedding was over, I remember thinking—so clearly—*my God, you've ruined this poor man's life.* I knew I *would* run, eventually, or, worse, that I'd make him so miserable by not running. He'd realize who he married. *What* he married. He thought he'd gotten poetry and paladins and he'd wound up with a depressive mess who can't even do her own dishes!" She slammed the cover down.

"Of course, he'd never do a thing about it. Paul would stick with me— no matter what I did, no matter what a mess I made of things, no matter how much he hated me. He'd go on loving me, loving me *on principle*, be- cause he'd made a promise and he was going to stick to it, no matter what, until one of us died! I could stand it if he left me, I thought. I've been left before. But that I couldn't stand. Being the occasion of the Martyrdom of St. Paul!"

"He's not a saint, Cecilia!" Rose said it more roughly than she meant to. "He's not a martyr. He's just a *person*. That's all."

A sad smile flickered across Cecilia's face.

"Maybe," she said. "That's worse."

"You could go back—" Rose forced herself to say it before she could think better of it. "If you wanted."

Cecilia turned back to the piano.

"I can't go back," she said. "I *won't*."

"Why not?"

"Because," Cecilia said, "I made a promise. To Morgan. To the others. Because I'm useful here. Because I'm needed. Because I've never made a vow in my life I didn't break, and if I break this one, too, then I'm the same wreck of a person I always have been. And *nothing*, nothing about this place mattered at all."

She looked so frail, there in the lamplight. You could almost believe she was still sixteen.

"Don't feel sorry for me, Rosie," Cecilia went on. "Really, don't. I'm happy here—at least, I'm as happy as I'll ever be. I do good things here. The others—they're kind. They're good, even. And we have each other." She smiled up at Rose. "It's like old times—isn't it?"

"You're sure?"

Cecilia hesitated.

"Sometimes," she said, "I let myself think—if it had only been different. If *I'd* only been different. If I'd asked him to dinner that first night. If we'd gotten to know each other, that way, the normal way. If I hadn't thought of the whole thing as some great, romantic experiment." She shook her head. "But I couldn't have done it, like that. *He* couldn't have done it, like that. It was what we loved about each other. It's what drove us both out of our minds." She steadied herself.

"It doesn't matter," she said. "What's done is done."

A small, bitter smile escaped her lips.

"It's funny, Rosie," she said. "If you think about it."

"What is?"

"I've finally done something," Cecilia said, "that I can't undo."

She turned back to the piano. She began, once more, to play.

"Good night, Rosie," she said. "I'm all right, really. Let's not think any more about it."

Rose left her there, still playing. She was still playing when Rose undressed in their bedroom. She was still playing—those same halting bars—when Rose slipped into the bed; when she closed her eyes; when she woke, five hours later, at dawn.

CHAPTER FIFTEEN

Fall grew cold.

Cecilia returned to rehearsals the next afternoon. She went out on a cabaret two days later. She played as beautifully—maybe more beautifully—than she had before. She swept the parlor floors. She chopped the dinner onions. She weeded the garden. If you didn't know her, the way Rose knew her, you would have thought her happy.

It will pass, Rose told herself. *Let it pass.*

Cecilia had said it herself—hadn't she? She was fickle—she had always been fickle; if she ran to Paul, on a whim, who was to say she wouldn't regret it a week later; hadn't she run to and away from so many others? Maybe Cecilia's love for Paul was like her love for the falconer or the writer or the poetess on the houseboat: something that would burn itself out and disintegrate into ash. Sometimes Rose hoped it would. Better, she told herself, that Paul go back to Maine or to England; better that he move on, get therapy, learn to love the way ordinary people love, and not people in books. Better, she told herself, that he remain somewhere where she'd never have to see him again, where he could not make her remember the sound of the Scottish fiddle or the smell of whiskey on their breath.

—

"It was an awful coincidence, of course," Jenny said to Rose on the veranda one crisp afternoon. "I can't imagine what she must be feeling right now."

The wind was blowing chestnut burrs across the pathway.

"But I guess that's the thing with love. With *that* kind of love, I mean." Inside, Cecilia played another clanging variation on her aria. "It can't last. It makes people too selfish."

Her eyes fell on Cassidy, pruning the primroses in the garden. He gave them a genial wave. Jenny waved back at him, a little too eagerly. She saw Rose notice, and flushed crimson.

"At least," Jenny went on carefully, "that's what Morgan says."

"You don't agree?"

Jenny hesitated.

"I think," she said at last, "that we're lucky to have found our kind of love."

She sipped her coffee.

"At least you know," she said, "it's something that can actually last."

Rose thought, once more, of Sunny's.

"You're probably right," Rose said.

Of course Jenny *was* right. What they had at the Avalon was worth whatever sacrifices a person had to make to hold on to it. How could anything, back in that other world, compare to those moments when you were out on the open water, breathing in the stars and the lights and the places where you could not tell the stars and lights apart; those moments when you fell in love all over again with the moon and the waves and—if you looked close enough—the waves in the moon? How could any life hold up to the moments when you looked into the bewildered eyes of a stranger and made them believe that the waves were full of angels?

Only, among those moments, there were now discomfiting ones: like false notes in a melody. The moments Rose was on deck drawing a visitor, for the fifth or tenth time that month, and suddenly she felt her mind wandering to a vague memory from her old life or an item from

Thomas's grocery list. The moments Rose, repainting the yellow side-boards of the house, started to take less care over keeping clean and even lines. The moments, even, that Morgan's waltzes and Morgan's ballads and Morgan's arias started to run together, until you could no longer tell the sparrows from the swallows, or the ghosts from the girls. They were rare, of course. They passed quickly. Still, Rose had never expected them to happen at all.

—

"It's time," Cassidy said, in the garden one afternoon. "You can feel it in the air. When we all get a little too used to seeing ourselves through our own eyes."

"What does that mean?"

"What it always means," Cassidy said. "We need a better audience."

Her name was Jane. Cecilia had been the one to find her: wandering colt-legged in fishnets and a pink wig around the East Village at three in the morning, after a live screening of *The Rocky Horror Picture Show.* Her first cabaret, she was so overcome by Robin's song about a boy who sails to the moon in a paper plane that she ran up before he had finished and threw her arms around his neck.

"My whole life," she told Rose, in a single breathless monologue, as Rose tried to get her to hold still long enough to sketch the way her pigtails rippled over her shoulders, "I've dreamed of people like you. I never doubted—not for a second—that you existed."

She was seventeen. Her parents were divorced. Neither one of them, she'd always known, had really wanted her; now neither one of them took much notice of her, except to remind her to study for her SATs and that good colleges cared about extracurriculars and that the connections you made there formed the basis of the rest of your adult life. Jane didn't mind. Her life—she told Rose, with shining eyes—had always been best lived in her own head.

"I've had wildly passionate love affairs," she chirped, "and the most *devastating* adventures. All without leaving the Upper West Side."

Maybe, she said, it was just that she'd been born in the wrong century. In the old days—Jane wasn't sure when, exactly, but maybe after the Middle Ages and before the Second World War—there were so many people like her, people who felt too deeply and cared too violently and were willing to die for causes people in the modern era hardly understood, because nobody, she raged, had convictions any longer. But it wasn't so bad, being born in the wrong century, because it meant that all you had to do was curl up in a corner of the upstairs room of the used bookstore on Broadway and 74th Street and you could magic yourself into the right one.

"But of course"—Jane caught her breath at last—"it was nothing, *nothing*, compared to this!"

Everybody agreed that it was the best cabaret they'd done in months. Maybe even the best one since Yvette Thornbill, or since the first they'd done for Rose herself. They sent Jane a clue for her second cabaret the very next morning. Rose deposited the next envelope—at Cecilia's suggestion—at the foot of Charlotte Canda's grave.

That day even Cecilia seemed cheerful.

"Poor girl," she said. "I know exactly how she feels."

"But of course," Cassidy said, when Rose remarked on the Avalon's renewed enthusiasm. "That's always the way. Or haven't you figured it out by now?"

"Figured what out?"

"We need them," he said. "As much as they need us."

The days after Jane's cabarets, Rose could still hope. Those days she could still make herself believe that everything was as it had been during those phantasmagoric days of early spring and summer; that Rebecca had been wrong; that Rose's distractions were momentary; that the Avalon would last forever. She could believe that Cecilia's heart would settle, once more, to rest.

Only, Cecilia stopped eating.

She was no less assiduous in her chores. She was diligent at rehearsals. At cabarets she never missed a note. But there was a pallor in all her movements, now, as if she were a ghost who lived among them. Behind her smiles, at every cabaret, was a shadow.

"I'm fine, Rosie," Cecilia insisted. "Really. You don't have to worry about me. It's just the weather. That's all."

Rose stopped believing her.

—

At last, when the leaves in the apple tree had turned crimson, and the last of the summer flowers lay desiccated in the garden path, Rose went to Morgan's room for tea.

"I need to talk to you," she said, as Robin set down the trays before them. "About Cecilia."

"I was wondering," Morgan said quietly, "when you would come to me."

Rose laid it all out as simply and straightforwardly as she could. Cecilia was—she was clear about this point—devoted to the Avalon; there was no question of her loyalty, or of her commitment to the promise she had made. If nothing was done, Rose knew, Cecilia would remain at the Avalon for the rest of her life.

Morgan listened to Rose.

"Then what," Morgan said, when she had finished, "is so very different—from how it was when you came?"

"She loves him!"

"And what do you want me to do about that, exactly?"

"I don't know," Rose admitted, defeated. "Talk to her? Release her from her promise?"

"There is nothing I could say to help her, even if I wanted to. Her promise was to the Avalon, not to me."

"Then—" Rose spoke wildly. "Couldn't you bring him here?"

"That's impossible."

"I mean, Jenny found him on a raid, didn't she? He came with an invitation. Fair and square," she added, stupidly, as if the Avalon operated on the same rules as a children's game. "She said so herself—he's one of us: he's a seeker; he isn't at home in the world, not really; that's what's so wonderful about him."

"And when your sister tires of him?" Morgan lifted her chin. "Or—just as likely—he tires of her? When he finds that the woman he's dreamed of, for so long, and who has made him suffer so deeply, is within his reach at last—that he can finally take the revenge he doesn't know he wants? Or do you really know so little of love as that?"

"Paul wouldn't take revenge—he's not like that!"

"They're all," Morgan said, "*like that*."

"They love each other," Rose tried one last time.

"And you love him."

Rose froze.

"I saw you, on the boat that day. Do you really think you can hide it from them forever?"

Rose could not summon the strength to deny it.

"If he didn't come to hate her," Morgan went on. "If she didn't come to hate him. Do you really think you wouldn't wind up hating them both? Do you really think he wouldn't wonder—looking at you, side by side, if he hadn't met the wrong sister, at the wrong time? Do you really think— even for a moment—you wouldn't *want* him to wonder?"

"I wouldn't!"

Rose didn't stop to consider whether she meant it.

"You say that now," Morgan said. "But picture the three of you. On the boat. In this house. Loving one another one minute. Despising one another the next. Could I really do that to the others? Could I risk *them*, for the sake of your sister's changeable heart?" Her expression softened. "There's a reason, Rose, why nobody ever falls in love, at the Avalon. That's the world's love, not ours. That kind of love corrodes. And is always corroded. That's the kind of love that brings visitors in tears to us. It's the kind of love we protect people *from*."

"But she's so unhappy!"

"Nobody can be unhappy here," Morgan said, "for very long. She will forget. She will come to see that what she loves is a mirage: a *what might have been*, that's all. She will remember that the world has never been kind to her—and that she has never been kind to it. She's not the first of us to have her doubts. But she will learn, from the others, to forget them. She will pretend, at the cabarets, until one day she feels again the way they do." Her gaze met Rose's. "The way you do."

The hardest part was: Rose still felt it. Even as the moments of distraction became more numerous, and closer together, Rose was still happier than she could ever remember being in New York. Still, when she sat with her easel in the garden, trying to catch the way the leaves looked, at dusk; when Nini came up beside her, to link Rose's arm in hers; when Rebecca closed her eyes and leaned into the microphone, Rose felt so wildly, savagely happy that the thought of leaving the Avalon seemed to her intolerable.

Morgan is right, Rose reminded herself. Morgan was always right. Morgan, who knew everything, who had seen everything, who even now so often seemed as ethereal and unreal to Rose as she had that first night on the boat, had promised that one day Cecilia would suffer less; that this was best for both of them. Rose let herself believe her.

In any case, it didn't matter. Cecilia wouldn't go. Paul wouldn't come. Rose would never grow to hate them. Cecilia grew pale and drawn, and there were dark circles under her eyes most mornings.

"For God's sake, Rosie, just let it go!" she cried, when Rose tried—for the last time—to reach her. "I've got what I deserve, haven't I—and I've made my peace with it—and I can't stand to hear another word from you!"

—

Jane came to the Avalon a second time, and then a third. She did the Charleston with Jenny. She flirted ostentatiously with Ralphie, in the manner of someone who has only ever read in books what flirting might look like. When Nini sang she wept into the folds of Morgan's dress, and when Julius at last brought out his marionettes to tell the tragic story of Tristan and Isolde her face lit up with such ecstatic astonishment that it made the multicolored flames look pale.

"It's more real than real," she breathed into Cecilia's shoulder. "Isn't it?"

Cecilia hesitated. She drew back, looking down at Jane with her old inquisitive stare. Then she smiled and kissed Jane on the cheek.

"It's exactly as real," she said, "as we need it to be."

"What did I tell you?" Cassidy said, as Jane staggered at dawn onto the pier at Domino Park. "We'll have to put another bunk in Jenny's room, at this rate. You know she plays cello?"

"You mean we might keep her permanently?" Rose rounded on him in surprise. She had reveled in Jane's cabarets; nevertheless, it had not occurred to her that Jane might be asked to stay. "She's a child!"

"Eighteen in two weeks." Cassidy shrugged. "Legally, we're in the clear. And it's not exactly like her parents have been keeping the closest eye on her, up to now."

"Still . . ." Rose faltered. "That's—I mean, that's young, isn't it?"

"Robin was eighteen, too, wasn't he?"

"That's different—his parents kicked him out!"

Cassidy shrugged.

"She's better off here with us," Cassidy said. "Besides—" His smile was sardonic. "We could use a cellist."

—

Jane's fourth cabaret came in the height of autumn. The leaves had started to fall from the apple trees; the garden was full of asters and chrysanthemums. Jane and Jenny lay on their backs, on the deck, and compared constellations.

"Is it true?" Jane let her arms fall over Rose's shoulders at the easel. "Are they really letting me stay? Cassidy said they might, next time. Once I'm eighteen."

"Ask me no questions"—Rose had gotten so good at evasion now— "and I'll tell you no lies." She added color to Jane's cheeks.

"Rose!"

Jane pursed her lips into a mock pout.

"If you're very good," Rose said, no less lightly. "And you eat all your chocolates. And you drink all your champagne." She added a few more tendrils to Jane's pigtails.

"Rose!"

"Do you *want* to stay forever, dear heart?" Rose tried not to betray her wavering.

"Of course I do! More than anything."

"And you wouldn't—miss what you'd left behind? What you could have had?"

"Like what?"

"College, say, or . . ."

"Not for a second!" Jane laughed. "What would I miss in *college*? Hooking up at frat parties? Going to *recruitment events* for jobs I don't want?"

"Love?" Rose put flecks into Jane's eyes.

Jane scoffed. "I don't believe in love," she said. "I mean, I don't believe in *consummated* love."

She threw back her head. She said it with such conviction.

"Why not, dear heart?"

"It never lives up to what you think it'll be. It's why all the greatest love stories are the unconsummated ones. That's why I've decided that I want to dedicate my life to Art."

"Hear hear!" called Cassidy, as he passed across the dance floor, with Rebecca in his arms. "Beauty must be protected!"

"But—" Rose waited until Cassidy was out of earshot. "Wouldn't somebody miss you?"

Jane fell silent.

"Well . . . ," she began. "Maybe at first. But not for long." She smiled brightly. "I haven't *done* anything yet, you see. To make me worth missing."

She let Julius wheel her into his arms.

Rose finished the portrait. She drew back. She considered it with displeasure. Something, she thought, was wrong with it. Jane did not look like Jane.

It took Rose another moment to realize why.

She had made Jane look exactly like Cecilia.

That night, when they got back to the house, and the bedroom door had been firmly shut behind them, Rose took Cecilia into her arms. She held her tightly, ferociously; she clung to her, the way you might cling to driftwood to keep from drowning.

"Rosie!" Cecilia looked up at her in surprise. "What's wrong?"

Rose didn't say anything.

CHAPTER SIXTEEN

They scheduled Jane's journey with no return. Jenny and Cassidy worked out the clue, their heads bent together in the parlor, before the fireplace they now kept lit. It would lead Jane to the Metropolitan Museum of Art, that Friday, at half past five: to the portrait of Joan of Arc on the second floor, the one where she casts her eyes upward, with rapture and terror, toward the angels who have come to tell her what to do next. Someone would meet her there, walk her one final time through the city, bring her to the boat, where Thomas would be waiting. They would—Morgan had decided—do one final cabaret, to welcome her: in the garden, while the last of the fall flowers bloomed, with candles and bowers and Ralphie's bird-painted scrim fluttering in the breeze. It was what they had always dreamed of doing, in New Orleans.

Rose would be the one to bring her in.

"It's only fitting," said Morgan, when she informed Rose. "She trusts you particularly. You understand her."

Rose did not sleep that night, either. She lay awake, listening to the sounds of Cecilia's piano, echoing up from the parlor.

—

On Wednesday, the boat went out for a raid. Rose and Robin were paired together.

Thomas assigned them to Red Hook.

"No switching," Thomas said, when Rose tried to protest. "This rota's giving me enough of a headache as it is. Anyway, Sunny's is always good for finding lonely hearts."

It was the first time Rose had been back to Sunny's since her night there with Paul. When she entered, her knees buckled under her. It was just as she'd remembered it: the Christmas lights, the painted sign, and the statue of St. Francis in the garden. The air still smelled of barrel wood and mulled wine. The same man with the metal detector was displaying his treasures at the bar.

"You okay?" Robin turned to her.

"I'm fine," Rose said. "Just—stomach trouble, that's all."

She took a seat at the booth overlooking the garden where she and Paul had sat the first night they had come. She wondered if this was the booth Paul had sat in the night Jenny had come to him; whether he had known, at first, who she was, or only hoped; whether he had gone searching or if the Avalon had found him, the way they always found the lost and the lonely and the ones who took things too seriously.

The band was playing "Wayfaring Stranger" in the back room.

Rose decided.

"I'm not feeling well," she told Robin. "I need some fresh air. Cover for me?"

"But we're not supposed to—"

"Just a couple minutes," Rose said. "Please."

Rose walked, steadily, out the front of the bar.

Then she ran.

She tore up Conover; she turned right at Dikeman; she dashed across Van Brunt so recklessly that a delivery driver had to screech to a brake at the crosswalk. She pressed the buzzer for apartment number 4. Her heart was pounding so furiously in her ears that she could not even hear it ring.

Maybe, she thought, *he is not even here*; maybe he had moved, gone back to England, or maybe he was out, on a date, because only an idiot would still be pining for Cecilia or the Avalon, after that scene on the pier. She rang a second time. There was no answer.

I will go back, Rose told herself. *I will get on the boat; it will be as if nothing has happened.* She was almost relieved.

Then the front door opened.

"Rose?"

Paul was staring at her in astonishment. He looked older, thinner, than Rose had remembered. He still had the same searching eyes.

"What in God's name are you doing here?"

"Hurry," Rose said. "We don't have much time."

They barreled up four flights of stairs. Rose locked the door, panting, behind her.

"Friday," she gasped. "The Metropolitan Museum. By the portrait of Joan of Arc, on the second floor—five fifteen—*sharp*—you can't be late."

"What?"

"It's the only time—" Rose caught her breath. "I'll be alone—I'll figure out what to do with Thomas."

"What do you mean, the only time?"

"The only time we can get you on the boat!"

For a moment there was anger in his eyes. Then he softened.

"Rose." It was a sigh. "Rose, what are you doing here?"

"She loves you!" Rose spoke without thinking. "She loves you—and she won't leave; she's made a promise to them, Paul, and she's stubborn; and she's afraid—God, she's terrified, but she's always loved you, Paul; she's loved you from the beginning; that's why she left."

"For God's sake, Rose!" Paul looked so immeasurably tired. "What do you want from me?"

Rose fell silent.

"To try again," she said, at last. "To come to the Avalon. To see for yourself—or to make *them* see." She wasn't even sure which one she wanted. "You have to see each other again," she said. "Face to face."

"Why?"

"I don't know!" Rose grew desperate. "You just—have to, that's all."

Paul sank down onto the futon.

"I can't keep doing this, Rose."

"Paul—*please*?"

"Why? So we can keep up the canard that there's such a thing as *true love*? So I can make a fool of myself once again?"

Rose wasn't sure if she'd ever seen him this angry.

"You don't know what it was like, Rose! God knows, I tried when I went back to Maine. And I couldn't bear it. I kept thinking of her—of you." Rose's head jerked up. But Paul had sprung to his feet without looking at her. "Of that bloody boat! And so I once more blew up my professional life, and I came back in midsummer, and I tried to work out what to do, with the wreckage of my life." He paced the room. "I became one of those sad old men who closes out the bar, every night, and I don't even know, myself, if I was looking for her or looking for you or looking for *them* or just looking to drink myself to death and forget the whole thing. And then, once again, I'm standing like a laughingstock on a pier, watching the two of you sail merrily along, without me, to fairyland or never-never land or wherever it is you keep going, where I'm too much of a fool to find the way!"

He was standing so close to Rose now. His breath smelled like bourbon.

Rose was close enough to kiss him.

For a moment, she wanted to.

It would be so easy. She could take his face in her hands; she could pull him to her; she could tell him so many true things about her love and her loyalty, and omit the true things about the changes that had taken place in Cecilia; she could leave Cecilia to the Avalon, where she was happy enough, or at least almost happy; she could stoke the embers of whatever complicated thing had burned between them, until they kindled to love; maybe there would be a time, two years from now, or ten, when they could pretend that it had always been that way, that she had always been the one he'd really loved.

Only: Rose was so tired of lying.

The Paul she had loved—strange, stubborn Paul; saintly Paul; Paul, who was maddening and confounding and infuriating all at once—had been Cecilia's Paul, who loved too long, and too strangely, and too well.

"For God's sake, Rose," Paul said. "We both know exactly how this is going to end!"

He was right, of course. Almost certainly he was right. People didn't change, no matter how much you wanted them to; probably one morning Paul would wake up to find the bed empty and the window open, as if Cecilia had been alchemized into air; probably there was no such thing as true love, in New York or Maine or England or anywhere else, and the best that you could hope for was a minute or two of forgetting, and then a lifetime of remembering that there had been a time when you forgot, and then one day you stopped remembering and forgetting altogether. Rose would have been a fool to believe anything else. Cecilia knew it, too, deep down. Hadn't she said at Bemelmans that life was probably a tragedy when you came down to it, and whatever Cecilia had promised Paul, under some cherry trees, some rainbow-sheened spring, whatever *have* or *hold*, let alone *love*, wasn't something any human being could ever live up to, *God, even Paul couldn't do it.* God knew how Rose ever would, and even if Rose looked into Paul's eyes, the way she looked into the eyes of so many strangers, now; even if she fixed her gaze and curled her lips and let the glitter shimmer on her cheekbones and said *but darling, the story keeps going, you never know how it's going to turn out, that's the thrill of it,* all that really meant was that maybe, sometimes, people managed to keep the promises they made.

"She's your wife, Paul."

He didn't answer her.

Ten minutes had passed since Rose had left Robin.

"I have to go," she said. "Five fifteen. Friday. St. Joan. Don't be late."

Rose drew up on her tiptoes. She kissed him on the cheek. She did not look at him again as she sprinted out the door.

Rose rushed down the stairs. She fumbled with the doorknob. She bolted into the night air. She was grateful for the chill. She tried to still her heartbeat.

"You lied to me."

Rose started.

Robin was standing before her.

"I knew it. I knew you were lying . . ."

"Robin—" she began.

"Who lives there? Was it your fiancé?"

"No—Robin—listen."

"We have rules for a reason!"

"Listen." Rose tried to buy time to think of an excuse. "Listen, Robin, it's complicated."

"Complicated? What's complicated about it?" Robin's voice notched higher. He sounded like a child again. "You missed him. You wanted to see him. To give him *one last kiss* or whatever. You wanted to have it both ways—you think you *get* to have it both ways."

"That's not . . ." Rose stopped herself. The truth, she thought, was so much worse. "Look—I'm sorry, Robin. It was a moment of weakness, okay? There were things I needed to say, and now I've said them, and it won't happen again!"

His lower lip was quivering.

"Listen—Robin—please, *please* don't tell Morgan."

"You want to lie to her?"

"Not lie—" Rose fumbled. "Just—don't say anything."

"That's lying!"

"It's not."

"We don't lie to each other!"

As if, Rose thought, it was so simple. She felt suddenly, savagely jealous of Robin. In her anger she forgot her pity. Ever since he'd come to the Avalon, they'd all made it so easy for him. He'd never had to make choices. He'd never have to wonder if their happiness was worth Lucinda

Luquer, floating in the bayou; if it was worth Jane's parents, frantic with fear and regret; if it was worth Francesca, with a sign in Tompkins Square Park.

"And you think Morgan's never lied to you?"

It came out before Rose could think better of it.

For a moment he was silent. When he spoke again his voice was small and low. "What are you talking about, Rose?"

"Francesca." She spoke quickly, as though if she slowed down the guilt would clog her throat. "Morgan never called her. She never spoke to her. She never gave her the chance—"

"That's not true!"

"I swear to you, Robin; I met her! When I was trying to find you. She's been looking for you."

"She hasn't!" Robin was ashen. "She gave up; she changed her mind . . ."

"She's been trying to find you this whole time! She tried to get me to help her! She stayed in Cypress Hill as long as she could, hoping you'd come back—she had a girlfriend in Philadelphia who wanted her to come stay; she wouldn't at first . . ."

Robin's face grew hard with recognition.

"Julia."

Rose barreled on.

"Morgan didn't tell you. She didn't want to burden you with the guilt, if you'd stayed; she didn't want you to have to choose."

Robin looked up at her. His tears, under the streetlights, had turned his eyes quicksilver.

"I see," he said. He spoke so calmly. He avoided her gaze.

"Robin—I'm sorry."

She put a useless hand on his shoulder. He wrenched it away.

Robin did not speak the whole way back to the boat.

He did not speak as they sailed home.

—

On Thursday night, they did a cabaret for a stranger. Robin claimed food poisoning and stayed home. To Rose's relief he seemed to have said nothing to Morgan at all. Rose quelled her guilt. She smiled, as ever, when Thomas played his flute; she smiled when she stretched out her arms, so extravagantly, and told a woman who'd been catfished by a married man that the moonlight made her look like a Nereid. She let the music wash over her, one final time, the music that even now, *God, even now*, made her feel like every goose bump on her skin had a corresponding star.

She let Morgan kiss her good night. She listened to the rising and the falling of Cecilia's breaths. She prayed that her choice was the right one.

—

Friday finally came. Thomas took Rose out on the boat in the late afternoon. She watched, more closely than ever before, the turns they took, under each successive bridge; she marked down the islands and the elevated trains.

"There's always something in the air," Thomas said, as the boat made its way through open water. "On the nights we bring someone in. Sometimes I think that's what keeps us going." He chewed, absentmindedly, on his pipe. "What keeps *her* going."

"Morgan?"

"Sometimes," he said, "I marvel at how lucky we all are."

"That she found you?" Rose pushed down her self-reproach.

"That she keeps believing. For all of us. When we can't—or won't."

"She *really* never doubts?" It would be so much easier, Rose thought, if she did.

"Not for a moment. Not even once."

"Are you sure?"

"You forget," Thomas said. "I knew Morgan before she was Morgan."

Rose was so surprised she almost forgot to keep her eyes on the route. "So—there *was* a before."

Even now there was a part of Rose that still believed the Avalon had always been there.

Thomas grunted.

"Who was she?"

"That's not my story to tell," he said. "Some things—Rose—they're sacred." He kept his hand on the steering wheel. "All I'll tell you is this. The first time I knew her, she was barely older than Jane. Always hanging around—" He stopped himself. "The places I hung around, with ten years on her. She was uncanny then, too. Had that same funny way of looking at you: like she knew your soul better than she knew her own."

"And the music? Did she write songs like that—then?"

Thomas made a noncommittal noise. "She wanted to. *More than anything in the world*, she said. *More than anything outside it*. She had talent—genius, even. I told her to be careful. The way of knowing doesn't come cheap, I said. You mess around with people's souls—you'd best be prepared to lose your own. She told me she'd keep that in mind. I lost track of her, after that. Twenty years, I lost track of her."

The Wonder Wheel appeared again before them. Rose tried to forget that it would be the last time she saw it like this.

"I had my own soul to throw away," Thomas said. "Made piles of money. Made every sacrifice you'd expect to make for it. And then I was a middle-aged Midas with an ex-wife who despised me and two children who wouldn't look at me, and for good reason. And then she found me, a second time.

"I don't know the details, of those twenty years. Morgan's never told me, and I know better than to ask. I don't know what she saw or sacrificed, what bargains she made, to be able to write songs the way she did. All I know is that, when I saw her again, across the bar, on the lowest night of my life, she showed me a song that shattered every lie I'd ever told myself about myself. All I know is that one night, walking alone with her through the streets of San Francisco, meant more to me than the past twenty years combined. All I know is that if it hadn't been the Avalon it'd have been a swan dive off the Golden Gate Bridge. And believe me when I say it came damn near close."

The boat slackened to a stop near Sunset Park. He handed her a wad of cash, a MetroCard.

"Me," he said. "I serve. That's all I want to do. I run the boat. I buy the beans. I put up the cash. I deal with lawyers and taxes and LLCs. I watched that girl in New Orleans slip under the water. So Morgan doesn't have to. So she can keep the magic, always—and never have to remember there's a world outside. It's the only thing I can ever do for her. It doesn't repay a tenth of what she did for me."

He cleared his throat. He hoisted Rose onto land. She could not look him in the face.

"I'll see you tonight," he said.

—

It was already five by the time Rose made it to the Metropolitan Museum.

She took a seat at the bench, by the painting of St. Joan. She waited.

He will come, she told herself. *He is the Paul you remember. He is the Paul you love. He will come.*

She still didn't know if she wanted him to.

At ten past five, Paul came into the gallery. He said nothing. He took a seat beside her. He reached out, without looking at her, and took her hand.

Rose and Paul walked out into the night. As they descended the museum steps, Rose saw Jane darting past her toward the entrance. Her face was flushed. Her smile was the most beautiful thing Rose had ever seen.

I will never know, Rose thought, *if I have saved her or destroyed her.*

Rose and Paul took the subway back to Sunset Park. She explained what she could stand to explain.

"I still think," he said, "that I've lost my mind."

"You probably have," Rose said.

Rose and Paul got off the train at 53rd Street. They waited, until it was almost time for the pickup. Then, at last, they walked toward the water. Thomas was standing by the boat. He was smoking his pipe.

Paul waited in the shadows, as he and Rose had planned.

Rose approached.

Thomas looked up.

"Bust," Rose said. "She didn't show."

Thomas's mustache twitched. His shoulders slackened.

"Shame," he said. "I really thought she was one of us."

"You never know," Rose said. "Maybe she got spooked. Or her parents found out."

Thomas blew out a cloud of smoke.

"You never know," he said. "About anyone."

"Do you mind?" Rose gestured at the pipe. "I've never smoked one."

He considered her. He nodded.

"Come on," he said. He took a few steps toward her. Rose led him, so casually, to the other end of the pier, so that he had his back to the boat. She had him light the pipe for her, show her how to inhale, how to hold the smoke in her mouth, and how to blow out rings. Out of the corner of her eye she could see Paul, slipping through the shadows. Paul boarding the boat.

"I don't look forward," Thomas said, "to breaking the news."

"We should drink first," Rose said, with forced gaiety. "To cheer us up. I think there's a couple bottles on the boat."

He hesitated.

"Why the hell not," he said at last. He looked out over the night.

"I'll just go get them."

Rose had hoped Thomas would not turn back, at least not until the darkness had shrouded his face. But as the boat pulled away from the dock, Rose saw it all. The shock, at first, and the understanding, then resignation. He didn't call after them. He just stared at her, with a wounded, animal look. It wasn't even angry. It would have been easier if it were.

It was a look, instead, of exhaustion, almost of relief: as if the end he had always expected had come at last, and at last he could rest.

He put his hands in his pockets. He leaned back on his heels. He kept his eyes on Rose.

He stepped back into the shadows.

Rose steered the boat into the darkness. Eight months now, she had watched Thomas do it; eight months, she had come to know the ways and turns of the water.

"So—" Paul said, at last. "This is the boat."

He walked, dazed, across the deck. He fingered the velvet of the divans.

"How did they do the flames?"

"Wires."

"And the flowers?"

"Paper. Motors."

"And the music?"

Rose didn't answer him.

—

Rose took them down to Coney Island. She rounded them past Brighton Beach, then the parkland of Sheepshead Bay. They crossed under the Marine Parkway Bridge. Starboard, Rose could make out the weed-strewn beaches of the Rockaways. They passed underneath the elevated train at Broad Channel, the uninhabited marshland beyond, the industrial piers. Then at last, she saw it, the little yellow house, with its blue veranda, with its fast-fading garden.

It might have been any other little house, any other garden.

Except for all the lights.

They were waiting, all of them, in the garden. They were all in white. They all held candles. Rose's breath caught in her throat.

They had rehearsed it, of course. Rose had known what to expect. But it had been daylight then, and Rose had been distracted with worry. It had not sunk in that their dresses, in the autumn wind, would look like the ripples of a river; that their lights, against the ink of sky, would look like falling stars. It had not sunk in that the false flowers, among the real ones, would make the garden look like it had in summer, or like it never had in summer, but how Rose would remember summers, always, from now on; that the color-changing flames would illuminate the pathway and the scrim Ralphie had painted and Jenny's trapeze among the beeches and Rose's easel, waiting for her by the blackberry bush, and Julius's marionettes, their wires invisible, dancing in each other's arms on the veranda, and under the apple trees, like there were so many more of them; like there was a whole world.

The boat drew nearer. Now Rose could hear them.

The wind blows out of the gates of the day, they sang, all together.

The wind blows over the lonely of heart

And the lonely of heart is withered away

While the fairies dance in the place apart

Paul stiffened beside her. He gripped the railing so tightly his knuckles had turned white. He closed his eyes. He breathed the music in. As if it held him, too.

The boat brushed against the dock. Rose could see them waiting: Nini holding the champagne tray, and Cassidy and Julius sprawled out over iron chairs, and Robin and Rebecca on either side of Morgan, enthroned in a chair at the top of the little hill that led to the house, the silk train from her gown, which Nini had lengthened, rippling halfway down the garden path. Cecilia stood, among the marionettes, her hair down to her shoulders.

"My God," Paul murmured, at Rose's side.

They had never looked more glorious.

Rose tried not to wonder what it would have looked like for Jane.

The boat came to a stop at last.

Rose led Paul onto the dock.

Cecilia was the first to see him. She started; she gasped; she froze, with her hand to her mouth. Her eyes darted from Rose to Paul to Rose again, as if confirming to herself that they were real.

"Darling!" Jenny was pirouetting toward them. *"We're so happy you finally—"*

She stopped. She saw Paul. Her mouth fell open.

"I—"

She looked back in confusion. Morgan had already sprung to her feet. Her eyes blazed. Her whole body tensed, like a watch spring. Rebecca followed like a shadow.

Morgan stepped, slowly, deliberately, down the garden path. Her train trailed after her. Her gaze did not waver. The others had fallen silent; Rose could feel it dawn upon them, one by one: the panic, and the betrayal. She bore their stares. She kept walking, past Jenny, down the dock, toward the garden, where Morgan was coming to meet her, Paul rigid at her side.

Then Morgan was before her—close enough to strike Rose, or to kiss her. Morgan's face was a mask. Her eyes were inscrutable. She took them both in. She searched Rose's face, as if in Rose's eyes or Rose's expression she might find the answer she was looking for, which Rose herself could barely have put into words, as if something about Rose's shame-flushed cheeks or parted lips or the tears she would not let come into her eyes could explain why Rose had betrayed her, why she had defiled this place that had embraced her, that had loved her, that had asked nothing from her but to give up the rest of the world.

Morgan turned to Paul. Decision crossed her face. She took a single, deep breath. She drew herself up to her full height.

Then she stretched out her arms.

"My dear one," she murmured. "My dear, dear lost one."

She seized his hands.

"We've been waiting for you," she said.

At first nobody moved. They all watched, dumbfounded, as Morgan pulled him toward the garden, as a fierce, determined smile spread across Morgan's face.

"We must have music! Lights!" she cried. "Nini, get our guest a glass of champagne!"

Nini spluttered, for a moment, with the tray.

Paul understood at the same time Rose did.

There was one rule at the Avalon. Rose knew this. You did not break the spell; you did not pierce the veil; you held on to the magic you had made, for as long as you could. You kept the music going; you let the champagne flow; you danced until your feet blistered, and then you kept on dancing, because if you stopped, only then would you feel the pain. The cabaret had begun; the guest was here; the Avalon would go on, as long as the world would let it.

Ralphie turned to the piano.

He began to play.

It was a light ragtime—jovial and buoyant—and as he played, Jenny scampered to Paul's side and kissed his cheek; Cassidy raised his glass in a toast; Julius bowed from the waist. Even Rebecca sprang to action, spreading out blankets on a chair and bidding Paul to sit as he looked around, flabbergasted.

"You're very lucky, old chap," Cassidy said. "We've got quite the show for you tonight."

"A corker!" Julius cut in.

"Nini's got a ballad that will knock your socks to smithereens!"

Only Cecilia did not move.

She was still standing, among the dancing marionettes, watching them. The shock on her face had faded now, replaced by disbelieving joy.

Nini poured Paul a glass of champagne.

He took it, with shaking hands.

He downed it in a single gulp.

Now Cassidy was at the microphone; now Cassidy was announcing the *carnival of lost souls, the priory of drifters*; now Ralphie was starting the flourish that would introduce Madame Nini and the "Ballad of a Rover's Homecoming"; now Nini was setting down the champagne tray on the veranda and making her way toward the piano.

Cecilia was already there.

She caught Nini's eye. A timid smile crept across her lips. She put a hand on Ralphie's shoulder.

He rose. He turned to look at her. His smile, too, was gentle, and sad, and slow. It was a smile of parting. He kissed her on the cheek. He whispered something inaudible into her ear.

Then he beckoned her to the bench.

He joined Nini, standing halfway along the path. He put an arm around her shoulders. He watched. He waited.

Cecilia said nothing. She sank down onto the bench. Her hands, too, were trembling. She turned—for a moment—to Paul, and fixed him with that stare of hers that even now made Rose think of some medieval mystic, or a holy fool.

Then she turned back to the piano. She began to play.

It was not one of Morgan's. It was too gentle, too simple, the melody too straightforward, as if it were something Cecilia had hummed absent-mindedly to herself, on a walk or in the shower, and had only later put into notes.

Rose had heard it before, but only ever in pieces. She had heard echoes, fragments, bars worked and reworked until the notes ran together. She had never heard it finished until now.

It was "Guinevere's Lament."

Cecilia's song was about a queen who has erred against the king. She loves him—she does not understand the way she loves him; she has chosen another knight, replaced his love with a worse one, something foolish, something simple and straightforward the way the chansons have told her love must be. She has gone away in shame to a nunnery; in her cloister things are at last clear to her. She knows better than to think he will come back to her. There are laws, she sings, and there are rules, and you must pay for what you take, and you must bear what you have broken.

Have we not heard the bridegroom is so sweet, Cecilia sang.

O, let us in, tho' late, to kiss his feet!

No, no, too late! Ye cannot enter now.

Rose could not take her eyes off Paul.

He was staring at Cecilia with astonishment, with wonder.

As if he had seen her dead and come back to life.

Cecilia kept singing. Her voice was low and sweet; it was the sound of autumn or of salt pools or of the last embers on a fire. It was the sound of midnight walks, through a near-empty city.

The others did not move. Nobody made a sound.

Rose turned to look at Morgan's face.

There was no trace, any longer, of anger. Instead, she was watching Cecilia, transfixed.

As if, Rose thought, she were a visitor, come to a cabaret for the very first time.

Cecilia played the last notes of the song. She kept her eyes on the keys, as if she did not dare to look up. She remained like that until Paul put his hand upon her shoulder.

Finally, she looked up at him.

"I'm told," he said, "there would be dancing."

Now Ralphie was at the piano; now he was playing one of the old, slow songs; now the marionettes were dancing; now the candles had all been set down; and now they were all dancing, too, Jenny and Cassidy, now Rebecca and Julius, now Robin and Nini, now Paul and Cecilia, under the light of the moon. They swayed, and they pulled each other closer, and Cassidy pressed his fingertips into Jenny's shoulder, and Paul pressed his lips to Cecilia's forehead, and if they whispered something to each other, as the music played, as the breeze made the candles flicker, Rose could not hear them.

Rose stood there, at the edge of the garden, watching them.

If only, she thought, *it could be like this forever*. If only there were some spell or some secret or some esoteric solution that would keep them all here, with Cecilia's head on Paul's shoulder and Rose still insensible to the pain; with Morgan still watching, rapt, and Jenny's lips on Cassidy's lips. If only Rose had had more time, or had asked the right questions, or had asked the same questions but in a different order, maybe there would have been a way to end it, a better way, the one where Jane was here dancing and also safe in her own bed, the one where Francesca had gone wherever Robin had gone, where Lucinda Luquer had not lain unburied in the water. If Rose had been cleverer, she thought, or wiser or better—if she had only loved more or had loved less or had loved in the right way—maybe she would not be wondering, now, if she had done right. Maybe, she thought, in wild and ecstatic hope, Morgan would see, now that Paul was here, that there was a chance that Paul and Cecilia might salvage something from the shipwreck of their love; she would let them stay; *oh, God*, Rose thought, *but only let me stay*.

Then she heard the sirens.

They were faint at first.

Then the flashing lights cracked the sky open.

The sirens grew louder, then louder still. Rose could hear a voice, muffled, in a megaphone—incoherent, at first, then one unmistakable word: *police*.

Then a buzzing—a hideous blaring bell—from the other side of the ivy-shrouded gate.

It drowned out the music. Then the music stopped.

Rebecca burst forward. Her fist was in Rose's face.

"What did you do? What the *hell* did you do?"

"I—I didn't . . ."

They buzzed a second time. The whole gate seemed to tremble. They knocked at a door Rose couldn't see.

Open up, the voices were saying, *NYPD*.

Jenny let out a whimper.

"You called them!" Rebecca went on. "You called them, didn't you!"

"Rebecca, I swear—"

Then Robin fell to Morgan's feet with a strangled scream.

"Robin?"

Robin began to weep. Fat tears sprayed the hem of Morgan's dress.

"I'm—I'm sorry," he gasped. "I'm so sorry, Morgan—I don't . . ."

"Robin!"

Rebecca rushed to him. She seized him by the shoulder.

"What do they want, Robin? What did you tell them?"

Robin kept kissing Morgan's ankles, Morgan's knees, Morgan's wrists. Rebecca yanked him so hard he fell backward.

"What did you tell them, Robin?"

When he spoke, he was calm at last.

"Lucinda," he said.

—

Everything happened so quickly, after that. They moved as one: grabbing the flowers, the motors, the stray furs. Seizing the microphones, the lighting gels, the blankets. Julius was hauling the marionettes; the police were battering, now, at a door beyond the ivy; Rose could hear the iron wrench. Their movements were as elegant, as rehearsed, as when once they had taken Rose in their arms, one by one, and steered her so expertly across the floor. Then Jenny was crying out; then Cassidy had put a hand over her mouth; then her knees gave way and he had to pick her up into his arms; then Morgan was crying *the dock*, and Robin was rocking back and forth on the grass, his head between his knees, and Cecilia was burying her face in Paul's chest; then the others were running to the boat; then Cassidy was unfurling the rope, and the boat was pulling out into the water.

It took Rose a moment to realize that Rebecca had not gone with them.

She was standing at the entrance to the house. Her face was pale and determined.

She turned to Rose.

"There's a side exit," she said. "Between the apple trees. It unlocks from the inside."

The battering ram gave one final, wrenching blow. The main door gave way. Robin let out another ravaged yelp. The police were shouting, once more, into the megaphone.

"It's time," she said, "to pay the piper."

Rebecca turned and walked toward them.

Rose grabbed Paul with one hand, Cecilia with the other. They swung the side gate open. They ran.

The last thing Rose saw, as she looked back, was Morgan: standing on the prow of the *Avalon* as it sailed out into the darkness.

Then Rose, Paul, and Cecilia were alone on a narrow suburban road. The sky was gray. At first the street was empty. They walked onward in silence: toward industrial lots, then, eventually, toward houses—squat, pale colonials, almost indistinguishable from the ones they'd left behind. They passed parked cars, mailboxes, a gas station. All the ordinary hallmarks of an ordinary street.

It was only when they reached Beach Channel Drive that Rose realized where they were. How many times, she thought, had she been here before—taken the Rockaway Rocket on languid summer Fridays with Caleb and Grant and Lydia; how many times had they closed their eyes and opened cans of rosé and stretched out their limbs into the sand, just across an ivy-covered gate from a world that could not exist.

They walked all the way to the A train. They hopped the turnstile. They rode back toward the city. Cecilia leaned her head on Rose's shoulder. She gripped Paul's hand. They did not speak.

A couple got on at Nostrand. They were tipsy and falling against each other, and they staggered onto the seat opposite. They took in the three of them: Paul's sweat-damp suit, Cecilia's white, shimmering dress, shredded by thorns when they'd run, and Rose's velvet dress, which was shattering along the seams.

"Jesus," the man said. "What in the hell happened to you?"

Nobody had an answer.

—

They got off the train in Downtown Brooklyn. Paul fished change from his pocket for a coffee cart on Fulton Mall. Dawn had just started breaking. All around them the city was waking: lawyers in suits were hurrying to Borough Hall, and two delivery cyclists were waiting for a dollar slice at a counter. There was an old woman drinking vodka out of an airplane bottle. There was a Russian man explaining crosswalk lights to his son.

Paul motioned to a bus shelter outside a Kingdom Hall.

"This is where I get on," he said. Cecilia nodded. She was still shivering. When she spoke, it was with difficulty.

"Maybe—" She cleared her throat. "Maybe tonight—if you're not." She swallowed. "If you're feeling up to it. You could come by. You know." She looked down. "Dinner?"

"I'd like that," said Paul.

He kissed her, gently, on the cheek.

He turned to Rose.

"I—" His words dissolved. "Thank you," he said.

They shook hands.

Then he boarded a bus and was gone.

Rose and Cecilia stood side by side, watching him go.

"Come on, Rosie," Cecilia said. "Let's go home."

—

It was morning by the time they arrived at Tudor City. Cecilia had broken a heel off her shoe. Rose's dress had shattered entirely.

The doorman gave Rose an incredulous look.

"You've got mail," he said.

He dropped an enormous bundle into Rose's arms. RealReal packages. Copies of the *New Yorker*. Rent receipts.

He handed Cecilia the spare key.

The apartment was just as Rose had left it. Falstaff was still nestled in Cecilia's pillows. Cecilia's clothes were still hung neatly in the closet. Rose's sketchbook still lay on the windowsill. Aside from a thin layer of dust that had settled on the mantelpiece, they might have only been gone a day.

They sat on the sofa.

"You want to know something stupid, Rosie?"

"What?"

"I'm *starving*."

Rose realized, with a start, that she was hungry, too. It had been almost a day since she'd eaten.

"So am I."

Cecilia rose.

"Have we got anything?"

Cecilia went to the kitchen. She rummaged through the cabinets. She returned, after a moment, with a can in each hand.

"Could we make it work, do you think?"

It was a can of pumpkin puree and another of cranberry sauce. The ones Cecilia had bought for Thanksgiving and never used.

Rose considered them for a moment, astounded.

Then she started to laugh.

She laughed, so long, and so hard, that she began to shake; until her laughter became crying, and then turned to laughter again; until Cecilia started to laugh with her, and Rose could no longer separate Cecilia's laugh from her own.

"I mean," Cecilia said, when at last they had regained control. "You could do worse."

They heated the pumpkin puree in the microwave. They added sugar to the cranberry sauce. They ate, facing each other, at the dining table, and then they cleared the dishes away.

"You should get some sleep," Cecilia said, from the kitchen sink. "You must be exhausted. I'll finish up here."

Rose could barely feel her feet.

"Don't worry," Cecilia said. "I'll be in, soon enough." She smiled up at Rose. Rose couldn't remember the last time she'd seen Cecilia smile, like that.

Rose went to her bedroom. She closed the door behind her.

Rose sat alone, for a moment, on the bed. Then she went to the window. She opened the blinds. She looked out over the city. Somewhere, she thought, there they all were; somewhere Paul was making a cup of tea; somewhere Lydia was trying on a wedding dress; somewhere Jane was sobbing into a pillow, convinced that the only beautiful thing that had ever existed in all the world had dissolved into memory. Somewhere Yvette Thornbill was gazing at her husband, across the breakfast table; somewhere there was a nihilist who sobbed in piano bars because nobody understood the world was ending; somewhere there was a father whose children hated him; somewhere a ballerina who could not stand her own skin. Somewhere there was a man, with a gray mustache, wandering alone through a city that was a stranger to him. Somewhere there was a woman, in a police station, telling the story of a body in a bayou; somewhere a boy, rocking back and forth upon the grass. Somewhere there was a boat, breaking through the dawn.

Maybe, Rose thought, *Morgan was right*; maybe it was the same story, every time. Maybe Cecilia would run from Paul, in a week or in six, the way Cecilia always ran; maybe he would tire of her, when at last she'd settled into his arms; maybe, maybe, Rose would grow to hate them. Maybe, Rose thought, maybe the greatest love stories were the unconsummated ones, maybe nothing was ever as good as you wanted it to be, maybe Rose would spent the rest of her life looking for a man or a midnight that would make her feel the way she'd felt the night she first heard flute song coming out of the darkness. Maybe she would spend the rest of her life running after the holy grail; maybe she, too, would come home, at defeated intervals, with hollow cheeks and hollow eyes and unwashed luggage, too stupid or too stubborn to admit that it didn't exist at all.

Or maybe she would find it.

Rose stood by the window. She pushed it open. She watched the city. She watched the cars swarm the highway, and the people who biked and skateboarded and walked dogs along the Esplanade, the East River grow thick with boats. She listened to the sound of the sirens, and the foghorns, and to the sound of Cecilia's piano, soft at first and then bold, echoing across the threshold. She said a prayer for the fathers and the bolters, for the lost girls and the old men, for the nihilists, for the lovers, for the man with a metal detector, for Jane. She said a prayer for the boat, maybe making its way, by now, to another city, for all those who mourned for it, and for those whom it had made mourn.

Rose leaned out the window. She opened her sketchbook. She began to trace the outlines of a shape whose contours were already fading, of a face she'd already half forgotten, of a dissolving dream. Already there were errors—Rose could not remember, now, where the boat's anchor had been, or how many windows there had been on the second floor of the house, or the colors of the flowers of the garden, or the flecks in Morgan's eyes.

Still, Rose set them down. An elegy, maybe, or an invitation.

Something to hold fast to.

ACKNOWLEDGMENTS

I'm incredibly grateful to so many people in the conception, the writing, and the editing of *Here in Avalon*—to my editor, Carina Guiterman, to my agent, Emma Parry, and the incredible team at Simon & Schuster. I'm also deeply grateful for my husband, Dhananjay, for his careful reading, his attentive support, and for his patience as I wrestled with draft after draft of this novel.

I'm grateful, too, for the people who have shown me versions of my own Avalon, in my life and, in particular, to the cast and crew of *Sleep No More*, and all those who took me there; to Sorrel and Massimiliano Mocchia di Coggiola, who showed me that life could be a carnival, and to all those who shared and share those February nights with me; and to Susannah Black, who reminded me when it mattered most that *another life is possible.* And to those who gathered and gather with me, under a cherry tree, for the past few years, and with whom I hope to gather still.

A note on the text: the lines of the poem that leads Rose to the Cloisters are taken from a 1946 poem, "The Unicorn," by Nancy Bruff, published in her sole collection, *My Talon in Your Heart* (Dutton, 1946), which is now out of print, and which I encountered as a photograph of a printed page posted to a Facebook group dedicated to the film *The Last Unicorn.*

ABOUT THE AUTHOR

Tara Isabella Burton is the author of the novels *Here in Avalon*, *The World Cannot Give*, and *Social Creature*, and of the nonfiction books *Self-Made: Creating Our Identities from Da Vinci to the Kardashians* and *Strange Rites: New Religions for a Godless World*. She has written on religion and culture for the *New York Times*, the *Washington Post*, the *Wall Street Journal*, and more. She lives in New York City.